MW01146786

Laura Smith Thril... opening… I couldn... ...this book fast enough ♡

4m 127 likes · Reply

—— View 7 more replies

Julia Shkolnik This book was literal catnip for me! Scary and surprising, the ultimate reality thriller ♡

1d 80 likes Reply

—— View 2 more replies

Jenn Heater A compelling tale of the dark side of social media, of the realities of what we tell our followers and how it often differs from the less glossy reality. The core mystery delivers many shocking twist, right up until the very end. Five stars for this compelling, ultra-entertaining read ♡

1d 182 likes Reply

—— View 6 more replies

Kathleen Hughes Exposing the underside of the world of influencers… how far would you go for money, fame and glamour? ♡

1d 732 likes Reply

—— View 2 more replies

Dena Martin The Tradwife stuff is delicious. I mean, it skewers! ♡

2d 134 likes Reply

—— View 10 more replies

THE TRAD WIFE'S SECRET

LIANE CHILD

ONE PLACE. MANY STORIES

HQ
An imprint of HarperCollins*Publishers* Ltd
1 London Bridge Street
London SE1 9GF

www.harpercollins.co.uk

HarperCollins*Publishers*
Macken House, 39/40 Mayor Street Upper
Dublin 1 D01 C9W8, Ireland

This edition 2025

25 26 27 28 29 LBC 5 4 3 2 1
First published in Great Britain by
HQ, an imprint of HarperCollins*Publishers* Ltd 2025

PB ISBN: 9780008744106
US PB ISBN: 9780008755003

Set in Sabon LT Std by HarperCollins*Publishers* India

Printed and bound in the United States

For
Cicely
My perfect #filter

Prologue

Let's take a deep breath. We all deserve a moment of calm amongst the chaos.

As I'm sure you'll understand, the @_TrulyMadison_ Instagram account will be closing with immediate effect. Over the last decade, Madison March has been an inspiration to millions of women in the United States and across the world. She chose to share her life and beautiful family with us all in the hope that others might embrace the all-American values that she held so close.

Thank you to everyone who has followed Madison's story with such positivity and support. It's a tragedy that this wonderful journey has been cut short in such an abrupt and violent way. But please remember Madison as I will – a beautiful soul who loved her family above all else. And whose only mistake may have been loving them too much.

RIP @_TrulyMadison_

Erica

@daisymaisie16 I'm heartbroken! How can this ever make sense?

@kateaidavine I can't believe it. I mean, I know it's true. But it's just too awful.

@bonnieliveson8 Full respect to that lady for doing what she could for her family.

@barneylovell43 Stupid bitch deserved everything she got.

Chapter 1

Madison

@loufromlouisiana You have a beautiful home and a beautiful family. God bless you all.
#homemaker #tradwife #familyfirst #truefemininity #inspiration

I give the camera my signature smile, holding it for a second longer than feels comfortable. This always feels a little false, but I know it's what my followers expect, and I don't want to disappoint them. 'Don't you love summer mornings?' I say in my honey, breathy voice. 'Wow, the sun is just peeking out over our mountains, full of promise. I just know today is going to be a good day.'

I rise onto my tiptoes and pull open one of the high kitchen cabinets. I know some of my less savory followers will get a kick out of this, watching my calf muscles lift and bulge, maybe rubbing their groins as they stare. But in my knee-length, floral smock dress, I'm hardly encouraging it, and what happens in the darker corners of the internet isn't my responsibility.

I reach for a bag of oats, then four different mason jars with handwritten labels, and turn back to the camera. I pause for a moment, knowing from experience that the early

3

morning sunshine will light up my eyes, then reach forward, stop the video and exhale. These dawn reels, making the most of the golden hour, might be high currency on Instagram, but filming before seven a.m. every day is exhausting.

I grab a ceramic mixing bowl from the cupboard and tip in most of the ingredients. Then I scoop a handful of dried fruit from a jar and position it on the wooden chopping board to look like it's just been dropped there. I shift the board until I find the right angle for the cherries to be drenched in sunshine – the red is mesmerizing when it gleams – then pull a knife out of the block and place it next to the fruit. One final check, a deep breath and a quick practice smile, then I press record.

'It's breeding season on the ranch,' I say, not looking at the camera now, but knowing the video will pick up my profile, my best side. 'And Michael has got a tough day ahead of him, so I'm making something super nutritious for breakfast. Homemade granola. And a lot of the ingredients are grown right here on the homestead. You might remember the children picking cherries and apricots last weekend. We set a few handfuls out in the sunshine, and I think they've turned out pretty well.' I roll the knife blade over the fruit, hoping the new external microphone picks up the faint squelch as the soft centers split open (because at over five hundred bucks, it really should). Then I add the dried fruit to the mixing bowl and eye the jar of honey.

Normally I'd stop filming now to set up the next scene. But the honey is exactly where I need it. Did Lori place it there last night for me? I don't remember telling her I planned to make granola this morning. As I ponder this, I realize I'm frowning, so I reach for the stop button. Honey or no honey, I need a moment to compose myself.

I breathe, thank the Lord for editing software, and press record. 'You know, our beautiful honeybees have been busy this summer,' I say, scraping thick honey out of the glass jar. 'We've had two harvests already, and I wouldn't be surprised if there's more to come. I think they might love the Montana sunshine as much as we do.' I let the honey ooze into the mixture. As I catch the last drop with my little finger, I turn to the camera and lick it off with a mischievous grin.

I pick a long wooden spoon from the wobbly utensil pot that Molly made as a gift for me last Christmas and place the mixing bowl against my hip. Making sure its contents are directly in line with the camera, I stir in wide circles. It's more physically demanding than it looks, but I keep up the rhythm until it's all blended together.

After another break to line two trays with parchment paper, I set up my final shot, then transfer the mixture, one gloopy dollop at a time. 'You don't need to bake it for too long, fifteen, maybe twenty minutes.' I have learned over the years what works best when I'm explaining recipes, and accommodating rather than bossy always gets me more likes. 'Which is lucky,' I go on. 'Because I don't think Michael is going to be in the mood for waiting around on such a nice day. Oh, and let me know in the comments if you'd like the recipe, and have a truly gorgeous day!'

I pause for one final smile after my trademark sign off, then reach forward to stop the video. I fight the urge to watch the footage back because I'm bound to see imperfections – a shadow somewhere, or possibly even fine lines around my eyes – and I know that's what editing is for. I wash my hands – my little finger still feels sticky from that honey – and head for the door. These days, I spend as little time as possible in the kitchen.

'Lori!' I exhale, as I find our housekeeper loitering in the hallway. She's wearing a long denim skirt, sneakers, and a white sweatshirt that's been washed so many times it's now a pale gray. When we first moved here, I bought clothes for Lori, floaty dresses and colourful skirts. She was only twenty-seven, even though she has always acted older, and she deserved to look beautiful too. But the feminine clothes rarely made it out of the closet, and eventually I gave up. 'What are you doing out here?'

'Sorry, I didn't mean to startle you,' she says. 'I wasn't sure if you were still filming, and I didn't want to mess things up by getting in the way.'

'It's fine. I'm finished. The place is all yours. The granola needs to come out of the stove in about ten minutes, if that's okay. So can you leave it to cool and let Erica know to come film it? And do you have time to cook some steak and eggs for Michael?'

'Yes, of course,' Lori says. 'And I'm sure the children will eat the granola if I give them free rein over the maple syrup.'

'Have you seen them this morning?' I ask with that familiar mix of gratitude and envy. Lori is great with the children, but I sometimes worry that they prefer her company to mine.

'Myron had a nightmare last night, poor thing,' Lori says. 'But he's fast asleep in my bed now. Matilda is wandering around in her cow costume; I think she's trying to impress her daddy. And I haven't seen Molly or Mason yet.'

'Okay, thanks. I'll go round them up. I need them looking their best this morning.'

'Oh?'

'The new tutor is arriving today,' I explain, not quite holding eye contact. 'And she'll be here soon. She flew in from Boston last night, stayed at the airport hotel. Bill's picking her up about now.'

'A new tutor?' Lori raises her eyebrows into a question. 'I thought you said that you were going to homeschool the children yourself after the last one left?'

'I wanted to, initially,' I say smoothly. I try to blot out the memory of holding back tears as I threw the girl out, screaming at her to never set foot on our property again. 'But Michael persuaded me to try again with a new one.'

'Michael did?'

I hear the unspoken meaning behind her question and push my lips together in annoyance. 'He wants to make sure I have plenty of time for him,' I say, taking care not to sound defensive. 'Because we all know that's the secret to a good marriage.'

Lori searches my face, and I flinch slightly as I see sympathy in hers. 'Are you sure this is the kind of life you want, Madison?'

I smile. 'This is the perfect life, Lori. And I'm truly grateful for it. You more than anyone should understand that.'

Chapter 2

Madison

I sit on the edge of our Alaskan King bed, the sheets still mussed from last night, and listen to the shower running in our en suite bathroom. I think about the times I've followed Michael in there, slipping off my dress and panties as I go, the grin on his face as he realizes what's coming. I wonder what would happen if I tried that now. Would he lift me up, let me curl my legs around his torso, hold me against the limestone tiles, and make love to me? Or would he disentangle himself, remind me about his busy day, and leave me smarting with embarrassment?

But the shower noise stops, ending my dreamy conundrum, and a minute later, Michael walks into the bedroom. His thick chestnut hair is wet, pushed off his face, and he's wearing a white towel knotted around his hips. He gives me one of his languid half-smiles. Easy as breathing to him, but even now, after over a decade of marriage, it makes my insides twist. 'So what was it this morning?' he asks. 'Banana bread? French toast?'

'Granola.'

He nods. 'Happy with it?' Michael is a barrel of a man. Muscular, strong, but thickset rather than ripped. More heavyweight boxer than track sprinter. He drops his towel on the floor and wanders over to his underwear drawer butt naked. Michael has never been prudish about his own physique, although it's a different story when it comes to women's bodies, and the biology that goes with them.

Thank goodness.

'I think it'll turn out well,' I say. 'The light was perfect.'

'Sounds great.' Then he twists towards me, his eyes narrowing. 'I take it there's something more filling for me?'

'Of course,' I say quickly. 'Lori's making you steak and eggs.'

He nods. 'Good. Cattle breeding starts today, so I need a proper breakfast. All being well, I'll have fertilized one hundred ladies by dusk.' He lets out a crack of laughter, then reaches for me. I go willingly into his arms, arch my body into his, give him my most seductive smile. His bulge expands against my dress, and I feel a frisson of excitement – laced with power. I might be in my thirties and a mother four times over now, but I can still arouse him. I'm not like Rose, and I never will be.

But then my sense of power vanishes, because Michael pulls back, gives my ass a light slap, and returns his attention to his underwear drawer. 'Will Lori make me a packed lunch too? And can you make sure, between you, that dinner is ready at six? I'll be starving by then, and you know how I hate to wait for a meal.'

'Of course. I'll let Lori know.'

'And what about you?' he says, pulling on a pair of jeans. 'You got much on today?'

He says it so dismissively that I have the crazy urge to goad him. To remind him that I'm the one who has built a global brand. But the compulsion evaporates as quickly as it arrived. 'Oh, just the usual. Helping Lori in the kitchen. Spending time with the children. And, um.' I swallow. I find that I don't want to tell him about the new tutor, even though it was him who pointed out that we needed a replacement, that our children deserved someone more qualified than me to teach them. But he's going to find out soon enough. And at least I took precautions this time.

'What's up, Madison. Cat got your tongue?'

'The new tutor is arriving this morning,' I say. 'Ready to start lessons next week.'

He stops buttoning his shirt. 'I didn't know you'd hired someone.' His voice cools. 'You didn't think to speak to me about something as important as that?'

My cheeks sting with the error. Why did I let my pain at his straying blind me to something so obvious? 'You're right, I should have done.' I wring my hands in frustration at my own stupidity, hoping it looks like humility. 'But you've been so busy working on the ranch; I wanted to take some of the burden of running the home off your shoulders.'

'Hmmm.' He resumes doing up his shirt and it gives me the impetus to keep going.

'And I used an agency that specializes in finding tutors who hold traditional family values. People like us.' This is a lie, but I can't tell Michael the truth. That I chose an agency in Boston exactly because the area is liberal, progressive. Full of people who are different to us. Young women that Michael won't want to sleep with. Because I knew a male tutor was out of the question.

'You interviewed her?'

'Yes, absolutely. She'll fit in, I promise.'

'If she doesn't smell right to me, she's gone, you understand? I don't care how much it will cost me.'

'Of course, honey.' This is a familiar dance for us. I never mention the huge paychecks I get through my brand deals and advertising revenue, and in return, Michael turns a blind eye to the hours I spend developing my social media presence. While we can pretend it's just a wholesome hobby – even though he knows exactly what I earn because those dollars go straight into his bank account – our marriage can stay strong. But sometimes that pretense is harder to maintain. Needing to give staff a sweetener in return for their discretion is one of the ways it spills over into our family life, but there are trickier obstacles to navigate.

Like security. The fence around the homestead is designed to keep animals out, not people, and whenever I get a particularly creepy message, I ask about hiring a security detail. But Michael always says that defending our family is his job, and that me suggesting otherwise questions his masculinity. Of course I never want to push things after that – Michael's masculinity is more important to him than oxygen – but I do wish I could ask him about all the time he spends on his ranch, away from the homestead, and who would defend us then.

I walk over to him, run my open palm across his broad chest. 'A word from you, and she's gone; you've always been a better judge of character than me.' I look up into his face and give him my most alluring smile, while internally praying that he doesn't decide to get rid of our new tutor. I need this one to work out. I can't let him replace her with yet another blonde-haired, wide-eyed good girl.

Chapter 3

Cally

I gaze out the half-open passenger seat window, my eyes wide. I thought the coastline around Boston was beautiful, but this is scenery on steroids. Snowcapped mountains. Lush green fields. High-definition blue sky. Vast swathes of pine trees that make the whole place smell like air freshener.

I had mixed feelings about this new chapter in my life when I flew out of Logan with just a heavy backpack for my year away from home – because having zero choice is never a good starting point. But with every hour that passed, fidgeting in an American Airlines middle seat, I became more excited about my new adventure. And now – with this incredible tableau – I'm even starting to feel a bit optimistic about how things have turned out.

I uncoil my spine and lean back against the seat cushion. Finally, I've had some luck. And jeez, it's been a long time coming. I didn't make it into an Ivy League university like my brother Luke did. And I got my grandma's creative brain rather than either of my parents' scientific ones, halving my earning potential in one DNA irregularity. And then I make one stupid mistake, and suddenly I'm exiled from my own city.

But none of that matters now. Because not only have I found a way to solve my own problem, I am deep diving into the crazy, wild world of tradwife influencers. And not just any influencer, but Madison March, the absolute queen. I'm not buying the lifestyle she's selling, all that saying grace before dinner and kowtowing to your husband. But wow, that house. Those cute kids. The amazing food she makes from scratch. And she's got to be one of the most beautiful women on the planet.

When I started tutoring sixth- and seventh-grade children in my neighborhood back home, it was just a way to earn some pocket money while I decided what to do with my life. But after some false starts on the career front – marketing wasn't for me, and apparently, I wasn't right for human resources – suddenly my two years' tutoring was my only solid employment history. Then one day, the tutoring agency said they had an interesting opportunity to run past me. I had nothing else on the horizon, so I agreed to an interview. And by the time that came around, I would have taken any job that took me out of state.

'So I hear you're the new tutor.'

I turn and stare at Bill, the driver. I have watched enough Westerns in my twenty-four years to know that cowboys wear Stetsons and plaid shirts in the movies. I just hadn't realized they dressed that way in real life too. 'That's right.'

'They're livewires those kids,' he warns, his Montana accent like a slow smile. 'I imagine you'll have your work cut out for you there, Cally. Getting them to sit still for more than five minutes.'

I look at Bill with renewed interest. His description of the children is news – they always seem super well-behaved on Madison's reels, and I thought children and animals were the two things you couldn't stage-manage – but it's more that Bill knows them well enough to make the comment. 'It sounds like you spend plenty of time with the Marches then?'

'I'm there most days, yeah. Depending on Mrs. March's schedule.'

'Oh, right.' Of course a woman with four children, ten million Instagram followers, and a husband who's never changed a diaper has a schedule. Madison must spend a ton of hours editing her reels to make her life look perfect. But I guess I assumed the rest of her day would be spent getting through the mush of raising kids and keeping home. I look back at Bill. 'So what's it like then, her schedule?'

Bill taps the steering wheel. He's quiet for a moment, a frown forming on his face. 'I take it you've signed the legal stuff?' he finally says.

'What legal stuff?'

Her tilts his head, then shakes it. 'Ain't no way the Marches employed a new tutor without getting you to sign a confidentiality agreement.'

I dredge up a memory of the offer letter that arrived in the mail a few weeks ago, a large envelope stuffed with papers I skimmed rather than read. My interview had been via a Zoom call with Madison in mid-July. It wasn't easy. I had to pretend I shared her views on how children should be educated – and decide if I had any red lines on the issue (which, once my bonus had been explained, it turned out I didn't). The conversation had then widened to questions I found easier to lie about. The only sticking point came when I let slip that I was vegetarian, but it clearly wasn't too much of a problem, because a couple of hours later the tutoring agency phoned to say I'd got the job.

And a week after that, the paperwork arrived. Once I'd seen my pay confirmed in black and white – my living costs covered plus a fifty-dollar weekly allowance, and then a fifty-thousand-dollar bonus if I completed one full school year – I realized someone up there was soundly coming to my rescue, and nothing was going to stop me taking the job. So I signed the rest of the forms without paying much attention to the detail.

'I guess maybe I did,' I admit, shrugging, trying to hide how dumb I feel.

'Listen, we all sign it,' Bill says, the warm voice back. 'It's for our benefit as well as theirs, just so everyone knows what's what.'

'All?' So Bill and I aren't the only ones on the payroll? Madison never mentions having staff on her social media posts, and she always gives the impression that she does the domestic stuff herself. Originally, I thought that she homeschooled her children, but I'm not an avid follower, so I wasn't too surprised when I discovered I'd got that wrong. But now Bill's talking like there's a whole team behind her.

My surprise must show on my face too, because Bill cackles with laughter and shakes his head. 'I think you're going to learn a few things about the Marches, Miss Cally.' Then he turns up the volume on the car stereo and starts swaying in time with the music, a vaguely familiar country and western song.

I stare out the windshield and try to swallow my embarrassment. Of course Madison has an entourage. My parents only had two children, and Mom still talks about how hard it was when we were little, how going out to work felt like a rest – and she's an emergency doctor. Madison has got double the number of kids, and enough money to hire all the help she needs.

And if she wants to pretend that she does everything herself for gullible followers to lap up, then who am I to judge? I've made a fair number of morally questionable decisions in my time too.

Suddenly the truck screeches to a halt and I'm flung forward, the seatbelt cutting into my shoulder. My head ricochets back up to the sight of a huge black cow staring at me through the windshield nostrils flaring. I sense Bill reach forward, then watch him pull a pistol from under the dash. Jeez, the ease with which he handles that thing. Then my shock morphs into a hot, sick feeling as I realize he's going to shoot the cow. My eyes bulge as he maneuvers the gun out the window.

But instead he cocks his arm and aims at the sky. As he pulls the trigger, a deep boom rips through my eardrums. The cow tilts, then flees.

And Bill carries on driving as though nothing has happened.

Chapter 4

Cally

A long, bumpy track finally gives way to a smooth tarmac driveway. Bill parks up in the shade of a giant pine tree and nods for me to get out. I'm still shaky from the cow incident, but seeing my home for the next year proves to be a powerful antidote.

I stand next to an imposing stone water feature and stare. The March Homestead is like a ranch from the movies – there are even horses grazing on the lawn. The walls are made of stripped logs, stacked horizontally, and there's a huge stone fire pit out front plus a life-sized bronze statue of a stag. The March home is also bigger than I imagined. And swankier. There's a grand, double-height entrance way with manicured flowerbeds either side, and an intricately carved oak front door.

It hits me that Madison never posts pictures of the outside of her home. There are plenty of valid reasons for that – protecting her privacy for one; there are probably hundreds of crazies out there who would stalk her if they could work out where she lives. Or she might not think it's appropriate to flaunt her wealth – even Madison must know about the cost-of-living crisis. Yet I can't help thinking that social media's favorite tradwife hides her lavish home because she wants her gazillions of followers to believe she's just a simple homemaker.

But Truly Madison can be as false as she likes for all I care, I remind myself. She offered me a way out, and I grabbed it. What her fans believe is none of my business.

'I've got some errands in town, so I've got to run,' Bill calls out from inside the cab. 'I'll drop your cases in your room as soon as I'm back, Cally, if that's okay. But everyone's expecting you, so head on in.'

I just have time to nod before he swings around the wide drive and disappears down the track, a puff of dust trailing after him. I walk towards the house but when I reach the front door, I pause. Because it's already open.

'Excuse me.'

I turn around. A woman in jeans and a navy blazer with blonde hair cut into a sharp bob is standing behind me, nodding impatiently at the doorway. She seems out of place here, her pink loafers more suited to East Coast city streets than bear country dirt roads.

'I need to get inside, if you wouldn't mind?'

'Sorry, yes,' I mumble, stepping aside. I watch the woman march into the entrance hall but then she stops, turns, pushes her sunglasses onto her head.

'Are you the new tutor?'

'I am, yes.'

'Okay, follow me.' She resumes her pace, and I scurry to keep up. There's no time to take in my surroundings in any detail, but I clock more wood, a wall of sparkling gray stone, and a black and white cow hide hanging down from the ceiling.

'Have you seen Nathan yet?'

'Nathan? No. I've met Bill,' I offer, but that's clearly not helpful because she rolls her eyes.

'Wait in here. I'll find Nathan. I'm Erica, by the way. But I've got a million things to get through today, so I can't hang around.'

'Okay,' I stutter. 'But I think I'm supposed to meet Madison? Is she around?'

Erica sighs. 'Yes, she's here, somewhere.' Her shoulders drop a couple of inches and her features soften. 'Sorry, this isn't much of a welcome, is it. Once you've had your meeting with Nathan, everything will fall into place, I promise. Now if you can hang here for a few minutes, I'll find him for you.' She gestures to a sitting room at the back of the property, gives me a bright and almost genuine smile, then strides back down the hallway.

I drop into the chestnut-brown leather sofa and stare at the incredible view through the window. The glass is pristine, no little hand smudges anywhere, and I wonder if that's because the children aren't allowed in this room, or because Madison is one of those obsessive cleaners. Or Erica, of course. Or Bill. Or Nathan.

'Good morning.' A large man with a thick moustache and bulbous nose stomps into the room. 'I'm Nathan, the March's lawyer. I assume you're Cally? Good to meet you.' I expect him to give me one of those bone-crushing handshakes, but he backs into the opposite sofa without proffering his hand and drops a briefcase on the coffee table between us. I listen to the click-click of the catch, then watch him pull out a file.

'It's great to have you on the homestead,' he continues. 'The kids are really excited to meet you. Michael and Madison too. So I'm just going to run over the legal stuff, and then we're good to go.'

I give him a tight smile. Bill talked about legal stuff, and now Nathan, but I still don't really know what they mean.

He smiles back. Somewhere between a cat and a wolf. 'Of course you've signed all the paperwork, so this is just a quick reminder of the obligations you agreed to. You remember signing the lifetime non-disclosure agreement on August 15th 2024?'

'Um, well . . .'

'Luckily it's very easy to remember what it covers,' he goes on. 'Because it's anything and everything that happens during your time here. That means no posting on social media. No talking to journalists. And no spreading gossip amongst your friends back home. Oh, and it's ad infinitum, which means it lasts forever.' He rolls his tongue over the last word, making my stomach churn. 'I'm going to level with you, Cally,' he continues, leaning forward. 'If you break this contract, spill a word of what you see here, on any medium, it's going to be jaw-droppingly expensive for you, do you understand?'

I swallow. 'What about my family?'

'Not a word. You know the phrase, "loose lips sink ships"?' he adds. 'It's like that. Keep your mouth shut, and there won't be any trouble.'

I tell myself that Madison has every right to protect her image, her privacy, as well as her home. She has millions of followers, who knows how many of them are obsessive weirdos. I'm sure this is totally normal. And anyway, it's not like I have much choice.

I dredge up my best fresh-faced smile. 'All fully understood,' I say. 'I won't breathe a word.'

He beams. 'That's my girl.' Then he reaches over and pats my knee faster than I can swing it away, setting off another wave of nausea. 'Now we've got that sorted, Madison will be along any minute. See you soon, Cally.'

Once he's gone, I pull out my phone and tap into Instagram. There's a new reel from Madison and I find myself wanting to watch it. As though, after everything I've just heard, I need to see this side of her again. Yes, it's a fantasy, but it doesn't stop me sinking back into the sofa and letting her soft voice wash over me.

Chapter 5

Madison

@debbiecolts47 I'm sorry but that man needs more than granola to fill him up!!!
#hothusband #ranchlife #manneedsmeat

She's prettier than I remember her looking on Zoom, but I'm not worried. She's still not Michael's type. Dark hair rather than blonde, and worn in a choppy bob rather than long and neat. Her brown eyes are framed with black eyeliner, but without contouring or blush, it makes her look both too made up, and not enough. And the only sparkle on her face comes from a small stud in her nose. I know Michael will take one look at her and think 'East Coast Gen Z progressive', and I allow myself a small inward smile. I did good.

'Hi, Cally, wow it's so lovely to finally meet you in person. How was your trip?'

'Oh,' she stutters. 'It was fine, thanks.'

There's a reticence in her voice that wasn't there during our Zoom interview. This will be Nathan's doing, I imagine, his heavy-handed approach to guaranteeing her discretion. Secretly I can't stand the man, but there's no way I could tell

Michael that. Nathan has worked for the March family for decades, and of course it's not my place to have an opinion about those kinds of things.

'And you're not too tired?' I ask. 'Can I get you something? I've just made some lemonade, although I can't guarantee there'll be any left now that Matilda's worked out how to climb onto the counter. You know, I'm not sure if I should be impressed or worried by her new acrobatic skills.'

The wariness on Cally's face fades, replaced with a smile. I love that I can do this. Erica, my social media manager, is always telling me that my ability to get people on side is a rare talent. But social media is just numbers. My adoration measured in views, likes, shares, comments. Even with ten million followers, being able to see my influence unfold in real-time gives me a warm feeling in my chest.

'I can't wait to meet her,' Cally says. 'And the others of course. Molly and Mason. And Myron.'

'And they can't wait to meet you too, so how about we go find them?'

Cally unfurls from the sofa, nodding, and as she stands up, I realize how petite she is. An inch or two shorter than me even, and maybe a size four. I ready myself for the wave of panic that I know will come – Michael likes them small – and ride it well, but the mix of curiosity and confidence on Cally's face makes me wilt. When did I last wear that expression? Feel excited about discovering something new? Except of course I know exactly when it was. And why I now know better.

'Great! Follow me.' I take a meandering path through our home, but only for effect. In truth, I know exactly where the children are, where I asked Lori to entertain them until I appeared. I'm not a fan of leaving things to chance.

'Ah! Found you,' I say as I push open the door to the craft

room, taking in my four children plus Lori, who's building a tower of wooden bricks with Myron.

Molly is at the easel, a stick of blue chalk in her hand, filling in the Montana sky on the picture she's drawing. My heart melts a little at the sight. Molly is so pretty. While I know it's not a kind thing to say, lots of girls have lost their looks by ten years old. Too old to be cute, suddenly afflicted by oversized teeth and early signs of puberty. But not Molly. Before she was born, I worried that she wouldn't look like me. And that as a result, I might even find her difficult to love. But perhaps all parents have those concerns with their firstborn, because on the day of her birth, with Michael by my side, love came easily.

'Hey, Mom!' Mason shouts out, dropping the stick he'd been whittling with a penknife that is possibly too sharp for an eight-year-old boy to be playing with, a present from his father. 'Is this our new tutor?' He stares at Cally, and for a horrifying moment I wonder if he's assessing her in the same way I did. Deciding whether she's going to make his mom cry like the last one. But I relax when he blurts out his question. 'What's that in your nose?'

Cally laughs, and it's a nice one. Light and contagious. Lori must think so too because her face softens at the sound. 'Well, it's a little stud,' Cally explains. 'Sometimes I pretend it's a diamond, but it's actually rhinestone. Do you know what that is?'

'I do!' Myron shouts out, lifting his hand. 'Daddy shot one in Africa.'

'That was a rhino, dumbo,' Mason says.

'Mason, don't call your brother a dumbo,' I say, while wondering whether dumbo is cute enough to not be offensive. And whether I should be filming this exchange between my children – editing Lori and Cally out of course.

23

'Isn't pretending like lying?' Matilda asks suspiciously. 'Because lying is bad.'

'Oh.' Cally's cheeks flush. 'I didn't mean . . .'

'No, Matilda,' Molly says, shaking her head at her sister. 'Pretending can be okay if you do it for the right reasons. That's right, isn't it, Mommy?'

I tense, but then remember that Cally has signed an NDA. She's one of us now. 'As long as we always put family first, that's the most important thing,' I say smoothly. 'Now, I think Cally would love it if you introduced yourselves. Who wants to go first?'

As I listen to each of my children step forward in age order and reel off their name, age, and what they love to do on the homestead – from collecting eggs from the coop in the morning, to swinging on the makeshift tire swing that Michael set up for the summer – I feel a swell of pride. Michael, Lori, and me. Between us, we've done a great job raising them.

'And this is Lori,' I say when Myron has finished talking about butterflies. 'Lori is our housekeeper, so she's the person who's really in charge.'

Matilda giggles. 'I thought Daddy was in charge, Mommy! That's what you always say.'

'Of course, that's right, honey,' I say, slightly flustered by being pulled up by my six-year-old. 'I just mean that Lori is the best person to show Cally the ropes.' I turn back to our new tutor. 'You might have seen from my content that I love cooking, and working the vegetable patch, and of course hanging out with the children. Well, it can get a little exhausting at times, so Lori is here to help me out when I need it.'

'Hello, Cally,' Lori cuts in, instinctively knowing when I need a little help. 'Welcome to the March Homestead. Your room is ready, and Bill just dropped your bags in, so you're all set. Maybe this afternoon I can give you a tour of the place, but right now I need to get on with making . . .' She slows to a stop. Thank goodness. I need to ease Cally into our set-up gently, she doesn't need to know that I can barely cook. 'Anyway, Madison, are you okay to mind Myron for a little while?' Lori finally continues.

I look at my three-year-old son. His shoulder-length curly blond hair is so adorable that it's hard to believe it's the subject of such furious exchanges. Erica loves its cherubic aesthetic while Michael rails against its femininity. I secretly agree with Erica – covertly encourage her, I suppose – but I don't dare oppose Michael's wishes. Even the thought of challenging him directly exhausts me. I feel my hand move to my belly.

'Is there any chance you could take him with you today, Lori? You know how the first couple of months always knock me out.'

Lori gives me one of her understanding smiles. 'Of course, I wasn't thinking. Let's go, Myron.'

'Wait, you're pregnant?' Cally blurts out, then blushes. 'Sorry, that's none of my business.'

I smile at her. 'Of course it's your business. You're one of the family now. And yes, all being well, there'll be a new March before March.'

Chapter 6

Madison

@tradlife.bestlife wow your kids are so cute! I hope I get lots of babies like you!
#tradlife #tradwife #bigfamily #familyislife #blessed

A new March before March.

Michael came up with that little quip when I told him about the baby, and Erica practically salivated at the prospect of using it to reveal my fifth pregnancy. But I'm not ready to share the news with the world just yet. I want to keep this one to myself for just a little while longer.

Because I think this will be my last.

I drop down onto my huge mattress and stare at the imposing rosewood ceiling fan above me. The quiet whir is verging on hypnotic, but it doesn't calm me. I don't exactly feel old – I'm barely into my thirties – but I have this sense that things are slipping away. That I've reached my peak, and there is now only one direction for me. Downwards.

I pull out my phone, open the camera, and switch it to the reverse lens. I stare at my face. I know it's a form of self-torture, that iPhone cameras are brutal in the wrong light, but I take note of every new blemish and unfamiliar fine line. I wonder how I will look in a year's time, after the baby is born. Older? Too old? An image from this morning appears behind my eyes. Michael's fading interest, his gentle slap on my backside. Like I'm one of his more likeable cows.

Then I think about Rose, his ex-wife. I don't know her personally – we've never spoken – but I've seen her around town often enough, and she's earned herself quite a reputation over the years. Old, unattractive, unfeminine. Either angry or morose. She works in the grocery store in the mornings, but spends most afternoons drinking liquor in the bar. I couldn't understand how Michael could choose someone like that, so one day, I begged Bill to explain it.

And then I wished I hadn't. Because Bill told me that when Rose and Michael were married, she'd been beautiful. Long blonde hair like mine, piercing blue eyes, bright smile. Not the woman I see now with her cropped white hair, darting, faded eyes, and heavy crow's feet. But when I pointed out the change in her appearance, Bill just shrugged and went quiet, as though women are a puzzle that he never expects to solve.

I know it's crazy, but I've never asked Michael what happened between them. There are plenty of rumors I've heard over the years – that Michael found hidden birth control pills, even that she hounded him about wanting to work on the ranch. But in over eleven years of marriage, I haven't dared ask him directly. In case the truth is that he simply got bored of her.

I flick the camera closed, shuffle up onto the pillows, and open Instagram instead. My post this morning is doing okay. Only two hundred thousand likes, but over a thousand comments. I scroll through a few, and for every nasty one, there are twenty good ones, and it lifts my mood. They love my dress, my granola, my utensil pot, my positivity.

I sigh, wonder if that's the biggest lie of them all.

Except it makes no sense to feel down. I have everything I have ever dreamed of, things I fought so hard to get. A successful husband who provides generously for his family. A brood of adoring children. Money to buy all the dresses I want, the expensive face creams, the little luxuries that remind me how far I've come. And millions upon millions of fans.

But somehow it feels like it's all resting on a precipice. And that one wrong move could bring it crashing down.

I click out of my notifications and start scrolling my feed instead. I set up my Instagram account while I waited impatiently for Molly to be born, over ten years ago. I was in full nesting mode at the time, so my early posts were of cute, knitted mitts and socks, or the homemade stencils Lori made to decorate the nursery. I wasn't called a tradwife back then, I was just a homemaker fresh on my journey. But a lot can happen in a decade.

Now I give talks at conventions. I'm quoted in articles, interviewed on podcasts, invited to judge beauty pageants. Feminist commentators discuss how oppressed I am while drooling over my plantation shutters, and Californian boss bitches miss work deadlines to find out how long I leave my sourdough to rise. I am the First Lady of tradwives. I lead, and every wannabe tradwife follows.

Except they don't anymore. The new audiences – young women rejecting the lose-lose working mom lifestyle their own mothers chose, disillusioned women finally prioritizing marriage and family over their failing careers – are joining the movement without knowing its history. They discover Sky Anderson or Alice DeMille, or any of those Mormon blondes on #momtok and think that these new tradwives know best. That their Marilyn Monroe looks, or botox-filled lips, or hypnotic voices mean that their content is better than mine.

And of course the algorithms prioritize their posts because they're all younger, fresher, more tech savvy than me. Jumping on every viral trend going. I thought bringing in a social media team – Erica and Noah – would change that, but it's like these platforms know that I'm cheating. They can sense my desperation. I take a deep breath to prepare myself, then swap to one of my other Instagram profiles – so I can keep my snooping under the radar – and click on Alice DeMille's latest reel. Seven hundred and eighty thousand likes. And for what? Making her own toothpaste? I click back into @_TrulyMadison_.

I'm about to throw my phone on the bed in despair, when I notice the messaging icon is showing new messages. Maybe that's what I need. A reminder that I'm still the main inspiration for millions of women. With my messaging profile set to public, it's guaranteed there'll be some weird ones, but I've got better at brushing those off, pretending they're just bots.

I click in and count twenty-three messages in total. Five of them are military veterans who want to screw me, three are African doctors who want to marry me, and there's a few sales pitches plus one death threat (which I delete and block), but the rest seem to be genuine followers. I snuggle down into the pillow and let their words sink in. How much joy I bring them. What an amazing wife and mother I am. It works like a balm. The sun is shining through the window now too, so I stretch out like a cat and feel its warmth settle on my skin.

When I get to the most recent message, the name of the account makes me pause. I run my fingertip over the screen. The message is from someone calling themselves Brianna Wyoming. With a mix of curiosity and nervousness, I tap into the message.

I love that your DMs are open.

That tells me a lot about you.
I won't take up your time, I know you have four kids
and a husband to look after.
I know everything about you!
But I just want to say that you're an inspiration to me.
After seeing how life worked out for you, I'm doing something
a bit risky, and I'd love to get your blessing.
Love Brianna

I frown at the message, trying to decipher any hidden meaning. But it reads like a genuine fan reaching out, showing gratitude, like so many others I receive. I usually delete my messages after I read them so that my account doesn't get too clogged up, but destroying this one feels wrong. The bare optimism of it perhaps. Deep in thought, I run my free hand along my belly, from hip bone to hip bone. It feels empty in this position, hollow, so I push up to sitting, and my belly curls into my hand.

Then I slide my finger along the message to delete it.

I don't have time for newbie tradwives anymore.

Chapter 7

Brianna

I stare at the hunk of sourdough bread and sigh. Because it looks more like cow dung than anything we might want to eat. Why didn't it rise? I followed the recipe. I even cheated this time, stealing a sourdough starter kit from the store when Jonah was too busy in the hardware aisle to notice. But still it went wrong.

I don't want to put the bread in the bin, in case Jonah sees what a mess I've made, so I drop it in the pocket of my sundress and walk outside. I can see him in the distance, unrolling wire mesh to cover the new chicken coop he's built, and the sight makes my chest swell. He's working so hard for this, for us. Soon this place is going to be a palace, I know it.

As I walk through the long grass, a gentle breeze cooling my skin from the sun's rays, I wonder what my friends back home are doing now. They're probably at work, grafting in a hot, airless office to raise money for their college funds. Wishing they could take my place, out here with our beautiful views, our acres of land and no schedule to follow. No nagging parents or handsy bosses to worry about. I suppose there's always the chance they'll be at the lake on a day like today, water skiing maybe, or just hanging out in the sunshine. But their pleasure will only be fleeting, while mine and Jonah's is a way of life. That's the difference.

When Jonah first brought up the idea of homesteading, after football practice one evening, I didn't think that way of life could be possible for two eighteen-year-olds with only a few hundred dollars of savings between us. But the more we talked about it, the more excited I became. We drove west from Buffalo and found these old homesteads in deep farming country that had been gradually abandoned over the last century as people moved to the cities for jobs. Each one was huge, and grand, and the crazy thing was that the state was selling them off for a dollar because they wanted people to bring the properties – and the land – back to life.

Jonah and I had been dating for nearly two years by then, and I knew without question that he was my forever man. Just like Dad was to Mom when they met as teenagers, and it worked out pretty well for them. Twenty years married, five kids, a family home on Prairie Drive. Jonah was Buffalo High's star football player, and I was the captain of our cheerleading squad. It was a match made in heaven, that's what everyone said, so when we found this place, with all its potential, I knew this would be our little piece of paradise. I sorted the paperwork and as soon as we finished school, we came out here. Rejecting the hustle, sticking it to the man. Living our best life on our own terms. It really is a dream come true.

Our land spreads out in every direction. It's flatter on this side of Bighorn Mountain, and if I look north or west, I can see for miles. But there's dense woodland to the southeast that starts only a few hundred feet from the homestead. An easy place to hide a failed lump of bread. But when I reach the edge of the treeline, I hear someone behind me. Jonah.

'What are you doing?'

I turn around, blush at getting caught.

'You weren't going to throw food in there, were you?' he goes on, his brow furrowing. 'Jesus, Bri, we may as well put up a sign saying, "Bears welcome".'

'You're right, I'm sorry, I forgot.' At home, I throw garbage in the trash can, and it disappears. Period. I need to remember things are different here.

'It's fine, don't worry. We're both still finding our way. Just remember that food needs to be eaten, used for compost, or burned, okay?'

I hang my head and nod.

'You know, you could just tell me that you mucked up the sourdough again.' Jonah gives me his wide, lopsided grin, the one that's impossible to resist. 'I take it that is what happened?'

'Honest to God, Jonah, can we not just buy Wonder and save on the cooking costs? Not to mention the ton of ingredients I've thrown away. I know we've got to be careful, but maybe we can cut some corners?'

He walks closer. He's naked from the waist up and there's a sheen of sweat across his chest. Blond haired and blue eyed, he's normally pale, but six weeks working on the homestead under the summer sun has toughened and tanned his skin. I smell his natural odor and feel myself stir. While the Lord (and my parents) won't be impressed, this might be what I love most about this place, being able to have sex outdoors, knowing with liberating certainty that no one will see us. No sneaking around, waiting for our families to be out of the house.

My parents were horrified when I told them I was moving away with Jonah. Not because we were choosing a homesteader lifestyle, or that I'd changed my mind about going to college, but because I was doing it without a wedding ring on my finger. I mean, what would people think? What would the church think? But that would mean staying in Buffalo for months to prepare for the Big Day, and we were too impatient, too excited about our new adventure to wait for a piece of paper.

'That's a little defeatist, don't you think, Miss Homesteader?' Jonah removes one strap of my dress, then the other. I suddenly remember that it's been two days since I had a hot bath, and I wonder if I smell bad. I eye the metal tub on the ramshackle deck. Maybe I can take a rain check on lovemaking until I've cleaned myself up.

'Soon we'll have chickens,' Jonah goes on, nuzzling into my neck, seemingly oblivious to any two-day-baked aroma. 'And dairy cows to churn butter. And pigs. How amazing will that be, scrambled eggs on grilled sourdough with bacon on the side. Made by your fair hand. This life here, with you, it's going to be perfect.'

I feel my dress slide down to my hips, my breasts exposed to the breeze. 'And you'll fix the house up for me,' I murmur.

'It's going to be a palace.' Jonah pushes my dress all the way to the ground. 'There'll be six bedrooms, for all our beautiful children, and a huge kitchen like those ones in the magazines you like, and a parlor, so you can have your new friends over for tea.'

I smile at that. 'Can we get a piano?'

'You'll be able to have whatever you want, my love, I promise. And that's without you ever having to work a day in your life. Doesn't that sound good?'

I push away the frustrations of that sourdough. The hours it takes me to light a fire. And also the summer I'm missing out on at home, the sleepovers with girlfriends, binge watching our favorite Netflix shows, going to the beauty salon with my mom. 'Yeah, that sounds good.'

I watch him unbutton his denim cut-offs with a sense of anticipation, and as we sink to the ground, all thoughts of stodgy bread, missed baths, and lumbering bears disappear.

Chapter 8

Cally

Matilda slides her hand into mine. 'Come on! You need to meet Clarabelle!'

'No, let's take Miss Cally to see the chickens first. I bet she can't catch one!'

'Shut up, Mason,' Molly says. 'Of course she can. She's an adult. All adults are faster than chickens.'

I smile serenely at the children. In truth, chickens freak me out. The feathers. Their jerky movements. The squawking. But I don't think it would be a good idea to admit that to the March children. Not unless I want to lose all their respect before school lessons even start. 'Who's Clarabelle?'

'She's our pet cow,' Mason explains.

'That's sweet.' A scene from one of Madison's reels comes to mind. Molly and Mason milking a cow, then trying to carry the pail between them but spilling most of its contents because it's too heavy. All topped off by Madison giggling out of shot. 'Do you milk her?'

All four children look at me quizzically for a moment, then burst out laughing. 'No, silly. Clarabelle's kind of like our sister,' Matilda says.

'She has the prettiest eyelashes,' Molly adds wisely, as though that explains everything. 'Come on.'

Still holding Matilda's hand, we run as a pack through the long grass and wildflowers.

The last twenty-four hours have been the craziest of my life, no contest. I have witnessed the kids act like the polite, helpful – bordering on submissive – children that I see on Madison's reels, but only when Michael's around. The rest of the time they're cheeky, loud, hyperactive. Mason sulks and Matilda does the opposite of what she's asked. And it feels surprisingly special to be behind the scenes, like I've been given an Access All Areas pass to the hottest show in town.

And also, the homestead is officially gorgeous. Lori was true to her word and gave me a tour after lunch yesterday. The main house has ten bedrooms, twelve bathrooms, and what feels like a dozen living spaces over its three floors. And there are three big barns outside. One has been set up as a stable for their six horses. The second was empty, but based on the pink bunting, I'm now guessing it's Clarabelle's home. And the third barn is full of gym equipment, which I can't pretend to get excited about.

On our walk around the grounds, I saw beehives, fruit trees, and a huge vegetable patch. I also noticed a weird structure beyond the barns, a dark green door cut into the hillside. Mostly, Lori was warm and generous with her knowledge on our tour, but she clammed up when I asked what that was.

Yet for all the positives, there have been some less comfortable moments too.

As the clock moved closer to six p.m. yesterday evening, I felt a rising tension in the air. Lori upped her pace in the kitchen. Madison came downstairs, looking amazing in a white dress and shimmering make-up, but with a nervous expression underneath the shine. The children scrubbed their hands and faces without being asked, and Molly glared at the youngest two every time a suppressed giggle rose too close to the surface.

And then the door banged open, and Michael stomped in. And I felt a mix of awe and discomfort as everyone submitted to his every whim. Me included.

'Here she is!' Matilda calls out proudly when we arrive at a small fenced-off meadow.

'Clarabelle!' Myron shouts gleefully, jumping up and down.

I take a tentative step forward and look at the March family pet. Pink nose, white face, black patches over each eye. And Molly's right: weirdly long eyelashes.

'Hey kids. Whadya doing?'

I spin around. Michael is walking towards us. His gait is purposeful but slow, like he's used to people waiting for him.

'Oh, hi, Daddy,' Molly says. I sense her take a few micro steps towards me.

'We're showing Miss Cally around,' Mason says. 'Mom says lessons don't start 'til next week, and that Miss Cally needs a few days to settle in.'

'Have you done your chores?' Michael asks. 'Tuesday's laundry day, isn't it?'

'Lori said she wasn't ready for us, that we could play for a bit first.' But Mason's voice is losing its conviction under Michael's hardening stare.

'Did she now.' Michael rubs his chin, and a noise like sandpaper on stone filters into the air. 'Well, you know my feelings about that.'

'We can go now,' Molly suggests. 'You know, she's probably ready for us.'

'Matilda, what are my feelings about work and play?' Michael asks, ignoring his eldest daughter.

'Oh, um . . . work before play?' she offers in a wobbly voice.

'That's right, sweetie.' His face finally breaks into a smile, then he widens his gaze. 'Now if a six-year-old girl can get it right, why is it that you two can't work it out? Now go!' He claps his hands, like a crack of thunder, and the four children run, Molly dragging Myron across the bumpy ground.

I stand awkwardly, not knowing if his command was meant for me too.

'You probably think I'm too strict with them,' Michael muses, staring after his fleeing children.

I think about Madison's Instagram reels, how I love watching Molly lift a heavy pot off the stove or Matilda chase chickens for eggs. Why have I never wondered if they're too young for such tasks? 'No, not at all,' I say, because I know it's what he wants to hear, then add, 'You and Madison have raised four great kids.' Because it seems like they have.

'Thank you, Cally.' His gratitude sounds more genuine than I was expecting. 'You know, I love those kids with all my heart, so that means a lot.'

I turn to look at him. If I asked any of my friends to describe Madison March's cowboy husband, they'd call him a classic misogynist forcing his wife to live a life of child-rearing and servitude. But in my two years of tutoring, no parent has ever even hinted that my opinion might be of value. And it's not like any of my friends have actually met him.

'Well, you've given them a pretty idyllic life here. You have a beautiful home.'

'It is special,' he says, nodding. 'And Madison does a great job of keeping it that way. But its real beauty runs deeper than the timber and stone. This homestead has been in the March family for five generations, built in 1870 following the Homestead Act eight years earlier, and it's that legacy that gets me up every morning, makes me work hard for my family, you know?'

I'm surprised by the sense of envy that floats through me. Because the answer is no, I don't know. I've lived in five different homes in my twenty-four years. In our latest house, my parents redecorated my bedroom when I left for college, and I'm still not a fan of the Japanese *sakura* feature wall. I wonder if I would feel less uncertain about my future if I had stronger roots to hold onto like the Marches.

'And you're settling in okay?'

'Um, yes, thank you.'

'That's great.' He's quiet for a few moments, and I find myself drawn to the sound of his breathing. And his scent, some heavily spiced aftershave that I normally can't stomach but seems to smell different in the fresh Montana air. 'And Madison gave you the list?'

The List. He uses such an amiable tone that it's hard to reconcile it with the thin folder Madison handed me last night. Because The List is an uncomfortable read. All the topics I should avoid in my lessons, and the ones I should focus on. It's like a curriculum from the 1950s. 'She did, yes.'

He beams at me again, and I feel slightly better about the directive to skirt over the Clinton presidency.

'Anyways, I've got work to do,' he says. 'It's good to have you here, Cally. The kids already seem to love you and I'm sure you'll fit right in.'

As I watch his large frame shrink into the distance, I wonder if that's true. And why fitting in is starting to feel like a compliment.

Chapter 9

Madison

@barbiegirlee99 Damn girl, how do you look so hot with all that delicious food you cook?
#tradwife #homecooking #inspiration #dieting

I look inside the toilet bowl. There are still tiny specks of vomit in there. Isn't this stage of pregnancy supposed to be over by now? I shudder, sigh, then hit the flush and try to erase the image from my mind. I can't be distracted by thoughts of babies, or morning sickness, or Michael's disapproving expression if he'd spotted the mess before I did.

Especially today, after I checked my engagement stats this morning. My last post got less than fifty thousand likes; I can't remember the last time that happened. I swear it's that Alice DeMille stealing my followers. I really feel this is crunch time. If I don't come up with some fresh ideas, my brand is going to disappear into mediocracy forever. And I can't allow that to happen.

It doesn't help that the weather has cooled. It's only September but the vibrant skies and warm sunshine of summer have already transformed into patchy clouds and faded colors, causing Erica to mumble about unflattering light whenever she walks past a window.

I wash my hands and make my way into the kitchen. With the children in the classroom with Cally, it's quiet in this large room, and I take a moment to watch Lori at work. She looks tired too, and I feel a rush of affection for her. Lori has always done so much for my family, but whenever I tell her to slow down, she promises me that she's fine, that she enjoys being busy. I wonder if it's more than that, that it's her way of paying penance, but I'm not about to start discussing that.

'Morning, Lori,' I say, breaking the silence.

'Oh, hey, Madison.' Lori stops chopping onions and turns towards me. Her eyes are red-rimmed, which I assume is down to the task she's undertaking. 'How are you feeling?'

I shrug. 'Oh, you know.' Lori has played a key role throughout all my pregnancies, looking after me, making sure both me and the baby are healthy, so I don't need to say much for her to understand.

'Want a coffee?' she asks. 'I dug up the chicory root yesterday, ground it fresh this morning.'

'Sounds delicious, thank you.' As I watch Lori drop a filter into the hourglass-shaped flask and add a spoonful of the tan-colored powder, I process her words. 'Is there any root left to dig up?'

'No, I got it all,' she says with pride. 'In case we get an early frost. There's enough to last us through the winter, and then I'll get the kids to help me sow more seeds as soon as the ground thaws in the spring.'

It's smart of her to think ahead, but still, a spike of annoyance tightens my shoulders. I know it's unfair. Lori has done a good thing. But I wish she'd taken two seconds to think. My whole brand is built on wholesome tasks like digging up flipping chicory root, and I'm in desperate need of some good content.

'I was going to collect the chicory root today,' I lie, making my face look sad. 'Erica and I had it all planned out. Me and the children digging it up, then roasting and grinding it into coffee. I've been waiting six months for this opportunity, and now it's gone.'

Lori's eyes grow wide. 'Oh, I'm sorry, I didn't think . . .'

She looks crestfallen, but I find I'm not ready to let her off the hook yet. I listen to the drip-drip-drip of the coffee. 'You've been part of this family from the beginning, from before in fact,' I say. 'Can you not be a bit more aware of what I need? How my followers expect constant updates?'

'You know I've never had much of a social media presence,' Lori reminds me in a whisper. 'Just Tumblr. We agreed it would be safer for me to stay off grid, after . . .' Her voice trails off as she passes me a ceramic mug filled with coffee.

As I stare at the steam snaking skyward, I wonder if it will ever be time for Lori to leave the homestead. I can't imagine surviving without her, but I have Michael now, and it's his job to look after me and the kids, not hers. Finding a new housekeeper would be easy enough. And maybe it's right that this strange, complicated relationship I have with Lori finally comes to an end. Perhaps it's long overdue. I take a sip, feel the liquid scald my tongue.

'I'm really sorry, Madison.'

'Now I have to come up with a new idea.' I privately shudder at the petulance in my voice.

'You could make sourdough again. You said everyone loved watching Myron poke his finger in the bubbles.'

'It's been done a thousand times, which you'd know if you took more interest in my work. Same with banana bread and cheese and flipping homemade lemonade.' Damn, why am I being such a bitch?

A gray cloud wafts in front of the window, sending a dark shadow across Lori's face. 'Maybe Erica could come up with something,' she says. 'Or Noah. They're supposed to be good at this stuff.'

I sigh dramatically, but then feel tears burn my eyes, so turn my attention to blowing on my drink. If anyone should be able to come up with content ideas, it's me. I'm the influencer with her finger on the pulse. Supposedly. So why is my mind blank?

'I think I'm losing my touch,' I admit quietly. 'Other influencers are doing it better than me.'

Lori shakes her head. 'No, you're the original.'

'The numbers don't lie, Lori. I'm not getting close to the level of engagement I used to get.'

'It must be a blip then. You're the one everybody knows, the biggest and the best. There's no way anyone could take your place.'

'I can't stop time though. I'm thirty-two, soon to have my fifth child. What if I'm past my prime? And what if Michael thinks so too and throws me out like he did to Rose? No beautiful homestead then. My followers would abandon me, the brand deals would dry up, and there'd be nothing left.'

'Michael loves you.' Lori pauses. 'At least, he loves having you as his wife.'

'Well, I imagine he liked Rose in that role too once.'

Lori shakes her head. 'Madison, there's no comparison. Rose is a sour-faced drunk who always looks a mess. You can't blame Michael for wanting to get rid of her.'

'Except Bill says she wasn't like that before. He told me that she used to be beautiful, happy, respectable. That she used to look like me.'

Lori doesn't say anything, as though she's run out of reassurances, and the silence makes my stomach lurch.

'I need to find a way to build my social media profile back up and keep hold of Michael,' I say. 'But I don't know how. It's such a tightrope as it is, being the perfect wife for him, and then acting the perfect wife for all my followers.'

Lori's brow crinkles in thought. I listen to her soft breathing, will her to help me. Of course Lori could never leave here, we're too entwined, too dependent on each other for that to be possible.

'Well, you know I've never been married, so I'm not exactly an expert,' she starts. 'But I reckon if Michael came up with the idea that rescued @_TrulyMadison_, you'd be killing two birds with one stone.'

I think through the wisdom of Lori's words. How Michael loves to be right. It is a good idea, but sadly, it couldn't work. 'Maybe, but Michael doesn't understand social media. There's no way he'd ever come up with a good idea in the first place.'

Lori gives me one of her proud motherly smiles. 'I'm pretty sure the Madison I know could make him think he had without him suspecting a thing.'

Chapter 10

Madison

@bethanywilliams_86 Do you ever think that your daughters deserve more than this?
#feminist #prochoice #equality #tradwivesruinlives

I set the speed on the treadmill to a gentle jog and pick up my feet. Lori is right that I'm capable of twisting things to make my ideas come across as Michael's – it's not like I haven't done it before – but that's only part of it. I still need to decide how to breathe new life into my declining brand.

My content needs to be more clickbaity – that's a given – which means dialing down the wholesome living and zoning in on something controversial. But what? We're anti-woke, anti-vax, anti-immigration, anti-tax. And we're pro-guns, pro-oil, pro-family and pro-America, God bless her. But all these issues feel like Michael's rather than mine. In our family, we believe in traditional roles. I'm a wife and mother first and foremost, a caregiver, not a commentator on societal issues. It's not my place to have an opinion.

I keep running, but I can't think clearly, the sound of my sneaker soles against the rubber treadmill belt is too distracting.

So after twenty minutes, I admit defeat. I slow it to a stop, grab my phone, lower onto a stability ball, and start scrolling.

And that's when I realize something. Alice DeMille might look like she's just making toothpaste, but there's other messaging going on too. In one reel, she mentions her neighbor being burgled in the same sultry sentence as a new immigrant family moving in. Then she giggles with delight while showing off her new pink pistol pouch in another. Her politics are subtle, but they're there – and on-brand.

I turn at the sound of the gym door swinging open, and watch Molly walk in. I know I'm not supposed to have favorites, but secretly Molly is mine. I love my boys, but I know they're only mine temporarily. Mason is already turning into his father, and while Myron may be cute as pie now, he'll follow in his brother's footsteps soon enough. There's hope for Matilda, I guess. She has great spirit. But she's a tomboy who doesn't care about her appearance, so we're not exactly kindred spirits.

Although Molly doesn't look her usual sweet self this afternoon.

'Hi, sweetie, is everything okay?'

Molly doesn't speak, but she walks over and wraps her arms around me. I need to hold tightly onto my core to stop us both toppling over, but once we're stabilized, I return the hug and wait for her to explain what's going on.

Eventually she pulls away, but there are tears bubbling in her eyes. 'Daddy disciplined me,' she whispers. She turns over her hand and I see the familiar red stripe across her palm. The mark of Michael's spank paddle that he had carved for himself soon after Molly was born. It might not be as painful as the thin whip that his father used on him, but it's painful enough. Thankfully, Michael is around so little that it doesn't see much use.

'What did you do?' I ask calmly. It's hard to stay loyal to my husband sometimes, but vows are vows.

'I mentioned Aunty Madeline.'

'Oh.'

Michael is the eldest of four siblings, excluding Mason – our firstborn son's namesake – who died in a car accident when he was seventeen. Michael's brother Matthew runs a milling plant in Great Falls, and his younger sister Macie moved to Colorado after meeting her husband Jeff at a ranching event down there. We see them both from time to time, but never his other sister. Madeline's first crime was going to college out of state, to Caltech, to study computer science with law. Her second crime was staying in California after she graduated, and then getting pregnant without a ring on her finger. But what severed the link with her family for good was Madeline getting herself a high-flying career. She's now on the board of one of the biggest tech companies in the U.S., and probably earns more than Michael and Matthew combined.

'Miss Cally told us that her brother works for Cisco,' Molly explains. 'And I remembered that's where Aunty Madeline works. So I asked Daddy if she might be Miss Cally's brother's boss. But he got mad at me for asking, and then started saying that my cousins from Aunty Madeline were abused children, and then I cried, and he told me off for crying about people who bring about their own downfall.' She pauses to catch her breath, then drops her eyeline. 'And that's when he took me to his study.'

I stroke Molly's hair, wipe the tears away with my thumbs. But as I do what I can to console my daughter, a small smile grows on my face. Because Molly might just have given me an idea.

*

47

I try to concentrate on Michael's story about a group of local kids trying to steal one of his cows, but my mind is elsewhere. I know tonight is my best shot at convincing Michael that he's the man to save Truly Madison. I've prepared well. My make-up is perfect, my usually iron-straight hair is curled. I'm wearing Michael's favorite dress, not one he allows me to wear in public – too low cut, too sexy – but one that gets him hot under the collar behind closed doors. The diamond earrings he gave me on my birthday are sparkling in my ears. And Lori has made a romantic meal for two, complete with candles and a bottle of wine – not that I can partake in that. I can sense Michael relaxing in front of me. I just need to find the right moment.

'Anyway, Aaron taught them a lesson, so I doubt they'll be back in a while.' Michael finishes the story and leans back in his chair. 'By the way, that steak was incredible. You know, when you told me that you came as a pair, I was pretty dubious. But it's turned out to be the best decision I've ever made. Lori is one hell of a cook.'

There was a compliment in there somewhere, and on another evening, I'd go fishing for it, but I have a job to do tonight. 'That's true, but I reckon the steak tasted great because you raise the best beef cattle in the world.'

His face spreads into a lazy smile. 'Anyone would think you're after something, Mrs. March.' He leans forward, raises an eyebrow. 'Care to enlighten me?'

My skin fizzes with pleasure. This evening couldn't be going any better. 'Nope, nothing at all. I just happen to believe in credit where credit's due. You run a very successful ranch, and that's because you work damn hard at it.'

'Well, I couldn't do it without you. Raising our beautiful children, looking after my home.'

'And your gratitude is my most powerful motivation, but,' I sigh, 'I just wish that everyone could have what we have. I feel so sorry for those children whose mothers go out to work. They're suffering because of the selfishness of those women.'

He nods, his face souring at the image of women in suits and sneakers flinging their babies through nursery gates. 'Well, we both know that's where things went wrong in the first place, telling women they should go out and work. And then they make up some bullshit narrative about households needing two salaries.'

'Is there any truth to it nowadays?' I ask, knowing just how to prod the bear. 'I mean, I guess there has been inflation lately. Maybe women genuinely do need to work now?'

'No!' Michael's fist slams on the table, and even though I was expecting something like it, I flinch. 'It's just lies put about by those scheming feminists. Every household can be run on a man's earnings. These women are just too damn lazy. They don't want to cook meals, or clean their houses, so they order takeout and line the pockets of immigrants, and then claim they're broke. It's close to criminal in my book, and do you know why?'

'Why?' I pretend to be oblivious while waiting for the line I know is coming.

'Because those poor children are being neglected to the point of abuse.'

I nod sagely. 'It's shocking really, the state of our country. Some of the comments I get on my videos, it's like these women don't know how brainwashed they are.'

'Well, you should tell them!'

I tip my head to one side. 'What? Tell who?'

'All your followers! You've got thousands of them, so tell them what they're missing. People are like cattle, Madison.

They need a firm hand to guide them in the right direction. This country is full of people who have no idea how families should be run, how to raise hardworking, God-fearing American patriots. But we do. And you can teach them that.'

I hold back from pointing out that it's millions, not thousands. 'Maybe you're right.'

'Damn right, I am. The Lord expects us to stand up for what we believe in, and this is what we believe in, isn't it, Madison?'

I nod.

'You show those selfish working mothers how much damage they're doing to their kids and country. You've got my complete approval.' He leans forward, strokes my hair, then pulls my head towards his. 'And I'm assuming I have yours,' he adds with a husky chuckle.

But I don't have a chance to answer before his lips land on mine, and his hand slips inside my dress.

Chapter 11

Cally

'Kids, this morning we're going to have a geography lesson,' I say, leaning back onto my desk. 'We're going to learn about all the different states in America, which also gives me a chance to tell you a little bit about where I'm from.' Educating the March children on America sits high on The List, so I know this is a safe lesson, but my reason for choosing it is personal. I've been feeling a little homesick lately, and knowing I can't go back yet, that I'm exiled from own city until next July, only makes it worse.

'I thought you were from England?' Matilda asks, chewing on a yellow pencil.

'It's New England, silly,' Mason says. 'Which is owned by America.'

I smile sympathetically at my three students, or four if you count Myron who is currently racing wooden cars under Molly's desk. Geography clearly isn't their strong point.

'New England is an area of America,' I explain. 'It's made up of six states on the northeast coast, including Massachusetts, where I'm from. The first settlers came from England, which is a country in Europe, about four hundred years ago, and they gave the region its name.'

'That's not a very exciting name,' Molly notes, scrunching her nose in distaste.

'I'd have called it Mason's Country, if I'd found it.'

'Well, I come from a city called Boston, in Massachusetts, which I'm afraid is also named after an English town.'

'Boss town,' Mason says, nodding approvingly. 'I like that.'

I screw my face up, wonder why I'd never thought of that. 'So who knows how many states there are in total?' I ask.

'Fifty!' Mason shouts out. 'Everyone knows that.'

I shouldn't let emotion guide my teaching, but I do find his smug expression slightly triggering. 'How about you name them all for us then?'

He narrows his eyes like a cartoon villain. 'That's too many. I know all the ones I need to know.'

'Oh?'

'Montana, Idaho, Wyoming, Utah.'

'You're talking about the western states,' I say, feeling oddly proud that I know this.

'Nah, they're the red states. The real red states that you can always count on.'

'Red's my favorite color!' Myron shouts from under the table, stretching down his red T-shirt. 'See?'

'Yes, those states do tend to vote Republican,' I say. 'But there are Democrat-leaning states in the area too . . .'

The door flies open. Madison steps inside. 'What an interesting topic, Cally. What was it you were saying about the Democrats?' she asks, her words more friendly than her tone.

My cheeks flood with heat. 'Oh, nothing. We were having a geography lesson. On America,' I add quickly. 'Anyway, is everything okay?'

'I see,' she says, sweeping further into the room. 'You know, I heard most of America will be voting Republican this time.'

She pulls a chair from behind my desk and positions it in front of the children. Then she sits down, laces her fingers, and smiles. I have a strange sense of being thrust into the shadows, even though I'm standing by the window.

'And yes, everything's fine,' she continues. 'But I've decided I'd like to get a little more involved in the children's education, so I thought we could share lessons.'

'Mommy's going to teach us!' Matilda exclaims, clapping her hands.

'What can you teach us?' Mason asks suspiciously. 'Does Daddy know?'

'Of course Daddy knows. It was his idea in fact. Cally will still be your tutor, but I'll teach you things like social studies.'

'What's social studies?' Molly asks.

'Well, we learn about society, and what makes a good one.'

'Daddy says we're upstanding members of our society,' Mason says proudly.

'And that's because we're a good family,' Madison says. 'We have a daddy who does a really important job, a mommy who stays at home and looks after her family, and four, soon to be five, beautiful children who are learning how to live right.'

'Will I be a mommy one day?' Matilda asks.

'Of course you will. You and Molly. And you will raise beautiful, well-behaved children because you've been taught the right values about family life,' Madison says.

'Do you want to get married and raise babies, Miss Cally?'

I turn to look at Molly and the concern on her face makes me want to cry, like being a mother is the only thing that matters in life. I don't even know if I want kids, but I do know I shouldn't get involved in this discussion.

'Maybe,' I say, slowly, as though testing the ground for an explosive device. 'But I want to get my career off the ground first.' I wait for a bomb to go off, but Madison looks more pleased than offended.

'What career is that?' she asks, without a hint of disapproval. Which is strange, based on The List. I have a discomforting sense that I'm stumbling into a trap. 'I think you mentioned marketing in our interview,' she goes on. 'Or was it human resources?'

'Well, um, I've tried both, actually. But they weren't for me.'

'Maybe raising babies is for you after all, Miss Cally,' Matilda offers. 'Like Mommy.'

'Deciding what to dedicate your life to can be hard,' Madison says. 'That's why we turn to the Bible for guidance. Mary dedicated herself to Jesus, and that's good enough for me.'

'But that was two thousand years ago,' I point out, apologetically for some reason. 'There are other options now.'

'Like what?' Molly asks.

'Well, you could be a nurse, or maybe a chef.' I want to say politician or journalist, but I know that would be pushing things.

'You could, yes,' Madison says, her tone still full of honey. 'But you would have to make sacrifices if you chose that path. Like leaving your children in other people's care. You wouldn't get to raise them, and your children might love those carers more than you.'

'I wouldn't like that,' Molly whispers.

'And working every day has its challenges, wouldn't you say, Cally?'

'Well, yes, but there are rewards too.'

'How was your journey into the office when you worked those jobs?'

'Well, yeah, that was pretty bad,' I admit. 'I'd take the bus,

54

but the traffic was always gridlocked, and sometimes I'd have to wait for ages for one to show. But my office had free coffee when I did eventually arrive.'

Mason looks nonplussed. 'Who pays for coffee?'

'And how did you find your bosses?' Madison asks, her voice heavy with compassion.

I sigh. 'Well, my boss at the marketing agency hated me from day one, to be honest. She was one of those single middle-aged women who needed to wield power just to justify her existence.'

I stop. Almost gasp at the words that have just fallen out of my mouth.

'My boss at the human resources firm had three children,' I blurt out. 'And she only hated me because I sent an email about layoffs to the whole business rather than the management team by accident,' I gabble on.

But I can see by the triumph on Madison's face, and the kids' sympathetic expressions, that I've well and truly lost this argument.

When I barely even realized I was engaged in one.

Chapter 12

Brianna

Something is wrong.

I sense it even before I see the coop, its wire mesh pulled away from the wooden structure, two of its planks smashed and broken.

Maybe it's the smell of blood in the air.

All six chickens are gone, and the damaged coop looks like a scene from *The Texas Chainsaw Massacre,* blood smeared across the ground and up the sides, some feathers stuck to it, others suspended in the air by the wind. I shiver as I stare at the brutal sight, wondering what to do, hoping that Jonah will magically appear beside me and tell me that clearing up the detritus of dead chickens is a man's job. Wondering if I can pretend that I haven't noticed the carnage until he does.

The irony is Jonah is usually the first up, sometimes by hours. I think my natural sleep cycle has always favored sleeping in, but I never had much opportunity when I lived in Buffalo. Cheerleading practice on Saturday, church on Sunday, school during the week. But now we're here, with no noises to wake us and no place to be, I sleep to midday sometimes.

But that didn't happen today. I woke up early and found I

was too cold to drift back off. So I came downstairs to get a fire going and make myself something hot for breakfast. Now that I've worked out how to make bread rise – it turns out it's about strength and patience, like most things in this place – I was thinking I'd cook some poached eggs on toast. But now the chickens are gone, and the eggs they laid before they were taken are all smashed and mixed in with the blood.

I feel my face crumple. I've cried a few times lately. Jonah doesn't like it, says it makes him feel guilty. But the truth is, I don't like crying either. I wish I could be stronger, more stoic like my great-grandma when my great-grandpa went off to war. She took over the family farm, that's what my daddy told me, and raised seven kids at the same time. While all I've got to do is clean up a broken chicken coop.

I hear a noise behind me and jerk around – an irrational fear that whatever killed our chickens, a racoon or a bobcat or a coyote, has come back for me – but of course it's Jonah, ambling down from the deck, yawning. But as he gets closer, his pace slows, giving himself time to process what's happened.

'Oh, shit,' he murmurs. 'Are they all dead?'

I feel a spike of annoyance. Of course they're all dead. Did he expect me to save panicking chickens from the jaws of a wild animal? 'It must have happened while we were asleep,' I throw back, my instinct to retaliate. 'I guess the coop wasn't secure enough.'

He tenses up beside me. 'It's hard doing all these jobs by myself. Would be nice if you helped me out a bit more.'

I pull my coat tighter around my body. There'll be snow in a couple of months, and then we'll really notice the cracks in the woodwork, the lack of insulation and central heating. The isolation. Those pictures in magazine articles, the homesteading posts on social media, they never show this side of it. The sun always shines in their photos – even in winter – and the whole aesthetic screams of abundance. Food, space, time, family. They seem to be overflowing with it all. So why do I feel like my life is shrinking and shriveling?

'Sometimes I wonder if we're ready for this,' I say quietly. The thought that has simmered softly in the back of my mind for a while, now bubbling with a new intensity. 'We could press pause for a little while, go home, have some fun with our friends. Come back in the spring maybe. There's no sell-by date on dreams after all.'

Jonah edges away from me. 'What do you mean by fun, Bri?'

'You know, be teenagers. Hang out, watch TV. See friends, go to parties.'

'Laze around at your parent's house, you mean? Expect them to bankroll you?'

'No, of course not.'

'Then you'd have to get a job. And would you really prefer to work in a stuffy office than be here, with me, working together to make our dream come true?'

'No, I . . .'

'Listen, we knew this wasn't going to be easy.' His voice turns warm and soft, and it reminds me of the luxury bath towels my mom bought in the spring sales. 'The best things in life never are. But we made a promise to each other, didn't we? Us against the world? Don't let a few dead chickens destroy our dream.'

He reaches for me, and I lean my head against his chest, listen to the constant thud of his heart. 'This is our home now, Bri,' he goes on. 'There is no turning back. I told my mom I was going to make something of myself, like my eldest brother did when he went into the army, and my middle brother taking that job on an oil rig in Texas. I'm not going back on my word.

And remember, you didn't leave on the best terms, did you? I doubt your parents would welcome you back with open arms.'

I bite my chapped bottom lip. It's true that my mom begged me not to go, and my daddy said if I chose this path, brought dishonor on my family, he'd disown me. And they never call to check how I'm doing. But would they really turn me away if we came back? I've been Daddy's little girl for eighteen years. Mom made the pajamas I'm wearing now. They can't have meant it.

'Listen, this isn't women's work,' Jonah says, pulling away from me. 'I'll clear up this mess, you get the fire on and make us some coffee. Then I'll build a new coop. I reckon we've got enough money for a couple of new chickens at least.'

'Are you sure?' I ask, hoping it's a rhetorical question.

Jonah kisses my head. 'Of course. Now go get warm.'

I'm so relieved that I'm practically skipping by the time I reach the deck. It doesn't really make sense. The house is still freezing, there's nothing exciting to eat, and I have a list of jobs to get done that will take all day. But not having to deal with dead chickens has sent a surge of joy through me.

Perhaps that is the attraction of this lifestyle. The bad is so bad that the smallest positive feels like Thanksgiving and Christmas Day all rolled into one. But I don't want to feel grateful for the small pleasures in life. I want to go after the big pleasures, the beautiful home and piano in the parlor.

I create a pyramid of kindling in the hearth and set it alight. Once it's hot, I add bigger logs, just like Jonah taught me, and watch the bark catch and flare. Then I fill the iron kettle with water and place it on the shelf above the fire.

As I wait for the water to boil, I pull my phone out of my coat pocket. When we were planning our adventure, sitting on those empty bleachers after Friday night practice, Jonah suggested that we go fully off grid, no phones, no internet. But I told him that I couldn't live without a connection to the outside world, so one of the first things he did when we moved out here was buy a secondhand diesel generator and set up a basic electricity rig. It's not reliable, but it's enough to give us light at night and charge my phone every day. I thought signal might be a problem, but it turns out the wide Wyoming plains can pick up a lot from those satellites in space.

Jonah isn't into social media, but he doesn't mind me scrolling once I've got my chores done. I look at them all, but Instagram is my favorite – all those beautiful people with beautiful things, and I love taking inspiration from the amazing #homesteading women. I've even messaged a couple of my favorite accounts, although I haven't heard back yet. I guess they're busy – I now know how much time this lifestyle takes up.

And maybe Jonah is right. Maybe our dream is worth working for. Then one day I'll be posting photos, and people will be coming to me for advice.

Chapter 13

Madison

@momofgirls1992 STOP poisoning your children and don't you dare poison mine!
#progressive #feminist #socialjustice #tradwivesruinlives

I run my fingers through my dresses, pick out a lavender smock dress with pale yellow flowers, and sneak a thermal vest underneath – essential for what I've got scheduled in this morning. To be honest, I don't have high hopes for this content anymore, but I can't tell Lori that after the effort she's put in. And it was me who made a fuss about digging up the chicory root, I suppose. I have a few minutes until Bill picks me up, so I sink onto the bed and reach for my phone.

My pivot towards controversy is taking off on an impressive scale. In the last three weeks, I've gained one hundred thousand new followers, my reels are regularly getting more than half a million likes again, and my media requests have doubled – even Fox News contacted me for comment. My loyal followers love me for it too. They tell me that I'm speaking truth to power, standing up for true American values, doing God's work by taking on those dangerous progressives.

And this shift has sparked new life into my marriage too. At least for now. Michael loved my post about sad cat ladies and even opened a bottle of champagne when #felininity started trending. That enthusiasm did start to fray after a couple of weeks of Erica calling me a genius, but then I filmed my latest reel, a direct to camera piece about the importance of being submissive to your husband. He watched that lying in bed one night, and seconds after it finished, my panties were flying off and I was submitting for real before my brain even had a chance to register what was happening. Which I guess is a sign that our marriage is still healthy.

But as I scroll through the blur of fifteen thousand comments, I wonder if my surging popularity has some downsides too. While my posts have always drawn some bitchy comments, or condescending ones about the lifestyle I've chosen, the vast majority have been glowing compliments. But that's changing, and my latest reel has sparked a ton of hate. People calling me evil, uninformed, a domestic abuse enabler, even a white supremacist – I mean, what? I mention that women are put on this earth to bear and raise children and suddenly I'm a Klan supporter? I like sharing these truths because it's so clearly needed, but some of the comments are so hateful and violent, I can't help wondering if I'm putting myself in danger.

A frisson of something unpleasant passes through my body as I think about what I've done, the can of worms I've flexed open with my pretty white teeth and honey smile. But I can't think like that. People are listening to me again, watching my reels, talking about me offline. And that means the algorithms will have picked up on my renewed popularity too.

To hell with my critics. What is it Mae West said? It's better to be looked over than overlooked.

I stand up, smooth down my skirt, grab a cream knitted cardigan, and head outside to Bill's Chevy Silverado.

Half an hour later, Bill drops me at the front door of the Stuarts' homestead and promises he'll wait – this visit might be at my behest, but I want to spend as little time here as possible. The door opens and I steel myself.

'Madison! So lovely to see you, it's been too long.' Jemma Stuart's cheeks are rosy, and her blue eyes sparkle with wholesome energy. But tufts of coarse red hair have escaped from her side plait, and her dress looks like it's from the thrift store.

'You too, Jemma. And thank you so much for today,' I say, taking care to sound as effusive as she does. 'I really appreciate your generosity – and your discretion.' The words stick a little because I really don't want to be indebted to this woman. I know Lori thought she was doing me a favor, arranging for me to dig up the Stuarts' chicory root and pretend it's ours, after she took away my opportunity to do it at home. But everything about this twee homesteading family makes my teeth itch.

'Oh, honestly, it's nothing. I love being part of your little conspiracy.' She giggles. 'Now come on in. It's getting cold, isn't it? Winter's knocking. Not that I'm complaining. The kids love the snow, and we're well stocked up for the cold months. And there's nothing like hot chocolate around a toasty fire with a jigsaw puzzle to conquer, is there?'

'Nothing at all.' I walk inside with my tripod clamped between tense fingers. My facial muscles are twitching with the effort of fake smiling too, so I'm relieved when Jemma turns and leads me through the house and out the back door. But my gratitude quickly slides as a barrage of different-sized children come running at me.

'Whoah, slow down!' Jemma calls out, laughing. 'Anyone would think you haven't seen another human being before.'

I count eight children in total, five girls and three boys. How does Jemma not look exhausted with this huge brood to contend with?

'Hi, Mrs. March,' the middle-sized girl says. She's around Molly's age but fatter. 'I made bran muffins this morning. Would you like one?'

'That's very kind of you. They look delicious, but I'm still full from breakfast.'

Her face drops a little, then recovers.

'Now kids, Mrs. March is here to do some filming for her homesteading blog, so we need to give her some space, okay? So go play while I help out, and then we'll head inside for Bible reading afterwards.'

'Yay!' a couple of the smaller children shout in unison. Then they all veer away, like an unrehearsed murmuration.

'Those kids just adore you, Madison!' Jemma says, radiating life on a disconcerting scale. 'Now, Marty has set up everything you need to dig up the chicory. He sends his apologies for not being here; he's gone to buy a new goat this morning. His goat cheese is really taking off in the general store and poor Gerty can't keep up!' She takes a breath, then relaunches. 'And you'll be pleased to know I'm getting pretty good behind the camera – you know, I've been accepted on a couple of those image websites, and my Montana skylines are selling like hotcakes.' She shakes her head. 'Who would have thought someone like me could make money online?'

Who indeed.

I smile. 'That's great, Jemma. I'm so happy for you. If you could just hit record when I give the word, that would be perfect.'

Twenty minutes later, I have enough footage for my reel. Jemma asks me to stay for lunch and for a fleeting moment, I find myself wishing I could. Jemma and Marty are well-known around town as the local do-gooders, which is why I generally keep my distance, helping strangers not really being my thing. But a few years ago, when canning started trending on Instagram in a big way, I asked Jemma if she'd teach Lori and me about preserving food. And she didn't hesitate. After our lesson, we were invited to stay for dinner. They didn't treat me like a global influencer, which normally might irk, but I remember how relaxing it felt that evening.

Except I am a global influencer of course. So I tell her I need to take a rain check, grab my tripod and head off to meet Bill at the car.

Chapter 14

Madison

@anonX7659 I will come for you when you're sleeping and cut your pretty little throat
#promise #incel #blackpilled #watchout

'Back home?' Bill asks as he starts the engine.

I shake my head. 'I'm due at Shelley's salon at midday so could you drop me in town?' It's been a while since I had my hair and nails done, and with the Montana Business Awards coming up, it felt like a good time to book an appointment.

But instead of smiling, Bill's forehead creases. 'Town?'

'Is that a problem?' I ask.

Bill shrugs and sets off. 'No, of course not.' We drive in silence for a while, but eventually he finds his voice again. 'It's just that Michael said you'd been talking some on your Instagram. And not all folks are best pleased about it.'

'Well, I guess that's true.' I pause, focus on not letting that unpleasant feeling from earlier find a way back in. 'Is Michael worried about me?'

'Well, no, not exactly,' Bill says, embarrassed now. Bill's

never been much of a talker. 'He's proud of you though, he said that, telling everyone how it is.'

'Oh. That's good.'

'But it does make you think, doesn't it? About being out in town on your own? I mean, I know these keyboard warriors make threats all the time, and they're probably too spineless to crawl out from behind their computer screens, never mind do anything. But it only takes one, doesn't it?'

I feel blood drain from my face. Because Bill's right. At least a dozen people have told me that I deserve to die just this morning. What if one of them is crazy enough to come after me in real life? I shuffle in the seat. 'But those kinds of people don't live around here, do they? This is Montana, not New York.'

Bill turns to me and – finally – smiles. 'Yeah, you're right. I'm being a numbskull. If Michael's not worried, I'm not worried. You sit back, and enjoy the drive.'

I lean back against the headrest, but Bill's words have put me on edge.

I pull out my phone and tap straight into Instagram. Five thousand more likes since last time I checked. My face breaks into a smile, until I see that there's another message from Brianna Wyoming. I've had a few now. I haven't blocked her yet, which is what I normally do when interest tilts towards obsession. In fact, that is exactly what I will do, just after I read this one.

Hey, it's Brianna again.
I watched your reel, and I wanted to say thank you for reminding me, because you're right, a woman should submit to their man.

I love mine very much, but sometimes I forget that he knows best.
Have you ever gone against Michael's wishes?
Or kept things secret from him?
I know you're so famous now, but I'd really appreciate you messaging me back.

I judder out a breath. It's a stupid message from someone I've never met, but something about it has struck a nerve.

You're right, a woman should submit to their man. I think about the sex Michael and I had the other night. Of course I wanted it – I know intimacy is the key to a successful marriage – but I didn't actually tell him that. I didn't get the chance. But that's because our marriage is so perfect that we can communicate without words. Isn't it?

I look down at my engagement ring. The one and a half carat diamond solitaire that I remove or twist out of sight on my @_TrulyMadison_ posts. When Michael threw me and a bottle of champagne into his truck, then drove us into the middle of a cattle field and pulled me down onto his one knee, I thought life couldn't get any better. This gorgeous, rich man wanted me to be his wife. And I have no regrets.

But did Rose wear this ring before me? Did he rip her panties off whenever he felt like it? And what did she do to make him stop?

Ask him to?

I drop my phone into my pocket and stare out the window until Bill pulls up outside Shelley's salon on Big Timber's Main Street.

'I hear congratulations are due,' Shelley says a while later, jolting me out of my daydream. My hair is in foils, my nail

68

varnish is barely dry, and no one is supposed to know about the pregnancy. 'Nancy told me,' she goes on. 'Nathan's wife. She said you were due in February?'

'Yes, that's right,' I stutter, smoothing out the skirt of my dress like a nervous tic. I asked Michael to keep our news quiet for now, but of course he'd tell Nathan, and our morally defunct lawyer wouldn't have any qualms about telling his wife.

'Well, you look amazing,' Shelley says. 'What number is this? Fourth? Fifth? Sweet Jesus, I wish I knew your secret.'

I smile. I'm not stupid – she's being nice in the hope that I feature her salon on my channels – but I've never been able to resist a compliment. 'It's my fifth. And thank you. Just between us, my secret is having a home gym.'

'I don't know how you find the time. Looking after your family, cooking all those delicious meals. Making it look easy. You're an inspiration to millions of American women, Madison. You certainly are to me.'

'Thank you, Shelley.' I half wish I could tag her salon on my next post now, but I know Erica will persuade me otherwise. 'And my more recent content?' I ask tentatively. 'Have you seen any of that?' I've never been good at guessing ages, but Shelley must be mid-twenties by now. And she's here, working, childless, as far as I know. I really hope she doesn't own a cat.

'Oh, yes, and I couldn't agree more. I mean, I'm still waiting for Mr. Right, but when he comes along, there's no way I'm working twelve-hour shifts in here. I want someone to look after me the same way Mr. March takes care of you.'

I lean back against the plastic seat cover and smile. Of course there's nothing to worry about, here, surrounded by my people.

An hour later, my hair is natural blonde all the way down to the root, and my nails are smooth and shiny. I leave Shelley a big tip – it's the least I can do – and head outside. As I look up and down Main Street, I spot two old guys heading for the bar and watch them disappear through the saloon doors. I check the time on my phone. I've got another twenty minutes until Bill picks me up. I wonder if she's in there now. She will have finished working at the store, and everyone knows how partial she is to a bourbon.

Could I?

Should I?

Without giving myself a chance to change my mind, I stride across the road, then slow my pace and slink inside the bar, plunging into near darkness. When Lori and I first arrived in Big Timber, we came here a few times. Now I only come once a year, on Labor Day, when they host a party for local working families. But in a dozen years, it hasn't changed. I walk deeper into the gloom, ignoring everyone – the bartender, and the smattering of daytime drinkers.

And then I see her. She's sitting on a stool at the end of the bar, head down, an empty tumbler glass by her hand. She's wearing jeans and an old Bobcats sweater. Slowly she looks up. We stare at each other for a few seconds, until I can't stand the tension anymore.

'Hi, I'm . . .' I start.

'I know who you are.'

'Oh. I've been to the salon. I got thirsty, and . . .'

She nods. 'If you're buying, mine's a Dry Hills, no ice.'

It's not like me to be speechless, but I nod mutely, then turn to the bartender and order Rose's drink, plus a lemonade for me.

'So he's looking after you?' she asks as I set her drink down.

The directness of her question creates a strange desire to confide in her. To tell her about my flying panties. The welts

70

on Molly's hand. Mason's rudeness. I shake my mane of salon-polished hair. 'Absolutely. Michael is a wonderful man.'

She releases an almost silent laugh. 'Yes, he is,' she says, swilling the rusty liquid around her glass. 'Until he isn't. And I hope you're ready for that because, trust me, it's a stinger.'

I feel conflicting urges to burst into tears and punch her in the face. Although isn't that how people describe Rose's erratic behavior? I shouldn't have come here. 'We're different, you and me,' I say, with more confidence than I feel.

'Not so different,' she murmurs. 'I used to look a bit like you once upon a time. Hard to believe now, I guess, but it's the truth.'

'Oh, I heard that. But that's not what I meant.'

'No?' Rose shifts slightly to face me.

'I'm smarter than you, Rose. I know how to keep hold of a husband.'

Rose looks at me – an unsettling mix of sympathy and distaste – then downs her drink. 'Oh, honey,' she says, her voice raspy from the fiery spirit. 'It's not me you need to be smarter than, it's him. Take care of yourself, Madison.' Then she swings off her bar stool and a moment later, she's gone, the saloon doors swaying to a stop behind her.

I stare after her, suddenly feeling exposed in this place built for men. The two old dudes are deep in conversation, but I can sense another man watching me from the corner booth.

Instinctively I know not to turn towards him, but the intensity of his gaze still makes my cheeks burn. I need to leave. I feel his eyes tracking me as I walk towards the exit. But as I push on the saloon doors, breathe in the daylight, and see Bill waving from across the street, my nerves settle.

I'm Madison March. Of course men are going to stare at me.

Chapter 15

Cally

I look at the caller ID on my phone – Luke – and feel my heart rate tick up. Even though we're polar opposites in lots of ways, we've always been close. But I haven't spoken to him since that night – the Fourth of July – when I made the not-to-be-recommended transition from dumb idiot to actual criminal. He saved my butt when I begged him to, but that didn't stop him kicking it once the dust settled. And it's been the silent treatment ever since. Not that I deserve more.

I take a deep breath and accept the call.

'Hey, Luke,' I say breezily. 'How's life in SF?'

'Good, I guess, when I'm allowed out of Palo Alto.'

He goes quiet, and I know I need to say something. But what? Sorry? I'm a changed person now, so you've got nothing to worry about? 'It's good to hear from you.'

'I thought I should check in,' he says. 'You know, make sure you haven't resigned yet. It's been two months, and I figured that was about your usual limit.' He chuckles, but it fades away because we both know he's deadly serious.

'I guess I have more of an incentive this time.'

When he doesn't respond, I close my eyes and remember that

terrible night. Luke picking up my call, somehow deciphering my hysterics, getting an Uber from the bar he was in, arriving on the street like my knight in shining armor.

'Listen, of course I'm going to stick it out,' I continue. 'I promise. I'm going to be the best tutor the March children have ever had, earn my big fat bonus, and be home before the Fourth of July to make everything okay again.'

'You're sure?'

'One hundred percent.'

He sighs, and I can tell by its sound that I've semi-convinced him, which I'm taking as a win. 'So how is it, living with a famous influencer?' he asks, and I silently thank him for the change in subject. 'Have you convinced her that you should star in one of her reels yet?'

'What, with my nose stud?'

He laughs, and I like the sound of it. 'What about her hot rancher husband then. Has he force-fed you slabs of cow?'

'No, although the veggie gravy does taste suspiciously beefy,' I admit. 'But overall, it's pretty good. The kids are better behaved than most of the entitled terrors I tutored in Boston. Madison is everything you'd imagine. Beautiful in that good girl kind of way. All demure and grateful.'

'Well, that's dull. What about their marriage? Please tell me the husband beats her, or at least locks her in a cupboard in between Instagram reels?'

'That's a bit dark.'

'Yeah, sorry,' he says sheepishly. 'I forget that they're not Netflix characters. Is he just an upstanding loyal husband like she makes out?'

I pause to consider Luke's question. Michael is charming. He rough and tumbles with the kids if they catch him in the right mood, and I saw him give one of his farmworkers a fistful of dollars when he announced that his wife was having a baby. But he also expects total obedience from everyone. And there are those welts I've noticed on Molly and Mason's hands from time to time.

But either way, I signed Nathan's form.

'Pretty much, I say vaguely. 'Traditional, you know. But that's fine because Madison loves things that way. And she adores him.'

'True love, hey. Looks like I need to do some work on my cynicism.'

We talk for another five minutes, about nothing, which is what I've missed most, then we say our goodbyes. Without giving it too much thought, I tap into Instagram, and Madison's latest reel is the first post I see. She's sitting in the classroom with the children all gazing up at her, rapt. I know Erica will be somewhere out of shot, bribing them with something illicit like M&Ms. Making them perform like circus monkeys for a few extra likes.

Madison is talking to the children about family life, and how it needs protecting. There's a transition to Matilda and Molly baking cookies, splatters of the mixture on their faces. I would have smiled at that once, but knowing the scene will have been carefully constructed by Madison takes the shine off. The next clip shows Mason outside chopping wood and Myron stacking the logs. Enforcing stereotypes before any of them have learned long division.

I shuffle up against the headboard and tip my face towards the ceiling. I always thought Madison March was harmless. Maybe not someone to admire, but laid-back entertainment, an antidote to real life. Her soft voice and brood of sweet, innocent children like a lullaby after a long day. But does that send some brain cells to sleep? Specifically, the ones that believe in smashing the patriarchy?

74

And I swear she's getting worse. Like that reel she made a couple of weeks ago, direct to camera, not her usual style, but still delivered in that honey-coated voice. Submitting isn't losing, she'd said, it's winning. Because the secret to a good marriage is both of you knowing your place.

I mean, seriously? Didn't those views die with birth control and LSD?

But there is the awkward truth that I'm her children's tutor, complying every day with The List. Does that make me part of this? Madison has already used my failed careers as currency for her cause. But there are worse things than dwindling employment options (hopefully). Women's reproductive rights, Andrew Tate's manosphere, Harvey Weinstein. How would I respond if Molly asked me what consent meant?

A knock at my bedroom door makes me sit up. My room is on the same floor as all the March family bedrooms, but at the far end, so no one ever walks past it. 'Hello?' The door opens, then closes, and I feel a jolt of panic. 'Is everything okay?'

'Yeah, all good,' Michael says, leaning against the heavy wooden door.

He's blocking my only route out of here, I notice, which feels a little overdramatic, but still, there it is. 'Does one of the children need me?'

'No, nothing like that. They're all fast asleep. Madison and Lori too. But I was outside, seeing to the horses, and I noticed what a clear night it is out there. Not a cloud in the sky.'

'Oh, I bet that looks pretty,' I say carefully.

'Pretty doesn't do it justice, Cally. Nowhere close.' He gives me that lazy smile, which, I'm horrified to discover, makes my stomach flutter. 'I promise there is nothing quite like a clear Montana night sky. You really need to see it.'

'Well, um . . .' I can't go out there, into the dark, alone, with

Madison's husband, can I? But maybe it is more appealing than scrolling myself to sleep.

'And I've got the firepit roaring, so it's not cold. Come on, no excuses.'

I did a whole psych module on coercive control, so it's not hard for me to pick up that Michael has smoothly turned an invite into a demand. But it's less clear why I unfurl from the bed, pull my UGGS on, and follow him outside.

I can't drag my eyes away. It's like nothing I've ever seen. There are the stars, yes, hundreds of them, like pure white dust floating around pearls in the darkness. But it's the sky itself which is truly mesmerizing. The epic, expansive size of it. I feel so small and insignificant, but also special to be its witness.

'Worth coming out for?' Michael drawls next to me.

'It's amazing,' I whisper, feeling like an awestruck seven-year-old. 'It's hard to believe we're on Earth, never mind still in America.'

'I've never understood why anyone would move to the city, not when so much of what's great about America is hidden behind concrete and artificial light in those places. Hey, see that?' Michael leans closer towards me and I feel his hand rest on my back, but it's between my shoulders, more fatherly than flirtatious, and I'm shocked to feel a slight disappointment at that. He uses his free hand to point at the sky. 'It's a shooting star.'

I watch what looks like a sparkling droplet of water descend and disappear. Then another one. 'Wow,' I murmur, the word floating away, my mouth too spellbound to close.

'How about I get us a glass of wine?' Michael says. 'Then we can sit by the fire and take it all in.'

'Yeah, sure,' I manage, still staring skyward. But as Michael's hand leaves my back, and his shadow disappears, I find myself lowering my gaze, becoming more aware of my surroundings. It's not only the sky that goes on forever. The homestead stretches into the darkness, and with only the faint crackle of wood burning behind me, I can hear the eerie cry of wild animals in the distance. It sends a shiver through me, and I back up towards the warmth and light of the fire. By the time Michael returns, I'm curled up on one of the small outdoor sofas directly in front of the fire. He hands me a glass of wine and sits down next to me.

'You know, we've always had tutors who come from states closer to home, Utah and Idaho. I wasn't sure about you at first, Cally, but now I'm glad Madison hired you.'

'Um, thank you.' I take a mouthful of wine. I don't ever drink red wine, but this is potent and heady. It suits my mood.

'Showing city folk this way of life feels like God's work, and I reckon I'm doing a damn fine job with you.' He chuckles, then clinks his glass against mine and takes a long gulp.

I manage an eyebrow raise and sardonic smile in response to his words. But as I push the glass against my lips again, I wonder if it's pride that I'm feeling, for making Michael think he's won me over. Or worry that I am, in fact, being taken in by his charm.

Chapter 16

Brianna

I look at the rancid fish peeking out of the plastic bag, listen to Jonah throwing up upstairs, and wonder what to do.

He was so excited when he came back from the lake yesterday evening. He'd positioned himself close to where the river flows in and used crickets that he'd caught over the summer as bait. It only took him three hours to catch two cutthroat trout. And they were a good size too. At least two dinners' worth.

Gutting that first one was gross. Chopping its head off. Slicing it down the middle then pulling out its insides. Trying not to retch at the smell. But I looked up how to do it on Google, and followed the instructions, so I don't understand why Jonah is so sick now.

Did I do something wrong? Or was the fish bad in the first place?

The whole experience of preparing the fish put me off eating it, so Jonah had the lion's share. And the small portion I did give myself got pushed around the plate. So it's not surprising that he's the one vomiting this morning rather than me, but Jonah didn't see it that way. He even accused me of poisoning him on purpose. Which is pretty unfair after all the effort I went to.

And I know he only accused me because of our argument yesterday. Our first proper full-throttle fight in two and a half years of being together. And over what? A couple of half-price dresses?

I should burn the second trout. That's what Jonah said we should do with old food. I'm not stupid enough to put it on the fire in the living room, so I pick up the bag with an outstretched arm – trying not to think about its slimy polka dot skin or glassy dead eyes – and head outside. The icy wind hits me instantly. Even now, after weeks of it getting colder, the first blast of the day takes my breath away.

I lower my face into my jacket collar and keep walking. Jonah has set up an old oil drum about two hundred yards away from the house for burning stuff, and I drop the fish in there, amongst bits of splintered wood and fallen branches. I wonder for a moment if I should try to smoke the fish. Does that get rid of the poison? Then I shake my head, throw some diesel into the drum, and set the lot on fire.

As I stare into the flames, my vision blurs. I can't keep denying the truth. Our new life isn't the dream it was supposed to be, it's a nightmare, except worse than that because it's not something I can wake up from.

But it's the life I chose, I remind myself, as the smoke stings my eyes. Jonah is determined to stay, to make it work somehow, and he's my forever man. We might not be married but we made that commitment, for better or worse, when we ran away together. I can't leave him. But how can I stay here when me ordering a couple of dresses, using my own savings, causes World War Three?

I push my hands further into my jacket pocket and feel the cold metal of my phone. It's like I'm in a trance as my stiff fingers pull it out, tap into my Favorites, and choose the first contact on the list. But my mind jolts into focus as I read the name. Mom. Should I just call her? Will she have moved on from the argument we had in July? Forgiven me?

I guess there's only one way to find out.

As I listen to the familiar ring, my heart begins to race. What will I say to her? I could admit that I'm not happy, tell her that I don't think I'm cut out for homesteading after all, and she'll come and rescue me, I'm sure of it. But can I be that disloyal to Jonah? Maybe I should stick to his narrative instead, say that I love it out here, and hope the sound of her voice and snippets about what they're all up to back home is enough. But what would be the point of making a Mayday call, then pretending everything is fine?

The line clicks into voicemail and after a second of indecision I cut the call.

A gust of wind whips under my dress and I ride the sting of it. I love to look feminine for Jonah, like my mom does for Daddy, and I know he prefers me in dresses too. But it's not so easy in winter, when I have a daily list of outdoor chores. With a sigh, I turn back to the house. I walk in through the back door and reach for the ancient kettle, hoping there's enough water for a coffee. With a swell of relief, I feel its weight and place it on the shelf by the fire.

As I wait for the water to heat, I open up the Tumblr app on my phone. I only set up an account last week, but I've already posted four times. I didn't think I had a story to share – not like those beautiful homemakers on Instagram, or those bragging vacationers on Facebook – but when I started writing, it turned out I did. I use a different username too, so I can say what I want without worrying that Jonah, or people back home, will know that it's me. I click to open a new post and start writing.

Hey, guess what? J got sick. Food poisoning, I think, so if anyone has any tips on catching and eating cutthroat trout, I'd love to hear them. And it's an extra shame that it happened last night because we had a fight yesterday. He even said I probably poisoned him on purpose – which I'm pleading the Fifth on, ha-ha! (joking, ofc)

But guess what we argued about? Me ordering some clothes online. I figured that it was coming out of my bank account, so where's the harm, but he said it was wasteful, that we needed the money for new chickens. I pointed out that he likes me to look pretty, and I need to invest in that too, but then he said that I should have bought a sewing machine instead and then I could make my own pretty dresses. I hate it when he makes a valid point, especially when I'm crap at sewing, because it's just another example of me not being a good homesteader.

You know, I don't understand why I find this life so hard. I see other people's posts, and everything seems to work. The meals look filling and delicious. The wives are all beautiful. Nobody seems tired, or cold, or hungry, or grouchy. These women have chosen the exact same life as me, but it looks so completely different. And when I ask for their advice, or a little inspiration, even just a reminder that I'm not alone, they don't message me back. What is up with that?

It's messing with my health too. Yeah, we have clean air, and good soil, and fresh mountain water, but some days I survive on sourdough and radishes. My body shape has changed, my hair is always crazy from the wind. And I haven't had a period in ages.

Please, someone, tell me it's going to get better. Anyone?

Chapter 17

Madison

I turn sideways and stare at my body in the mirror. Should I wear this dress? It's elegant, handmade from Japanese silk, but it hugs my curves. Does it give too much away? I haven't gone public with the pregnancy yet, but it's five months now. I need to soon. Tonight is a big deal in Montana – the annual state business awards – and there'll be plenty of photos circulating online showing off the glittering event. Once my news is out, people are bound to pore over those images, analyze my tummy for clues, probably claim they guessed all along. I can't face it. I pull off the dress and pick a rose-pink chiffon gown with flutter sleeves and an empire line instead.

'So, do you reckon I'm going to win again?' Michael asks, smelling his armpits, then pulling a fresh shirt out of his closet.

'How could you not, honey? March steak is the best in Montana, everyone knows that.'

He chuckles. 'Yeah, you're right, should be a good night.

Especially with you by my side in that dress. You look like a princess.'

Heat rises in my cheeks at the compliment. I would love his good mood to continue, but I know I can't keep the rest of tonight's schedule from him any longer, can't risk him finding out during the ceremony with the great and the good of Montana watching on. 'You know, there's a new award category this year,' I start, trying to sound nonchalant.

'Oh, yeah?'

'For women in business.'

He sits down on the bed to pull on his cowboy boots, but pauses, one boot hovering mid-air. 'That doesn't sound good. It's like they're encouraging it.'

'I know, it's worrying,' I agree. 'But the thing is, I've been shortlisted. For @_TrulyMadison_.'

He frowns. 'But that doesn't make sense. That's not a business, it's an Instagram account. I mean, I know you have a fair few followers, but that's only because they want to see our home, our kids, how committed you are to raising a decent American family. It's not like you make or sell anything.'

I think about the hundred-thousand-dollar contract that Erica recently negotiated with a new fashion label, then push the thought away. 'Which is why I won't win,' I say. 'In fact, they probably only shortlisted me to make doubly sure you turn up.'

His face breaks out into a smile, the tension gone in an instant. 'Yeah, you're right. Can't believe I didn't think of that. By the way, I'm driving us tonight. Bill's otherwise engaged.'

'Oh?' It's a ninety-minute drive to Billings, and Bill always takes us.

'Yeah, something happened today, so I've sent him on a little fact-finding mission.'

'Sounds intriguing. What happened?' I wonder if it wasn't my place to ask, but he seems happy enough to explain.

'Bill spotted some drifter hanging around the perimeter fence. And when he told him to get lost, the guy stayed put, mumbling some crap. I reckon he had a few screws loose, I bet he got the vaccine, but Bill didn't like being ignored.'

'What did he do?'

'Pulled his gun.'

'Bill shot him?' My mind races, weighing up the pros and cons. With the right narrative, it's a strong example of doing what it takes to keep your family safe, but I guess it's also against the law.

'No, little miss airhead. The guy ran. Some random drifter is hardly going to risk death so he can make out with Clarabelle or whatever.

'Yes, of course. I wasn't thinking.' I pause for a moment, my mind wandering to all the death threats I've been getting online. Some from those ugly incels (not that they show their faces, but everyone knows what made them incels in the first place), but most from deluded progressives who call me a danger to society. I mean, they're the ones threatening murder and I'm the problem? 'So what did he want, this drifter?'

Michael pauses for a moment, as though weighing up how to answer. Then he sighs. 'How the hell should I know?' he says tightly, but then softens his voice. 'But that's what I've asked Bill to find out. He's going to the bar tonight to ask around, see if anyone knows him. The guy was quite distinctive apparently. I'm sure it's nothing, but I don't like surprises, or strangers near my home.'

I lower myself onto the bed. 'Did he say anything to Bill about why he was here?' I ask. 'Or mention me at all?'

Michael's face darkens. 'For Chrissakes, Madison, it's not always about you.'

Shit. I can't rile him, not tonight. 'I know, I'm sorry. It's just, these comments I'm getting . . . But you're right, it won't be about me.'

Michael's expression clears and he drops down next to me. 'Look, I'm sure it's nothing to worry about. Maybe the guy heard that I had a good survival set-up going on here and got nosey. Either way, Bill will get to the bottom of it.'

I give him a weak smile. 'Yeah, I guess.'

'You know that I'll always protect you, don't you?' he continues. 'I'm not letting any man near my wife. Whether they want to sleep with you, or kill you, they have to come through me first.' He puts his arm around my shoulder and pulls me into his chest. It's more gentle, more intimate, than I was expecting, and as I lean against his solid frame, I find myself wanting to cry.

But I need to pull myself together. It took me a full hour to get my make-up right, and I can't risk tears – especially as Alice DeMille lives in Montana too, so there's a good chance she'll be at tonight's ceremony. I need to look better than her.

'I appreciate that, honey, I really do.' I kiss Michael on his cheek, then draw away. 'But I guess we should get going. Don't want to be late for your award.'

'Oh, I doubt they'd start without me.' He chuckles, and I smile in response. But the muscles in my cheeks ache with the effort.

Chapter 18

Madison

@shelleyssalonBigT Congratulations Madison!! I knew you'd win! Can't believe Michael missed out :(
#MTBA2024 #Montanagirl #trueAmerican #influencer #inspiration

When I found out the event was being held in a converted train depot, I had visions of hard wooden benches and drafty high ceilings, but the room is sparkling. Midnight-blue sashes with diamante studs are draped across the walls and a mesh of lights twinkle above me. There's a dramatic floral centerpiece on every table – deep reds and violets – and more cutlery than most Montana folk will bother trying to figure out.

A waiter carrying a tray of drinks pauses beside us. I start to reach for a glass of champagne, but then I think about the baby and pick orange juice instead. I watch with envy as Michael reaches for a champagne flute and takes a large gulp.

'Ah, Michael March!' A thick hairy hand slaps my husband on the shoulder, then clasps it. 'Good to see you, it's been too long. How's things?'

'Hey, Dick.' Michael twists out of his grasp and shakes the

man's hand. Dick Winters is twenty years older than Michael, but he runs the second largest cattle ranch in Montana, so I bet his little hand bones are getting crushed to white powder right now. 'Yeah, we're all good, had a productive summer.'

'This little wife of yours keeping you busy behind the camera, is she?'

I swallow hard, watch Michael's face sour. I'm pretty sure Michael won't lose his cool in here, amongst friends and rivals, but I might extract myself, just in case. 'I'm just heading to the restroom, gentlemen, if you'll excuse me.' Without waiting for a response, I back away. I smile at other guests as I walk through the throng, some I know, others who no doubt know me, until I finally push on the restroom door.

And walk straight into an Instagram ambush.

'Madison March, wow.' Alice DeMille's reflection smiles at me in the mirror. She puts her lipstick – Rouge Muse would be my guess – in her purse and swivels around. 'What an honor.'

'Lovely to meet you?' I say, adding a question mark with my eyes, pretending that I don't check her grid at least twice a day.

'I'm Alice DeMille,' she says. 'And it's amazing to finally meet you IRL; you have been such an inspiration to me over the years.'

'Well, thank you.'

'I remember when I first found @_TrulyMadison_ on my Instagram, like maybe seven years ago? You only had Molly and Mason then, and Michael would whisk you off for romantic picnics on the ranch. It was beautiful, all of it. I was this gawky fourteen-year-old, too shy to even talk to boys at the time, but you gave me ambition. And look at me now.'

I smile tightly. Alice DeMille has nearly as many followers as me on Instagram, and more on TikTok. And she's only twenty-one? Eleven years my junior? 'You're an influencer too?' I smile, then click my fingers. 'You know what, I think I might follow you. Do you make your own toothpaste or something like that?' Forget a business award, I should be winning an Oscar with this performance.

Her smile broadens, exposing her perfect white teeth. 'Honestly, knowing Madison March follows me makes my skin tingle. Look, I've got goose bumps! That's how special you are,' she adds with a giggle.

'Huh.' I look at her arms, the fine blonde hairs are lifting up. I feel my stance soften.

'Listen, can we meet up later?' she goes on. 'Get a photo together? I'd do it now except this light won't do either of us any favors, and I promised my publicist I'd only be a minute, and I've already been five. She has a ton of people she wants to introduce me to before we sit down.'

I force a smile. Alice DeMille has a publicist? My palm feels clammy, and I realize I'm still clenching the glass of orange juice. I place it on a ledge next to a plastic flower. Why don't I have a publicist? What's the point of investing in people who can make my content look good if there's no one making sure people look at it?

A burst of rage rattles through me. Being a traditional influencer isn't supposed to be about blatantly conspiring with the corporate media machine. It's about being a good wife, putting your husband and children first. And if brands want to help us spread the word, then we gratefully accept. But we don't chase them. It's no wonder this woman is racing ahead of me; she's a barefaced cheat. With superior make-up.

I flutter my eyelids. 'Of course we can, I'd love that, Ally.'

'Oh, it's Alice, but that's awesome, thank you. See you later then.' She leans in, as though she's going to hug me, then changes her mind – perhaps it's the way I hold both my hands in front of my chest, like a shield with talons – and slips out of the room.

I take a moment to check that my own make-up is still perfect – and that my internal rage isn't evident on my face – then I follow Alice out of the restroom. When I see who she's talking to, I have an idea. I take my phone out of my purse and film the video content that I know will come in useful one day. Because all cheats get their comeuppance eventually.

I can see that Michael is still where I left him, now talking to a man I don't know in full cowboy get-up – handlebar moustache, Stetson, bolo tie. I should join them really, be the dutiful wife, listen to the cowboy lip sync his favorite MAGA lines, or lament the pitiful price of cattle, then nod along as Michael shares his valuable insight. But it will be time to sit down soon, and then I won't have any choice but to listen to the men, divide my attention between whoever the event organizers deem worthy of seating to my left and right. It's something I want to put off for as long as I can.

I notice a fire door that's wedged open, and I slip outside, onto a concrete platform with iron bars overlooking the old train tracks. It's arctic, and the night sky hangs heavy with cloud, but I must be protected from the wind on this side because the air is still. I stare out towards the Crazy Mountains, the snow on their peaks ghostlike under the shine of distant streetlights. I wasn't born in Montana; it was just the place I ended up when the gas in Lori's car ran out. But I've grown to love it.

Out of nowhere, a single snowflake lands on my hand. I study it for a moment, its intricate pattern, then look skyward. The first snowfall of the season. And it's beautiful. Picture perfect in fact.

I pull out my phone and take a mix of selfies, landscapes, and close-up shots. And when I check the photos back, there's one that's so gorgeous – snowflakes resting on my hair, a giggle-shaped smile on my lips – that I post it straight onto my grid. And that's when I notice there's another message from Brianna Wyoming.

Why didn't I block her? I have almost done it countless times – but something always stops me. Even though I know that keeping the line of communication open only encourages her. With fingers shivering from the cold, I open the message.

Why don't you ever message me back, Madison?
Do you think you're too good for me? Is that it?
Or are you scared that you might spill a secret?
Is your perfect life really a lie?

Chapter 19

Cally

It's only October 27th and there's already snow on the ground.

I throw open the window and breathe in the freezing air. The child in me wants to pull on my winter gear and race outside. Build a snowman or lie down and make snow angels. But twenty-four-year-old me is freaked out that the weather can get this cold before the real winter months arrive. And how it's going to make this place even more isolated. With a sigh, I close the window and pull on the warmest clothes I can find.

Before I got here, I assumed that the Marches went to church on a Sunday morning. I've watched reels of Madison getting the kids dressed in their Sunday best, then bundling them into Michael's shiny red truck. Yet church hasn't been mentioned since I've been here, and as a lapsed-to-the-point-of-comatose Catholic, I haven't felt it was my place to ask. But that means Michael will be around all day today.

The other night, under the stars, I found myself getting drawn in by his cowboy charisma. But when the sun rose the next morning, my error of judgement became high-definition clear. Michael thinks women belong in the home, and sees no problem with hitting his own children. How could I be charmed by that?

I want to believe it's just the loneliness that's been creeping in, that I'm not swayed by his masculinity, or his rock-solid belief in himself (or his rock-solid torso). But I can't wholly trust that to be true. Which is why I've made a big effort to avoid him since, and I don't want that to change now, so instead of going to the kitchen for breakfast, I head straight outside.

The sky is the blue of summer, but the ground sparkles white. There's no wind, and while the air is cold, when I turn my face skyward, the sun feels warm on my cheeks. I think about Michael's words that night, how city life hides what America has to offer. I guess even misogynists can be right about some stuff.

But I jolt as the stillness is broken by my phone ringing. It's bound to be my dad, he always calls on a Sunday, so I blindly click to accept the call.

'Cally Brown?'

Shit. Why didn't I check the caller ID? My heart thuds.

'Hello?' the voice continues.

Is it him?

'I know you're there, Cally. Fucking talk to me.'

I cut the call. My whole body is shaking. I wait for the inevitable ding-ding of a voicemail being left, then I quickly swipe to delete it. I feel a moment of uncertainty, like maybe I should have listened to it first, that it could have been good news, a reprieve. But I shake the fantasy away. There's no way this is being fixed until I can get hold of that fifty grand. Because that's why I'm here. Not to teach kids, or look at stars, or question the morals of misogynist cowboys. I'm here to free my brother.

With an unfamiliar sense of purpose, I step further into the snow, and then walk around to the back of the house.

I thought the kids would be out here, throwing snowballs or

building a snowman. But then I remember. *Work before play.* The man who talks up the great American wild west is also the father who won't sanction fun until all the chores are done, even after the first snowfall of the season. As I walk past the gym barn, I half expect to hear Madison's footsteps thumping on the treadmill – she swears by her daily workout – but that's quiet too. I'm pretty sure I wouldn't be so committed to working out if I was in her condition, but then again, I doubt our exercise routines have ever aligned.

I pause when a metallic click-click noise cuts through the silence. I can't see anything, but my instincts tell me it's a gun, so I slip behind a barn, out of sight. I walk along its back wall, in the direction of the sound, then peer around the corner. Michael is stood outside that weird mound with its dark green door and he's carrying a shotgun. It's slung over his shoulder, broken open with the top of the barrel resting on his collarbone. Nonchalant, like he's carrying an old sweater.

I watch him walk around the side of the house and then disappear from view. The only people who carry guns in Boston are the bad guys, but I need to remember that it's different out here. A gun is a God-given right, a crucial part of the American dream. Lori told me that it's hunting season at the moment, so that's probably where Michael's going. Killing yes, but a more civilized kind. Supposedly.

I look back at the strange little hill. I've been curious about that place since I arrived here, and with Michael not around, it's the perfect time to check it out. I wait a couple of minutes in case he comes back, then walk inside Michael's footprints so that I can keep my snooping a secret. As I get closer, I see that the green door is set into a thick slab of sand-colored concrete. The door is made of steel, and it's secured with a heavy-duty padlock.

Suddenly I know what it is. One of those post-civilization bunkers – I watched a Netflix show about them once. Which means Michael must be a doomsday prepper. Men who we laugh at back in Boston for being either weird or overdramatic. Is that what Michael is? The man who runs the biggest ranch in Montana, who rules his family with an iron fist, who can spot shooting stars in a blanket of natural glitter while swilling a glass of Shiraz. A crazy fool prepper? I can't believe it and yet it makes total sense.

I reach out and run my hand over the smooth concrete. I hope the end of the world doesn't happen before July. I really don't want to be stuck in there with the Marches.

When I'm in need of food and warmth, I head through the back door into the kitchen, and it's the exact opposite of outside. Warm, noisy, chaotic. Lori like a conductor leading an untrained orchestra, Madison playing the role of unimpressed audience member.

'Cally!' Matilda shouts, waving a knife in the air. 'I'm making garlic!'

'You're peeling garlic,' Lori corrects. 'Now, be careful with that.'

'I'm laying the table,' Myron says, clinking two spoons together.

'I'm tenderizing the steak,' Mason announces, before slamming a wooden mallet with a ridged head against a large piece of red meat. Molly gives him an envious look and then returns to turning the roast potatoes.

'It all looks delicious, especially those potatoes,' I say, winking at Molly.

'Michael's out for the day,' Lori says. 'Him and Bill have gone hunting. We're cooking lunch for the rest of us, aren't we, Madison?'

'What?' Madison looks up from her magazine. 'Oh, yes. Hi, Cally.' She smiles at me, but it's a weak attempt. Nothing like her usual sparkle.

'How was the award ceremony?' I ask.

'Mommy won!' Molly says with a proud smile. 'And Daddy came second in his category.'

'It was stolen from him,' Mason grumbles, hitting the meat harder. 'By that bastard Dick Winters.'

'Mason!' Lori reprimands.

Matilda giggles. 'It's lucky Mommy isn't filming today.'

I look back at Madison, then scan the room. I'm so used to seeing tripods set up in strategic places, usually with cameras attached to them, that I barely register them anymore. But they're missing today. I wonder why. With all the children involved in the cooking, and lots of homegrown produce on show, I would have thought that this was a perfect scene of wholesome family living. 'Is everything okay?' I ask, notionally directing my question at Madison.

'What? Yes, I'm good,' Madison stutters. 'Just tired after last night. Now, how about I help Myron with the table.' Without waiting for a response, she slides off the bar stool and walks over to where the water glasses are kept. There's something weird about her gait, I notice, like she's stiff.

'Did you go to the gym this morning?' I ask. 'I think it's so impressive that you train all the way through your pregnancies.' Sucking up to Madison makes me feel a bit queasy, but it seems to be the only way to get a decent response out of her. I guess ten million followers can do that to a person.

'No, not today.'

I frown. Normally her face lights up at a compliment like that.

'Are those steaks ready for grilling, Mason?' Lori asks, breaking the silence.

'Yes, ma'am,' Mason shouts, jumping off his stool and wielding the mallet above Myron's head.

'And leave your little brother alone.' Lori whips the makeshift weapon out of Mason's hand and drops it in the sink at the same time as she picks up the tray of meat. That woman has superhero powers, no question.

'Hey, Matilda, catch this!' Mason pulls his other hand from behind his back and hurls a cut-off from the steak at his sister's head. Matilda screams, and launches herself at Madison, wanting protection from the flying slice of animal fat. But the momentum carries her straight into Madison's midriff.

Madison gasps. Screws her face up in pain.

Matilda bursts into tears. 'Sorry, Mommy!'

'It's fine, darling,' she says, her face somewhere between a smile and a grimace. 'I had a little fall last night, bruised my ribs. Nothing to it really.' Her face finds full beam. 'But you know, I'm not that hungry after all, so I might sit this one out.' And then she turns and walks out the room.

Chapter 20

Cally

Lori hands me a serving dish dripping in warm water and I run a tea towel around the smooth ceramic.

Lunch was awkward. Matilda's sobs settled down quickly enough but were replaced by exploding hiccups. Molly spent the meal coaxing Myron to eat his green beans, and Mason moaned about being in a room full of girls and babies when he should be out hunting with the men.

And however much I tried to catch her eye, Lori hardly spoke at all. She filled her plate up with food and worked through it, slowly, deliberately, as though it was a challenge she was not prepared to fail at. When the ordeal was finally over, Lori told the kids to go outside and play in the snow. Molly was the only one to hesitate, stealing a look towards the stairs that Madison had disappeared up, but she was soon swept along by her siblings' enthusiasm, leaving Lori and me to clear up.

'It's a shame that Madison's winning night ended with her falling over,' I say, trying to cut through Lori's reverie. 'It looked like she was in a bit of pain.'

Lori stops scrubbing the meat tray for a moment, then

resumes with more gusto. 'High heels and snow, not a great combination, I guess.'

'Michael must have been distraught,' I continue. 'His pregnant wife hitting the deck like that.'

'I'm sure he was.'

It's clear that Lori wants to shut this conversation down, which adds to my suspicions. Michael won't have enjoyed watching his wife win an award after missing out himself, his ego bruised as badly as Madison's ribs. And it makes sense that a man who disciplines his children by hitting them takes his frustrations out on his wife in a similar way.

'It's also a shame that Michael didn't win his award,' I go on, undeterred. 'I imagine that might have been a bit awkward after Madison's success. Especially with it being a business thing.' As Lori places the clean tray on the drainer, I shift my gaze towards her face, but she's giving nothing away.

'No one likes to lose,' she says.

I turn back to the window. The white blanket, now punctured with footprints, reminds me of being outside earlier, the way Michael held his gun so casually, the bunker that shows how his mind works. Expect the worst. Every man for himself. 'Do you think Michael could have hit Madison?' I ask quietly, wondering how Lori will take it, whether female solidarity trumps employer loyalty or Montana madness.

Lori turns to face me. 'Can I give you some advice, Cally?'

'Sure.'

'Meddling in other people's marriages brings nothing but trouble. Trust me, I know.'

'But domestic abuse is a crime,' I remind her, not willing to give this up. 'And don't you and Madison go way back? Even if there's only the slightest chance that Michael hurt her, don't you want to find out?'

Lori turns away, but not before I see her eyes blinking furiously. 'Madison wouldn't thank me.'

'Why not? I mean, I know Michael is a persuasive guy, but gaslighting is a crime too, you know.'

'Cally, have you ever done something you've regretted? I mean, set the wheels in motion for something truly terrible?'

Wheels in motion. My eyes widen. My heart booms in my ears. Has Murphy found out where I'm working? When I cut him off earlier, did he call here instead?

'How do you know?' I whisper, the words catching in my throat. But then my phone starts ringing, and the noise sets my pulse racing so fast I think I'm having a heart attack. 'Jesus,' I exhale. Then I see the caller ID. 'Fuck.' I scrabble for the off switch.

'Cally? What's going on?'

Ding-ding.

'The answer is yes,' I blurt out. 'I have done something truly terrible. And now the guy is calling me, and I don't know what to do.' My eyes fill with tears, and I can't stop them bubbling and snaking down my face. I wipe at them roughly.

Lori's eyes soften with concern. She runs her hand down my arm. 'I bet it's not that bad.'

'It is!'

'Do you want to talk about it?'

'You can't tell Madison, I really need this job.'

'It happened before you came here? Before you met Madison?'

'Yes,' I whisper.

'Then you can trust me with your secret.'

Her voice is so thick with kindness that it makes my eyes burn again. I slump into a chair, drop my head into my hands. And it feels good to finally say the words. 'If I don't raise fifty thousand dollars by next summer then I'm subjecting my brother to a life of . . . I don't know really. Looking over his shoulder, being at the whim of a drug-dealing asshole, maybe even physical danger.' I hear Lori suck in a breath behind me. 'Yeah, exactly,' I continue. 'Pretty terrible.'

She steadies her breathing. 'What did you do?'

I close my eyes, remember that night again. 'I was at a house party,' I start. 'A fourth of July thing. There was this guy, dark floppy hair, fake tan, really full of himself. Kept name dropping actors and musicians that he supposedly hung out with it.'

'Sounds like someone to steer clear of.'

'Yeah,' I murmur, wishing I had Lori to advise me that night instead of my old school friend Lily. 'He drove a vintage Porsche 911, and everyone knew it because he kept dropping that into conversation too. So when he left his keys on the table, my friend dared me to steal it. Not permanently. Just take it for a joyride to get one over on him. I don't know why I said yes.'

'And he found out?'

'It was a stick shift. I've only ever driven automatics. I crashed it into a fire hydrant maybe one hundred yards from the party.'

'Oh, Cally.'

'It was the guy whose party it was who grabbed me out of the car. And the look on his face, how scared he was for me, was when I realized how badly I'd fucked up. He told me to run, but it was only seconds later that the asshole owner came outside.'

'And your brother was involved too?'

I shake my head. 'Not at first. But when the host told me who the man was, why he's so friendly with all those celebrities and how he makes his money, I panicked. I called my brother, who was in a bar not far away, and he came to my rescue. Somehow, Luke squared up to one of Boston's biggest cocaine dealers and bought me some time. But it came at a price. I've got a year to pay Murphy back for the damage I did to his car, and if I don't, he says he's going to make life very uncomfortable for Luke. Whatever that means. Luke's got a good job, so I could ask him to get a loan to pay Murphy, but I can't bear the thought of that. This is my fault, my debt, my problem to solve.' My face contorts again. 'And now the guy's calling me, and I don't know why.'

'And that's why you took this job, for the money.'

'Yes. And to get out of Boston. Luke was only there for the holiday weekend – he lives in California now – so he could keep out of the guy's way easy enough. But with my track record in luck, I worried that he'd find me, and probably when he was coked up and looking for a fight.'

Lori drops down next to me, reaches for my hand, and smiles. 'So what Michael says about city folk is true after all, that you're all a bunch of hoodlums.'

Maybe it's Lori's touch, or the shock of her choosing humor, or just the relief of getting things off my chest, but a giggle works its way up from my chest and escapes. And then Lori joins in, and soon we're sniggering like two naughty school kids. How did she do that? A fresh wave of gratitude – and fondness – sweeps through me. 'Will you keep my secret?' I ask when I find enough breath to speak.

'Of course I will,' Lori says. 'We're all allowed to make mistakes, as long as we face up to them. And as for you that means sticking it out with us crazy homesteaders, the least I can do is make it as enjoyable as possible.'

'You're a good person, Lori. I can't imagine you've ever made a mistake.'

'Oh, you'd be surprised,' she says. 'And if that drug dealer phones again, you pass the phone to me. I'm tougher than I look.'

Chapter 21

Madison

@justatexangal You look like Snow White in that picture, and Michael makes the perfect prince!
#princess #beautifulcouple #tradlife #wishwegotsnowinTexas

I gingerly pull up my top and inspect the injury. A bruise has started to form across my rib cage. I imagine it will spread over the next few days, and change color before it finally disappears.

How could I have been so clumsy? I suppose I was out of practice, both walking in heels and battling snow, but it's still not like me. The beam was my best apparatus in gymnastics when I was growing up, and my regular gym sessions have only improved my core strength.

And there's also how Michael tried to stop me falling. A hand on my back, grabbing the loose material of my coat. Of course he was trying to keep me upright, so why did it feel more like a push?

I prayed with every bone in my body not to win the women in business award. For a start, it really doesn't help my brand when I'm calling working moms the scourge of our society.

But I also knew it would upset Michael, especially after he missed out for the first time in five years. But my prayers went unanswered, and I had to climb onto that stage, with Michael glaring from the table. Of course Alice DeMille was full of whooping praise, and somehow managed to steal the limelight while I was busy trying to pacify my husband.

And then we left the venue, walked to the car, and suddenly I was toppling over, and landing on a snow-covered rock.

I run my hand across my midriff. The whole area is swollen. I think about the baby I'm bringing into the world – we're bringing, it's our baby, not mine – and feel tears well in my eyes.

Michael has never hit me. But that doesn't mean I've never feared his physical dominance. He's an intimidating presence when he's happy – tall, broad, solid – so when his face sours, or even worse, closes down, he can be terrifying. I've cowered when he steps towards me, felt my pulse race as I see his hands ball into fists. And I know he has a temper. I've seen him get physical with other men, use his beloved paddle on the children's palms. And I'm very conscious that if he turned on me, I wouldn't stand a chance.

There's a gentle knock at the door. I pull down my top, shuffle up the pillows, and call for whoever it is to come in.

'How are you doing?' Lori says, slipping into the room and closing the door behind her.

I consider smiling, but this is Lori. I don't need to pretend. 'It really hurts.'

'I brought you some arnica.' She hands over a glass jar with a dollop of thick greenish cream inside. 'I made it myself. Rub it on twice a day.'

'Thanks.'

I turn away, but Lori hovers. 'And it *was* just a fall,' she finally says. 'Nothing more?'

'Of course.'

'Good. I mean, not good, but . . .'

'But what?'

She exhales. 'I was worried that Michael might have done something.'

'Why would you think that?'

'Well, the award, I guess, but also . . .' She sighs. 'I thought it might be my fault. That I'd suggested you manipulate him into thinking he saved @_TrulyMadison_, and he found out somehow and got mad.'

Heat rises through my body. Inflammation, new tissue forming, dread, all burning together. 'Lori, we've been manipulating Michael a long time without him figuring it out.'

'But people get wiser as they get older. Life experience making them see things more clearly. What if Michael works it all out one day? Would it be more than a fall in the snow then?'

I suddenly think of Rose in the bar, her hands shaking as she necked her bourbon. *It's not me you need to be smarter than, it's him.* Then I shake the image away. 'He won't. He believes me,' I say with a confidence I've always felt. Yes, I worry that Michael might lose interest in me, toss me aside, and replace me with a younger model. But I'm a good liar. I've never worried that he could work out the truth about me.

'If you say so,' Lori murmurs.

'And what choice do we have anyway? Without Michael, I'm nothing. And that makes you nothing too.'

'We're not nothing. We could start again. You, me, and the children.'

'And leave all this behind? After everything I've sacrificed to get here?'

'Maybe we could go home.'

I click my tongue. 'You know, I've been getting these

messages,' I say, needing to change the subject, to stop Lori from saying crazy things.

'Oh?'

'From someone on Instagram who calls herself Brianna Wyoming.'

Lori's face pales. She walks over to my bed and drops down onto the end. 'What do the messages say?'

'It started off with normal things. How I'm an inspiration, how I make things look easy, you know, the usual. She's persistent though, and last night, she pretty much accused me of lying.'

'Have you seen a picture of her?' Lori says it nonchalantly, but I'm not stupid. I can hear the weight behind her question.

'No, her profile picture is a pine tree. But of course it's not the same Brianna. That would be impossible.'

Lori nods, and I see her shoulders tense and then slacken. 'You're right, I'm being silly.'

'Did you hear that Bill caught someone outside the homestead on Friday?'

'What? No.' Lori chews her lip. 'Who was it?'

I shrug. 'Michael sent Bill into town to ask around. I'm going to ask him about it when he gets back from hunting.'

Lori nods, but I know she's just giving herself thinking time. 'It's probably nothing to worry about,' she says. 'I mean, men defending their territory, it's in their blood, isn't it?'

Despite everything, I smile. 'You're probably right.'

'Do you mind if I go for a nap? I'm exhausted today.'

'Of course I don't mind – you work too hard, Lori. I wish you'd slow down.'

She gives me a sad smile then turns to go. I lean back against the headboard, run my hand over my swollen midriff again. We're going to announce the pregnancy tomorrow, but Erica and I filmed the content last week, so at least I don't have to worry about how I look now. On autopilot, I pick up my phone and switch to one of my snooping profiles on Instagram. Alice DeMille is there again, a cute reel from last night. There's some footage of me accepting my award, but weirdly she hasn't tagged me. I push up to sitting. Watch the reel again. Then I read the description underneath.

> Had the best time at #MTBA2024 last night.
> Jack wanted to go to support his boss who was up for an award, so of course I was there by his side. Major highlight was meeting #MadisonMarch #trulyMadison. She won a business award which seems crazy to me, especially as poor Michael @MarchranchMT missed out. I would never put Jack in the shadow like that, but we are all on different journeys, and I'm not going to criticize the original #tradwife for her choices.
> #loveyouMadison #tradvalues #montana #homemaker #husbandfirst #nojudgement

I sling my phone across the room. Scream. Hot tears burn my eyes. My midriff throbs. I need to destroy that woman, make her regret the day she crossed Madison March.

But I need to be clever about it, not get into some petty tit-for-tat like a pair of underdressed rappers. I pick my phone off the floor, click into my photos, and find the video content I filmed last night. There's a much smarter way to do this. And if I can deceive my husband for twelve years, I don't think I'm going to have much trouble with a twenty-one-year-old airhead.

Chapter 22

Brianna

'I'm just going to chop some wood!' Jonah hollers up the stairs. 'Chickens need feeding, Bri, and the water container is empty!'

'Do it yourself,' I murmur, staring at myself in the cracked bedroom mirror, knowing he won't hear me. My wavy hair looks more unruly than ever, and there's a cluster of new pimples on my chin. I listen to Jonah whistling before the back door bangs shut and feel an irrational rage pulse through me. Doesn't he see how hard this lifestyle is? Why is it only me who misses Wendy's burgers and Starbucks' iced coffees and going to the movie theater on a Saturday night? Now my only highlight is eating stolen chocolate bars and scrolling through my phone, trying to live out the fantasy that my life will soon be worth sharing on social media. Because I know it's a fantasy now.

I blink away tears and turn to look at my topless body in profile. There's no hiding it anymore. As my limbs have shrunk and my cheekbones have sharpened from lack of food, my belly has grown. If that was the only sign, I might think that I'm suffering from malnutrition, like the children in those UNICEF adverts with spindly arms and pot bellies. But there is something else going on too. A fluttering sensation inside me.

107

A baby.

A brood of kids is supposed to be the most joyous part of the homesteading dream. But right now, it just makes the nightmare scarier.

I spent a week wondering whether I'd tell my mom about my pregnancy suspicions when she returned my call – I didn't leave a voice message, but she would see my number in her missed calls. As it turned out, I didn't have to decide, because she never phoned back. I don't know whether my dad demanded it, or if my mom cut the apron strings all by herself – she's still got another four children to get it right with. But there's no clearer sign that I'm on my own now. That I made my choice when I ran away to live in sin.

I haven't told Jonah about being pregnant yet either, and amazingly, he hasn't asked. We still have sex regularly enough, so he's had plenty of opportunity to notice my thickening middle. But we do it at night now, both of us too lost in our chores during daylight hours to feel sexy. Which means it's dark, he's half dead with exhaustion, and I'm not sure how much he really sees me at all these days.

But he deserves to know, and more than that, it's about time I'm treated with a bit more care. As the precious mom-to-be.

I plod downstairs and pull on my boots. Jonah is right about the water, so I pick up the empty plastic container and head outside. Once again, I'm hit by that relentless, life-sucking wind. Winter in Buffalo is harsh, but it feels even more bitter here, and I can't work out if that's because the terrain is more exposed, or if I never realized how much my home comforts protected me.

Jonah is in his favorite corner close to the woods, where he's built a makeshift shed – well, three wooden boards butted up together and a worktable. He's focused on his task – balancing hefty logs on a tree stump and splintering them with an axe – and doesn't notice me watching. I could fill the water up first, then tell him about the pregnancy. But it's a boring, back-breaking job, and there's always the chance Jonah will offer to do it for me if I share my news first.

I wander over. 'Hey.'

He looks up, grins. But when he sees the empty container, his smile fades. 'Everything okay? You know, I'm pretty parched, this is thirsty work.'

I nod, his message clear. 'Yes, I'm going, but there's something I wanted to tell you before I do.'

His face tightens. He's waiting for me to make an excuse, and it reignites my anger. Fuck him. I work a hundred times harder than most girls my age, and I still make an effort with my appearance. He should remember that he's lucky to have me.

'We're having a baby,' I say, not bothered anymore about how I deliver the news. But still, I watch his expression carefully. Shock will come first, but then what?

His eyes widen, then soften as his face stretches into a broad grin. He drops the axe, strides over, takes me in his arms, spins me around. I smile back, giggle with nervous tension. Suddenly his optimism is welcome, not irritating, contagious even.

'Are you happy?' I ask.

'How can you ask that? Of course I'm happy! This is what we're working so hard for, Bri. A family of our own. And it's just the start. You watch, we're going to have six kids, ten maybe. This place is big enough!'

My cheeks flush. Because he's right. The house might be run down but it's huge, six bedrooms and loads of living space, and we've got enough land for all the animals and crops we dream of having. Have I been too pessimistic? Too focused on how hard the day to day is to see what we're creating for our future? Is everything going to be okay after all?

'Wait, let me get the water,' he says, taking the container off me. 'You shouldn't be carrying heavy stuff in your condition.'

'But where will the baby sleep?' I ask, not able to let his excitement sweep me fully away.

'I'll fix up a nursery, it only needs a few roof tiles for those back bedrooms to be watertight.'

'And what about money? Babies aren't cheap. We'll need a crib and a stroller and baby clothes. I can't make those, you know that, right?'

'I'll get a job. I'll work day and night if I have to.'

My stomach lurches. 'But how? I need you here. I can't look after the homestead by myself.'

'Just for a few months, before the baby comes. There's not much we can do here until the spring anyway, so I can earn enough to see us through until we can be self-sufficient.'

'But where will you get a job?'

He frowns, but then his expression clears. 'I'll talk to the guys in the bar in town. One of the farms is bound to have some winter maintenance work. Now you go inside, give our baby some rest.'

I nod, smile my gratitude, and walk back inside. But my head is spinning. Jonah getting a job was never in our plans. On the plus side, it means money not just to survive, but to actually live. No more radish dinners. But with Jonah not around, all the work on the homestead will be left to me.

I collect my phone from its charging point and tap into Instagram. I scroll through the accounts I follow. Sparkling kitchens, colorful crochets, cows being milked and chickens fed. One of the women I follow is suffering a pile-on in the comments; being called a liar, a fraud, for keeping quiet about sponsorship deals.

So it's not just us who needs cash to make their lifestyle work. I think about what we could buy if Jonah was earning. Things for the baby, of course, and materials for fixing up the house. But I guess there'll be enough left over for Christmas presents. Maybe a new duvet, a warmer, more stylish coat, even a trip to the hair salon. I smile. Maybe Jonah working is a good idea after all.

Chapter 23

Madison

@sallyann.sykes100 I'm so happy for you! You're such a great mom. Those kids are lucky to have you!
#newbaby #naturalbirth #tradwife #tradfamily #GodblessAmerica

I pull at my cashmere sweater, sink deeper into my office chair, and release a long, weary sigh. I didn't sleep well last night. Michael came to bed late, stinking of wood fires, and bourbon, and the distinctive metallic stench of animal blood. And when I asked him what Bill had found out on Friday night about the weird guy hanging around the homestead, he just barked, 'nothing, he's gone' and rolled over. A few minutes later, he was snoring beside me, while I lay on my back – my ribs too bruised to sleep any other way – and stared at the ceiling.

And the sleep deprivation has put me in a black mood today. Not even witnessing Alice DeMille get the fallout she deserves – I used another one of my secret Instagram accounts to post footage of her sucking up to the owner of Montana's biggest gold mine with her publicist clearly oiling the wheels – can pull me out of it. Even my staff are irritating me. Noah's skinny arms poking out of a ratty and faded Slipknot T-shirt and the East Coast arrogance of Erica's hot-pink 'New York, New York' sweatshirt.

'You posted the baby reel this morning?' I ask them, swinging on my chair and flapping at my sweater again. I pulled it on straight after my gym workout and I'm learning that cashmere and perspiration don't mix well.

'Yes, it went up at seven-thirty,' Noah says.

'So the commuters can see it,' Erica adds.

This is one of the ironies of what I do, how much of my anti-work content is hungrily consumed by followers on their way to the jobs they claim give them a freedom I don't have, but which they clearly hate. 'I assume it's doing well?'

'Yeah, pretty well,' Noah mumbles.

'It's doing really well,' Erica corrects, but she shifts her eyeline. 'The comments have been amazing; everyone is so excited for you.'

'That's lovely to hear.' I smile, wonder why neither of them will hold eye contact with me. 'And the stats?' I ask. 'Are they amazing too?'

Noah's face pales.

'Jeez, yes,' Erica says. 'Thousands of likes and shares.'

My shoulders tense, my skin dampens even more. 'Thousands? How many thousands?'

'Well, I don't have the data to hand but, you know, a lot.'

She's so transparent. The reel is tanking. How can that be? Pregnancy reveals have always been like catnip in the past. My post announcing that I was pregnant with Mason got more likes than Kylie Jenner's new lip kits. How can another March before March be of such limited interest?

I think of Rose, rotting in the bar. Alice DeMille's lipstick-coated smile in the mirror. God, it's hot in here. 'Get one of the other accounts to comment,' I snap, pushing out of the chair and pacing the floor. 'Something from the pro-choice camp, see if we can spark a debate.'

'Yes, good idea,' Erica says.

'And tag a couple of hardline pro-lifers to really ignite things.' I'm in full boss mode now.

Noah pulls the laptop towards him. 'I'm on it.'

'You know, I don't understand why it's always me who finds solutions.'

'I'm sorry, we'll sort . . .'

'I'm going to get coffee. And then I want you to film me with the kids. Something that will grab people's attention, like how we're donating ten grand towards weapons training for teachers.'

'Sure, Madison,' Noah stutters. 'I'll . . .'

I slam the door shut behind me. I don't really want coffee, but I do want to see Lori, to be reminded that I can do this, stay relevant, remain one step ahead of my rivals. And I know I'll find Lori in the kitchen.

But when I push open the door, I freeze. Because while Lori is in here, she isn't alone. And I don't like how guilty the pair of them look, like I've caught them stealing from the cookie jar.

'Cally, why aren't you teaching my children?' I give her my best boss-bitch stare.

'Oh, it's break time.' She sounds flustered, which doesn't help her cause. 'They're playing in the craft room. I was grabbing a quick coffee with Lori but I'm going back in a minute.'

I sink into the chair at the end of the table, the one reserved for Michael when he's home, still irritated. 'So what have you guys been talking about?'

Lori says, 'Christmas.' While Cally blurts out, 'The snow.'

I narrow my eyes, feel heat rising in my chest again. I circle my shoulders but the wool sticks to my skin. 'So which is it? Or are you both lying?'

'We were talking about it being a white Christmas,' Lori says smoothly. 'And how are you today? Is the arnica helping?'

'They posted the baby reel, and no one cares.'

'I saw it,' Cally pipes up. 'I thought it was great.'

'Did you like it?' I ask. 'Share it?'

'Um.' Cally's cheeks turn immediately crimson as she scrabbles for an excuse. 'I thought I wasn't supposed to post stuff on social media?'

God, couldn't she have come up with something better than that? I click my tongue. 'Come on, Cally. A fancy East Coast college education and you can't figure out what content we're happy for you to engage with?'

'Well, I . . .'

'The truth is you didn't care enough about the content to share it, and if my kids' own tutor isn't bothered, what hope have I got with anyone else?' I push out of the chair. My throat is burning now and my chest throbs.

'I do care,' Cally whines. 'I just didn't think. I can share it now.'

I listen to her tap frantically at her phone. 'Forget it. It's too late.' I yank at my sweater and pull it over my head. I feel instant relief. I close my eyes and enjoy the feeling of air on my bare skin.

'Madison.'

I open my eyes, see Lori staring at me intensely. Why is she looking at me like that? It's like she's mad with me for talking to Cally that way, but when did our dim-witted tutor become so important to Lori?

'I better go round up the kids,' Cally splutters. Then she twists out of her chair and launches herself at the door.

'What's up with her?' I ask as the door slams shut. 'She needs to toughen up if she's going to last a year.'

'I don't think it was your tongue lashing that bothered her.'

'Well, what then?'

'Your Lycra tank top, Madison,' Lori says calmly. 'And that washboard stomach underneath.'

Chapter 24

Cally

I'm too shocked to speak, but I hand out the math sheets that I found online and luckily the children start to complete them without any verbal instruction. Then I lean against the desk, grateful for its support.

I don't know much about babies, or pregnancies, but I'm pretty sure women who are five months into their term don't look like that. I mean, how could a half-grown baby fit inside a stomach that flat? Something freakishly weird is going on.

Could she have lost the baby? But no, she only posted about it this morning.

I think about the reel I watched over breakfast. Madison curled up on a floral sofa, wearing a floaty gingham dress and cupping her stomach, happy and grateful for being blessed with another child. She used the same phrase as she did on my first day here – a March before March. It sounded cute then, but this morning it came across more like a quarterly marketing campaign.

Her flat stomach flashes up in my mind again, and with it comes a rush of nausea. Is her pregnancy just that? A fake story to keep people tuned in over the winter? It's nuts, but what other explanation is there?

'I've finished!' Matilda shouts out, waggling her pencil in celebration.

I refocus on the children. 'Wow, that was quick. Let me see.' I go over to Matilda's desk and scan her math sheet, checking the answers she's written. My eyes rest on one of the sums. Four plus one equals five.

I look up. Molly and Mason have finished their sheets now too, and I take in their innocent, trusting expressions. These children are expecting a new brother or sister in February. Madison might be okay with making up stories for her followers, but she wouldn't lie to own children, would she?

An idea starts to form in my mind, a chance to work out what the hell's going on. 'Who wants to learn about probability?' I ask.

Mason's eyes narrow. 'What's proba . . . that?'

'I promise it's nothing complicated. Probability is the measure of how likely an event is to happen. If there's no chance, it's zero. And if it's definitely going to happen, it's one. Everything else is in between.'

'Like the chance you'll hit a target at shooting practice?' Molly asks.

'Exactly, Molly.'

'That's zero, in your case,' Mason murmurs with a smirk.

'Then maybe you should let Molly practice with your gun,' I suggest. I'm not sure why I'm encouraging shooting, but the more time I spend around this family, the more I feel Molly needs a wing man who believes in equal rights. 'You could give her some tips.' Mason looks suspicious for a moment, but when I smile, he returns it with a nod. He's not his father yet.

'And what about with your new sibling,' I continue, shame

beginning to needle between my ribs. 'Do you know if it's going to be a boy or a girl?'

'I want a girl,' Matilda says. 'But Mommy says we have to wait and see.' She drops her bottom lip and frowns like the lead in a Hollywood brat movie.

'Well, that helps me out with your math lesson because now we can talk about the probability of your mommy having a girl. What do you think it is?'

Molly tilts her head in thought. 'Is it half, so zero point five?'

'Exactly, Molly!' I smile at them all, then worry that it looks manic and straighten my face. 'So what does that tell us, Mason?'

He looks suspicious, and for a moment I worry he's guessed I'm fishing. But then he shrugs. 'It doesn't tell us anything. If there's the same chance of it being a boy or a girl, then we won't know until it's born.'

'Very good,' I say, giving him my proud teacher smile. 'And when is the baby due to be born again?'

'February,' Molly says. 'And I'm so excited; I don't care whether it's a new brother or sister.'

I nod, smile. But my head feels like fudge. The children are definitely expecting a new sibling in a few months, and Madison is very obviously not pregnant. So what's going on?

'Umm, so, does Mommy let you listen to the baby kicking inside her tummy?' I know I've sunk to a new low with this question, but I can't help it. I need to get to the bottom of this.

And it seems I've hit some kind of jackpot because the children look at each other, sharing a silent conversation.

'Mommy's baby doesn't live inside Mommy,' Molly finally says.

I blink. 'Sorry?'

Molly sighs. 'Mommy really wanted to carry us all; she tells us that a lot. But it's not possible, so she asks Lori to look after her babies instead, inside her tummy, until they're ready to be born. Lori has carried us all for Mommy.'

I feel frozen, all except for my heart which is pumping faster than feels healthy. Images of Lori fly through my mind. Her looking pale and exhausted. Wearing shapeless jumpers. Working her way through Sunday lunch like it was a task not a pleasure.

'Lori is a surrogate?' I whisper. I search three blank faces. There are a dozen other questions swirling around my head – does Lori carry Madison's eggs? Or is she the children's biological mother? Is there any medical intervention at all, or could Lori be Michael's lover? But I can't ask the children.

'Can we go now, Miss Cally?' Mason asks. 'Now we know what that proba-thingy is?'

'Yes, absolutely,' I whisper, grateful. 'You should go.'

I listen to their chairs scrape back, watch them jostle each other as they race for the door, grins on their faces, our conversation about Madison's pregnancy already forgotten. How can they be so okay about this? Except the children are isolated here, their world entirely informed by the few adults they interact with. Madison and Michael, and then the rest of us – Lori, Bill, Erica, Noah, me. But what influence do the rest of us really have? Every day I follow The List. We all commit to total confidentiality. Michael uses his cowboy charm and physical presence to control us, and Madison does the same with her honey smile and covert ruthlessness.

And the longer I'm here, the more toxic I realize it is.

Especially now. With this.

Lori is pregnant, not Madison. And this isn't a one-off. Molly said that Lori has carried all of them. What must that do to Lori? Having to give up the child she's carried, four times, soon five, and then watch on while they're raised by someone else. Someone like Michael who thinks it's okay to hit a child. I've got nothing against surrogacy, but even I know it's complicated. It needs rules and scrutiny and impartial experts. Not lies and cover-ups and an imbalance of power.

It's clear that Lori is being exploited, but by whom? Madison and Lori are supposed to be friends, but it's clearly not an equal friendship. And yet it's Michael who makes all the big decisions. Does that mean they're in it together? Or does Michael force his demands on Madison too? But if that's the case, why is she so smug about her perfect life online, so happy to promote it to the world when it's all a lie?

And here I am, in the middle of it all. I feel dirty. Complicit in a shameful secret. But I can't leave; I need the money. Instead of instantly deleting Murphy's second voicemail, I dredged up the courage to listen to it. He wasn't calling the debt in early, thank God, but he was making it clear that he hadn't forgotten. That he was still angry. And that my brother would be made to pay if I didn't give Murphy the fifty grand I'd promised by the Fourth of July, 2025. I need to make that Luke's Independence Day.

Which means staying with the Marches until the bitter end.

Chapter 25

Madison

@mommazilla90 How do you carry all those babies and still have that amazing body? What's your secret??!
#6kids #stretchmarks #bigmomma #noregrets

I stare at the calendar on the wall. Saturday November 30th. How can it not be December yet? It already feels like I've been holed up in this place forever, but it's only been a month since I announced my pregnancy. Going out in public means wearing a very uncomfortable fake bump that I swear makes me look like I'm having twins, so I try to avoid it. But that means I've still got weeks of hibernation ahead of me.

I reach forward, flip the pages. It's a homemade calendar – of course – and I move through photos of a family Christmas, and then Mason fishing, before I reach February, my due date circled in sunshine yellow – as though I might be able to entice spring with a marker pen. Clarabelle stares back at me from the photo, and I smile at her.

Because Clarabelle's predecessor Bluebell is how I sold the idea to Michael in the beginning. Our precious, never to be impregnated, pet cow.

In the past, breeding cattle was a messy business. According to Michael, his dad would have to travel up and down the state to find the right bull, and then he'd come home every night during breeding season, sweaty and dirty, cursing the animal for not living up to its reputation, not earning its extortionate price tag. So when the industry introduced the practice of artificially inseminating the herd – a cleaner, quicker, and easier way to breed cattle – soon after Mr. March Senior died and Michael took over the ranch, he didn't hesitate to adopt the new method.

And if it works for cows, why not humans?

Michael wasn't sold on the idea initially. He's likes things to be traditional, which to him means plenty of sex until one day your wife announces that you need to go gentle. But in the end, it didn't take too long to convince him, persuasion being one of my biggest talents.

I talked mysteriously about the effect of pregnancy and childbirth on a woman's body, which I knew he wouldn't ask me to clarify, then pointed out how undamaged my body would remain if Lori carried our babies, how good our sex life would stay, and he buckled like a working mom in a toy shop. That was twelve years, three pet cows, and four children ago. Now he acts like there's no other way to become a father. A private room, a stack of porn magazines, and let the women sort out the rest.

It's Lori who I won't always be able to rely on. Yes, she owes me a heavy debt, but what is the cost of carrying a child for nine months and then handing them over like you played no role? Of course she has plenty of access to the children, and they genuinely love her, but like an aunty, not a mom. And I'm pretty sure that's a poor substitute. Will five babies be her limit? She'll also be forty soon, and at some point, her egg reserves are going to run dry. What happens if Michael demands a sixth child and she can't, or won't, deliver?

The door from the mudroom slams against the wall, and I turn to see Michael walk into the kitchen, blowing hard on his exposed fingers. 'Wind chill must be close to zero out there,' he mutters. I watch him grab two logs out of the basket and add them to the dying embers. The wood crackles and spits for a moment, then lights up.

'What have you been up to?' I ask, as lightly as possible. Michael hates any sense that I'm checking up on him, but he's been gone for hours. For all I know, he's been in the bar all day, drinking bourbon and shooting the breeze with his ex-wife. Or maybe he's been at the Stuarts' place, feasting on goat's cheese and bran muffins. I click my tongue in frustration. Of course he hasn't done those things. This is just me going crazy from being stuck here, my imagination running wild.

But Michael must think my disapproving expression is aimed at him because his face sours. 'Why?' he asks.

I give him an apologetic smile. 'You look cold. I don't want you getting sick.'

'I'm not scared of a Montana winter.'

'Sorry, you're right.' I sigh. 'Maybe this new baby is making me too protective, my nesting instincts kicking in.'

'Yeah, must be that.'

I hold back from rolling my eyes. I'm not pregnant, so there are no extra hormones racing around my body, no baby to guard with my life. My only sacrifice is four months of house arrest. For an intelligent man, Michael's ignorance about women's health has always been off the scale.

'If you must know,' he adds. 'I've been getting supplies. All this snow reminds me how important it is to make sure we're prepared for when the time comes.'

Doomsday. That's what Michael means. The end of the world. He's been predicting it for years, but an election campaign always spurs him on, even if the winner is as red as Santa Claus.

'And how's it going out there?' I ask. 'You making progress?'

'There's a lot to think about.' He's always like this when we talk about his bunker – our bunker, I suppose, but he never positions it that way – defensive, suspicious. Like I'm going to spread his secret around town, and then he'll be expected to save all those losers who haven't thought about the inevitable apocalypse. 'Especially with a newborn on the way,' he goes on.

'How about we just pray the baby's toilet trained and walking by the time the world ends.' The words are out before I can stop them. It's being stuck on the homestead, the weather dull and cold, making me lose my self-control. I tense, prepare for his dark stare, while giving him the most loving smile I can manage. 'Wow, that probably sounded ungrateful. But you know how thankful I am, don't you? You battling the cold to make sure we'll be safe, in the event of.'

'A man's most important job is protecting his family. And the world's in trouble, Madison. We might be needing that place sooner than you think.'

Despite myself, I feel a shiver of dread crawl down my spine. The thought of living in that gloomy bunker with Michael and the kids, eating his canned beef chunks, wearing the practical clothes he's probably chosen for me, is horrifying. I've been through too much to end up there.

But I need to remember that it's not actually going to happen. My daddy always said that if there's a Republican in charge, things are going to be just fine. And while I haven't seen him in close to fifteen years, he might still be the smartest man I've ever known. But I've played along with Michael's survivalist fantasies for a decade and there's no reason to stop now. 'I bet it looks good down there with all the effort you're putting in.'

His face lights up. 'It does, Madison. I've worked so hard on it, for you and the kids.'

A rush of warmth spreads through me. Despite the putdowns, the flares of temper, the infidelity, he can still do this. Remind me that I love him, in my own way.

'Hey, how about we go there now?'

My shoulders tense. 'What?'

'I'd love you to see what progress I've made.'

Chapter 26

Madison

@jennasimpsonMT So I've done a thing. Wish me luck
Madison!!
#quitmyjob #tradwife #familyfirst #husbandfirst

I have the hood of my coat up to fend off the wind, but tiny beads of ice have formed on its fur lining, and I can feel them grazing my cheeks. I silently curse Michael for making me come out here to see the prison he calls a safe haven. I pray I'll never have to spend more than a few minutes inside.

'Are you ready?' He nods towards the heavy steel door that he's painted forest green. For camouflage, he said, as though he's forgotten the three or four months of the year when snow turns the land white. I give him a half-smile of encouragement, and he turns, hunches over the handle to obscure the padlock. I listen to the metallic ticks as he lines up the code that he's never been willing to share with me. Like I'd ever come here of my own volition. A moment later, the door swings open with a high-pitched whine, and I follow him inside.

It's exactly how I remember it. Dark, claustrophobic, oppressive. There's a main living area with a sofa, wooden table and chairs, and a kitchen area, then three bedrooms off to the side, plus a bathroom, with some complicated system that brings water in directly from the well. The walls are made of concrete, and there are lights hanging on shiny nails, with long cables tailing down the wall. Power comes from either the solar panels Michael has installed or a diesel generator. At the far end of the living area, storage boxes are piled high, all of them labeled with important terms like medical supplies, dry goods, cleaning products, ammunition.

There are guns on the wall, and I count two rifles, a shotgun, a small pistol, and an old-fashioned revolver. And in case that's not enough weaponry, there's also a crossbow. So many ways to kill, I can't pull my eyes away. I think about my fall on the night of the Montana business awards, Michael's hand on my back. If I was forced to live down here, with him, would he ever get mad enough to turn one of those weapons on me?

'Impressed?' Michael asks. I turn to face him, take in his proud expression.

'It looks like you've thought of everything,' I lie. There's no soft down pillows or fluffy duvet. No hair straighteners or anti-wrinkle cream or bergamot diffuser. There's not even a mirror.

'It's not too hard. My dad taught me young that I need to be self-sufficient. When this country goes to the dogs, and mark my words it will, we'll be ready for it.'

I run my hand over my stomach. Even though there's no baby in there, I feel the weight of it. 'Not everyone will fit though,' I note carefully. 'Only three bedrooms.'

'Bill will be fine; he's got his own thing sorted. And I'm not babysitting those East Coast computer geeks of yours.'

I could point out that Noah comes from Wisconsin, but I don't. I don't mention Cally either because the last thing I want is her at close range. I hate the way she looks at me now, like

I'm exploiting Lori, her new best friend apparently, when she knows nothing about what brought us here. Just as I hate the way Michael looks at her. Like all things considered, he'd prefer her to be naked. All the effort I went to to recruit a tutor with repellent values appears to be pointless in the face of pert tits and a pulse. 'And Lori?' I ask, the one person who does matter.

'If it happens before the baby comes, we'll find a way to fit her in.'

The dense walls seem to suck in the air's oxygen as the meaning of his words sinks in. 'And if it happens after?'

He shrugs. 'Lori's not part of this family. I can't save everyone.'

I can't save everyone. Michael's words catapult me back thirteen years, to the start of my messy, sometimes ugly, but enduring friendship with Lori. Could I let Michael banish her? I imagine her trudging down our snowy track, head low against the wind, all alone, destined to perish.

'Did you see I got your tech sorted for you?'

Michael's voice brings me back to the present, and I scan the room. It was during one of his long monologues about the inevitable collapse of law and order that I brought up the subject of connectivity. He was dismissive at first – preached about how social media would become obsolete in such circumstances, and that he had his ham radio for emergencies.

But then I changed my angle, brought up his potential as an apocalypse-savvy influencer. I said that people might not care about sourdough if civilization ended, but they'd be desperate to know how to hunt, make a fire, defend themselves from thieves. That it might even be Michael's God-given duty to help them if the internet did indeed survive, and any good prepper knows that the fundamentals of their role involve prepping for all eventualities.

And it sounds like my angle worked because I spot a tripod in the corner with a smartphone attached, a power cable snaking towards a multi-socket panel. I walk over, touch the phone screen, and watch it light up. The familiar app logos calm me a little, and I tap into Instagram. My account profile pops up, and I feel both grateful and annoyed that he knows how to login to what is supposed to be my private business – albeit shared with ten million followers. I notice that there are thousands of notifications and hundreds of new messages – I've managed to reignite my engagement stats by subtly backing a couple of conspiracy theories – and I itch to check them, but I know Michael won't allow it, so I turn back to face him.

'Thank you, honey. That's reassuring,' I say. A shiver runs through me, and I realize there's no heating on down here. 'But I guess we should get back inside now, warm up.' Then I notice that Michael's eyes have become glazed. It's a look I recognize, and I drop my eyeline to his pants. Shit.

'I can think of a way to warm you up,' he says in a deep, gravelly voice. He walks towards me, then hooks one leg behind mine. It could be a romantic gesture, our limbs entwining, but it also means that I'm trapped. If I take one step backwards, I'll fall.

'How about we go back into the house, the bedroom,' I say seductively. I want to have sex with my husband, just not here in this dark punitive room full of guns. And possibly rodents.

'You don't mean that,' he says, nuzzling my neck, curling his arm around my back, and pushing his groin against mine. 'You wouldn't deny me, would you?'

He moves me over to the wooden table, pulls my dress up.

And I discover that indeed I wouldn't. Couldn't. Can't.

Chapter 27

Brianna

I hand Jonah his packed lunch. It's not that exciting, our usual staples mainly, but I did bake some cherry pie for the occasion and I'm proud of how it's turned out. But he takes the box without comment, without saying thank you, which isn't like him. 'How are you feeling?' I ask.

'Fine, good.'

'Not nervous or anything?'

'I'm fixing fences, Bri, not performing eye surgery.'

'Yeah, I know, but it's still new, isn't it? Working a full day, having a boss.'

'It's not the dream, for sure. But the sacrifice is worth it, for you and the baby.'

I nod, bite my lip, chastised. 'And you'll be back by six?'

He sighs, but his shoulders soften. 'Yeah, around then.' He takes a few steps closer and strokes the gentle curve of my belly. 'And you two will be fine by yourselves, I promise.'

He leans down and kisses me, and it's a lingering kiss, so I wrap my arms around him and return it. Jonah has got himself a job on a farm west of town, mending broken fences before the cattle go back outside in the spring. He's being paid two hundred dollars a day, cash, which is proper money, enough for food, and the baby, and a dairy cow, and doing up this house. And hopefully a few treats. That's what I need to focus on, not being stuck out here on the homestead with only a bump for company.

I watch him drive away, then reluctantly turn back to the living room. Jonah gave me a list of chores before he left – he's kept up his promise to collect water every day, but otherwise he seems happy for me to continue as laborer, cook, cleaner, and seamstress – but he's going to be gone for hours, so there's no rush to tick them off. And there's still one Twinkie left from the multipack I stole on my last visit to the grocery store.

I grab it from its hiding place at the back of the kitchen cupboard and return to the living room. I put another couple of logs on the fire – the ground has been covered in snow for the last few weeks, and the freezing temperatures leak through every crack and gap of this place – and watch the flames roar with a sense of pride. There's some stuff I'm getting good at.

I collapse into the sofa, peel off the wrapping, and sink my teeth into the Twinkie's soft sponge. God, it tastes good. I savor its synthetic sweetness in my mouth until my stomach can't bear the teasing anymore and I swallow it down. Two more mouthfuls and it's gone. I feel a sudden urge to cry, but I can't cry over an empty packet of Twinkies, so I screw the wrapper in my fist and throw it onto the fire.

I know I need to stop stealing from the grocery store, especially with Jonah bringing in a wage now, but I'm getting so good at it that my pulse doesn't even register it when I swipe a chocolate bar off the shelf and slide it up my coat sleeve. It's funny. When I lived back home, with a cupboard full of snacks and treats, I would choose to eat salads and fruit. Now I'll risk my liberty for a sugar rush.

As I lean forward to grab another log for the fire, I eye my pile of wool. I'm supposed to be making a blanket for the baby's crib, and really how hard can knitting a couple of dozen squares be, but I drop more stitches than I catch, and I'm not sure how cozy it's going to be when it's finished anyway. Knitted with scratchy, cheap wool. I've begged Jonah to buy all the baby's bedding instead, but he says it's not the same. That our baby deserves something homemade, by its mom, and anyway, what else am I doing with my time?

Maybe I should make some headway on that, make Jonah proud. But then I notice my phone which is resting on the sofa, never far away. Maybe just ten minutes on that, I think, and then I'll start on the knitting.

'Brianna?'

I open my eyes. Shit. It's dark. How long have I been asleep for?

'Is dinner ready? I'm starving. And why did you let the fire go out? It's freezing in here. It would have been nice to have a bit of warmth after working my ass off in the snow all day.'

'Jonah.' I sit up, rub my eyes with one hand, subtly touch my phone with the other. But it must have run out of battery because it doesn't light up. I have no idea what time it is. 'I'll go make something now,' I stutter. 'And hey, how was your first day?'

But my attempt at defusing his anger doesn't work. He narrows his eyes. 'Are you saying you haven't made anything?'

There's an unusual smell on his breath. Unusual for Jonah, that is, but a smell I recognize from Sunday afternoons in my daddy's company. 'Have you been drinking?'

'Sorry?'

'I can smell it on your breath.'

'What the fuck? I have one beer with the guys after work and you want to preach about my behavior when you've spent all day lazing around here? I bet you've been on that fucking phone.'

'I haven't,' I say, which is the truth, for once. I've spent most of the day sleeping.

'Jesus, Bri, there's a real world out there!' he shouts, flinging his arm towards the window. 'In case you hadn't noticed. And real people like me and the baby who need you to step up.'

'Step up? Seriously?' I'm fully awake now. 'I'm pregnant, remember? That's why I'm tired. Pregnant with *your* baby. Are you really going to begrudge me one day of rest?'

'One day? Come on, what do you actually do around here, Bri? Yeah, you cook, most of the time. But the place is filthy. The chicken coop is rancid. You haven't fixed any of my ripped shirts. And the baby's blanket is still a flipping ball of wool. Actually, I'm going to eat in town. I've got money now, hard-earned, and I'm going to spend it on some proper food – and with people who don't moan about being tired all the time.'

'Tonight?' My voice wobbles, anger replaced by fear. 'But you've been out all day. You've just got back.' I feel the baby shift inside me, and I rest my hand on my growing belly. This baby is both my biggest fear and my best friend.

He shrugs. 'Treat it as a lesson. An incentive to have my dinner ready when I get home from work tomorrow. I'm doing this for you, remember. The least you can do is put food on the table.'

'Jonah, please,' I whisper. 'Don't leave me on my own tonight.'

He hesitates for a moment, and I wonder if he'll change his mind, remember that it's his job to protect me, that this is our shared dream. But then his expression hardens. 'Sorry, Bri, but you brought this on yourself. And my car is warmer than this fridge, so I may as well sleep in there and go straight to work tomorrow.'

Tears sprout in my eyes and my stomach churns as I watch him leave for the second time today. Of course the Twinkie and the fire's warmth were going to make me sleepy this morning, and then I let those images of influencers with pretty dresses and perfect homes send me into a dreamworld.

But why do I still fall for it when I know it's bullshit? And why do they spread these lies in the first place?

Do they not care that they're ruining my life?

Chapter 28

Madison

@briannawyoming Why do you spread lies Madison? What do you think people would say if they knew the truth? Can't believe I fell for your bullshit. I hope you die.
#tradwivesruinlives #falselyMadison #lovedyouonce

I stare at the comment. It's not like this is the worst thing anyone has ever written about me, but it's from her. Brianna Wyoming. The girl whose messages were once full of awe. *I hope you die.*

What did I do? Okay, I didn't respond to her, but I have millions of followers; surely she can't have expected me to single her out for special treatment? It makes me think about another Brianna from a long time ago, and how she grew to hate me too.

'You need to block her,' Lori says, her tone half reassuring, half pleading. 'And then forget about it. For both our sakes.'

We're sitting opposite each other at the kitchen table and Myron is asleep on Lori's lap, his growing limbs draped around her curves. We don't know whether the next one will be a boy or a girl – Michael's isn't a fan of antenatal scans; it's in God's hands, he says, although I doubt he'd react well if it came out less than perfect – but I hope it's a girl. Mothers need daughters.

'Do you think I should have responded to her messages?' I ask.

Lori shakes her head. 'You don't owe her anything. And neither of us need to be reminded of what happened before.' She gestures towards my phone which is resting on the table between us. 'Just block her, and the problem will go away.'

Lori's right. Of course she's right. I pick up my phone and do what's needed. Brianna Wyoming won't be able to contact me again. So why do I still feel uncomfortable? 'If she wants me dead, maybe she'll try to hurt me for real.' I say, voicing my fears at last. 'It happened to that actress, didn't it? Her stalker waited until she came off set, and then threw acid in her face.' I shudder. 'There are some evil people out there.'

I want Lori to rebuff me, remind me that keyboard warriors barely leave their computer screens, never mind cross state lines. But instead, she sighs. 'I wish Michael wasn't so stubborn about not having security. Not because I think this Brianna's going to show up,' she adds. 'I mean, her husband probably doesn't let her leave the house. And there's no one from your past life who would be able to find you after the effort you've put in. But there are other threats out there.'

I think about the drifter Bill confronted last month, and how I haven't asked about him since Michael's gruff rebuttal after his day's hunting. 'You remember me telling you about a strange guy hanging around the homestead the day of the business awards?'

'Sure I remember. Did Bill find out who he was?'

'I don't think so, but I haven't asked lately.'

'Well, why don't you check with him now? He's outside washing Michael's truck. I could get him to come in?'

137

'I guess it can't hurt,' I murmur, wondering if, in fact, it could.

Lori lifts Myron up and shifts him onto my lap without waking him, then heads in the direction of the back door. I look at my slumbering angel – I love them when they're asleep, especially when they get those little pink flushes on their cheeks like Myron has now. As I gently stroke his soft warm skin, I wonder if my children love me back, and if they had to choose between Lori and me, who they would pick.

'Hey, Madison, how are you?' Bill's easy Montana drawl spreads through the kitchen. 'Long time, no see. Michael said you had a fall a few weeks back and were taking things easy?'

I smile. Bill is a true gentleman. I just wish he wasn't quite so enamored by my husband. 'I did, yes, but I'm all fixed now.'

'We were just talking about that stranger hanging around here a few weeks back,' Lori says. 'The one you were forced to pull your gun on. Madison wondered if you ever found out who he was?'

Bill's face clouds over. He chooses the kids bench to sit on and straddles it like a horse. 'No luck, I'm afraid. You know, even on the afternoon he came, there was something about him that scratched at my brain. But it was only when Michael got me to ask around in the bar that I worked out why. There's this guy I'd seen in there a couple of times before that day. I couldn't tell you what his face looked like, but he wore a hat that stood out, just one of those regular trapper hats, but he had it really low to his eyeline, and he was wearing it indoors. And I realized that the guy who tried to get onto the homestead was wearing the same hat.'

I lean forward. 'So he did try to get onto the homestead? It's just that Michael said you spotted him wandering around.'

Bill looks embarrassed. 'Sorry, yeah. He was just hanging

around, staring up at the house. But I assumed that he would have come closer, if I hadn't stopped him.'

'It's an impressive house though,' Lori muses. 'Maybe he was just admiring it.'

'Well, if that was the case, why was he talking about Mrs. March?'

Bill's words are like an electric shock. 'What do you mean? What did he say?' Myron is suddenly like a furnace burning a hole in my chest. I hand him back to Lori, but the movement wakes him, and he releases a howl of indignation. Lori quickly hands him a chunk of banana bread, and he falls quiet, thank goodness.

'Nothing that made much sense, to be honest. He just kept repeating your name, Madison March, Madison March, and peppered with a few extras that aren't repeatable in front of you ladies. He was intense too, like he was angry about something. I wouldn't have let him get past me though. You know that, right?'

'Of course, Bill,' I manage, although it's hard, my lungs struggling to regulate. Michael didn't tell me any of this, as though my safety being in question wasn't as important as protecting his ego.

'You're a good man, Bill,' Lori says for me.

'When I didn't get anywhere in the bar, I mentioned to Michael about maybe getting the sheriff involved,' he goes on. 'But he didn't think it was necessary. He thought the guy was more crazy than dangerous, and that my gun would have done enough to scare him off.'

Lori's face darkens but she holds her tongue. She's been part of this world her whole life too – never question men, however questionable their decisions.

'And do you think it did?' I ask. 'Scare him off?'

Bill shrugs. 'I was doubtful at the time, I'll be honest. There was something freaky about the guy, like my gun didn't faze him, and those are always the most dangerous types, aren't they? Like animals, I suppose, too stupid or desperate to care about self-preservation.'

'You're scaring me,' I admit in a whisper.

'Hell, I'm sorry, Madison. That wasn't my intention. Because the thing is, it looks like I was wrong, that I have run the guy out of town after all, because he hasn't been seen since.'

'You're sure?'

Bill nods. 'I asked Drew to let me know if he showed up – Drew's the bar manager down there – and nothing yet. It's been six weeks now, so I reckon he's gone for good.'

'So Drew knew who you were talking about then,' Lori says. 'But he didn't know him?'

Bill shakes his head. 'He remembered the guy for the same reason I did, the hat, but Drew said he wasn't the talkative type. He'd just order a beer, wait for it to be poured, and slope off. The only thing Drew did say was that he'd seen the guy talking to Rose a few times. But Rose and me aren't exactly on friendly terms, so I couldn't ask her about him.'

'Rose,' I mumble. A woman I can't quite purge from my life.

'But he's not been back since you pulled your gun on him?' Lori pushes. 'A full six weeks?'

'Nope.'

'So it sounds like we've got nothing to worry about, do you think, Madison?'

I lean back against the hard wooden chair. With everything going on, it's a struggle to appear unworried, but I'm a professional.

'It sounds that way,' I manage. And even follow it up with a smile.

140

Chapter 29

Cally

'So today we're going to talk about five of the most important women in history.'

I lean against the back wall, my arms crossed, and watch Madison deliver her lesson at the front of the classroom, her slender frame – visible through her cotton smock dress – sending another spike of outrage through me. Names run through my head – Marie Curie, Rosa Parks, Eleanor Roosevelt – but I doubt any such women will feature on Madison's list. I already know who Madison's role model is.

'Is the camera rolling, Noah? I can't see the red light flashing?'

'We're all good,' Noah says, emerging from behind his tripod to my side. 'Just do your thing and I'll make it look awesome.'

'Mommy, I need to go pee.'

'Not now, Matilda,' Madison says. 'Make sure you cut that out, Noah.'

I smile, despite it all. Despite Lori being exploited, and these poor children being indoctrinated with lies. Despite Madison lying to the American people and me having no choice but to cheer from the sidelines.

'So who do you think is the most important woman in history?' Madison asks, her honey tone back. The children stay silent, nervous about giving the wrong answer. 'How about I give you a clue,' she continues. 'Her name starts with the same letter as our names.'

'Um, is it Michelle Obama?' Molly asks.

Shit. My cheeks flare. I turn my head towards the window so that Madison can't make eye contact with me, but I feel her stare burn holes in my skin. It's my one act of rebellion since I found out about the fake pregnancy, and I only risk it with Molly, dropping little hints about banned subjects. But it's clearly leaving an impression, which means I need to be more careful.

'No, Molly, it isn't. I mean Mary of course. The mother of Jesus.'

'But why is she important?' Mason asks, screwing his nose up. 'She didn't make miracles, or have disciples, or stand up to the Romans. She didn't even save Jesus from Herod, because that was Joseph, and he wasn't even related.'

'You'll take all this out, right, Noah?'

'You're the boss, Madison, you have full editorial control.'

Madison nods. Smiles. 'Mary is important exactly because of those things, Mason. Her purpose was purely devotion to her husband and son, which she carried out with God-given fortitude. If she had turned her attention to other things, she would not have been carrying out the work God intended for her.' She takes a deep breath. 'Now let me do that again, and this time you keep quiet, Mason.'

As she repeats the question and Molly and Matilda dutifully give the right answer, I silently click my tongue in protest. Except it can't have been that silent because the five of them turn to look at me.

'Do you have something to say, Cally?'

'What? No.'

'Do you not think that Mary, mother of our Holy Father's son on Earth, is a good role model for my children?'

I look at three expectant faces and one hostile one. Noah has disappeared behind the camera again. How do I answer this? Think about Luke and say yes, my bad, of course she is. Or grow a backbone and find a way to let Molly and Matilda know there are options beyond diapers and meal planning.

'Yes, of course she is.'

'Good. Now who wants to know who the four other most important women in history are?'

I zone out as Madison lists more names, women I've never heard of. But perhaps that's the point. People become famous for doing noteworthy things, but in Madison's eyes, noteworthy is a sign of women shirking their true duty. Instead, I watch the children take it all in, wide-eyed, three sponges absorbing Madison's poison.

Michael came to my room again last night, said it was another incredible night sky, that I should have a glass of wine with him again, and that he wouldn't take no for an answer. Since finding out about their freaky pregnancy arrangements, I can barely look at him, but he batted away every excuse I could think of, and I found myself following him outside.

We sat around the fire with our glasses of red wine. I looked at the sky (which he wasn't lying about) while he seemed more interested in staring at me. He drank fast, while I swilled the dark liquid around the glass. He talked about family life and how he'd do anything for his kids, while I focused on not bringing up Lori, or asking if he's proud of himself for ruining a woman's life. I even had to shuffle away from him on a couple of occasions, his wandering hands no longer giving fatherly vibes. But I survived it, and eventually he let me go to bed.

'So was that a good lesson, children?' Madison asks. 'Is it fun being taught by Mommy?'

'It was great, thank you,' Molly says.

'I still need to go pee, Mommy.'

Madison lifts her hands in surrender. Then she shifts her gaze to the back of the room. You've got enough for a reel, Noah?'

'Plenty, we're good.' Noah releases the camera from the tripod. His eyes flit to mine for a second, then away, towards the floor. Perhaps I'm not the only one struggling with my principles.

'Excellent. Well, you are all excused. But make sure you get your chores done before going out to play, otherwise Daddy will be very angry.'

Chairs slide under desks with a screech and the children file out. There's no denying they're better behaved when Madison's teaching them, but they're more enthusiastic with me, and I know which I prefer.

'You don't normally stay for my lessons,' Madison says, holding the door open for Noah without acknowledging him, then almost clipping his heels as she closes it.

'Well, there was something I wanted to ask you. I thought I could grab you at the end of the lesson.'

'Oh?'

'I know that my contract runs to July 1st with no holiday.'

'That's correct.'

'But I was wondering if I could have some time off over Christmas. Just a few days. I figured the children wouldn't be having lessons, and I'd love to spend a bit of time with my family.'

This is a lie. I can't risk going back to Boston yet, but I'm desperate to get away from here, somewhere, anywhere, like a detox but with less milk thistle and more alcohol. Madison prioritizes family over anything else, so I figured she wouldn't be able to refuse.

'Oh, I'm sorry, Cally, but I'm afraid that's not going to be possible. Lori's not going to be able to do as much as usual, which is understandable of course, but it means we'll need your help with childcare, cooking, and so on.'

You could help, I want to scream. You and Michael could look after yourselves for once. 'I could batch cook some meals before I go?' I say. 'And there'd be one less mouth to feed too?'

'That's kind of you, really, but Michael prefers his meals fresh. I'm sorry, but this conversation is over. As per your contract, your generous contract remember, you're not leaving the homestead until June's over.'

'Sure,' I whisper. The walls of the classroom seem to draw closer, compressing air into a solid mass. This place is a palace. Every room is warm, comfortable, beautifully styled. Every need is catered for.

But it's also a prison. With broken inmates like Lori and brainwashed ones like Bill. And wardens who pretend to be sweet as pie while happily crushing you if you refuse to follow their rules.

I watch Madison walk out of the classroom and slump, defeated, into a chair.

Chapter 30

Madison

Everything looks perfect, so why do I feel on edge? Bill found us an eight-foot tree with symmetrical branches, and the reel of the children decorating it is gorgeous. It's been liked by over half a million followers, and I've had countless good wishes. There's been nothing from Brianna Wyoming since I blocked her, of course, and no sign of that man. I even managed to sneak some bourbon into my eggnog when Michael took the kids to church – excusing my absence with pregnancy exhaustion, the oldest trick in the gestational book.

But I can't relax.

Perhaps it's Cally. I was so pleased with myself for finding a tutor who Michael was supposed to find repugnant that I didn't consider how I would feel about her. And it's not like my plan has even worked. Watching Michael drink wine with her through Myron's bedroom window, no doubt using his worn-out line about the beautiful Montana night sky, made my blood boil. Why the hell do I wear virginal dresses, and natural make-up, and hang off his every word, when all he wants to do is leer after a Democrat with facial piercings and unkempt eyebrows?

And it's not just Michael who she's sunk her talons into. Molly hangs off her every word, and even Lori seems to be under her spell. When I tell Lori that I don't like the two of them getting close, she says I'm imagining things and that I shouldn't worry. But then the next time I walk into the kitchen, lo and behold, they're drinking coffee together again.

Yes, Cally has got to go. But I don't want to give Michael more fresh meat to salivate over, so I need to bide my time. Other than me, Lori's the smartest woman I know, so she can become the children's tutor once this baby is born. I'll find a way to get Michael to agree to it. And then there'll be no temptation in anyone's way.

'I missed you at church,' Michael says, taking a long gulp from his tankard.

What he really means is that he missed having someone to keep the children in line, but I smile anyway. Then I lean forward, pick my glass of illicit eggnog off the coffee table, and take a slow sip. Bill took the kids off to Clarabelle's barn after church, helped them set up the nativity scene, and then we all applauded as they reenacted the story of Jesus's birth. It was a beautiful moment, made even more special by how exhausted they were afterwards, and consequently how quickly they all fell asleep.

And now it's just Michael and me in here, celebrating Christmas Eve together. The best thing about this room is the floor-to-ceiling window and the spectacular rolling views that go with it, but the sky is thick with cloud tonight and I can't see anything but darkness.

'Was church full?' I ask. 'Everyone there?'

'You know how it is. Everyone crawls out of the woodwork on Christmas Eve. Nathan sends his regards by the way.'

'No surprise he was there,' I murmur. 'I imagine he's got a lot to repent for.'

'Maybe you should mind your manners.'

I take another sip. Michael is so hard to impress. So easy to offend. 'And your ex-wife? Was she there?'

He looks at me quizzically. 'Why would you mention her? I thought this holiday was about peace and goodwill.'

I smile. I know I should rein it in, but I don't want to. Maybe the festive spirit is spurring me on. Or maybe it's the bourbon. 'It's been a long while since you broke up, a lot of water under the bridge, so I figured you might have built some kind of friendship.'

He leans forward, rests his forearms on his wide knees. 'Are you testing me? Because if you think I've still got feelings for that old hag . . .'

'Why did you split up?'

'You've seen her, how unattractive she is.'

'Bill said she used to be beautiful, that she looked like me once upon a time.'

'Bill told you that?' He shakes his head. 'If you must know, she's barren.' He looks down at his hands, but whether in shame or anger, I can't tell. 'But she omitted to tell me that until I put a ring on her finger. I mean, she must have known that I wouldn't marry her if she'd told me before. But she forced me into putting my dad through all that divorce drama, and with his heart problems, I'm sure it's what killed him. I couldn't let her get away with that.'

I think about the broken woman, her shaking hands and words of warning. I swallow, bite my lip, drain the eggnog.

'You know, when you first floated your little idea by me,' he goes on. 'I thought history was repeating itself. That you didn't function properly down there either.'

I smile, raise my eyebrows like I can't believe he'd jump to that conclusion. 'I did it for us,' I manage. 'To keep things exciting.'

'Yeah, I know. And I realized it was smart, once you'd explained it.'

I feel my cheeks blush at the compliment, but the stakes are too high for me to relax. If he ever found out the truth.

'But I was thinking,' he goes on. 'Lori is getting on a bit now, isn't she? And it's not like we're at it like rabbits anymore. I reckon we should do the next one the traditional way. You never know, I might even like you fat.'

The lights on the tree flicker and I will them to go out, anything to distract us from this conversation. But they stay stubbornly bright. 'Or we could thank God for giving us five healthy children,' I suggest. 'Show him how grateful we are by not asking for any more.'

Michael screws his face up. 'Five? You're kidding right? Even Matthew's got six and he's four years younger than me. You're still young, Madison. We can have ten babies. Think how proud the Lord would be of us then.'

A whimper escapes from my lips, but before I have a chance to cover it up, or excuse it, the room erupts with bright light. I blink, my eyes taking a moment to adjust. When I can see again, I realize it's coming from outside, and Michael is standing by the window, staring out.

'That's the security light,' he says. 'Someone must be out there.'

'Do you think it's the same man as before?' I ask, my voice rising a few octaves. 'Has he come back for me?'

Michael gives me a withering look. 'It's not always about you, Madison.'

He walks out the room before I can defend myself, tell him that I've talked to Bill, and I know the guy was here for me. Once again, I need the reassurance of Lori, her big belly and soft arms, so I scurry down the hallway into the kitchen.

But the room is empty. I hover, unsure where to go. The children are sleeping, Bill went home, Erica and Noah too, and Cally could never be a comfort. But I don't want to be alone either. The answer is obvious. I pull my phone out of my pocket and click into Instagram. I don't check my comments or messages, just in case, but I swipe through other people's stories, try to lose myself in sparkling lights, blue-eyed children with tinsel in their blonde hair, and the sweet sound of carol singers on driveways.

Someone has posted about a Christmas pageant in Buffalo, Wyoming, and it makes me think about Brianna and what kind of Christmas she's having. Her early messages were so full of hope. I wonder if she really had been stupid enough to think homesteading is possible without money behind you.

Suddenly the front door bangs open. I hear the unmistakable thud of Michael's footsteps in the hallway and the high-pitched clatter of something metallic against the floor. I click out of Instagram. He storms into the kitchen, and Lori is with him, walking silently behind, her head down.

'Are you okay?' I ask, staring at his clenched fists.

'You were right; it was the same stupid bastard as last time. I caught him leaning on the fence, like he was biding his time until we all went to bed.' Michael is breathing heavily. 'And I found a knife on him.'

'Oh, my God!' I feel a rush of nausea. I look over to Lori, needing her familiar smile. But she's still staring at the floor.

'Don't worry. I scared him off.'

'What happened?' I whisper.

'I shoved the barrel of my gun into his chest and told him that I wasn't afraid of shooting a man at close range.' Michael chuckles. 'You should have seen his face. He went white as a sheet.'

'And then he left?'

'Yep. I told him he was a pussy and that he better not come back else I would shoot him straight off.'

'And the knife?'

Michael looks flustered for a moment, then his expression hardens. 'I'm not a thief, Madison.'

I scream silently. 'Why do you think he was here?'

Michael sighs. 'Who cares, Madison? I showed him who makes the rules around here, and protected you, and you haven't even said thank you.'

'Thank you,' I say, on cue. But I'm too numb to feel gratitude. Because all I can think about is who the man is, what he wants with me, and why the hell Michael didn't take his weapon off him.

Chapter 31

Brianna

I look at my phone again, check the date for the hundredth time. But it doesn't change.

How can it possibly be Christmas Day?

The house is silent, Jonah still dead to the world, sleeping off whatever made him stumble rather than walk up the stairs in the early hours of this morning. And it's freezing cold because I forgot to bring any wood in last night so it's all damp, and the logs I put on the fire are smoking rather than burning.

Our Christmas tree is a four-foot cut-off that Jonah dragged up from the woods. I tried to decorate it, making snow with flour and water for the tips of the branches and entwining it with paper chains, but without lights it looks more like it's caught some kind of fungal disease. Tears prick at my eyes as I turn away from it, towards the window. But there's nothing much to see there either. Just misty white clouds and snow-covered fields as far as I can see.

I pull the blanket tighter around my shoulders. My blanket until the baby is born. After Jonah's first day at work, him finding me asleep on the sofa, I resolved to try harder. To figure out how to knit and do one thing right for a change. I knitted one square, and over the next couple of weeks, found the patience to repeat the process twenty-three times. Then I sewed the squares together in one day, suddenly excited to see what I'd made. I was right about the wool being scratchy, but I still love it, because it shows that I can make something beautiful. I drape it over myself all the time now, like a cape, as though it might give me a superpower one day.

I look at my phone again. Not to check the date this time, but to see if I have any messages. But it's the same result. Disappointment.

We received two Christmas cards in total, delivered by a mailman I didn't know existed until he showed up a week ago – a nice guy, as it turned out, willing to take a hastily made card without a stamp – but neither of them was addressed to me. Jonah's mom's card had a nativity scene on the front, and a long paragraph inside about how proud she was of him, some loose references to Mary's hardship in Bethlehem working out for her. The other card was from a Mary, but a different one, Jonah's only sister. Fewer words in that, but a message that made me pause. *Let me know if I can help*. Mary had left home by the time Jonah and I started dating, so I haven't met her, and Jonah never talks about his sister. And yet, she still finds the time to write.

Unlike my family. There's been nothing from them.

I wonder what they'll be doing now. Christmas Day in the Nelson household. They're probably on their way to church. My baby sister Cora will have a new dress for the occasion, some new patent ballet pumps, and I wonder if Mom has let her paint her nails yet. Mom will look beautiful too, despite having been in the kitchen since dawn, her pre-church to-do list getting ticked off with holy diligence. Daddy will be letting my three brothers get away with more bickering than usual, mellowed by his morning whiskey and pride in the family he built with his high principles and hard-earned dollars.

Will they be thinking about me? Mourning the empty space in our Grand Cherokee? Or have they made their peace with my disappearance, decided a family of six is legacy-building enough?

I check again. Still no messages.

But a noise at least, something to distract me. Jonah's thudding footsteps on the stairs.

'Fuck, it's freezing in here. Again.'

'Merry Christmas,' I say, somewhere between an olive branch and an accusation.

'What? Oh, yeah, you too.' He pauses for a moment, then rallies. 'Even more reason to treat ourselves to some actual heat though, don't you think?'

'There wasn't any dry wood.'

'There must have been, I chopped loads. And you know to bring fresh logs in every evening, dry them by the fire so they're ready for the next day.'

'I forgot.' I want to say more, to ask why it's always my job to remember, but I don't want to fight. Not today. 'Sorry,' I add, and try to sound genuine.

He rubs his forehead with the heel of his palm. His eyes are bloodshot again. Having one swift beer after work with his work mates has evolved into full-on drunken nights out, although he still expects a plate of food to be waiting for him when he gets home.

'But you sit in front of the fire all night,' he goes on. 'How could you forget?'

I look away, back to the window. It's started snowing, and I watch a snowflake descend and disappear.

'You know, I reckon it's that phone,' he goes on. 'I bet you spent the whole night scrolling through that thing again, your head lost in some make-believe crap. Man, my mouth is like the Nevada desert, my whole body hurts. I really didn't need to come down to this on Christmas Day.'

'It's not make-believe. It's people's lives.'

'Well collecting firewood is your life, so it would be nice if you could start living it.'

'But it's a shit life, Jonah! Don't you get it? The dream we had, it's not coming true! We could be at home with our families, opening presents, eating roast turkey and salted ham and mashed potato and pumpkin pie.' Just saying the words makes my mouth salivate. 'Don't you want that?'

'Jesus, Bri! Of course I do! But do you not realize why it's not coming true? You're the problem, not me! You want the dream, but you're not prepared to work for it like I am.'

'How the hell would you know when you're never here?!' I throw back. 'And what's the point of you having a job when you spend half your earnings in the Ranch Inn? Leaving your pregnant girlfriend to fend for herself?'

He takes one, two, three strides towards me. His hands are curled into fists. Our bodies don't touch, but I can feel the warmth radiating from his, his stale breath filling my nostrils. Jonah played fullback for our school football team. He may have a narrow frame, but he's six foot one, and weighs a hundred and eighty pounds. I've never known him to get in a fight, but that doesn't mean anything. Is Jonah going to hit me now? And if he does, who will stop him?

I take a step back. 'I'm sorry, I shouldn't have said that.'

Jesus, am I scared of Jonah?

'Damn right you shouldn't. We only have a Christmas dinner at all because I'm out working.'

'I know, I wasn't thinking straight.'

155

'It's that phone.'

'What?'

He nods. 'It's putting ideas in your head.'

'No, it's not. What ideas?'

'Women's rights; equality; my body, my choice. All that shit.'

'I'm not interested in those causes!' I say, horrified that he could think that I might be. I was not raised to treat family values with contempt. 'I follow other women like me, homesteaders, wives, and mothers who like to do things the traditional way. They're my inspiration.'

'I don't believe you.'

'What? Why not?'

'Because those women wouldn't tell you to disrespect me, or to sit around expecting everyone else to do the hard work either.'

'Jesus, Jonah, I'm pregnant! That's why I need you to do more.'

'Give me your phone.' He reaches out and I flinch, his closeness now a source of fear, but he just hovers his hand in front of me, wriggling his fingers. I grip my phone tighter. His face sours. My heart rate ticks up.

'My phone, my choice,' I say – but silently, inside my head – and then I hand it over.

His voice instantly softens. 'Listen, Bri, I know it sounds like a punishment, but I honestly think I'm doing you a favor. Without your phone, you can concentrate on the baby, on our home, on us.'

I nod. My baby kicks, maybe in protest at my yearning for a slab of glass and metal. 'Maybe you're right,' I whisper.

His face beams with that lopsided grin I used to love so much. 'That's great, Bri. That's really great.'

Except it doesn't feel anywhere close to great to me.

156

Chapter 32

Madison

@adelemeadows1996 Merry Christmas to you and your beautiful family. Did you make those pajamas or can I buy them some place?
#tradwife #familyChristmas #sleepwear #cutekids

'Madison? Are you okay?'

I look up. Erica is staring at me with a concerned expression. How long did I zone out for? Did I say anything? I barely slept last night. Every time I closed my eyes, all I could see was a faceless man in a trapper hat with a knife in his hand. And I'd only just drifted off when Matilda started running up and down the landing, squealing that Santa had been. Michael hollered at her to get back into bed, but that woke Myron, and soon the whole household had decided that five o'clock in morning was the right time to get up.

'Sorry, I was just taking a moment to reflect,' I say. 'On how lucky I am to have such a wonderful family.'

'Right, okay,' Erica says, her expression a mix of confusion and suspicion. God, why am I acting with Erica? She knows the real me. I need to sort myself out.

157

'Mommy, can I eat this?'

I turn towards Matilda whose fingers are hovering over a plate of deviled eggs.

'No!' Erica calls out. 'Sorry, just give me a minute, I haven't shot it yet. Where's Noah?'

'He's fixing the Christmas tree,' Lori offers from the other side of the kitchen. 'Mason knocked it over and the lights went out.'

'Has he set up the tripods?' I ask, my heart rate kicking up a gear. Why have I not been more on it this morning? Made sure this stuff is in place before we sit down for lunch? Only Michael, Lori, and I know about last night's events, and the three of us agreed to draw a line under it, so I can't let it affect me now. 'Michael will be down soon, and we can't be delaying Christmas lunch to get the tech right.'

'Don't worry,' Erica says. 'It's all ready. And this morning's reel is gorgeous; I know matching pajamas is hardly novel, but using the same material in different styles was a genius idea of yours, Madison, especially that cute nightie for Molly. Thanks for making those by the way, Lori.'

'No problem.'

'And we're all set for the Christmas lunch reel,' Erica goes on. 'I've got some footage of the kids from earlier, and Michael even let me film him putting the turkey on the barbecue. We've got two cameras set up for the meal, one with a portrait lens for head shots of you, and the other panning over the middle section of the table. You can put the rest of us wherever you prefer. We could be dinner guests, pretend to be family, or we could sit out of shot. Obviously we'll put Lori out of the way.'

I pretend to think about it for a moment, when in reality there is no way Erica, Noah, or Cally fit my @_TrulyMadison_ aesthetic. 'You know what, I think it might be best to keep it to a family Christmas. And put Bill on the end next to Mason, to give us a margin of error.'

'Sure, Madison, whatever you say.'

'Please, Mommy, I'm starving!'

I watch Erica take a few snaps of the plate, then wink at Matilda, who takes two egg halves and stuffs them in her mouth, adding the second while still chewing the first. Lori appears with a damp cloth and wipes fluffy egg yolk off Matilda's chin.

'What would I do without you,' I say. Lori seems distant today, and I don't like it. She might be tired from the pregnancy, or freaked out by what happened last night, but I'm worried this is Cally's doing. That she's driving a wedge between us. If she's whispering in Lori's ear about Stockholm syndrome or exploitation, I swear I'll hang her on the Christmas tree by that nose ring of hers.

'I'm not sure,' she answers quietly, not looking at me.

What is wrong with her?

'Do you need any help with anything?' I go on. 'I could set the table?'

'It's already set, Molly did it earlier.'

'Oh, right. Are there potatoes to peel then? Carrots to baton?'

'It's all done, Madison. Once Noah has fixed the tree, he'll film Michael bringing in the turkey. And all the rest of the meal just needs moving from the stove to the table. You can manage a dish or two with the camera behind you I guess?'

Is that a dig? I search her face, looking for clues. But she just looks tired. 'Of course I can do that.' We stand in silence for a while, me trying to draw her gaze, Lori's eyes darting every which way to avoid mine. 'Do I look okay?' I finally ask, twirling in my new freebie floral dress that's come all the way from Liberty in London.

She sighs. 'You look beautiful, Madison. As always. Shall I go round up the children?'

'Sure,' I say, but I pause, still not satisfied. 'Listen, are you okay?'

Finally, she looks at me, and her face softens. 'Sorry, yes, I'm fine. It's probably just the pregnancy, and Christmas, feeling a long way from home, I guess. Do you ever get like that?'

'No.' I shake my head. 'No.'

'Sorry, of course you don't. That was a stupid thing to ask.' Lori dips her head once more, then disappears into the hallway.

An hour and a half later, Noah turns the camera off for the final time, and we all breathe a sigh of relief. The Christmas lunch reel will look good, I think. Molly looks stunning in the sage-green ballerina dress I bought her, with its chiffon skirt and spaghetti straps. I'm glad I experimented with make-up too because the mascara really lifts her blue eyes. Mason is dressed as a mini-Michael, which always goes down well, and he didn't bicker too heavily with his sisters – probably due to the ongoing threat of missing out on apple pie. Matilda looked cute serving up the purposefully mis-sized stuffing balls, and Myron's delight at eating the huge turkey leg might be the shot of the day.

'Do you need to go, Noah?' I nudge, using my honey voice so I don't offend. 'Is it time to get the reel edited?'

'What?' Noah looks up from the glass of red wine that Michael poured him without checking if he wanted any. 'Oh, yes, cool. I'll do that.'

Out of the corner of my eye, I watch my husband shake his

head in disgust – a man taking orders from a woman – then take a long gulp of his wine. I don't care what Michael thinks about Noah, but I know how his mind works, and I don't want to be to blame for his darkening mood.

'Actually, it's your Christmas Day too, so why don't I check the footage, work out which clips I want, and you can come down when you've finished your wine?'

'Really?' Noah looks at me with suspicion, then turns his face towards Erica, who gives a small shake of her head. 'How about we both go?' he says. 'Then you can tell me what you like, and I'll edit it. Many hands and all that.'

I look at Michael, who seems happier, me agreeing to Noah's suggestion. 'Great idea.' I stand up and give the table my signature smile – saving my most genuine flash for Bill who is, unsurprisingly, cutting himself another slice of baked ham. Then I follow Noah into my office-cum-editing suite.

Noah loads the footage onto his Mac, and I select the bits I want, making sure my flat stomach doesn't feature – I couldn't face wearing the silicone bump today. We discuss exposure, saturation, and background music, until we're both happy with the ninety-second mix of video and stills. Then he asks me what text to write.

'I think, "Christmas at the March Homestead. Both special, and everyday",' I say. 'Then add the hashtags #tradwife, #homemaker, #stayathomemom, and #notjustforChristmas. Does that sound okay?'

Noah chuckles. 'It sounds perfect. You really are the master of this.'

I feel my cheeks glow. 'Thank you, Noah.'

'Oh, by the way, did you get that card?'

I frown. 'What card?'

'Yeah, I found it in the mailbox this morning, but it had

slipped down the side, so I'm not sure how long it had been in there. It didn't have a postage stamp, but there was ink on it, like it had come through the system. Really messy handwriting too.'

'Noah, I don't know what you're talking about.'

'Oh, right. Well, I gave it to Lori; she said she'd pass it on. I guess we've all been busy though.'

Chapter 33

Cally

'Lori, sit down, I've got this.' I give Lori my best teacher stare, and it works because she lifts her hands in defeat and lowers into one of the kitchen chairs. I turn back to the sink and continue washing the pans. At home, Luke and I play rock, paper, scissors to decide who does the dishes after Christmas lunch, and I always lose, so I'm quite the expert.

'How has your day been?' Lori asks, her voice floating over my shoulder. 'Spending Christmas with the mad Marches rather than with your family?'

From nowhere, my eyes grow hot. I blink, stare at the rolling white view out the window until they cool. 'It's fine, I mean good,' I add, remembering that she's an honorary March. 'It's not like I can go home anyway, not with Murphy on my case.'

'Is he still calling you?'

'No. I messaged him back after the last time, promised that everything was on track for getting him his money on time, and it seems to have worked, for now at least.'

'Well, I'm pleased you're here for Christmas,' Lori says quietly. 'For your help, and your company. Each pregnancy seems to get harder.'

I attack the stainless-steel tray with the scourer, rip at stubborn balls of congealed animal fat left behind by the prime ribs. 'But you still do it,' I murmur. 'This surrogacy thing, or whatever you call it.'

'I do, yes.'

As I rinse off the tray and stack it on the drainer, I notice my hands are shaking. 'Can I ask why?'

'I think it's too complicated to explain properly.'

'You could try, and see how we do?'

Lori releases a soft chuckle. 'Well, let's start with I've never had strong maternal instincts of my own, and Madison is a great friend, so why not help her out.'

I twist around, lean against the cool ceramic sink, and look at Lori. 'Really? But you're great with the kids.'

'Perhaps I am now, but I was never one of those girls who dreamed about meeting Mr. Right and having a brood of kids with him. Which was unusual where I come from.'

'What did you dream about?'

Lori runs her hands over her bump, then stills them underneath, fingers intertwined like a cradle. 'Can you keep a secret?'

I wipe my hands on the tea towel and sink down into the chair opposite Lori. 'Well, you know mine, so I guess it's only right that I keep yours.'

'I wanted to be a cowboy.'

'A cowboy?' I laugh. 'Like Michael?'

'I suppose so, yes.' She leans forward, lowers her voice. 'But a nicer one than him.'

I'm not sure if this is how loneliness works, but I feel a surge of joy that Lori – a woman fifteen years my senior with zero shared life experience – has become my friend. I match her movement. 'I don't think that would be very hard,' I whisper back.

Lori rests her hand over mine, squeezes it, then settles back against the chair. 'Is he causing you problems?'

I shrug. 'You know.'

'Making you feel uncomfortable without quite doing anything you can call him out for?'

'You've known him a long time.'

'Over twelve years.'

'But you're still willing to carry his baby?'

Lori's expression darkens and I worry that I've pushed her too far, that she's offered me the hand of friendship, and I've pulled her fingernails back. But then she sighs. 'Madison's baby. That's why I agree to carry them.'

'Well, you're a very special person. I'm pretty sure I wouldn't make that kind of sacrifice for my best friend.'

'There's joy in helping others, especially those you love.'

'And you love Madison?' I don't add the rest. That the Madison I know only seems to love herself. And that Lori is worth a thousand of her.

'She deserves to be happy,' Lori says. 'To have this kind of life.'

'The children say that's why you do it, for love, but I'm guessing there must be a medical reason too?'

Lori looks away. 'Madison couldn't cope with losing Michael,' she eventually says. 'I know she comes across as confident. But he is her oxygen. Nothing works without him.'

'Are you saying that Michael forces this arrangement?' I ask, leaning forward again. 'He wants a big family, and will do anything to get it, screw anyone who gets hurt in the process?'

Lori looks uncomfortable. 'I'm sorry, Cally. I've probably said too . . .'

'Because if that's true, it's fucking selfish.'

'Cally, please . . .'

165

'I'm sorry for swearing, but doesn't he make you want to curse too? Michael is taking advantage of your friendship with Madison, with zero thought for how emotionally damaging this whole thing is, for everyone involved.'

Her face flushes like I've slapped her. 'Michael isn't a saint, far from it, but this isn't manipulation, not in the way you think.'

'You're talking in riddles!' I push air through my lips, exasperated. 'Why can't you just tell me? I already know that Madison lies to her followers. That she pretends to be this wonderful homemaker, when in reality she has a bunch of staff who do everything for her, including you. That thousands of women are choosing to give up their jobs, or be submissive in their relationships, because she's duped them into believing her lifestyle is all home-baked bread and soft-focus honeybees. And what could be worse than that?'

'You'd be surprised,' Lori mumbles, turning away from me.

I open my mouth to respond but hold my tongue. She looks scared, I realize. Is all this talk of love and altruism actually bullshit?

I think about Michael. His size. The casual way he carries a gun. How his charm gives way to coercion when he doesn't get what he wants. And then I think about his doomsday bunker, and why it needs a massive padlock on the outside.

'Why has Michael built a bunker?'

Lori looks up. 'Michael believes the apocalypse is coming, at least he's convinced enough to spend thousands of dollars getting that thing built.'

'And why the padlock? I mean, doesn't he just need a lock on the inside?'

'Michael's a suspicious guy. He doesn't talk about his bunker because he thinks all the townsfolk will come knocking when

Russia sends a nuke, or big pharma turns us into zombies, or whatever. I imagine the padlock is to keep people he doesn't trust away, which is most people.'

'I saw him outside it once, with a shotgun slung over his shoulder.'

'Michael believes he's the next Rick Grimes. I imagine he stocks quite a few weapons in that bunker.'

'And that doesn't worry you?'

'You've spent too long in Boston, Cally.'

'That doesn't really answer my question.'

Lori looks down, strokes her bump again. 'There are dangers everywhere, Cally. It's rarely the obvious ones that you need to worry about.'

Chapter 34

Brianna

I push my fingers into my lower back, circle them against my tight muscles. I have worked like a maid today – cleaned the house, made a stew with the turkey leftovers, even collected the water. And I've sewn up the rips in Jonah's shirts. But while I've been doing these chores, Jonah has been sitting on the sofa with a book that one of his drinking buddies lent him – something called *Mandate for Leadership*, which sounds a lot duller than his usual Lee Child novels – plus a bottle of whiskey.

When I asked if he was going to pull his weight at any point, he bit my head off. Told me he'd been given a few days off work over Christmas, and it wasn't my place to question how he spent it. And that him raising a few toasts to the man who'd gifted him a bottle of Jack Daniels was a sign of respect, so I should quit giving him daggers for it. I didn't push things because I need Jonah in a good mood, and maybe him being a bit loose from the booze could work in my favor.

It could get me my phone back. Because I can't survive another day without it.

At least my hours of hard labor have given me a chance to work out my argument, and it's a good one. Jonah spends hours away from the homestead, so having a way to communicate is safety 101. And if I need to know how to preserve fish or mend clothes or unblock our ancient drains, I always use Google to find out. How will I do that without access to the internet? And most importantly, we had a deal. When we spent those afternoons planning our new life together, I was clear that having my phone was a must, and if that trust is broken, what's left?

It all adds up. I just need to find the right moment to ask.

'Stew smells good,' he murmurs as I sink down next to him. 'Is it ready? I'm starving.'

'Five minutes,' I say. 'Just cooking some vegetables to go with it.'

He nods, takes a large gulp of his drink, then leans forward and places his glass on the wooden crate we use as a coffee table. 'Listen, about yesterday,' he starts. 'I was thinking that maybe you're right.'

My stomach lurches. This is my chance to say something. 'About my phone?' I blurt out, leaning forward too. 'I can have it back?'

'What? No.' He clicks his tongue. 'There are more important things to talk about than your stupid phone, you know.'

'Oh, right.' I look away. Personally, I can't think of anything more important. 'Like what?'

'Like our homestead? For fuck's sake, Bri.' His words are crisp and clear, not slurred from the whiskey yet, but they still sound unfamiliar. Cold as the frozen ground beyond the window.

'What about it?' I whisper.

'I think it's time I stopped working on Jacob's farm, dedicate myself to our home before the baby comes. I mean, you're only going to get bigger, aren't you? Less capable?'

He's right, and this is what I've been praying for, so I don't know why his words sting. 'I guess.'

'I'll tell Jacob when I go in on Monday, give him a week's notice so I stay in his good books. And I can keep in with the guys, go for a drink with them sometimes, just in case I need a job in the future.' He shuffles forward to the sofa's edge, pours himself another generous shot of whiskey, swills it around the glass for a few moments, then necks it.

'Okay,' I whisper. But my head is spinning. I wasn't sure about him taking a job, but now I don't know how I feel about him giving it up. Yes, it will be good to have him around to do the chores, but can we afford it? And more pressing than that, how will I ever get my phone back if he's here, watching over me twenty-four seven?

He looks at his watch. 'That dinner ready now, do you reckon?'

'What? Oh, yes.' Shit, I'd forgotten. The vegetables will be soft and watery now. I quickly push up to standing, but something happens. A twang. A jolt of pain explodes in my back like an electric shock. I gasp, drop onto my hands and knees.

'What the hell?'

'My back,' I stutter, breathless. 'I've done something to my back.'

'Bri, you just stood up.' His words are slurring now, I notice. Or maybe the pain is messing with my hearing. 'Stop being such a princess.'

'No, honestly, I can't move. Can you help me onto the sofa?'

I can't see him from this angle, but I can sense him frowning. 'What about dinner?' he says. 'I thought it was ready to serve up?'

I tense with irritation, but that sets off another spasm of pain, and I gasp again, louder this time.

'Jesus, Bri, your acting skills are shit. At least try to make it look genuine.'

'It is genuine!' My eyes blur with tears. I give up hoping that Jonah will come to my rescue and twist tentatively until my side reaches the floor. The hard, cold, termite-puckered floorboards.

'Are you really just going to lie there?' Jonah's blue eyes blaze with indignation.

'I can't move, Jonah.'

I stare at his socked feet, the frayed edges of his jeans. His toe bounces on the wooden floor, Jonah's tic when he's thinking, and I pray that he finds some compassion. But a moment later, he slaps his foot flat on the floor – a decision clearly made – and walks into the kitchen. With the door open, delicious smells seep through and my stomach growls with hunger as my back sparks with pain. And all I can do is cross my fingers and hope that Jonah returns with a plate of food for me.

Chapter 35

Madison

@ashleycoltrane92 Not just for Christmas? Seriously? Maybe you should get down off that high horse your millionaire husband bought you and check out real life #workingmom #lovemykids #twowagefamily #tradwivesruinlives

I peer around the kitchen door and frown. Where's Lori? I blow out an exasperated sigh and turn on my heel. I search the rest of the ground floor, but the only sign of life comes from the craft room. The kids sound like they're having fun, but I'm not ready to engage with them until I've worked out why Lori is still acting so strangely, so I head upstairs instead, both flights.

I can't remember the last time I was in Lori's room. We have a couple of young girls from town who do all the cleaning and laundry that the children aren't tasked with (and get paid well to keep quiet about their jobs), and Lori spends so much of her time in the kitchen, that there's never a reason to visit. But something's going on with her, and I'm losing my patience. I knock on the door, then push it open.

'Madison,' she says, her eyes widening. 'Is everything okay?'

Lori is fully dressed, her hair neatly braided. The curtains are open, and her bed is made. But she's sitting on top of the bedspread with her back pushed against the wall and there's a musty smell in the air. Then I notice that one of Lori's hands is hidden beneath her pillow, and it makes me think about my conversation with Noah yesterday. Did she just slide something under there? A card addressed to me perhaps?

'I thought you'd be in the kitchen,' I start.

She laughs, then looks shocked by her reaction. 'Sorry, I'm coming now.'

'Are you sick?'

She draws her hand back – it's empty – and rubs her palm along her jawline. 'Not really, but I do have toothache,' she says. 'I've rubbed some clove oil on it, so hopefully it will settle soon.'

I nod, realizing what the smell is, then shift my eyeline back to the pillow. 'I didn't get a chance to ask you last night, but Noah said he gave you a card that arrived for me.'

'What kind of card?'

I shuffle with annoyance at the deflection. 'I don't know, a card kind of card, I suppose. He said the handwriting was messy. That there was no stamp on it.'

'Oh. Maybe.' Lori shrugs. 'You and Michael get so many Christmas cards; I don't pay much attention to the envelope.'

'You really don't know what card I'm referring to? It was the only mail in the mailbox on Christmas Day. He thought maybe it had been there longer because it had slipped down the side.'

'No, sorry.' She gives me an apologetic shrug. 'Maybe it's this toothache, messing up my memory. Anyway, I guess the kids will be hungry soon, so I better get myself in gear.' She pushes off the bed and looks at me expectantly, like she wants me to leave first. I consider reminding her whose house this is, but that's crazy, I can check under her pillow whenever I want. So I back out of her room with a gracious smile and walk downstairs, Lori trailing just behind.

'You know, Madison, I might need to go to the dentist about this tooth,' Lori says as we take up our usual places in the kitchen – me sitting down, Lori preparing lunch.

'But you can't leave the homestead until the baby comes,' I point out. 'And you've always said clove oil performs miracles.'

'It does, sometimes, but I'm worried the tooth might get infected if I don't see someone about it.'

'I'm sorry, Lori, but you're six weeks from giving birth. There's no way you could hide the pregnancy now. What if people in town see? Put two and two together?'

'I'll wear one of Michael's big coats, and keep it done up the whole time. People will just think I'm a middle-aged woman who's eaten a bit too much yule log. And I'm an invisible kind of person, you know that. Barely anyone will notice me anyway.'

'I don't know. It feels risky.'

'Please, Madison!'

Lori's plea jolts me. She sounds so desperate. Does her tooth really hurt that bad? I drum my fingernails against the wooden arm of the chair. Letting Lori go into town feels like the wrong thing to do, but if her tooth gets worse, she could end up in hospital, and that would be bad. She has managed to give birth to all our children at home, with only the help of the same private midwife, Kate, a woman whose silence is easily bought due to her lifelong shopping addiction. I don't want to mess up Lori's unblemished track record for the sake of a dodgy tooth.

'Okay, fine. But don't engage anyone in conversation. Strictly tooth talk only.'

'One hundred percent, I promise. Thank you, Madison.' There's so much relief in her face that it's as though me agreeing to it has taken the pain away. But that's not possible of course. It's the clove oil.

'I might go hang out with the children,' I say, suddenly feeling restless. Although when I say children, what I really mean is the girls. Both Molly and Matilda love having their nails painted. In truth, Myron loves it too, but the only time I gave in to him, Michael nearly had a heart attack when he saw Myron's gold toenails, so that is off the table now. Because Lori knows me better than anyone, I wait for her to offer to mind the boys.

'Great. Have fun.' Lori walks over to the fridge and pulls out the leftover turkey. 'I'll prepare lunch.'

'Right, okay.' I hesitate. I'm not used to having to work at these things. 'Myron might want to hang out with you though,' I finally say. 'And Mason could be sent outside to chop wood or something.'

'Sorry?' Lori's brain calibrates. 'Oh, yes, of course, I wasn't thinking. Send the two of them down here and I'll sort them out.'

'Lori, is anything wrong?'

'What? No, not at all. I'm completely fine.'

'Apart from your tooth.'

'Exactly.'

I linger for another few seconds, trying to make sense of this change in Lori, then give up and head towards the craft room. But I have a detour to make first.

I walk slowly up the first set of stairs and then quickly up the second. I push open Lori's bedroom door, walk over to the bed, and slide my hand underneath the pillow. My fingers connect with paper almost instantly. I was right. I allow myself a triumphant smile as I pull the envelope out, but that morphs into a frown when I realize there's nothing inside it. The envelope is as Noah described it: messy handwriting, no postage stamp, but a smudged ink postal service stamp, although I guess the envelope could be secondhand. And they've only written a partial address – *Madison March, March Homestead, Montana*.

I drop onto the bed, not caring if I ruffle the bedspread, half wanting Lori to know I've been here. Why did she steal mail that was addressed to me? What has she done with the card inside?

And who sent it?

Chapter 36

Madison

@angel_mckenzie97 Hey! We're mom twins – I'm due in February too! But damn, how come your jawline is so defined still? I have hamster cheeks!
#momlife #newbaby #3kidsandcounting #familyislife

My mind is full of noise about what a bad idea this is, but I focus on the road and keep driving. I can't believe Lori is forcing me to take these risks. But how can I let her go off by herself with my baby inside her after the lies she's told? The weird way she's behaving?

I thought there'd be an easier way. That I'd get Bill to drive Lori into town and then give me a rundown about what she got up to later. Bill might save most of his loyalty for Michael, but I know there's some left over for me. If I asked him to report back with an account of exactly where Lori went and who she spoke to, he would do it without questioning why. But Bill is visiting his mother today, in a care home near Yellowstone, so he's not around to help. And there's no one else I can ask.

So here I am, trying to keep Lori's car in my eyeline without making her suspicious, while also trying to figure out how all the different buttons in Michael's truck work. Michael's pride and joy, which I'm not – under any circumstances – allowed to drive. I wonder what he'd do if he found out.

But he won't find out, I remind myself. Michael has gone away for a couple of nights on a hunting trip. His brother Matthew drove down from Great Falls first thing this morning, and they headed out to the Gallatin forest in Matthew's Chevy. They're not due back until late on Sunday, so even if Michael decides there aren't enough elk, or grows impatient with the park's pointless rules, and cuts the trip short, he won't be back anytime soon. I just need to make sure I get the truck back to the homestead without it picking up a scratch.

My front wheels spin on some black ice and I grip the steering wheel to steady it, my heart racing so fast that it takes my breath away. I learned to drive when I was sixteen, but the way my life has turned out, I haven't had much opportunity to practice. Michael doesn't even like me driving around the ranch in case I injure myself. At least that's what he says. I suspect it's more to do with him not trusting me to navigate around his precious cows.

The truck straightens and I breathe a sigh of relief. Lori drives a brightly colored Buick Encore, a tiny car compared to most on these roads, so it's easy to spot. I watch as she signals right, towards town, and when she disappears around a bend; I follow.

Lori pulls up outside the dentist and despite this being where she said she was going, I feel a sense of anticlimax. I've risked Michael's anger for this, and Lori might have been telling the truth after all. To query a tooth infection. But I'm here now, and I think maybe she's smart enough to factor in covering her tracks if she has a secret agenda. So I drive past, and when she disappears inside the building, loop back and park where I can see the door.

Twenty minutes later, Lori emerges. Michael's old parka is still buttoned up like she promised, and the sight makes me soften. But instead of getting back in her car, Lori starts walking up Main Street. I frown. There are a dozen reasons why Lori might want to take a detour – she comes into town even less often than me – but she knows how uncomfortable I am about her risking exposing her pregnancy. What could be important enough for her to go against my wishes?

I slide out the car, pull my hood over my head, and follow.

I've done everything possible to fade into the background and not be recognized. Yes, I'm wearing the wildly uncomfortable silicone baby belly, but it's too big for my frame, and I don't want Michael to find out I've been off the homestead anyway. So I've scraped my hair into a ponytail and I'm wearing my least fashionable sunglasses. I'm dressed in a long gray skirt over black boots, a darker gray roll-neck sweater, and a wool coat from three seasons ago. I look terrible in fact, so that's another reason why I need to stay incognito.

There are a few people around – desperate for some time away after two days holed up with their families, no doubt – but no one seems in the mood to stop and chat, thank goodness, so I'm free to watch Lori. She passes Shelley's beauty parlor, crosses the road, and walks into the bar.

My mind instantly goes to Rose. I imagine her sitting at the bar, nursing a Dry Hills, no ice. Has Lori gone to meet her? But that's silly. Lori doesn't even know Rose. And two days after Christmas, there'll be dozens of people in there. Lori could be meeting any one of them.

Except, who does Lori know? She spends all her time at the homestead, has dedicated her life to looking after me and the children. She's estranged from her family, and there's been no time for friends, or lovers, or any kind of life beyond the Marches. A lurch of guilt runs through me, but I shake it off. If Lori feels like she owes me, that's her call.

Except she seems to be walking a different path today.

I stare at the matching saloon doors, gently swinging in a wind that's whipped up. I desperately want to go inside, to find out who Lori is talking to. But that would mean blowing my cover. I don't care if Lori knows I've been following her, but what would I be walking into?

This must have something to do with the Christmas card Lori stole, it's too much of a coincidence not to. But what? I don't know who the card was from, or even whether it came through the mail or was hand delivered.

Could the card have been from Rose? Some threat, or warning?

Maybe Lori intercepted it to protect me. She could be in there now, telling Rose to stay the hell out of my marriage. My eyes swell with tears as I imagine that conversation, Lori always looking out for me.

But then I shake my head in frustration. The truth is, I don't know why she's in there, or who she's with.

'Madison?'

I freeze at the sound of the familiar voice. Then slowly turn my head. 'Oh. Hi, Jemma, Marty.' I look at the pair of them, holding hands, smiling with those simpleton faces of theirs. 'No kids today?'

'We've got them working,' Jemma says with a wink. 'We're dropping in food packages for the needy, it's a church thing, and we've split the kids into two teams, put our eldest, Lettie and Rory, in charge.' She tilts her head and her smile weakens. 'Are you okay, Madison? You look . . . different.'

'I'm not well,' I whisper in a hoarse voice, thinking on my feet, like always. 'You shouldn't get too close.' But I underestimated Jemma Stuart.

'Don't be silly.' She takes a step forward, touches my arm. 'What can I do?'

God, she's going to hug me, realize my baby is a lump of silicone. 'Nothing. Thank you.' I step backwards. 'And Michael's waiting, so I should probably go.'

'Oh.' Her eyes widen, startled by my brush-off. 'And the baby's okay?'

'Yes, it's fine. Bye, Jemma.' I turn away from her and do my best waddling impression back towards the truck. Lori is still in the bar, talking to God knows who. But I can't wait around to find out. This whole trip, the risks I've taken, feels like a waste of time. But it isn't.

I've found out that Lori is lying. That the dentist appointment was just a cover. And when she gets home, I'll get the truth out of her.

Chapter 37

Madison

@ringofroses16 Your life is so perfect. Do you ever worry about it falling apart?
#blessed #beautiful #bigfamily #liveeverydaylikeitsyourlast

'So how was the dentist?'

Lori looks up from the rocking chair. She's sitting by the fire in the den, knitting something wholesome, maybe a jumper for Myron. I think about how good the image would look on my grid, the burnt-orange-colored wool against the backdrop of logs and flames, then I remember why I'm here and narrow my eyes at Lori.

'Oh, it was fine, thank you. A false alarm, no infection, but I'm glad I got it checked out.'

'I bet you are.' I flash her one of my fake smiles and Lori responds as I hoped, her bottom lip quivering and eyes widening, because my expressions are like Lori's first language – and she's the only one who can spot a fake.

'And have you had a good day?' she asks, trying to change the subject, to put off the inevitable. She also resumes her knitting, except that her hands are quivering now too. I listen to the irregular click clacking for a moment, draw some pleasure from the number of stitches she must be dropping.

'An enlightening day, I'd call it.'

'That's nice. Oh, dammit.'

I gesture towards the point of her needle, now empty, an orange loop of wool suspended in the air. 'I know I'm not much of a knitter, but I guess that isn't good?'

Lori bunches the whole ensemble together and drops it on the side table with a deep sigh. 'I'll sort it out later. It's time to start supper anyway.' She starts to push out of the chair, but I take a couple of steps towards her and rest my hand on top of hers. She stiffens.

'I took a trip into town today, Lori.'

Half of Lori's face is flushed from the fire, but the other half pales. 'I thought Bill was visiting his mother,' she whispers.

It takes me a moment to realize what she's saying. Lori must have put the idea in Bill's head, a Christmas visit to see his ancient mother in her care home. Having Bill out of the way meant Lori could drive herself to town, and also that I would be stranded on the homestead. It's almost impressive.

'I took Michael's truck,' I tell her. 'Followed you. I wanted to check you got to the dentist okay.'

'I did, thank you,' she whispers.

'And then you went to the bar.'

She curls her arms around her bump, and I fight the urge to pull them away, to tell her she's lost the right to hug my child. 'You weren't supposed to know,' she finally says, her voice low.

'Of course I wasn't! Because if I did, I'd also know that you were willing to put my whole life, my brand, in jeopardy! But for what? That's what I want to know.'

'I didn't take my coat off. No one could tell I was pregnant. There was no risk to you.'

'In that case, why lie about it? Why tell me you were going to the dentist?'

'I did go to the dentist . . .'

'Was Rose there?' I throw back. 'In the bar. Did you meet her?'

Lori looks up at me, and the guilt in her eyes is so clear that I know I've hit the jackpot.

'What the hell have you and Rose got to discuss?!' I shout.

'Madison, I don't want to talk about this. I need to make supper.'

'No way you're getting out of this. Why did you meet her? What did she want with you?'

Lori runs her hands along her thighs, like she's calming a child who's desperate to run. 'It's better if you're kept out of it, safer for you. I talked to Rose, but you don't have to worry about her.'

'How do you know? What did you do to convince her?'

'It's complicated.'

'So tell me!' I start pacing the room. 'Was that card Noah gave you from her? I know you stole it. Where is it?' I pause, point my finger at her. 'I demand you give it to me!'

Lori looks at the fire. 'I'm sorry, I can't.'

I follow her gaze. 'Wait, you burned the card?'

'You don't want to read it. It's better this way. Destroyed.'

'Oh, God.' I drop onto the sofa, suddenly exhausted. Part of me is furious with Lori, and desperate to know what she's been doing behind my back, with Rose. But another part is grateful, relieved that she's sorting out my problems, like always.

Lori pushes out of the rocking chair and lowers down next to me. She takes my hand, and I find myself resting my head on her shoulder. 'Life is messed up, Madison,' she says quietly. 'You think you can control it, and my goodness, you have done an amazing job of that over the last thirteen years. But no one can, not forever. Things happen that we could never predict, never plan for.'

'You're scaring me.'

Lori strokes my hand. 'Do you trust me?'

I think about what we've been through together. How people died on that terrible night, the innocent and the guilty, but not us. We were the only two who survived, and Lori the only one who came out unscathed. She made a promise to me then, that she would make up for her mistakes, help me get the life I deserved. And I have had no reason to doubt her commitment in all that time. 'I do, yes.'

'Well, trust that I'm handling it. You have nothing to fear from Rose, or anyone else.'

I lift my head off Lori's shoulder and drop it back against the sofa cushion. I stare at the ceiling, the colonial-style wooden fan, stilled for the winter. I could keep on at Lori until she tells me everything, I'm sure I have that power over her. But Lori has been living the difficult, uncomfortable parts of my life for over a decade. Why would I want to change that now? If she says she's handling it, what's the point of exposing myself to it?

I sit up straighter, twist to face her. 'There is one more thing before I let you go make supper.'

Lori looks at me with anxious eyes. 'Yes?'

'Can you fix your knitting so that I can take a photo of it by the fire? Those oranges look gorgeous together.'

Chapter 38

Brianna

'Jonah! It's nearly eight!'

I stare up the empty staircase, will Jonah to respond, but the silence continues. I rub my lower back in frustration – five days on, the pain still niggles, not that Jonah has given me an ounce of sympathy. Where is he? He used to be the one who got up early, who laid a fire and made sure there was hot water for my morning coffee. Now it's like dragging a walrus through mud. He says it's the hours of physical labor that make him tired, but I reckon it's the hours of drinking he fits in around it.

'You're going to be late for work!'

Suddenly there's a crash, then low-level mutterings, and finally Jonah appears, swaying at the top of the stairs. 'Quit your screeching, woman. I know what time it is.'

'I just thought . . .'

'What? That I might get fired? I've given Jacob notice, remember? I'll be gone by the end of the week, so what's he going to do?'

I sigh. I still haven't decided whether having Jonah back here full time soon is a blessing or a curse. 'Do you want some coffee?' I mumble. 'Breakfast?'

'What have you made?'

'Um, nothing yet,' I admit. 'But I could do some French toast?'

He clicks his tongue. 'Forget it, Bri. I don't have time. I guess I'll just go out hungry again.'

My face smarts. But I don't understand why him being late is my fault. 'Will you come straight home from work today?' I ask, choosing to change the subject.

He shrugs. 'Maybe.'

'It's New Year's Eve,' I remind him. 'I was thinking we could see the New Year in as a family – you, me, and bump. Talk about what we can get done before the baby comes, now that you're finishing work.'

He pauses, and I watch his shoulders slacken. 'Yeah, okay. That sounds good.'

I smile with relief. Then I sidle over, wrap my arms around him, move them up and down his back. 'I love you, Jonah.'

'I love you too, Bri.'

I follow him outside, then wave him off until his car disappears down the drive. For once, the wind has stilled to a gentle breeze, but the snow on the ground has doubled in thickness and the temperature is brutal. As I search the vista for some color, my eyes fall on the rusty mailbox at the end of our long drive. I think about the mailman, who I didn't know existed, delivering those two Christmas cards for Jonah, and the hurried homemade card I gave him in return. I walk over to the mailbox. I'm not expecting anything, so I'm not sure why my eyes sprout tears when it's empty. I turn back towards the house and the paltry warmth inside.

But I need to focus if I'm going to find my phone. Jonah finally went back to work yesterday after the Christmas break, and I was certain his twelve hours away from the homestead would give me long enough to recover it. But I searched the house and found nothing. I know it isn't in his car – I got up in the middle of the night, risked all kinds of predators, to check that. And now I know it's not in his pockets either – my drifting goodbye hug doubling as a pat down. Which means it must be outside. It was snowing a blizzard yesterday, too heavy to find anything, but it's much calmer today.

I pull on my coat and gloves, and head straight to Jonah's work area. There's lots of junk behind the boards of plywood. Rusty tools, fishing equipment, ripped newspapers, an old cashbox with a few coins inside. I kneel on the frozen ground and pull a wooden crate towards me. It's covered with a slab of heavy stone, but I use all my strength and manage to slide it onto the ground with a thud.

The crate is jam-packed with stuff and it's hard to find purchase in the bulky gloves, so I pull them off. My fingers instantly burn with cold, but I ignore the pain and keep searching. I touch cool, curved metal, and my heart slows. Carefully, I pull out a pistol, hold it in my hand. My daddy has guns, even my grandma shot a rattlesnake once. But I've never held one myself. I find I like it, the sense of power it gives me. I aim the gun at a tree in the distance and pull the trigger. It clicks. Not loaded, of course.

But it's not the only weapon in here. I pull out a smooth, rigid handle. A hunting knife. It's covered with a black leather sheath, and I slide it free. It's maybe a foot long, the blade serrated on one side and smooth and sharp on the other. Gleaming. Deadly. I grip the handle tighter, draw a cross in the air, then stab at nothing. If an intruder came here when Jonah was out, could I use this to fend him off?

I shake the dark thoughts away and push the knife back into its sheath. But as I bury it in the box again, I keep digging, because I'm sure my phone will be in here now. This is clearly where Jonah keeps his most precious things.

And finally, I find it. I breathe a sigh of relief, but it's more than that. Joy, desire, sustenance. I'm prepared for it to be out of battery, so the black screen doesn't frustrate me too much, but it gives me a sense of urgency. I shove the wooden box back where I found it, heave the stone slab across, and then run towards the house and my charger which has been dangling forlornly from the plug socket for five days.

Ten minutes later, my phone finally has enough power to switch on. I check my messages first, ride the sting of disappointment. No season's greetings from my family, or anyone else. I blink back tears and check my social media. It's torture of course, but I still devour it all. Sparkling trees. Brightly wrapped presents. Big families around long tables, platters stacked high with delicious-looking food. Eggnog in frosted glasses. Laughter. I read the posts, the hashtags, the comments from other accounts. And I silently mourn what I'm missing, what I deserve after all the work I've put in.

I move to my Instagram messages, but that's a sad sight too. A short list of people I don't know in real life, and only messages in one direction. From me to them. Some ignored completely, others with the soulless standard reply: I'm not accepting messages right now. So much for #blessed and #grateful and #allGodschildren. Those navel-gazing bitches don't care about anyone but themselves.

With a jolt of rage, I click into my Tumblr account, and my mood instantly lifts. There are seven comments on my last post, which I wrote late on Christmas Eve. Jonah wasn't back, which wasn't unusual, but it hit me hard that night, knowing how my family would be celebrating back in Buffalo. I scan my post, feel the loneliness all over again, then read the comments.

None of them have any time for Jonah – or J as I call him on my blog. These seven women – because I can tell they're women – are mad on my behalf. They think he's either a fledgling alcoholic or just an asshole, but either way, I should leave him, go back home, ask my family for forgiveness, beg if necessary, but move on. They tell me that everyone is allowed to make mistakes, and while yes, a baby makes things more complicated for an unwed mother, it doesn't need to be a deal-breaker, if I'm humble enough.

But the problem is, I don't want to beg. I don't want to be grateful for someone's pity. I am Brianna Nelson. Straight A student. Captain of the cheerleading squad. Prettiest girl in twelfth grade.

There must be a better way.

Chapter 39

Cally

I scroll through my phone. Somehow there are both too many messages, and not enough. My parents, Grandma, my college friend Cassie, even Luke, making me feel homesick with their Happy New Year GIFs, their plans for tonight, and questions about what I'm doing. And then there's the message from Murphy. Reminding me what my only resolution needs to be this New Year.

But there are also the people who haven't been in touch. I don't care about Lily – our friendship ended when she hightailed it out of the party after giving me that stupid dare. But Tasha, Flo, Nix, Conor. These are people I used to hang out with most weekends, but I haven't heard from them in months.

I can't blame them though, because it was me who stopped responding when they kept asking how things were going with the famous Madison March. I didn't know how to even begin to explain, so I took the easy way out and avoided them altogether. All being well, I'll be going back to Boston in the summer. But will we pick up where we left off? Or am I too different a person now?

My phone buzzes and I grab it, suddenly desperate for more contact with my old life. But it's a message from Madison.

Dinner will be ready soon and Michael has just popped open a bottle of champagne, so I need to get down to the formal living room quick. She finishes off with *Remember, I'm pregnant*, which is weird under the circumstances, but I log it and do as I am told.

My mood sinks even lower when I hear Nathan's booming voice leaking under the door. I sneak into the room without making eye contact with him, or the woman next to him, who I assume is his wife from the way her shoulders hunch with disappointment. Erica is perched on the sofa arm, watching Noah carefully as he distributes drinks, and I suppose it's good to see some role reversal in this place, even if it is from the two people who were born out of state.

'Do you want some fizz, Cally?'

I take a glass from Noah's tray. Other than those two glasses of wine with Michael, I've barely drunk since I've been living here. Partly because none of the women seem to drink – although Erica is sometimes slow to remove her sunglasses on a weekend shift – but also because I feel I need to be on my guard, just in case. But it's New Year's Eve. All my friends back home will be getting bombed, and it might just be the only way to get through an evening with Nathan. I gulp a few generous mouthfuls, and then proffer my glass to Noah for a refill.

'Hey, Cally.'

I turn around and smile. 'Hey, Bill. How are you?' Bill was the first man I met in Montana, and as it's turned out, the only one worth meeting so far.

'Things aren't too rosy, to be honest,' he says.

'Oh? I'm sorry to hear that.'

I've never heard Bill complain about anything, and my concern must show on my face, because he shakes his head and gives me an apologetic smile. 'Listen to me, bringing my favorite Yankee down on New Year's Eve. It's just my mom. I went to see her the other day, in her care home, and I don't think she's much longer for this world. But she's eighty-four, and hasn't ever missed a Sunday service, so she'll be going someplace better when the time comes.'

'Still hard for you though,' I say, not letting him get away with the men don't cry act. 'We only have one mom.'

'Yeah, true. But the sun will still rise in the morning, the stars come out at night. Life goes on.'

'What was that about stars?' Madison slides between us. She's look predictably stunning in a shimmering gold dress, but that's not what draws my attention. I'm more taken aback by her huge ball-shaped midriff. She gives me her shut-up-or-die smile, then looks at Bill quizzically. If he has clocked her new appendage, he doesn't mention it.

'Just talking about the Montana night sky,' Bill says.

'Ah, the best in the world,' Madison purrs, then shifts her eyeline to me, and I know categorically that she saw me with Michael around the fire. Shame explodes on my cheeks, but then I start to feel angry. Why should I be embarrassed when it was her husband who dragged me out there?

'I guess there are other amazing night skies though,' I say, wanting to rebel in some small, pathetic way. 'You know, in the African deserts, or the Andes mountains. Or those countries in Europe that see the aurora borealis.'

'You don't have to go to Europe to see that,' Bill says.

Madison tips her head. 'Is that the green and pink light show? Do we get that in Montana?'

Bill smiles. 'We sure do, from time to time, when the atmospheric pressure is right. In fact, they were talking about it on the radio this morning. Apparently, it's happening soon.'

'Really?' I ask. 'When?' This is something I can get excited about. As long as I make sure it's not just Michael and me gazing at the colorful sky, his arm snaking somewhere it shouldn't.

Bill scrunches his nose. 'I think they said the seventh. Yeah, a week away, that's it. You should get the kids out too, Madison. It'll blow their mind.'

'What? Yes, good idea.' But Madison has clearly lost interest in our conversation because she's too busy tapping on her phone to listen.

'Right, everyone, drink up,' Michael hollers. 'We've got venison for dinner – deer I hunted myself, I might add. And I don't doubt Lori has rustled up something pretty special to go with it. So shall we sit down?'

'Lori and I,' Madison cuts in, resting her hand on her fake bump. 'Mainly me, though.'

'Where is Lori?' the woman who I guess is Nathan's wife asks.

This must be why Madison's pretending to be pregnant, I suddenly realize. This woman doesn't know about the surrogacy. And that's also why Lori isn't here. She's been hidden away, like a leper rather than a mom-to-be. I bet she prepared all the dinner – I haven't seen Madison cook more than toast since I've been here – and now she's been banished to her room to see in the New Year alone. I can't believe I have to let this exploitation go unchallenged, especially to someone as lovely as Lori. And all because I can't drive a stupid stick-shift car.

'She's minding the children,' Madison says. 'Lori isn't a fan of dinner parties, and I didn't want to force her.'

'Of course,' the woman says, looking at Madison with a doting expression.

'Shall we go?' Michael suggests again, and this time there's a clear edge to his voice, so we all file quickly out the room.

Chapter 40

Cally

I sigh when I see there are name cards on the table, then louder when I find mine. I'm sitting at one end, next to Michael and opposite Nathan. I thought my New Year's Eve was going to be dull, now I know it's going to be hellish.

'Don't look so nervous, Cally,' Nathan booms. 'I don't bite.'

Michael leans towards me, our shoulders touching, and whispers, 'I might.'

Then they both burst into laughter, and I need to grind my feet into the floor to stop from running away. I take a mouthful of wine and pray for intoxication to get me through.

The evening feels like it goes on forever. Nathan's wife – who I discovered is called Nancy – apparently wants to be an influencer. She has talked constantly about handmade Christmas decorations, and monopolized Erica and Noah's time. Bill and Madison are sitting at the other end of the table – Madison not holding court like I'd expect, maybe she's pretending to be tired from the pregnancy. And I've been listening to two big egos go head-to-head all night.

'Guys and gals, it'll be midnight soon,' Nancy exclaims, her words sliding into each other. 'Michael, is there any special champagne to see in 2025?'

'Nancy, you're being rude,' Nathan says. His voice carries an icy undertone, and Nancy pales in response – literally sobering up in real time. God, this place. Why can't a dinner guest politely request another drink on New Year's Eve just because she's female?

'Well, I would love a glass of champagne too.' I regret my comment almost instantly, the rebuke it might bring. And why am I sticking up for a woman who can talk about Christmas wreaths for a whole evening?

But Michael seems more pleased than put out. 'Well, in that case, let's go!'

I frown. 'Go where?'

'To get some very special all-American champagne. I take it you're not too important to help me collect it from the cellar? Or do you East Coast types expect to be waited on?' He winks at me, but if that's meant to put me at ease, it doesn't work.

'No, I . . .'

'Come on then. Otherwise we'll miss the big countdown.'

Michael cups my elbow and stands, levering me up with him. I send a Mayday signal to Erica – she's my best bet without Lori here – but she looks away. I don't dare turn to Madison for help, and Nancy is too busy digging herself out of her own hole to notice my developing crisis. I feel Michael's hand on my back, his fingers spreading, but I have no choice but to let him guide me out of the dining room.

It's darker in the hallway, just a table lamp for light, and I feel Michael's arm around my waist. 'You know, it's really great having you here,' he murmurs, his hot breath spreading over my neck. 'I don't usually have much time for women who sabotage their face like that, but it didn't take you long to

196

change my mind, Miss Cally. You're damn sexy, but you know that, right?'

I hide my growing horror behind a grimace-tinged smile. Then I wriggle, try to disentangle myself, but he holds on. 'Shall we get the champagne then?' I squeak, anything to distract him. 'So that we can get back to the kitchen with plenty of time to pour it before midnight?'

He slides his arm away, and I almost cry with relief, except that his eyes light up. 'Yes, let's go.' He claps his hands, then walks towards the cellar door. He's swaying, drunker than I'd realized, but I follow because what other option is there?

He opens the door to a set of stairs and gestures for me to go first. My legs are shaking so much that I have to grip the banister to keep myself steady. I pray to a god I desperately hope is real to make all these frenzied red flags just false alarms.

But as soon as my feet hit solid ground, he's there too, his hands on my arms, turning me around to face him. He walks me backwards towards the cold stone wall.

'Michael, we should get back.'

'Come on, don't pretend you don't want this too. After all our romantic stargazing.'

'No, I don't . . . Please, Michael.' But I can't say any more because his mouth is on mine, his tongue prizing my lips open. His hands are everywhere too. Panic makes my head swim. I can't stop this.

'Michael!'

He pulls away. I suck at the air, try to get some purchase over my breathing. Madison is standing at the top of the stairs, hands on her hips, biting fury on her face.

'What's going on?'

'Ah, nothing for you to worry about,' Michael says, wafting one hand in the air while pulling at his groin with the other.

The sight makes me want to vomit. 'Cally and I were just having a little private celebration.'

'Cally, go to your room.'

In other circumstances, I might rail at being treated like a child, but I'm so grateful that I scrabble up the steps with my head low and don't stop running until I'm in my bed with a chair butted up against the door handle. I stare at the ceiling through a glaze of tears until I finally cry myself to sleep.

Chapter 41

Madison

@Madonnafangirl456 I wish I was as beautiful as you, then maybe my low-life #mfkg husband might stop screwing around
#faith #marriage #commitment #judgementday

It takes every morsel of energy I have to hold my head up and my tears back. I did everything to avoid this. Found a tutor that was supposed to be the opposite of Michael's type. Made sure I was available to him, always.

But here we are.

'Why are you looking at me like that?' Michael demands, on the defensive. 'We're celebrating the start of a new year, for Chrissakes. I can't believe you spoke to Cally like that, in front of me, like you're in charge around here. You're taking liberties, Madison, you need to watch your step.' He clicks his tongue, then starts stomping up the stairs towards me.

An apology bubbles on my lips, my instinct to survive, to keep him happy. But I'm tired. Tired of him treating me like his possession, the trophy wife and model mother, too unimportant to have opinions or feelings. Because I'm the one with ten million fans, not him. I'm the one who put the March Homestead on the map, not him.

As he gets closer, I steel myself for an argument, but he just pushes me out of his way. Knocked off balance, I stumble, but he doesn't slow down, either to check I'm okay or to mock my clumsiness. He just sails past like he hadn't noticed I was even there. I feel his absence, and I'm both heartbroken and enraged.

I breathe, try to find some strength. Use every new burst of oxygen to remind myself that I need to let this go. Barely anything happened between Michael and Cally because I got there in time to stop it. And these loose women who pass through his life mean nothing in the end. It's me who has the ring on my finger, and access to his wealth, his name, the lifestyle his money provides. I am the true winner here.

But after more than a decade, that logic is so faded, so withered, that it curls and dies almost instantly.

I hear a noise from the hallway. Michael yanking open one of the drawers by the front door. Then the jangle of keys. Shit. The sound spurs me into action, and I race to catch him up.

'What are you doing?' I ask in as steady a voice as I can manage. 'Why have you got the keys to your truck?'

'I'm not staying here, with you, and that weird techy crowd of yours. I'm going for a drink with the guys from the ranch. Men who know to respect their boss.'

The only place to go for a drink around here is in town, the bar, which will be open for hours tonight. But it won't just be Michael's cowboys in there. I think about Lori, the card, her asking me to trust that she's dealing with Rose. But what if Rose is as drunk as Michael? Everyone knows she's unpredictable, wild. Will she blurt out whatever she and Lori talked about?

'It's late, Michael,' I say, trying to sound both conciliatory and suggestive. 'And you've had plenty to drink already.'

'Don't you dare tell me how much I can drink!'

I raise my hands, part apology, part self-preservation. 'I'm sorry, you're right, I shouldn't have said that. But it's only ten minutes until midnight,' I try instead. 'And town is at least a half-hour drive in this weather. You don't want to see the New Year in all by yourself in the truck. Why don't you stay? Come back to the table?' I reach out, run my hand down his arm, then try to curl my fingers around his.

But he whips his hand away, then grabs the door handle and pulls it open. 'You can't tell me what to do, Madison. You know that.'

I look past him, through the open front door. Our Christmas lights twinkle against the navy-blue sky, as big balls of fluffy snow drift towards the ground. It's beautiful, but also deadly. Michael's truck is built for weather like this, but not when its driver is drunk, and any natural light is hidden by heavy cloud.

As I watch Michael stomp outside, I wonder if I should just let him go. Go upstairs and kneel by my bedside. Pray for God to take him early, for him to drive too fast, and hit black ice, for Michael to be spun into a centuries old tree or an uncompromising wall of snow.

But I shake the images away. Michael is my husband, my one true love.

And what would I do if he's left his entire estate to Mason?

I scurry after Michael, taking care not to touch him, to rile him again. 'Please, Michael. The roads will be treacherous in this snow, and you're too important to me to risk your life like this, too loved.'

'I've been driving these roads for thirty years,' he growls. 'Snow up to my waist sometimes. You think I can't handle a few flakes?'

'No, I don't mean . . .'

'Listen, Madison,' he cuts in. 'Can I give you some advice?'

'Sure,' I whisper.

'If you want forgiveness for undermining me in front of Cally, you need to step aside now. And you better hope I have a good time tonight, because the more fun I have, the more likely it is I'll be in a forgiving mood when I get back. Does that make some sense in that pretty little head of yours?'

I don't speak – I can't trust myself not to verbalize what's actually swirling around my pretty little head – but I nod and take a step back. I watch him climb into the truck and rev the engine. As the wheels spit out gravel, and his taillights shrink to pinpricks, I think about my own journey in that truck, only four days ago. How proud I was to be outsmarting Lori. And then later, the relief of knowing she was taking care of whatever dangers lurked out there for me. Now I feel helpless. Despite my fame, my huge brand value, my survival feels like it's in the hands of others – Michael, Lori, Rose.

I hear rustling in the pine trees that border our driveway, and I turn towards to it. It's too dark to see anything, but as I stare into the snow-spattered blackness, I think about the man Michael confronted on Christmas Eve. Who was he? Bill said he kept repeating my name when he came across him, but I've never seen him. And if he's only come here twice in two months, he's hardly an obsessive stalker. Michael said he was carrying a hunting knife, but most men around here carry some kind of weapon. Was he planning on using it on me? Would I be dead now if he hadn't tripped the security light?

The thought makes me walk back inside. But I turn towards the stairs rather than my guests. I know I won't sleep, but I can't face them now, after everything that's happened. Bill will see everyone out.

Chapter 42

Brianna

Jonah promised he'd come straight back after work, but it's close to ten and there's no sign of him. It's not like he hasn't spent nights away from the homestead before, and he's sometimes slept in his car rather than making the journey home. But this feels different. It's New Year's Eve, for Chrissakes.

That's why I made a big mac and cheese for supper and apple pie with custard for dessert. I even found a candle in the drawer when I was looking for my phone yesterday and I've stuck that into an empty beer bottle.

It was supposed to be a special evening, but now the pasta is cold and half eaten – it's been a long time since Jonah's absence stole my appetite – and the candle is just a stub, its melted wax making bulbous patterns on the glass.

The weather has got worse too. The blizzard has returned, dropping snow in clumps too big to look pretty. Jonah's car was a seventeenth birthday gift from his mom, a two-wheel drive Ford something more suited to Buffalo gritted tarmac than icy rural tracks.

Is he stuck out there somewhere? Could he have run out

of gas? Is he so exhausted from repairing fences that he's lost control of the car and crashed?

I look at my phone – it hasn't left my side all day, I'm planning to hide it at the last minute – but it can't help me now because Jonah sold his phone a few days after moving in here. He called it liberating – I kept my phone in my bra for a full forty-eight hours after that. But there is a way to communicate with him – theoretically – because Jonah has a ham radio in his car, and we also have one here, in the room we call Jonah's study.

As I walk into the moldy room on the front corner of the property, I remember when we gave all the rooms in the house grand names like the parlor, the library, Jonah's study, and it makes my eyes burn. Because now all I see are six dilapidated prison cells. I pull my blanket tighter around my shoulders and walk over to the makeshift desk. The ham radio is battery powered, and I breathe a sigh of relief when I turn it on and a light flashes. Jonah has told me how to use it a dozen times, so I should really know, except I'm not great with hardware, or instructions, and all I heard when he talked about it was white noise.

I remember that I need to set it to a particular frequency, so I twirl the dial, hoping that more details will come to me. But as I listen to static rise and fall, nothing does. Unfamiliar voices fade in and out, so it must be working, but no one stays on long enough for me to ask for help, and the frequency remains a jumble of numbers and letters in my head. I whack my palm against the cold metal in frustration. What if he's trying to get ahold of me, and freezing to death, because I didn't pay attention to his instruction monologue?

But that isn't fair. I can't be the villain when it's Jonah who spends hours, sometimes whole nights, away from home.

And deep down, I know he's not stuck on the side of the road anywhere. He's at the Ranch Inn, just like he always is. Celebrating New Year's Eve by getting wasted with his buddies.

I switch the radio off, wander back into the living room, and stand in front of the fire. I'm tired. I could curl up here, fall asleep, face reality in the morning. Except things will be worse then. The fire will have burned itself out, so I'll be stiff with frozen bones. And my baby will be a day closer to being born into this nightmare.

I look at Jonah's two Christmas cards on the mantelpiece, the constant reminder that his family love him more than mine love me, even though he's proving himself less loveable by the day. I pick both cards up and read them again. Try to digest Jonah's mom's obvious pride in a son who lets his pregnant girlfriend lie on the cold floor while he eats his dinner. His sister's easy offer of help, as though we might need a room painting or a pair of curtains made. They have no idea.

Unlike those women on social media who know exactly what this lifestyle is like but make up a fantasy anyway. As though they're sociopaths spreading a lie, making my life hell, for no other reason than because they can.

But maybe that's not fair. Because not all social media is equal. The love and loyalty I get from my tiny follower base on Tumblr feels stronger than anything I get from Jonah these days. They might be anonymous, but sometimes I feel like they're the only people I can trust.

I pick up my phone, tap into the app, and open a new blog, starting with the title, *I need your help, now more than ever.*

Chapter 43

Madison

@loufromlouisiana HNY to you too Madison! My NY resolution this year is to be more like you
#hello2025 #lifegoals #beautifulfamily #inspiration

@momofgirls1992 My NY resolution is to expose the truth about you and your kind. The end is nigh . . .
#spreadingpoison #lastdance #tradwivesruinlives

I watch my New Year's Eve reel for the tenth time. Elvis Presley crooning 'The Wonder of You' on low volume, my smiling face sparkling under my new Chanel glow stick.

But how can I look like that? Happy. Relaxed. Yes, these photos were taken before Michael sneaked off to the cellar with our tutor, before he took off in the snow to drink liquor with God knows who. But the conversation I'd had with Lori after her little excursion was still banging at my temples, as was the memory of a weirdo with a hunting knife lurking around the homestead on Christmas Eve. I was distracted, not happy. Tense, not relaxed.

Is this Erica's editing skills on display, or my talent for deception?

I click out of Instagram and roll off the treadmill – I had plans for a workout, a way to release the stress, but I only got as far as lying on the soft rubber of the treadmill track and scrolling through my phone. I don't think I slept at all last night and my body feels five times heavier than it really is.

I push to sitting and admit defeat. I exchange sneakers for my snow boots and pull on my new Woolrich trench coat – a Christmas gift from Michael that Erica purchased from the link I sent her. It has stopped snowing now, but we got at least six inches of fresh snow overnight. The ground is thick with it as I pull the gym barn door closed behind me and wonder where to go next.

The children are building a snowman close to the deck, laughing and shouting, oblivious to their absent father. Lori is watching over them, a fleece blanket wrapped around her. From here, she looks like she's crying, but the wind is strong, so it could just as easily be her eyes watering. I could go over, praise the kids' building skills, help find pebbles for the snowman's eyes. But I'm too tired to deal with their boundless energy today, so I head away from the house instead, towards the animal barns.

I've left Michael two voicemails and sent him three text messages. I want to do more – keep prodding speed dial until he picks up. But I know how Michael hates being hassled by a nagging wife, so I've had to keep my discipline for now. I'm not going to call the police – there's no way I want that kind of scrutiny – but I could alert Bill, maybe Nathan. Get them to track him down. It would incense Michael though, and while it would get him home, it might be at too high a price.

We have six horses on the homestead, but I've never been a big fan – too sweaty, too skittery – so I walk past the stables and head inside the smaller barn next door. Clarabelle's winter home. I take in the scene with an approving smile. Clarabelle is lying down in her pen, a look of rapture on her pretty face. There's more bedding in there than a newborn chick gets, and the pink bunting wound around the railings give the place a rosy hue. I sink into the pink sofa outside her pen and do what I always do when I'm conflicted – pick up my phone and check my social media.

There's a new message on Instagram that catches my eye. Not from Brianna Wyoming this time – she's still blocked – but another account that makes my heart beat faster. @AliceDeMille. I hover over the message. We haven't had any contact since I posted the award night content from my secret account. The revelation that forced her to beg her followers for forgiveness, to promise to learn and grow into a better person. Content that no doubt stymied her earning potential too. And while the vast majority of Instagram might not know who @gossipgirlieee is, I'm willing to bet Alice DeMille has a pretty good idea.

But what harm can a private message do? I open it, then frown. Just a couple of lines and a video.

Sent this by a friend
Thought you should know.

I take a breath and press play. It's a bar scene. A load of drunk people trying to line dance, on, under, and around wooden tables. Bodies colliding. Chairs clattering. It takes me a couple of seconds to recognize the bar in town, and a couple more to spot Michael. It's proof that he didn't die on his drive over there, which is something, I suppose, but I don't think that's why Alice sent it. Michael's arms are around a young girl's waist – maybe twenties, possibly teens – and I watch as he pulls her towards him, then spins her away, never loosening his tight grip.

Her face is a tougher watch. Glazed eyes, slack smile. Her body curling and slipping in his grasp like overcooked spaghetti. Someone might watch this and see an innocent celebration. Others might see Michael taking advantage of a vulnerable semi-child. I swear at Alice DeMille and shift my gaze away from the uncomfortable scene.

But that doesn't help, because I see someone else that I recognize in the crowd. Rose. She's sitting in her usual place, alone at the bar. She seems to be watching Michael, but her expression is unreadable on this grainy video. Then another person catches my eye. A man, sitting behind the rowdy group of dancers in one of the booths, wearing a bulky hat, even though it must be baking hot in there. Bill said the drifter who came here never took his hat off. Is that him? From his gesturing, it looks like he's talking to someone, but I can't see who – they're out of shot.

I close the video down. I've got a more pressing issue to deal with first, stopping Alice DeMille launching her missile. But luckily, I've got some ammunition of my own, because there's no way Alice DeMille would forfeit the chance to appear on state TV. I type a message: *Thanks so much for your kindness, Alice. I'm doing a feature for KULR-TV about family life in a few weeks, and now I'm wondering if we should do it together?* I grimace slightly as I add a heart emoji. Then I send the message and reopen the video.

I slide my fingers to enlarge the man's face to see if I recognize him, but the image blurs all his features together. I lean back against the sofa cushion, look at Clarabelle. Her expression is always so free of worry that I have to fight a wave of envy – I can't be jealous of a cow. Is this the man who came to the homestead, who Michael pulled his gun on? And if it is him, what might he have done if he discovered Michael drunk and oblivious, just a few feet away?

I look at my watch. It's nearly midday. Twelve hours since Michael left. Seven since the snow stopped falling. The roads will be clear enough to drive on now, and that's plenty of time for Michael to have slept off the booze in the cab of his truck. Is he not home because he's with that young girl somewhere?

Or because a strange man in an ugly hat took the opportunity to exact his revenge?

Chapter 44

Brianna

'Where the hell have you been?' I hiss, tears already bubbling as I look Jonah up and down. He turns nineteen in a few days, but standing in the doorway, he seems both ancient and adolescent. His eyes are bloodshot, and his skin has a grayish pallor. But his blond stubble is patchy, like a teenager who isn't sure whether to start shaving or not.

'Whoah, easy,' he says, lifting his hands as he walks further into the house, like he's fending me off. 'My head is banging. I can't deal with you screeching at me the minute I get home.' He slings his car keys onto the table, rubs his hands together. 'Is there anything to eat? Any coffee? I'm starving.'

'What, so you're nearly a full day late for our New Year's Eve supper, and I'm supposed to just welcome you home without a word? Forget that you stayed out all night, after promising you'd be here, and just cook you a meal because you're hungry?'

'Actually, yeah, something like that. I worked yesterday, while you were sitting around here like a princess, and I don't expect to be balled out for adjusting my plans. I get that you're pregnant, but if it's not the baby, then it's your back, and if

211

it's not that, you're bitching about me having a beer with the guys. All you've got to do is cook and clean, for Chrissakes. Is it really that hard?'

My vision blurs. I feel unbalanced, and I reach for the wall to steady myself. I think about the blogpost I wrote last night, the comments that came back. 'And today?' I ask. I can't let him off the hook again, not when he keeps treating me like I'm nothing. 'Why are you not working today?'

'That's none of your business.' He glares at me. He reminds me of a landmine, a dense pack of explosive lying just below the surface.

'Too hungover, are you? Too desperate for another shot of whiskey?'

The punch sends me flying. I've never felt pain like it. My head ricochets back and I fall, land on the hard wooden floorboards with a thud. My face burns, my skull throbs. I close my eyes. All those times I've been scared that he might hit me, those false alarms that I've judged myself on, not him. And then it happens without a second's warning. I listen to him stomp up the stairs, slam our bedroom door shut with such force that I can see wooden panels splintering behind my eyelids.

I listen to my own breathing, short and ragged. How did I end up here, lying on a cold floor, unmarried, pregnant, living with a violent man? I knew my path once – handsome husband, cute children, church on Sundays. Organizing the Veterans Day parade every year, being thanked by brave men in uniform.

I thought our dream would give Jonah and me all that and more. I believed those women who told me that being a homemaker was the fastest way to happiness. But all it does is destroy people. Destroy love.

Jonah and I were both sold this lie, and there's no coming back from it now.

Eventually I find the strength to open my eyes. Everywhere is quiet. Jonah is probably fast asleep, exhausted after a night of celebrating, and a morning beating his girlfriend.

Moving one inch at a time, I slide my body along the floor until I reach the sofa, then use its solid structure to push up to sitting. My whole head feels like it's on fire. Nausea bubbles and flares in my stomach, but doesn't climb any higher, thank God. I need to get into the kitchen, find the Tylenol, hope there are still some left in the packet.

But there is something else I must do first. It's time.

I slide my hand under the sofa. My fingers catch the cool metal of my phone, and I pull it towards me. I hug it to my chest for a moment, then click into my camera and switch to reverse mode. I stare at my face. It's so swollen that I barely recognize myself. I can't imagine ever being pretty again, but I can't think about that now.

I take photos. My puffy eye. The bruises that are already forming across my cheek. The cut along my eyebrow where Jonah's ring caught.

When I'm finished, I take a few breaths, then push up to standing. My head feels too heavy on my shoulders, but I stand still for a while and slowly my body accepts the burden. I stumble into the kitchen, find the packet of Tylenol, and almost cry with relief when I see there are still four pills left in the pack. I fight the urge to take all of them – I have the baby to look out for – and swallow two down with some water. Then I sink into a kitchen chair and drop my head into my hands.

And when the pills have done enough for me to focus, I pick up my phone again, and connect with the only people I have left to trust.

Chapter 45

Cally

I peer around the banisters and breathe a sigh of relief. The coast is clear.

I woke up early yesterday morning, New Year's Day, and was instantly grabbed by a kind of panic as images from the night before flew in. Michael's solid body pushing against mine. How completely defenseless I felt. And then Madison arriving, saving me from a terrible fate, yes, but making me feel ashamed, complicit, in the process.

I then spent ages hanging around my bedroom, ignoring calls from my mom and deleting the torrent of drunk texts that my friend Cassie had sent me around four a.m. It was only hunger that finally dragged me out in the early afternoon. Luckily, I managed to get some food without bumping into anyone, and I took full advantage of the privacy to slide a small kitchen knife into the pocket of my jeans. I will do what I can to avoid Michael, but he will never make me feel that helpless again.

My second outing from my bedroom was more eventful. Matilda knocked on my door around five and begged me to play Chutes and Ladders with her. I tried to persuade her to bring the board game to my room, but she was adamant that we played in hers, so I eventually gave in and let her guide me down the long landing. The door to Madison and Michael's suite was closed, thank goodness, but Molly's bedroom door was open, and when we walked past it, I could see Madison in there with her oldest daughter.

Our eyes caught, and we froze for a few seconds, like actors in some daytime TV drama, or maybe a TikTok meme, *POV: your man's sleeping with the nanny*. The pause gave me enough time to see what she was doing too, and it made me feel nauseous. Molly was sitting in front of her vanity unit, and her face was covered in make-up. Yes, she looked exquisite. But she also looked eighteen, not ten. A woman, not a child.

As I finally pulled my gaze away, and turned towards Matilda's room, I heard Madison's sweet breathy voice telling Molly that she deserved the world, but the only way to guarantee getting it was by being more beautiful than her competition. How can a mother speak to her daughter like that? Especially after what had gone down the night before. I was so mad about it that I spent the next hour telling Matilda all about Greta Thunberg and her environmental activism. Something I may live to regret.

With no one in sight again today, I walk quickly down the stairs and along the hallway towards the kitchen. The door is closed, so I have no way of knowing who is in there, but I know that America's number one tradwife spends as little time as possible in any domestic setting, so at least I have irony on my side. I say a silent prayer that Madison isn't inside and push open the door.

And my prayer is answered because the only person in here is Lori. And while that isn't a surprise, the scene does look unusual. For one, she's sitting down – which isn't like Lori, even heavily pregnant she likes to be busy – and in the chair deemed to be Michael's, whether he's on the homestead or not. But more than that, Lori is staring at her phone. For most of the world's population, that's not a big deal. But I've never seen Lori use her phone to pass the time, or anything much else, now I think about it.

She has her back to me and doesn't seem to have noticed that I've walked in. I realize why when I see the earbuds poking out each side of her loose ponytail. Lori has earbuds?

I don't know how to announce my presence without making her jump. And the last thing I need is Lori being shocked into early labor. I'm still considering my options when Lori shifts her position, and I can suddenly see the screen of her phone.

My eyes widen. I look away, then back again. A conflict between respect of her privacy and morbid curiosity. Lori is looking at images of a young woman with a beat-up face. She's got dull blonde frizzy hair and gray-blue eyes, and her face is out of kilter, all bruised and puffy. She looks so young, maybe still a teenager. I don't usually get upset about a stranger's problems, but my eyes grow hot as I feel a rush of sympathy for whoever the girl is. I'm not sure what makes her look poor – the faded jumper perhaps, or the lack of make-up and pimples on her chin – but my instinct tells me she's got nothing. And no one to fight for her.

A noise distracts me. Lori's chair scrapes on the wooden floor.

'Cally!' she breathes out, tipping her phone face down on the kitchen table and pulling out her earbuds. 'I didn't hear you come in. How long have you been standing there?'

'I just walked in,' I say brightly, doing everything I can to convince her I haven't spent the last minute or so watching her stare at images of an assault victim. 'Is it okay if I make myself some breakfast?'

'Of course, go ahead. I was just . . .'

'Having a well-earned rest,' I say, finishing her sentence. I eye the granola for a millisecond – cereal used to be my go-to breakfast, but that was before I tried it with unpasteurized milk – then pull the half loaf of sourdough out of the bread bin and cut two thick slices. I turn on the grill – toasters don't fit the aesthetic of the March Homestead apparently – and wait for the bread to crisp up.

'How are you feeling?' I ask, still trying to wipe the images of the young woman away. 'I guess it's not long now.'

'No, not long,' she whispers.

There's an undertone of fear in her voice and I turn to look at her. For me, the thought of pushing out a fully formed human is beyond terrifying, but Lori has done it four times already. 'You sound scared. Are you worried about this one?'

'What? This baby, you mean?' She runs her hands over her bump, and it seems to relax her. 'Oh, no. I'm not worried. Sorry, my mind is elsewhere. How are things with you? I suppose you've heard Michael has gone AWOL?'

I turn back to my toast. Matilda mentioned last night that Michael wasn't at home, but I didn't realize it was an issue. I wonder if his absence is linked to what happened on New Year's Eve, whether Madison might have kicked him out. Lori was sound asleep at the time, so she might not know anything about it. 'I heard he wasn't here yesterday,' I say. 'But I don't know any more than that.'

'It's none of our business, I suppose,' Lori says. 'I imagine they'll work it out. They always do.'

'Does she love him that much?'

'That much?' Lori asks, dipping her head into a question.

'Michael isn't a respectful husband,' I whisper.

Lori sighs. 'Sadly, I doubt learning to respect women was a

217

priority in his upbringing. Like too many other men around here.'

'He tried to force himself on me the other night,' I admit quietly. 'New Year's Eve.'

Lori closes her eyes but doesn't speak.

'In the cellar,' I go on. 'When we were getting the champagne. If Madison hadn't walked in . . .'

'She does love him that much,' Lori cuts in. 'Or at least she's desperate enough for him to love her that she'll turn a blind eye to his faults. And not because he's got all this.' She waves her arm around the room. 'At least, not only that. I know Madison comes across as spoilt sometimes, selfish even. But there's another side to her. Behind the opulent home and the pretty dresses, there's a young girl who just wants someone to take care of her.'

'It sounds like you've known her a long time.'

'Long enough. From the day I met Madison, I think I knew she was destined for a life full of beautiful things, but what I didn't know then was how much getting it would cost her.'

'Do you think Michael has left her?' I ask.

Lori gives me a sad smile, then shakes her head. 'This was Michael's home long before the rest of us moved in. If he doesn't come back, it'll be because he's dead.'

Chapter 46

Cally

'Dead?' I repeat, mainly horrified, slightly hopeful. 'Why would he be dead?' I think about the relaxed way Michael carries a gun, how Bill used a deadly weapon to scare a cow on the day I arrived. Is this the way people in Montana settle their scores? 'Has he got beef with another rancher or something?'

'Beef?' Lori smiles and shakes her head. 'It's hard to believe we speak the same language sometimes, you Yankees and us cowboys.'

Despite everything, I laugh. 'You know, you should come to Boston one day. Find out how us East Coast types live. You might even like it.' I pause for a moment. 'I think maybe Boston could learn a thing or two from you too.'

Lori's eyes shine, with pride maybe, or a glaze of tears, but before she has a chance to answer, a loud noise distracts us both. The sound of the front door slamming shut. I eye the crumbs on the bread board, quickly brush them into the sink and turn the tap on to flush them down. Then I drop into the chair next to Lori, away from the door, my legs suddenly too weak to stand.

'Not dead,' Lori whispers. Then she reaches for my hand and squeezes my fingers. 'Don't worry, I've got you.'

A second later, the kitchen door flies open and Michael walks inside. His stubble has grown into the beginnings of a beard, and his eyes are slightly bloodshot. But otherwise, he's the same Michael who thought it was okay to ram his tongue into my mouth on New Year's Eve. A mix of adrenalin and nausea surges in my stomach, and I don't know where to look, but Michael's attention is directed at Lori. 'Where's Madison?'

'In bed, I think. She wasn't feeling great.'

Michael nods his head slightly, but doesn't move or speak, like he's having a hard time processing Lori's answer.

'And you?' Lori finally adds, filling the silence. 'Have you had a good, um, trip?'

'Trip?' Michael says, a scowl forming. 'What do you mean by that?'

'Nothing,' Lori says quickly. 'Only that you've been away for a couple of days. Madison wasn't sure where you'd gone.'

'And I suppose you've been filling her head with lies. Telling her I'm a terrible husband.' Michael takes a few steps towards Lori. I lean away, an involuntary reaction, but she holds her position.

'Madison's been worried about you. I bet she'd love to know that you're back safe and sound.'

'Sorry, Lori, let me get this straight. I've just walked inside my own house, and into my own kitchen, and you're telling me what to do?'

The threat in his tone is clear. I can't believe he's treating Lori this way. The woman who cooks for him, who carries his children, who never complains about anything. I put my hand in the front pocket of my sweatpants. The knife I took is in there. I curl my fingers around its handle and squeeze. God, how much I would love to drive this blade into his thick neck right now. If only I could stand the sight of blood.

'I'm sorry, that was rude of me,' Lori says, her voice calm, if a bit robotic. 'Can I get you something to eat first? Or a coffee?'

Michael blows air through his nose like a horse, but he's mollified. And Lori is a freaking saint. 'I don't like you sitting in my chair either,' Michael adds, needing to have the last word. 'But yeah, a coffee would be good.'

Lori pushes to standing and he takes her place. He's too close to me now, but I'm scared of moving, alerting him to my presence. So I keep my shaking hand on the hidden knife and my eyes focused on the table. A minute later, Lori hands him a steaming mug of coffee, and the traditional free pouring sugar dispenser that he loves. I watch him pour at least three spoonfuls in, then take a loud slurp. He smacks his lips, takes a few more mouthfuls, then tilts his head back and drains the rest.

'Thanks, Lori. Good coffee.' Then he pushes up to standing and slides the chair under the table. 'And now I think I'll check on Madison.'

I listen to him stomp out of the room, then turn to Lori when I'm sure he's out of hearing range. 'I don't know how you do it, be so submissive when he talks to you like that.'

'You think that being submissive is automatically a bad thing.'

'Yeah, because it is. Women's instinct to be submissive is why we're behind in everything. Salary rates, senior roles, representation in politics, the divvying up of household chores.' I don't add that my own failures in these areas are probably more to do with my default idleness than my gender. It feels good to stand up for the sisterhood in a place like this, so I'm embracing it.

Lori drops back into the chair that Michael has just vacated. 'Where I come from, we get wolves,' she says.

'Are you going to tell me a story about submissive animals?

Because I know wolves live in packs with a strict hierarchy. I might come from the city, but I did go to school.'

Lori smiles. 'Did you know that the dominant wolf chooses to be submissive sometimes?'

'Isn't that an oxymoron?'

'Wolves are clever enough to know that there are different ways to get what you want. That being dominant isn't always the best strategy.'

I lean forward, instill my voice with as much compassion as I can. 'But this can't be what you want, surely? Multiple surrogacies, looking after everyone on this homestead, having no life of your own.'

A tear bubbles in each of Lori's eyes. It shouldn't be a shock – she deserves to be upset about how her life has turned out – but Lori is usually so composed. 'I get to see them,' she whispers, her voice barely audible. 'Play with them. Raise them.'

'Are they yours?' I ask in a low voice, the question that's revolved around my head for weeks finally spilling out. 'I mean, are you their biological mom?'

Lori's eyes flit to the door, but she nods.

'How do you stand by and watch from the sidelines?' I ask. 'See Mason turning into a mini-Michael? The four of them petrified that he might find a reason to take them into his study and discipline them?'

'They're half his,' she murmurs. 'It's his sperm we use at the clinic.'

'And half yours,' I remind her. 'Did you know what I saw Madison doing yesterday?'

Lori looks up at me.

'She was teaching Molly to put make-up on. And I don't mean a sparkly tween lipstick or blush. She painted her ten-year-old daughter – sorry, your daughter – to look like a woman. She's teaching her that her only worth is in her looks. Is that really the future you want for her?'

'I can't . . . They're Madison's children, I made a promise.' Tears are rolling down Lori's face now.

'Why are you so loyal to her? What hold does she have over you?'

Lori drops her forehead into the heels of her hands. I'm worried I won't be able to hear her – she's already talking so quietly – but then she looks up, a new resilience in her expression. 'I did a terrible thing. Madison suffered for it, but she wasn't the only one, so I've made it my life's work to help others. And I get fulfillment from it, I promise. Living in this beautiful house, being with my children, never having to worry about money. It might horrify you, but it's much more than millions of women can even hope for.'

Strangely, I find I'm holding my breath. Lori's views are wrong, which isn't surprising because she's been brainwashed by the Marches for the last thirteen years. So why do I feel a rush of jealousy? Why does Lori's conservative way of life suddenly sound more appealing than mine? But I can't think like that. Michael is a monster. And women through history have sacrificed too much for me to squander my rights for a pretty kitchen.

'You've talked about making mistakes before,' I say. 'But you must have had your reasons for doing whatever that terrible thing was.'

'I thought I did. But thirteen years on, I'm questioning that.'

'Thirteen years is a long time.'

'It is, you're right.'

'Long enough to forgive yourself maybe? Finally put yourself first?'

Chapter 47

Madison

@justatexangal21 Hey honey, you ok? Not heard from you in a while . . .
#beautifulsoul #inspiration #homemaker #tradwifeMIA

The slamming of the front door reverberates around the house. There's only one person who causes that kind of racket. I stare at my bedroom ceiling and wonder how I feel about Michael being home.

The last time I saw him in person, he was kissing our tutor. The last time I saw him at all was on the video that Alice DeMille sent me, showing Michael pawing a girl even younger. For the last twenty-four hours I've boomeranged between imagining him cozied up with her, and worrying about him bleeding to death in some alleyway, the man he raised his gun to on Christmas Eve taking his revenge.

And now I know one of those scenarios didn't come to pass.

I push the duvet away in frustration. I should hate him. I do hate him. But he's my husband, the man who has given me this ten-thousand-dollar bed, this goose-down duvet, and Olivia von Halle pajama set, this perfect life that I sell to millions of other women every day. I can't get angry with him – because I'm the one who will end up suffering for it.

I take a deep breath, then exhale, and repeat. I'm not a fan of yoga, all those sinewy women drinking dairy-free smoothies, but I have found myself adopting a few of its breathing practices lately. Using cold air to put out the fire in my belly.

Michael doesn't come upstairs straightaway, which works in his favor, because by the time he walks into the bedroom, I'm much closer to zen. 'Hello, darling.' I flash him a bright smile, then take pleasure in watching his expression move from confusion to wariness. 'You look exhausted,' I continue. 'Why don't you take a shower, then maybe we can cozy up in front of the fire together. If you want to, of course.'

He coughs, a sign that he's feeling awkward, and I ride another swell of satisfaction. 'So you're not mad anymore,' he finally says, somewhere between a statement and a question.

'I can never stay mad at you, darling. You know that.'

He nods, settling into our familiar narrative, my advantage only ever fleeting. 'You did step out of line the other night,' he reminds me.

'I'm sorry,' I say, even managing to sound genuine. 'A marriage needs each of us to know our roles and I lost sight of that on New Year's Eve, I realize that now. But it won't happen again.'

Michael drops onto the edge of the bed, then twists to face me. 'We've been married for more than a decade now, and you've been a good wife up 'til now, I'll say that. But we can never take these things for granted.'

My mouth dries. 'I would never take you for granted. You know how incredibly grateful I am for the chances you've given me.'

'And you're clear about who makes the rules around here?'

225

'Of course I am.'

'Good. Because I've been thinking, and for the sake of our marriage, I want you to give up the social media stuff.'

I blink. I can't catch my breath. Can't think. My yoga zen crushed.

But I can't stay silent on this. Every woman around here knows that saying nothing means yes. 'But honey, isn't that how we spread our message?' I ask. 'Show the world how wonderful our way of life is? What they're missing out on?'

'It has been, yes,' he says, nodding. 'And we've done an amazing job of it. But you said there are lots of other families doing it now. It's time for you to step back, concentrate on our family, our marriage.'

'But why?' I ask, barely managing to keep my composure. 'I've always put you first, and that will never change. You know that my social media is just a thing I do while you're busy on the ranch.'

'I know, and that's why I've let you do it all these years. But it's encroaching now. I don't like it.'

'Is this about the man on Christmas Eve?' I plead, panic starting to take over. 'Do you think my fame is putting our family at risk? Did he find you in the bar, threaten you?'

Michael scowls. 'What are you talking about? It's got nothing to do with that loser. And you're not famous, Madison. You post videos of yourself online, same as billions of other people. I mean it's encroaching on us. The truth is, these last couple of days have made me realize that I'm feeling undervalued in our marriage. And that's not my doing.'

They're the words I have feared for so long, but now that he's said them, it doesn't feel real. How can he feel undervalued? I have dedicated my life to him, or at least the bits of my life that he cares about – my body, my agency. How can he just announce that I'm failing him and that becomes the accepted narrative?

But then I think of Rose. And how this is the natural way of things between powerful husbands and their wives. And if I fight it, I'll end up like her.

'What can I do?' I whisper. 'To prove how much I value you?'

'You can stop treating every family meal like a photo opportunity for a start.' He sighs, then pushes off the bed. He shoves his hands into his back pockets and starts pacing the bedroom. 'You need to stop posting stuff on social media completely. You need to remember that I'm Cally's boss, not you. And you need to give me a bit more attention. And then we'll see.'

'We'll see?' I repeat, struggling to keep my voice in check.

'Well, I can't guarantee that it'll work, can I? We can only hope.'

Tears threaten to fall. Panic rises even more. He wants me to give up my influencer role, the one thing that proves I'm a real person and not just someone's puppet, and won't even guarantee that it will be enough. Could I end up with nothing? How do I stop that from happening?

'We'll have a new baby in a few weeks,' I say, finding my only bargaining chip. 'And Lori is convinced it's a boy.' This isn't true – Lori says her pregnancy is a carbon copy of when she carried Matilda – but the truth has always been less important to me than survival. 'I thought we could call him Michael Junior.'

Michael stops pacing. 'Oh, yeah?'

'A son to carry your name, like you carry your daddy's, and Mason carries your brother's.'

Slowly, a smile starts to form on Michael's face. 'Yeah, I'd like that, and so would my dad, God rest his soul.'

I sense my opportunity, push to standing, and run my hand down Michael's arm. 'This baby will mend our marriage; I just know it.'

'Maybe it could.' His voice has lowered, become huskier, and I step closer, brush my breasts across his arm. 'And then we can start making some babies of our own,' he finishes.

And as he leans down to kiss me, it takes every ounce of self-discipline not to splutter in his face.

Chapter 48

Brianna

I hear the rumble of an engine and straighten up. It's not Jonah – for once, he's home, grumbling and cursing as he tries to build a crib from scratch. It's still biting cold out here, but at least the sun is shining today, and I wonder if the approaching vehicle is bringing good news too.

I fling the last of the chicken feed into the coop and walk up to the house. I head in through the kitchen and make my way to the front door. But before opening it, I pause to look in the hallway mirror. It's been five days since Jonah hit me and the bruising has finally faded enough for the concealer he bought me – the most bittersweet of apology gifts – to be of some use. He is still saying sorry multiple times a day, but every apology seems laced with the residue of blame. And I'm finding that quantity is a weak substitute for quality.

I pull the door handle and walk straight into a woman on our front porch. 'Oh,' I exhale, taking a step backwards. I glance behind her and see a canary-yellow car parked up. It looks alien in this drab black and white setting. 'You're not the mailman.'

'No,' she says gently. 'I'm Mary. Jonah's sister.' Then she tilts her head and her expression shifts. 'Have I got the right place? It wasn't easy to find.'

Let me know if I can help. 'Um, yes.' I'm flustered now, uncertain how to act. 'Jonah's out back.' I rest my hands on my bump, an instinctive gesture, but it draws her eyes.

'And you must be Brianna. It's nice to finally meet you. I can't believe I never met you back in Buffalo, but I was away studying for a while, and I didn't get home much.'

I give her an awkward smile. I don't want to tell her that I had almost forgotten she existed until her Christmas card turned up, that Jonah has talked about his two brothers plenty of times over the years we've been together, but rarely mentions having a sister. I also can't be sure what her views might be on her brother living in sin, his girlfriend six-months pregnant. But she doesn't seem fazed, and I smile my gratitude. 'So you went to college?'

She looks sheepish. 'Kind of. I went to catering college. My mom thought it might help me get a husband.'

Mary has intelligent eyes, but a plain face. I look down at her left hand. 'And how did that work out?'

She sighs. 'I dropped out after a month – I like cooking well enough, but not the regimental, recipe-following kind. When I discovered that I couldn't give a monkey's backside whether a soufflé rose or not, it seemed like the right thing to do.'

I start to laugh, and it makes me realize I haven't done that in months. I don't laugh anymore. Ever. That can't be normal for an eighteen-year-old, can it? 'Sorry, where are my manners. Would you like to come in?'

'Thank you, yes.' I stand to the side and let Mary walk inside. She makes it into the living room, then pauses. 'And you've been living here since the summer?' she asks.

I follow her gaze, and see what she sees. The fire has gone

230

out, so our breath is creating tiny clouds in the freezing air. There are big mounds of ash in the grate – I never seem to get around to emptying it – and dozens of burn marks on the hearth. The sofa is our sole piece of furniture, bought secondhand from a guy in town, other than the makeshift tables built out of crates. I hope she hasn't noticed the blood stain on the wooden floor.

I pick my blanket off the arm of the sofa and wrap it around my shoulders. 'I made this,' I murmur. 'I'd never knitted anything before. It's for the baby really.' It's a pathetic attempt to impress her, but she picks up on it anyway.

'That's beautiful. You should be really proud of yourself.'

I nod, but I can't speak, my throat constricted by a solid ball of regret.

'Did you say Jonah's outside?' she coaxes.

I nod again, then follow Mary out the back door. I watch her walk up to her brother. He doesn't realize she's there until she taps him on the shoulder. He twists around, then his eyes double in size. Of course he would be surprised to see her, but is it more than that? He looks uneasy. Jonah's real mom never appeared to hold much sway over him, she was always too sad, still mourning the death of her husband from his fatal accident at work when Jonah was young. Mary is a fair bit older than her brother. Was she forced into a proxy maternal role, expected to raise three unruly boys?

Their conversation starts friendly, but I soon notice a tension rising between them. Mary has her back to me, but I can see Jonah's features harden, his speech speed up. And Mary's hand movements grow bigger, gestures of appeasement, but also persistence. Finally, they walk over to me.

'I take it you've met my sister,' Jonah says.

I nod. 'It's nice of Mary to come and see us.'

'I was just saying to Jonah that I could stay over for a few days, help you get this place sorted in time for when the baby comes.'

'And I've told her that we're grateful for the offer, but we're not ready for guests yet.'

'To which I responded that I'm not really a guest,' Mary continues brightly. 'I'm family, which is different. You know, I pretty much brought Jonah up, so he's used to my meddling ways.' She laughs again.

Family. Tears burn the back of my eyes. Do I miss my own family? Or do I hate them for abandoning me? I run my hands over my belly. I've only known Mary for five minutes, but already I want to fold into her arms, soak up her offer of help. But if I want her to stay, I need to win over Jonah first.

'I don't think you realize how much you have done, Jonah. It may not be a palace yet, but you fixed the window in that end bedroom, didn't you? And you got the blow-up bed in that garage sale for a crazy good price. I bet Mary would be impressed if you showed her.'

Jonah looks at me with annoyance – he must know what I'm doing – but then his eyes soften, and I exhale. 'Fine, but I can guarantee you won't want to stay long.'

Mary beams. 'I'm not sure about that. This homestead lifestyle is the adventure I always dreamed about but was never brave enough to try.'

Jonah's expression brightens a notch at that – maybe she knows how to get the best out of him more than me – and he leads her back into the kitchen with almost a half-smile.

Chapter 49

Madison

@debbiecolts47 Are you and Michael on a romantic holiday some place? Pictures please!
#januaryblues #wintersun #trophyhusband

I run my fingers through the dresses in my wardrobe. They're all a similar style, and I love every one of them. They're mid-calf or longer, all made from natural fibres, cotton mainly, but linen and silk too. Most are light in color, and there's a mix of plain, striped, and floral patterns. It's a shame that there are going to be fewer opportunities to wear them now that Michael has served his diktat, but not none, I've made sure of that. I pick out a plain white peasant dress with a square neckline and push my arms through its puff sleeves. Then I turn towards the long mirror and appraise.

I look angelic. And sexy. The padded push-up bra has the dual benefit of keeping my pregnancy story on track and giving me a Marilyn Monroe vibe. The new anti-aging cream I'm trying has had a rejuvenating effect on my face (sadly not a freebie, but there was no way I was awakening that algorithm) and the full thirty minutes I spent on my make-up this morning has paid off. I give one final twirl in front of the mirror, then head downstairs.

And I need to look my best because this is my first chance to create content since New Year's Eve. When Michael dropped his bombshell about me coming off social media, I thought my life was over. I had to let Erica and Noah go – and while I put them on extended leave rather than firing them (never say never), it felt like there was no coming back. But their absence turned out to be more liberating than confining. I've always had a sneaking suspicion that they don't approve of me – which is rich coming from a woman approaching thirty-five without a husband, and an aging manchild who's scared of cows. So being back in the driver's seat has given me an unexpected boost of confidence.

Especially now that I've worked out a way to hold onto my status as one of the world's most popular influencers without Michael knowing a thing.

I've always known Michael's Instagram login details because I set up his @MarchranchMT account in the first place, soon after I started posting my homemaker content when I was waiting for Lori to give birth to Molly. So it was easy to access his account and unfollow @_TrulyMadison_ without him knowing – which means he'll stop seeing my posts, and assume that it's because I've stopped making them. I love it when genius is simple. And while I'd never risk filming or posting anything when Michael's around, he spends most of his time on the ranch, so I felt there'd still be plenty of opportunity.

What I didn't factor in was Mason, or how readily he'd agree to spy on me for his father. Luckily Molly warned me – it seems that Mason is a more willing spy than a discreet one, telling his sister – so I haven't been caught in the act. But it has reduced my window of opportunity to a sliver. Cally is taking all the children on a nature trail this morning – Lori's idea apparently, I imagine for my benefit – so now is my chance. It's the Epiphany today, so I'm going to film myself taking down all our Christmas decorations. Hopefully there'll be some cute angles I can use to keep my midriff out of shot – I don't want to spoil this look by trying to wrestle a silicone ball underneath my dress. I've got a plan for tomorrow's content too, which I'm also excited about.

The kitchen is empty, which is disappointing because I had hoped Lori (the only person I confided in) would be here to help with the filming. I pause for a moment, drum my fingernails on the counter. I think about her little excursion last week, her changing mood. I think I'll feel better if I know where she is before I start.

I check the whole of the first floor, and when I don't find her, I take both sets of stairs to the top floor. I suppose, with only five weeks to go, there's always the chance Lori's in labor, and a lurch of panic twists in my gut. I knock at her bedroom door first, but when she doesn't answer, I push it open. I'm immediately hit by a sense of emptiness. Lori isn't in here, but it's more than that. I narrow my eyes and scan the room.

I see an envelope. Propped up against her bedside light. For a moment, I think it's the mystery Christmas card – that Lori lied about when she said she'd burned it – but when I pick it up, there is just one word written on the envelope, and in Lori's neat handwriting. *Madison*.

Why is Lori writing notes to me?

My hands are shaking a little as I rip it open, like I already know it's bad news. There's a simple white card inside. I snatch it out, as I drop onto Lori's bed, and read.

My dearest Madison,
I'm sorry to leave you, but this is something I need to do.
The other night you said that you trusted me.

Trust me now.
And above all else, don't try to find me.
Your friend always, Lori

I scream. No one can hear me – I'm alone in this vast dungeon of a house – but I scream for help anyway. How can she leave me? How can she take my baby? Michael's baby? I clatter down the stairs, so distraught that breaking a fingernail on the banister barely registers. I jump around like a drunk flamingo trying to pull my snow boots on, then throw open the back door and run as fast as I can in my clumsy footwear to reach the garage. But what was I expecting to find? Of course her car is gone. She has left us – her note makes that clear. My Lori, who has been like a mother and sister melded into one, has left me. For a break? Or forever?

Ten days ago, I was mad with her for going into the bar without telling me. And now she's gone, and I have no clue if she'll ever return. Is this something to do with Rose? Has she persuaded Lori to leave? Lori knows all my secrets. She asks me to trust her, but how can I when she doesn't trust me enough to tell me where she's gone? Maybe she sees a new cause in Rose, another vulnerable woman to fight for. To join forces with. Are they friends now? Are they going to expose the truth about me?

But I shake the panic away. I don't know anything for sure and I need to stay focused. Because even if Lori's disappearing act has nothing to do with Rose, how is Michael going to react to losing his fifth child, the baby he thinks is going to become his namesake?

And above all else, don't try to find me.

Lori must be crazy. Of course I'm going to find her! I just need a moment to think things through, to work out where – and when – she might have gone.

Michael has been on the ranch since dawn, but Cally only took the kids on the nature trail less than an hour ago. I thought Lori was creating an opportunity for me to film some Instagram content unobserved, but it must have been about giving herself the chance to run away. But at least it means she can't have gone too far.

I run back inside, fling my boots every which way, then race to the kitchen where I left my phone. I jab at Michael's number. *Pick up, pick up, pick up.*

'Yeah?'

'Michael, I need you!'

'What? Why?'

Michael's slow drawl sets my teeth on edge, but I need to find some calm. Make him understand how important this is. I breathe. 'It's Lori,' I say. 'She's left.'

'What do you mean, left? Where's she gone?'

'That's just it, I don't know.' The downside of dialing back the adrenalin is that it lets the emotion in. Tears carry Dior brown mascara down onto my cheeks. 'She left a note,' I whisper. 'Says we shouldn't go after her.'

'What the hell?' Michael's slow brain is finally starting to get it. 'She's run off with my kid in her belly? Michael Junior?!'

'We need to find her, bring her home,' I plead.

'Too fucking right, we do,' Michael growls.

The line goes dead. Suddenly exhausted, I drop my phone on the kitchen table and rest my head alongside it. Tears roll down my cheek.

But am I crying for my baby? For Lori? Or for how my whole life seems to be falling apart?

Chapter 50

Cally

I look at Molly. Her shoulders are hunched up to her ears and her body is shivering. But of course she's freezing in these temperatures – she might have a coat on but she's only wearing a thin dress underneath and frilly ankle socks so her legs are bare. I feel another wave of sympathy for her, and anger at Madison for making her wear these impractical clothes because they're supposedly more feminine.

'I think that's enough nature for one day,' I announce. 'Let's head back to the house now.' To be honest, I'm not only doing this for Molly's sake. It was Lori's idea that I take the children for a walk in the woodland beyond Clarabelle's grazing field. I wasn't surprised by her suggestion – Lori loves the outdoors and the colder the better as far as I can tell – but I was a bit taken aback when she suggested I take Myron too. Usually she's happy to mind him when Madison isn't around. And trying to keep all four of them in line is proving to be beyond my capability.

'But look, Miss Cally!' Matilda calls out, pointing at a snowy path through the trees which is puckered with holes. 'We need to follow the tracks; I think it's a bear!'

'A bear?!' Myron yells. 'I'm gonna punch him on the nose!'

'It's not a bear, you idiots,' Mason says. 'But you're right, we should follow the tracks. It could be a coyote.'

Matilda sighs. 'I'm pretty sure it's a snowshoe hare. I remember Daddy showing me tracks just like those ones last winter – and it'll be long gone by now.'

'Liar,' Mason throws back. 'Daddy wouldn't take you animal tracking without me.'

Matilda shrugs. 'Well, he did, so get over it.'

I guess – correctly – that Mason is going to lunge for his sister, and leap into his path to block him, but I knock into Myron and he wails as his head connects with my ribs. I suck in a breath to ride the pain, then feel Matilda's ice-cold fingers curl into mine as a shadow passes across her face.

'Hey! Cally!'

I twist around at the sound of Michael's voice. He's striding towards us, wearing an angry expression. Molly slots in behind me. Mason hesitates for a moment, then joins his sister. Myron grabs my other hand. 'Is everything okay?' I ask, trying to hide my breathlessness.

'Where's Lori?'

'Um, I don't know. In the kitchen, I guess?'

'Don't bullshit me! I'm on my way back from the ranch now, Madison's in pieces. So quit protecting that woman!'

My heart revs up. 'Lori was in the kitchen when we came out, wasn't she kids?' Shit. I can't believe I'm involving the children. How low can I sink?

'Yes,' Molly whispers, remembering she's the oldest, that she needs to be the bravest, despite Madison treating her like a dress-up doll.

'Well, she's not there now. Selfish bitch has run away.'

'Run away?' I repeat, shock making the words tumble out.

'Don't act surprised! You two have been thick as thieves lately. Did she tell you her plans, where she was going?' He takes two steps closer, leers over me. 'If she did, you better tell me. Remember who pays your goddamn wages.'

A few nights ago, I was scared of Michael because his eyes were full of drunken lust. Now they're full of rage, and I don't know whether I'm more frightened, or less. But my palms grow clammy against the children's soft skin as I remember my advice to Lori the other day. *Finally put yourself first.* Did she reflect on that? Has she decided to run away with her fifth baby because I encouraged her to?

'Honestly, I don't know, I promise,' I beg. 'She suggested I bring the kids out here this morning, and so I did. That's it.'

'Well, get back inside, because we're all responsible for bringing her home.' He shoves my shoulder. I stumble, slip in the snow, but regain my balance. We move as one, Matilda and Myron's hands coiled around my fingers, the older two clinging onto the back of my jacket. Michael's heavy boots crunch through the snow behind us. As we get closer to the house, Michael shoves past, opening the back door and clomping inside.

We trail after him, but he's already disappeared. We pause in the mudroom to take our coats and boots off. But then I hesitate. Where do we go? We usually hang out in the kitchen after playing outside, but that's because Lori is always in there, ready with a hot chocolate and homemade muffin to warm us up. On Instagram it always looks like the kitchen is the soul of this house, but it's not – it's Lori. And without her, it already feels like the March Homestead is being starved of oxygen. Suddenly I wish I hadn't been so vocal about her deserving more than this. I need Lori here; I can't survive these next few months without her.

240

'I'm hungry,' Matilda finally says.

'Me too. And thirsty,' Mason adds.

I blink. I don't want to bump into Michael, or see Madison, but these children are my priority. And I can't avoid their parents until July. 'Okay, let's go find something.'

I push open the kitchen door. Madison is sitting at the table, completely still, while Michael is marching up and down.

'And you have absolutely no idea where she's gone?' he shouts. Madison keeps her head low as she shakes it.

'Mommy!' Matilda runs towards her, but when Madison looks up, she pauses, and I can see why. Madison's eyes are red from crying and smudged with make-up. I've never seen her look so real.

'Where's Lori?' Matilda asks, tears now bubbling in her eyes as she picks up on the tense atmosphere. Madison pulls her in for a hug, but then seems to cling on.

'Don't cry,' Michael barks. 'Lori will be back soon, so there's nothing to get emotional about. I'm going to collect her now. Cally, look after Madison, make sure she doesn't do anything stupid.'

'Stupid?' My heart leaps. What does Michael think Madison might do?

'Like post anything on Instagram. I don't want the world knowing our business, any of it.'

'Of course I'm not going to post anything about Lori leaving us,' Madison spits out. 'I'm not an idiot.'

'And you?' Michael looks at me. 'Can I trust you?'

'Me? I haven't posted anything since I arrived,' I splutter. 'It's in my contract; I haven't broken it.'

'I didn't mean that. Are you going to message Lori? Tell her I'm coming for her?'

My cheeks flare. Because the thought had crossed my mind –

a warning to make sure she stays safe – and I can feel guilt shining on my face.

'Give me your phone,' he demands.

'What?'

'Quit stalling!' Michael shouts, walking towards me. He holds out his hand. 'Your phone, Cally.'

I bite my lip. I can't bear the idea of giving away my only connection with the outside world, but what choice do I have? Michael is a towering bully, and Madison would never stick up for me. And even I'm not unprincipled enough to expect the children to step in.

I pull my phone out of my jeans pocket and drop it in his hand.

Chapter 51

Madison

I shift my gaze to the wall clock but only five minutes have passed since I last looked, so I return to the window and the monochrome view. Even the trees look black through the depressing filter of heavy cloud cover.

It's funny. Usually I can't wait to get out of this room. Once I have enough content for whatever reel I'm filming, I find much more pleasant places to hang out until Michael gets back from the ranch. But I can't seem to drag myself away today. Michael left in a furor of anger and disbelief about five hours ago, Cally took the kids off to the classroom once she'd fed and watered them, and I've been sitting here by myself ever since. Drinking badly made chicory coffee.

I push my mug away. Why hasn't he found her yet? Why hasn't he called with an update? Why do I never feel able to call him?

And how will I survive if he doesn't find Lori? In truth, I care less about the baby she's carrying – I have four children already and they're enough for me – but there are a hundred other ways she looks after me. She makes me look like the best cook, the most thoughtful mom, the most successful homemaker. The perfect wife. And without her, I won't be able to hide the truth. Michael will throw me out, like he's already threatening, and my followers will abandon me. I'll have nothing.

Not even Lori.

Where has she gone? When I first read her note, my instincts jumped to this being Rose's fault, her toxic influence. But it could be a lot simpler than that. Lori has done everything I've asked of her for the last thirteen years. Maybe she has just snapped. Decided she wants to keep one of her babies for herself.

I think about the time she came to my room the day after the business awards, when I was lying on my bed, nursing my injuries, and wondering whether my husband was a clumsy hero or a sly abuser. She suggested then that we run away together. Has she been planning this since then?

Should I have said yes?

Lori is much more resourceful than me. And – ironically – richer too. We don't pay her a fortune, but she earns a fair salary, which is more than I do. All the brand deals I negotiate, my appearance fees, it all goes straight into Michael's bank account. I've always been grateful that he allows me a credit card – the opportunity to spend a miniscule portion of the money I earn – but I need his approval for large purchases, and more than that, I have no control over it. It would only take one click of his mouse for that tap to be turned off. My chance at independence gone.

Except I don't want to be independent. I want a husband to take care of me – it's what I've dreamed of since I was a little girl – and I already have that. I don't need to work out how to change my life to avoid its destruction, I need to work out how to protect what I already have. And I might not be resourceful in the traditional sense, but I'm shrewd; just look at what I've achieved so far.

Not being able to get pregnant could feel like a death sentence in a place where every lifestyle choice is measured against traditional family values, but I didn't let my biological limitations hold me back. I found a different way, a better way, and I'm married to the man once dubbed Montana's most eligible bachelor, and the mother to his children without anything demoralizing like stretch marks or reduced bladder control. It is also my personal genius that has allowed me to successfully navigate the path between traditional wife and world-famous influencer for years.

I am gifted. I can find a way through this. I have to.

I push out of the chair and walk towards the window. I lean over the kitchen counter and stare out. There's a thin break in the clouds, a blue line of hope in the sky.

Michael will find Lori, I'm sure of it. He owns a fair proportion of this county for a start, and he knows everyone who lives here. Lori's car is easy to spot, and while the roads are quiet, they're not empty. Someone will have seen her. And Michael is a hunter, he knows how to track animals, and he's always telling me that people are no different. I just need to be patient.

I should bake a pie. Distract myself. I consider looking up a recipe on my phone, but no. I'm going to do this from memory. I take butter out of the fridge; flour and sugar from the pantry; and a mixing bowl from the cupboard. I don't film it in case Mason walks in – now is not the time to be taking those kinds of risks – but more than that, I don't feel the urge to share this moment with anyone.

Which is weird.

It's more than a decade since I made my last pie without Lori's input, but soon my hands are moving without me thinking too hard. Cutting and weighing, sifting and rubbing. Rolling the pastry. An hour later, I pour a thick cherry mix into the pastry crust and slide it into the stove. I watch the red liquid bubbling through the glass, and the image reminds me of Michael, his face frothing with rage. What will he do with Lori when he finds her? Will her pregnancy – his baby – keep her safe?

I imagine him shoving her. Nothing too damaging, just a reminder of who's boss, a lesson in abiding by his rules. But Lori isn't a stranger to violence, and I can't imagine Michael's half-baked attempt at dominance would faze her too much.

I set the timer for forty-five minutes and settle back into the chair. The sky has darkened; it will be nighttime soon. An easier time to hide.

I eye my phone – just in case I put it on silent by accident – but there are no missed calls or messages from Michael. Damn him. How can he leave me in the dark like this?

I pick the device up, but swerve away from his number, away from enflaming his anger, and click into Instagram instead. As I look at all the beautifully edited posts, I feel a wave of annoyance crash over me – the Epiphany reel I planned but haven't filmed, my perfect make-up ruined by tears, my beautiful white dress now spotted with cherry juice. Then I brush it away; there's always tomorrow's idea for content, which will outclass my competition for sure – and Lori will be back by then. I have to believe that.

I don't look at my notifications – the drought is too depressing – but I start swiping through the stories. So many beautiful people, amazing homes, happy families, stylish couples. Alice DeMille on a beach in Florida. Sky Anderson skiing with her kids in Colorado. When I can't take the purgatory anymore, I click into my messages. There are dozens of them, but everyone wants to leech something out of me. Money, or tags, or parts of me I'm not willing to share. I almost miss those messages from Brianna Wyoming, her genuine emotion – good and bad – evident in every word.

A sense of foreboding descends on me, so heavy it makes my shoulders droop. Lori has left me. My marriage is teetering on a precipice. And less than two weeks ago, a strange man brought a knife to my home.

The timer goes. The pie is ready.

But I'm not sure I am.

Chapter 52

Brianna

Jonah closes our bedroom door. 'And what is she doing here?' he asks, his voice quiet but his tone menacing.

I bite my lip. Mary is his sister, not mine. Just because I'm grateful that she's here doesn't mean I should take responsibility for her visit. But the memory of his violence is still raw, and I don't want to antagonize him. 'I . . . I don't know. She offered to help on her Christmas card, didn't she?'

'Yeah, but people always write stuff like that,' he says. 'It doesn't mean anything. Don't you think it's weird, her showing up without an invite?'

I lift my shoulders into a shrug but then they want to stay like that, tight around my ears, and it takes effort to ease them back down. 'Maybe it was an impulsive thing, it's the season of goodwill after all.'

'Or maybe someone called her, asked her to come.'

Jonah's words make my heart race. Does he know that I found my phone amongst his stash of weapons? That I use it whenever he's out? I force myself to face him, to trust my own deception. 'Do you mean me? How could I have called her when I don't have my phone anymore?'

'Because the card arrived before Christmas, Bri. You had plenty of time to call her before I took it off you.'

Relief floods through me – he doesn't know I have it; he probably can't imagine I'd be that disobedient – but the rush of emotion makes my head swim. I lower myself onto the bed, fighting the urge to go further, to drop my head onto the pillow and close my eyes. I need food, and not homemade stew but something with instant energy. A Snickers bar or a Twinkie. 'I didn't contact her,' I say.

'Has she asked about the bruises on your face?'

'No.'

'Have you told her anything about what happened?'

'No.'

Jonah nods, drops down next to me. 'If I find out you're lying, I won't be happy. You know that, right?'

I run my hand over my hard round belly. 'I'm not, I promise,' I whisper.

'Either way, we need to get rid of her.'

I think about the hug Mary gave me, how she made me laugh for the first time in ages. 'Maybe she could stay for a few days, stick around until your birthday,' I suggest. 'She could help get the nursery ready, like she said. And she brought a stack of food too, so we can save our money while she's here.'

Jonah clicks his tongue. 'It sounds like you prefer her company to mine.'

'Of course not.' I smile to mask the truth. 'But she seems nice, and she is family.' I rest my hands on my bump. 'Our baby's aunt.'

'And what about us?' Jonah asks. 'Didn't we always plan this as our adventure? The two of us living out our dream without any interruptions?'

'It's just a few days,' I whisper.

Jonah stands up, then turns and stares back at me with a mix of suspicion and disappointment. 'I'm not sure you've ever cared about this dream as much as me.'

'What? Of course I have.'

'If there's any opportunity to cut corners, to offload your chores, you take it. You're asleep more hours than you're awake, and you'd spend all day on your phone if I let you.'

A white-hot rage suddenly rattles through me, and I push off the bed. How can he criticize me for sleeping late after what he's done? Going out and getting wasted whenever he gets the chance while I'm here all alone? But I can't bring up his failings because he might hit me again. Overpower me when I don't have the strength to fight back. That's what I hate the most.

'I'm pregnant, remember?'

'Sweet Jesus, how could I forget.'

'And I do more around here than you've ever given me credit for,' I go on.

'Well, if you're such a hard worker, you can have the job of getting rid of Mary.'

'She's your sister,' I remind him. 'If you're so desperate for her to leave, you tell her. Or do you not think she'd listen to her baby brother?' I wonder if I'm pushing him too far, if having Mary here protects me, or if I'm walking into trouble again.

'She understands her place in our family – yes, she's the oldest, but she's also got three brothers. But that's not the point. She knows I can take care of myself, so she must be here because she thinks you can't. Which means if you tell her to go, then she'll happily be on her way.'

'Why do you have to make it sound like I'm failing?! For Chrissakes, Jonah, I'm pregnant!'

'Don't raise your voice with me, Bri, or I swear I'll—'

'Do what?' I interrupt. 'Hit me again?'

Jonah takes two steps in my direction, hovers over me. Suddenly I'm back in the living room, feeling the explosion of pain as his fist connected with my face. I feel my body start to shake. 'Please don't hurt me,' I whisper.

He lets out a deep sigh, and his face smarts with shame. But as he twists away from me, his shoulder catches mine. I stumble, lose my balance, tumble backwards onto the floor. I hit the floorboards with a thud, my back first, then my head. I close my eyes to ride the wave of pain.

Someone knocks on the door. I open my eyes.

'Is everything okay in there? I heard a bang.'

'We're fine,' Jonah calls out, then turns to me and hisses, 'Get up.'

'Are you sure? Can I come in?'

Jonah grabs my wrist, yanks me up to standing. 'Yeah, of course.'

The door opens. I smile at Mary – some reflex instinct to pretend everything is fine – and she returns it, but she's not stupid. She knows we've had a fight. And as the three of us stand in awkward silence, I wonder whose side Mary will take.

Chapter 53

Madison

@ashleycoltrane92 Hey, who thinks Madison March is dead?
#tradwifeMIA #seeya #tradwivesruinlives

I went to bed around eleven, but it was pointless – I couldn't sleep – so I came downstairs, quietly, to make sure I didn't wake any tired, overly emotional children. And now I'm back at the kitchen table with a generous slice of cherry pie in front of me.

Around seven o'clock, when Cally was making grilled cheese sandwiches for the kids, and pretending it was a treat rather than the only thing she could cook, I gave in and finally called my husband. But of course, he didn't pick up. So here I am. Comfort eating in the early hours of the morning. I tip in another mouthful and catch the crumbs in my hand.

My phone flashes up in the darkness, buzzes on the table, making me jump. Shit. I chew madly, swallow, then grab it, breathless from the effort. 'Yes?'

'I've got her.'

Relief floods through me. Tears sprout. I take a silent gulp of water before speaking. 'Is she okay?'

'Michael Junior's okay, that's the only thing I care about right now.'

'Of course, that's what I meant,' I say quickly. 'How did you find her?'

'I saw Jonty Wilson in town, and he reckoned he'd seen Lori's car an hour before on the road out to Harry Fisher's farm.'

'And she was there? Why there?'

Michael clicks his tongue. 'We can talk about this when I'm inside. I'm just pulling onto the drive now.'

'Wait, what?' My brain takes a few seconds to process his words. He's been gone for a full day and half the night. Harry Fisher's farm is an hour away which means he must have found Lori ages ago. Why is he only telling me about it now?

'That a problem?'

I can hear the confrontation in his voice and remind myself that now isn't the time to fall out with my husband. We're allies tonight, Lori our common enemy. I need to remember that. 'No, that's amazing. Thank you so much for finding her, for sorting everything.' I end the call and, true to his word, Michael's tires crunch on the gravel a moment later. I expect the front door to burst open, but there's silence for a few moments, then the door from the mudroom flies open. He must want to keep his return low profile, which is out of character, but I'm grateful for it.

Lori's face is ghostly white, but her expression is resolute. Her arms snake behind her back, her hands tied I presume. There are no obvious signs of injury, but I know from experience how little that really means. Michael's fingers are curled tight around each of her shoulders, and there's a look of triumph on his face, like he's caught a prized stag.

I blink the image away and stand up.

'She was in one of Harry's outbuildings,' Michael says. 'And do you know what? She pulled a gun on me. My own fucking gun as well. The lying bitch must have taken it out of my study.'

For all the violence he inflicts, Michael rarely swears in front of me, and I'm surprised by how much it makes me flinch.

'She was freezing too,' he goes on. 'She could have died out there, taken our baby with her, if I hadn't found her. But instead of being grateful, she whips the gun out of her boot and aims it at me.' He shakes his head in disgust. 'It was only after I kicked it out of her hand that I realized it was my gun. It was loaded too. She'd have killed me if I hadn't been quicker than her.'

Lori tried to kill Michael? It feels so out of character that I can barely believe it, but maybe that's not right. Lori is the strongest woman I know.

'Was she planning on sleeping there?' I ask, not acknowledging Lori's presence – I'm not ready for that yet.

But Michael shrugs. 'I don't know, I found her around lunchtime.'

'Lunchtime? What the ff . . .?' I gasp, then push my lips together, the old saying about stable doors and bolting horses reverberating around my head.

Michael glares at me. 'If you must know, I took her to the ranch for a bit. Bill's got some stuff going on – his mom isn't well – so I was needed there, and anyway, I couldn't exactly bring Lori back here in handcuffs when the kids were awake.'

'Yeah, of course, that was dumb of me.' I don't add that he could still have called me, stopped me fretting for hours. That he doesn't need to be selfish all the time.

'I need to use the bathroom, so you think you can mind her? You won't lose her this time?'

I swallow. 'Go ahead.'

Michael pushes Lori down into a chair, then swaggers out

the kitchen. I wait a beat, then turn to the woman I once thought would always be there for me. 'What were you thinking, Lori? How could you leave me?'

Lori shrugs, looks towards the window. 'It felt like the right thing to do,' she murmurs, her voice raspy. 'It was worth a try.'

'How could it be the right thing when you have so much here! This beautiful home, a job you love. You can see the children whenever you want. I've given you so much, and you still betray me!'

Am I mad at Lori? Or Michael? The pie is making me nauseous.

'My children, you mean?' she throws back.

The comment, and the icy way she delivers it, takes my breath away. Where is my Lori? The one who does so much for me because she loves me? And because she carries a debt so heavy that she knows she'll never be able to pay it off.

'Who put you up to this?' I ask. 'Was it Cally? Or was it Rose? Has she been saying stuff about Michael, about me? Because she's just a bitter old hag, you know that, right? You shouldn't listen to the poison she spews.'

'We could have left together,' Lori murmurs. 'Back in October, when you started getting messages from Brianna Wyoming. Then it wouldn't have had to come to this.'

I pause, wait for the prickles of fear to run their path down my back. 'What does Brianna Wyoming have to do with this?'

Lori releases a faint laugh. 'Everything. And nothing.'

'What the hell does that mean?'

The door slams against the wall. I jump, then silently curse the interruption as Michael walks back into the kitchen.

'I'm beat,' he announces. 'Got to get some sleep.'

'What about Lori?' I ask. I've been so preoccupied with hoping Michael would bring her home, that I haven't thought about what to do with her when he did. Lori has lived here as long as I have, and I've always considered her part of the family. But she's never been a flight risk before. Do we need to lock her door every night? Keep her in handcuffs? How will we explain that to the kids?

'I'll put her in the bunker,' Michael says. 'It's secure down there, and I can handcuff her to something to stop her roaming.'

Lori's eyes widen. She turns to me. 'No, Madison,' she murmurs. 'I need to stay here, in the house, with you and the children.'

'Shut up,' Michael growls. 'You lost your right to an opinion when you almost shot me. Come on.' He grips the top of Lori's arms and hoists her out of the chair. Then he gives her a shove, and she staggers forward. They walk like this until they reach the door to the mudroom, but then Lori pushes back against his bulk. She twists around to face me.

'It's all going to come crashing down, you know, Madison. If you'd just let me go . . .' She sighs, looks down. 'I think you're on borrowed time now.'

I don't know what she means, or how to respond. So I just stare at her, silent, until Michael gives her a hard push and they both disappear out of sight.

Chapter 54

Cally

I can't sleep.

Of course I can't sleep. My only friend in this freakish hellhole of a homestead has run away, in freezing temperatures, eight-months pregnant. And my boss has gone after her, planning God knows what if he finds her. The children have been difficult all afternoon – missing their mom, because that's who she really is, we all know it, as well as picking up on the tension in the house. And Madison has been sitting in that kitchen all day, staring out the window in her floaty white dress, like the tradwife version of Jadis, the White Witch from Narnia.

And the worst thing is, I can't tell a soul about it.

I can't believe Michael made me hand my phone over, or that I did so without protest. There isn't a landline on the March Homestead – something about the government listening in – so I can't even call the two numbers I have memorized (my family home, and our local Thai restaurant who held off delivery apps for longer than most). Shouldn't having a means of communication in a back-of-beyond place like this be a human right? But then I suppose so should having agency over your own body, and that doesn't seem to be a priority here either.

I throw back the duvet and climb out of bed. I walk across my bedroom floor – warm, thick carpet underfoot – and into my en suite bathroom. As I pee – pretending this is the real reason I can't sleep, that an empty bladder will solve all my problems – I look around the room. The huge walk-in shower with its dinner-plate-sized shower head. The heated towel rail and backlit mirror. I have been surrounded by this luxury for five months, and I can't think of a place I want to be less.

I need to leave. But how can I? If I didn't need the money so badly I would find a way to escape, even if it meant walking to town in this freezing cold. Yes, I would be abandoning the children, and with Lori gone too, that's a shitty thing to do. But acting the hero has never been a personality trait of mine.

But the fact is, I do need the money. On the night I crashed Murphy's car, Luke *was* a hero. He came to my rescue without thinking for a moment about the risk to him. And then some macho honor amongst thieves meant that it was Luke who became the target of Murphy's anger. Of course my hardworking, reliable brother would be able to raise fifty grand if he needed to, but I can't let it come to that. This is my debt, not his. If I go home with nothing, what message would I be giving him? That I don't love him enough to put in the hard work that will get him out of trouble?

No, I can't walk away from this. Whatever happens to Lori, whatever Michael or Madison do, I have no choice but to stand on the sidelines and pretend to approve.

I flush the toilet, wash my hands, and walk back into the bedroom. Then I draw back the curtains and stare at the view. My room is at the back of the house, and when there's daylight, I can see miles of open fields and patches of woodland. In my first few months here, there'd also been some life to watch. The horses grazing in the paddock. Clarabelle sashaying around her dinky meadow like the adored family pet she is. But since winter kicked in, and the animals were moved inside for most of the day, it's been nothing but rolling hills.

And now it's a black nothing.

Or almost. The cloud cover must be patchy because the moon keeps appearing and disappearing, casting its eerie glow across the snow-covered fields, then hiding again. I'm about to go back to bed, and another pointless attempt at sleeping, when I catch movement at the edge of my vision. I straighten up, feel my muscles tighten. It's past one o'clock in the morning, but I'm sure someone is out there. The moon disappears again, and the view descends into darkness. I squint, but it's no use. I can't see anything but black.

Until a flashlight switches on. It's directed at the ground, but there's enough light bouncing off the snow to work out who's there. Lori with her hands behind her back, unbalanced as she shuffles forward. Michael gripping onto her arm, pushing her onwards. My breathing sticks but my heart races. I rub my eyes, wondering if I'm seeing things, but they're still there, getting smaller as he takes her farther away from the house.

What should I do?

Maybe I'm not surprised that he found her, a man like that, plenty of friends around here, ruthless in his determination to get what he wants. But treating Lori like a prisoner? The woman who is carrying his child, who has been part of his family all this time? I wonder if Madison knows. I heard her go to bed around eleven, so she could be oblivious to what her husband is doing. But equally, she could be behind this, wanting Lori punished for leaving her. I've lived with this family for five months, and I still can't work out whether Madison is a victim or the mastermind behind this whole toxic fantasy world. Or somehow both.

259

The moonlight returns, the flashlight turns off, and a moment later, their shadows disappear into the night. A wave of despair crashes over me. It's below freezing out there, and Lori has a growing baby inside her.

I need to stop this. Luke was brave enough to save me, and now I need to do the same for Lori, but without putting my brother's life at risk.

I know it's the right thing to do.

I just have no idea how to do it.

Chapter 55

Madison

@sarah.pilling72 You inspired me to give up my job. Now my kids are all grown, my husband's left me, and I'm so lonely I want to die. And where are you now, Madison? #tradwivesruinlives #tradwifeMIA

You're on borrowed time.

I turn the speed up on the treadmill and run faster. What did Lori mean by that? I shake my head, hoping it will clear my mind, but it just makes me dizzy.

I finally fell asleep around three this morning, with Michael snoring next to me. But then Myron started crying a few hours later. Molly got up with him, bless her maternal instincts, but I couldn't get back to sleep after that, and eventually I gave up trying, and tiptoed out to the gym.

I don't feel tired though, at least not in the normal way. My mind is so dazed that I could be in a dreamworld, but my body is overflowing with energy. So much that I need to burn it off in here. Get away from all that fear snapping at my heels.

Brianna Wyoming. What has she got to do with this?

Everything and nothing. What the hell does that mean?

When I started getting messages from Brianna in the late summer, I assumed it was a new tradwife looking for tips. Yes, it was a coincidence, but the movement is getting more and more popular across the western states, and Brianna isn't exactly an unusual name. Even when her messages got more intense, more critical, I still wouldn't let myself believe she had anything to do with my past. I blocked her and moved on. But Lori's comments last night throw lit gas on any innocent explanations.

So who is she?

The messages can't have been from the Brianna we knew – she died thirteen years ago – but someone sent them. Of course anyone can set up an Instagram account in a fake name, but who cares enough about the old Brianna to rake up the past like this?

I know there's an easy way to find out. Lori is locked in the bunker just a few hundred feet away from me. I don't know what state she's in, whether Michael gave her food and water, or a chance to use the bathroom before he tied her up. But either way, she must be desperate enough to do a deal. To tell me the truth in exchange for . . . what? I still need to figure out what I can offer her.

I bring the speed down and jog for another twenty minutes, until I finally feel calm enough to face her. But as I'm pulling on my fleece-lined sweatshirt, the barn door opens and Cally walks in. She looks worse than I do. There are dark circles under her eyes. Her raven hair is scraped off her face into a tight ponytail. And without her signature black eye make-up, she looks ghostlike. I still have no idea what Michael saw in her, or maybe sees in her, present tense. Who knows anymore.

'I'm sorry to interrupt your workout,' Cally says, rubbing her hands against her jeans nervously.

'Is everything okay?' I ask with fake concern. 'The kids?'

'They're fine, yes. I . . . I just wondered if you'd heard from Lori? If Michael has managed to find her?'

I drop onto the weight bench and pull on my boots. It's irritating, Cally asking after Lori like they're friends when she's only known the woman for five minutes, and Lori is worth ten of her. But my life is hanging by a thread already. I don't need to make an even bigger enemy of Cally. And Michael and I agreed on our story before he went to sleep last night, so I may as well use it. 'He did, yes,' I say, finding my Truly Madison persona. 'And they had a long heart to heart.'

'Oh?'

'I don't think Michael and I have fully appreciated the toll these pregnancies take on Lori. She's always so eager to help, but she's turning forty this year, and middle age isn't kind to women, Cally. I imagine we'll both find that out for ourselves one day.' I look wistful for a moment, then tilt my head and exchange it for a generous expression. 'Lori is going to take a few weeks out. Michael has found a gorgeous hotel for her to rest in and a little boutique maternity hospital for when the time comes. When you see Lori again, she'll be a different person, I promise.'

While Michael and I agreed on our public statement, we didn't find consensus on what we will actually do with Lori. We'll have to keep her locked up until the baby's born, but then what? Threaten her into staying? Banish her with a wad of cash and hope she keeps quiet? Or . . . well, the third option doesn't bear thinking about.

'Does that mean I can get my phone back?'

'Sorry?'

'Michael took my phone yesterday, remember? In case I warned, I mean, contacted Lori.'

'Oh, I'd forgotten that.'

'So do you think I can have it now?'

I smile. The idea of Cally having contact with the outside world unnerves me after what's happened over the last twenty-four hours. But I don't want to undo all my good work by refusing. 'Of course. I don't know where Michael put it, but I'm sure he'll be happy to oblige. Just as soon as he's back from work.'

Chapter 56

Cally

I can't believe the bullshit that came out of Madison's mouth this morning.

But is she lying to me about Lori's whereabouts, or has Michael lied to her?

And is she right that Michael will just hand over my phone when he gets back from work, or was that pure fantasy too?

I lurch forward on the sofa, grip my hands together, tense up as frustration pulses through me.

'Are you okay, Miss Cally?'

Molly's eyes are full of concern. The other children are busy playing. Mason is doing a jigsaw puzzle, a frown of concentration on his face – he's quieter than usual today and I wonder if he's missing Lori more than he's willing to let on. Matilda is building a tower of bricks and squealing with delight every time Myron rams his cars into it – a lesson in resilience if ever there was one.

'I'm fine,' I say. 'Just a little tired.' I pat the cushion next to me, and Molly drops down into it. 'And how about you?'

Molly shrugs.

'You must be missing Lori.'

She nods, her eyes starting to glisten. 'And Daddy seems real mad.'

'He does?'

'Mason saw him this morning, before he went to work.' Molly's voice is low and strained. 'He wanted to go to the ranch, hang out with Daddy and the guys but . . .' Her voice trails off.

'Your daddy said no?'

'He took him to his study. Said Mason was acting all entitled and needed taking down a few pegs. I mean, I know we're just stupid kids, and we need to be punished sometimes. Daddy says that a lot. But I don't really know what Mason did wrong.'

'He did nothing wrong,' I whisper. Unlike his father, I wish I could add. The man who forced his tongue down my throat. Who has taken Lori somewhere, in handcuffs. Probably to his apocalypse bunker with thick cement walls and heavy-duty padlock.

But Michael is also the person who calls the shots around here with his physical strength and crater-sized ego. The man who will decide if I get my fifty grand. Who has a hand in Luke's future.

I don't know what to do, how to help Lori without having to ask Luke to save his own skin. But I do know that I need my phone back, and that I can't rely on Michael to give it to me.

'Molly, can I leave you in charge for a bit? I won't be long.'

'Of course.' As she smiles, I see Lori's goodness so clearly in her features that I can't believe it took a washboard stomach in Lycra for me to work out the truth. I shake my head at my stupidity, then head into the hallway.

I stand still for a moment and replay yesterday morning in my mind. When Michael demanded my phone, we were in the kitchen, and then he came out here and left the house via the front door. My phone could be in his truck, flung there and forgotten about, but was there a reason he didn't use the back door? Did he make a stop somewhere before he left?

I've never been inside Michael's study, but it's off the hallway at the front of the house, so an easy detour on his way out. Its big oak door is always closed, but it doesn't have a lock on it. And Michael is on the ranch right now, so where's the harm in checking it out? I feel an unnerving spike of adrenalin as I push down on the handle, but when I slip inside and close the door behind me, it starts to settle. No one is going to find me in here.

The room has a large window overlooking the drive, which feels exposing, so I lower onto my belly and slither across the wooden floor, like I'm in training for the special forces. I stifle a laugh – fear can have this effect on me, hysteria, I suppose you'd call it – and climb up onto the desk chair. There are three drawers either side and I expect at least some of them to be locked – Michael is the most suspicious man I've ever met – but they all slide open on demand. Perhaps he believes no one would dare cross his threshold. The thought sparks another wave of terror, and I turn towards the window. But it's all quiet out there.

The top right-hand drawer has normal desk stuff – pens, paperclips, a couple of notepads. The drawer on my left has a wooden tool inside, like a flat shoehorn, which I guess is what Michael disciplines the kids with. There's also an empty black and gold cardboard box, with *handgun ammunition* written on the side. I close the drawer.

The lower drawers are full of paperwork – folders, files, loose bits of paper. I could probably find all manner of white-collar crimes in here if I knew what I was looking for. But all

267

I really want is my phone, so I rifle around, and then feel a crushing defeat when I come up empty-handed.

There's a desktop computer in front of me, and I wiggle the mouse, more out of frustration than intent, but when the screen lights up, I wonder if I can access my social media, send a Mayday message. It only takes a couple of seconds to realize Michael's computer is password protected. Of course it is. I consider trying *MichaelMarch* – the only person he really cares about – but I know it's too risky, so I lean back in the chair and try to work out what to do. Do I carry on looking for my phone? Try to find another device that doesn't ask for a password? The children aren't allowed phones, and I haven't seen Erica or Noah for days. But there might be options if I can get inside Madison's study.

Or do I prioritize finding Lori? Or risk trusting Madison with what I saw last night? Or get the hell away and try robbing a bank for Murphy's fifty grand instead?

Oh, my God, my head is going to explode.

Suddenly I hear a noise. Tires on gravel. Shit, shit, shit. I jolt with fear, my knees knocking against the underside of the desk. Is it Michael? I drop to the floor, slither across the wood. I pause – terrified that he'll walk into the house and catch me red-handed – then gabble out a prayer and lunge for the door.

And I'm just sinking into the playroom sofa – my heart clattering – when I hear a familiar voice in the hallway. Bill is here.

Chapter 57

Brianna

Steak. My mouth waters at the sight. Back home, we ate steak every Saturday night, my daddy cooking it on the barbecue in summer, Mom taking charge in the winter. But I haven't eaten one since I moved out here, so the sight of three ruby-red rumps is making me dizzy with excitement.

And steak wasn't the only gift that Mary brought. There are also fresh vegetables, meatballs, a couple of casseroles that we've boxed up and left outside to freeze, and a large bag of the juiciest oranges. Over the last three days, I've eaten so well that my snack cravings have almost disappeared. Although I have hidden the multipack of Twinkies she brought, just in case.

I set the bunch of rosemary on the chopping board and start pulling the herb off its stalks. There's garlic too, and butter, and with roast potatoes and broccoli, it's going to be a feast. When Mary turned up on our doorstep, I was bruised, scared, hungry, and hopeless. And here I am now, preparing Jonah's birthday dinner with a smile on my face.

And that's because Mary is a godsend. She gets up at dawn, drinks two cups of coffee, then starts work. And she doesn't let up until nightfall. Cleaning, cooking, mending, making.

And every time I protest, she reminds me that I'm six months pregnant, and that I shouldn't look a gift horse in the mouth. Yes, I've heard her mumble the saying 'if a job's worth doing, do it yourself' a few times, but I refuse to feel offended by that. Especially because she reminds me that we all have different skills. I'm only cooking tonight's dinner because she's outside helping Jonah finish the crib he keeps cursing over.

I look at them through the window, working silently, but without the animosity I sensed on the day Mary arrived. He seems to have accepted her being here. Realized what a help she is. I know this isn't forever, that one day she'll pack her bags. But I don't want to think about that right now. Happiness has been so sparse over the last six months that I need to hold on to whatever scraps I can.

I reach down, scrabble for the garlic hidden in the bag of vegetables, finally lay my fingers on it, and straighten back up.

But then I frown. Something outside has changed.

Jonah is standing tall, taut, staring at Mary. Mary is flapping her hands, her mouth spewing out words I can't hear. I place the garlic on the chopping board but don't pick up the knife. Instead, I grip the work surface and stare through the window, like I'm watching a dark thriller on mute.

Jonah starts walking away from his sister, towards the house. Mary follows for a few paces then reaches out, grabs his arm, and pulls. He twists around to face her, and for a moment I think he's going to hit her like he hit me, but he uses his spare hand to unfurl her fingers. I can only see the back of him now, so I can't work out if he's talking or not, but Mary starts shaking her head. *Please*, I lip read. *That came out wrong.*

My breathing shallows.

What did she say? Please, not our secret.

Jonah turns his back on her. Now I can see his face, and

it's blazing with fury. As I watch him walk towards the house, I think about searching for my phone on New Year's Eve, how I found those weapons in his makeshift man cave. The unloaded gun that I shot into the woods. The hunting knife with savage edges that I stabbed at thin air with. The power I felt when I held each of them in my grip.

Why didn't I take one of them?

I reach into the pocket of my dress and feel the smooth metal of my phone. I was so relieved to have it back that day that I ran to the charger forgetting all about the weapons I'd uncovered. My phone was supposed to be my lifeline. But now I wonder if it will be my downfall.

And if I should have taken the knife instead.

Chapter 58

Madison

@tradlife.bestlife Is it true that Michael has been having an affair? Is that why you're offline?
#sendinglove #solidarity #cheaters #tradwifeMIA

I stand in front of Michael's bunker and try to find the strength to open the door. Everything is going wrong, and it turns out even Bill isn't immune. He got a call from his mom's care home this morning to tell him his mother had passed away overnight. He appeared in the kitchen earlier, telling me he was heading to Yellowstone to sort out her things. He was calm, resolute. But his eyes looked redder than usual. I know him not being around makes things simpler with Lori being locked up, but watching him drive away, maybe the only man I've truly trusted since my daddy let me down, made me feel even more vulnerable.

But I need to do this, so I take a deep breath, line up the six digits Michael texted me – eventually, after I'd gently pointed out that our baby might need some sustenance in the ten hours he was away from the homestead – and listen to the padlock release. I pause for a moment to collect myself, or possibly a few minutes, a lack of sleep and an overload of stress hormones stretching the time continuum, just like those TikTok videos have always claimed. Then I push on the door and walk inside.

It's dark. No windows in here. Has Lori been lying in the pitch black all this time? I find the light switch that's pinned to the wall, and the line of bulbs hanging above me light up. Whoah. I suck in a breath, stumble backwards. I thought Lori would be in one of the bedrooms, but she's sitting in front of me, tied to a chair. Her eyes piercing mine.

'Lori,' I exhale.

She's not gagged – I would like to think that's because Michael wouldn't be so cruel, but it's probably because no one would hear her scream in his soundproofed dungeon – but she doesn't speak. Just stares at me like I'm Judas, even though she's the one who ran away.

'I'm sorry we had to do this,' I say, trying to actually sound sorry, when what I really feel is an intense mix of loneliness and fear.

'No, you're not. Because if you were, you wouldn't have done it.' Her words are spoken quietly, but they land louder. I start pacing.

'What was I supposed to do then? You ran away, Lori! With my child inside you! Why would you do that?'

'I had my reasons. Stupid ones, I see that now.'

'Exactly!' But there's such defeat in her voice that it drains the fight out of me. I pull a chair up next to her and sit down. I consider touching her arm, but I'm scared she'll reject me. Maybe we're finally past comforting each other now. 'I know you've done a lot for me over the years,' I say. 'And I'm grateful for it. But you did owe me. I thought you understood that. That you wanted to make amends.'

Lori's face pulls taut. 'It was a long time ago. Things change, we realize that maybe we remembered things wrong.'

'You didn't remember anything wrong! How could you possibly? What's going on, Lori? Why were you talking about Brianna Wyoming last night?'

'I need to use the bathroom.' She pushes her lips together – a clear message that she's not talking until I agree to her request – and I feel like crying. Of course I wouldn't deny her such a basic human right. I undo Michael's complicated knots, then grip her arm and lead her through to the bathroom. Once she's finished peeing, I do the journey in reverse, push her down into the chair.

'Don't tie my hands,' she begs. 'Let me see the children and I'll tell you everything.'

'I can't do that,' I say, pulling her hands back and contemplating the rope. 'Michael would kill me.'

'Yeah,' Lori murmurs. She resists my pull for a moment, then surrenders. 'I've always wondered how you've managed to pick two of them.'

I flinch. Lori's strike landing a direct blow. 'So now it's my fault that so many men are raised to abuse their wives and girlfriends?' I wind and twist and knot the rope.

'I don't know, Madison. But I do feel that I've sacrificed a lot for you to learn nothing from the past.'

'And what about the amount I've sacrificed? And all because of your loose tongue?'

Tears bubble in Lori's eyes, just as I knew they would. She's not the only one with a trump card.

'It was an accident,' she murmurs. 'The words just slipped out. But you know all this.'

I feel emotion rising in my throat. I have tried everything, including changing my entire identity, to put that day behind

274

me and still, the fear and trauma always takes over. I swallow hard. 'The one thing I made crystal clear in my text was that Jonah must never know I asked for your help.'

Lori releases a low moan. 'I know.'

'And I sent you those photos so that you knew that what I was asking of you really mattered, that your brother was a dangerous, violent man.'

Lori closes her eyes. 'We've been over this a thousand times,' she whispers. 'That's why I've kept the photos all this time.'

'And we'll go over them a thousand times more if I want to,' I throw back. 'My friends on Tumblr convinced me that you'd take care of me if you knew the truth, that you'd put my welfare before sibling loyalty. But they were wrong, you just threw me to the wolves.'

'It was a mistake!' she throws back. 'A terrible, tragic mistake.' She releases a long sigh, then looks straight into my eyes, almost confrontational. 'And then I made another one.'

My shoulders tense. 'What do you mean by that?' I demand. Because it can't be what it sounds like.

'It's taken me until now to realize.'

I shake my head. 'No, no way.' I push out of the chair, twist around to face her. 'Don't you dare call that a mistake!'

Chapter 59

Brianna

'You lied!'

Jonah shoves me, the heels of his hands slamming into my collarbone. I stumble backwards, away from the chopping board, from the kitchen knife, which I instantly mourn. I still don't know what's going on, how things have moved from idyllic to this, but all my senses are screaming that I'm in danger. Real danger.

'I'm not,' I gabble. 'I haven't. I don't know what . . .'

'You brought her here, after swearing to my face that you didn't!'

'What? No, I . . .'

'How did you convince her to come? What did you tell her?'

Mary clatters through the back door into the kitchen. My eyes dart towards her, but Jonah spins all the way around, his back to me now. I wonder if I could reach the knife without him noticing, without it making things worse.

'Jonah, no, please!' Mary calls out. 'I didn't mean Brianna, I meant Mom! She gave me the directions to find you; I just got my words mixed up.'

'Stop bullshitting me! And get out of my house! This is between Brianna and me.'

My stomach roils. I begin to shake, my muscles spasming. The baby kicks. 'Don't leave me,' I whisper.

'SHUT UP!

'Jonah, this isn't Brianna's fault,' Mary begs, breathless. 'You and me, let's talk some more, outside.'

Jonah strides forward, grabs Mary's arm. It's only now I realize how much stronger he is than her. She's tall, and capable, and for the last three days I've considered her indestructible. But her small, slim frame is no match for Jonah's size. She's as helpless as me. He drags her so forcefully that her feet slip and slide, skitter across the wooden floor, towards the back door. Then he flings her out, slams the door shut, slides the bolt across. I dip down, my knees giving way. It takes all my energy to straighten back up.

'Jonah, please. Yes, I asked her to come, but only because I'm pregnant, and you're never here. You're always at work or the bar.'

'That same bullshit narrative again! I'm sick of it. I work damn hard for you!'

'But that's not true! You get drunk all the time, and you hurt me, Jonah! You know you did.'

'Yeah, and you drove me to it,' he hisses. 'You've been punishing me every day with your lazy ways, your constant moaning. Do you know what it's like to have your dream ripped to shreds because your girlfriend gives up at the first sign of trouble?'

'Fuck you, Jonah. You're not perfect either!'

He walks towards me, jabs his finger at my chest. 'See. Disrespecting me again.' He shoves harder and my back connects with the solid ceramic sink, reigniting the old pain, making me want to vomit.

'Maybe I could forgive you for being useless, even for your

foul, disrespecting mouth, but shaming me in front of my sister and then lying about it? That's a new low, even for you.'

There's a loud banging from outside. Mary pummeling on the window with her fists. Jonah glares at her for a moment, then grabs my shoulders and pushes me once, twice, until we're out of the kitchen, into the living room, out of Mary's view.

There's silence for a moment, both of us shaking, me with fear, Jonah pulsing with anger. I look at the blood stain on the floor, remember the pain Jonah's anger caused that day.

And I surge for the front door.

Except Jonah is too quick. He extends his leg, twists his toes inwards. I trip over his foot, fall, sprawled on the floor. A pain flares deep in my belly. I release a low, guttural moan. 'I fucking hate you,' I say. 'This was my dream too, remember. You're the one who fucked it up, not me.'

'Still refusing to admit the truth!'

He kicks at my waist. Pain stings. I roll onto my side, stare up at him. His seething, contorted expression. His cold blue eyes, always bloodshot these days. How could I have loved him once? How could I have not seen the monster behind the lopsided smile?

'The only truth is that you're a bully,' I hiss with as much volume as I can muster. 'And a coward for picking on someone weaker than you.'

The next kick is so powerful that it lifts me off the floor. I drop back with a thud and close my eyes. I want to ride the pain like last time, but it's too much. My head swims. I feel myself losing consciousness.

But suddenly I'm moving. Jonah's fingers dig into my ankles, and drag me across the floor. Pain explodes in every part of my body. Where is he taking me? And what is that smell? Something pungent, metallic.

I hear a scream. Loud enough to rouse me. Mary is here, the front door swinging on its hinges, the rusty lock broken. She looks like Jonah, I realize. The blonde hair, pale skin. The ice-cold fury in her blue eyes.

Her arms are above her head, like a diamond, elbows out, hands clasped. The dregs of the day's sunlight sparkle through the gap. I wonder if she's an angel, if I'm dead, if Mary is here to welcome me into heaven.

She lets out another, more guttural scream, then brings her hands forward, exposing what she's holding. A skillet. A cast-iron pan, bought at a garage sale, dozens of years old, but heavy as a cauldron.

The skillet hits Jonah on the side of his head. He staggers. Mary hits him again. I stare, wide-eyed now. She lifts her weapon, brings it down for a third time. *If a job's worth doing, do it yourself.*

Jonah collapses onto the floor.

He rears up a few inches, and she hits him one last time. Finally, he's out cold.

The skillet slips out of her grip, thuds on the floor. She sinks to her hands and knees.

I close my eyes. Feel the damp wood beneath me. Listen to Mary's weeping. Taste blood in my mouth.

And that smell.

I sink under.

Chapter 60

Brianna

I surface in hospital.

For a moment, I'm twelve. My arm broken during cheerleading practice. Waking up from the operation that pinned it back together. I scan the room for my mom, then feel the wrenching loss as the image becomes a memory and drifts away.

I see Mary. Sitting in an armchair in the corner of the room. Her head resting on her hand, eyes closed, her face twitching. Floating in the twilight between awake and asleep.

It's light outside, and I wonder what time it is. How many hours have passed since I watched Jonah collapse under Mary's relentless blows.

Or did I dream that?

I look up at the ceiling, concentrate. I remember Mary begging me to get up off the floor, but not being able to move, then her dragging me outside when I didn't react. I remember her arms squeezing my rib cage, lifting me into the passenger seat of her car. The pain that rattled through me as she drove down our uneven track. Then nothing. Until now.

I jolt. I'm lying on my back.

The realization unleashes a spiral of panic. I push up onto

my hands. My shoulders lift, but then sag, my elbows breaking, the effort too much. But I'm in my third trimester, I shouldn't lie on my back. The doctors must know that.

Slowly, warily, I lower my hands to my belly.

It's still distended, but it's soft. Where's the baby? My eyes dart around the room, looking for a crib, any sign that my child still exists. But there's nothing. Just Mary, her eyelashes quivering.

I sink my fingers into the wobbly flesh. Hot tears burn my eyes. Then my hands travel. Dressings cover the lower half of my tummy. My skin feels both numb and on fire. What have they done to me?

I make a strange sound, a low moan, loud enough to wake Mary.

'Brianna.' She pushes out of the chair, crouches by my bedside, takes my hands in hers, starts gabbling. 'I'm so sorry. This is all my fault. I can't believe I was so stupid, that I let my guard down after everything you'd told me. And seeing it with my own eyes. My own brother. I'm so ashamed.'

I pull my hands away, return them to my belly. 'My baby?'

Mary shakes her head, shifts her eyeline away. 'I'm so sorry. They scanned you when we arrived, there was no heartbeat.'

Any wisp of hope that my baby is sleeping in another room, alive and healthy, shrivels and dies. 'A girl?'

'Yes. The doctors will tell you about her.'

'I don't want to know.' There's a new edge to my voice. I don't recognize it, but instinctively I know this is who I am now. Battle hardened. My icy tone matching the cold metal of an armory that I will wear forever.

I reach up, touch Mary's cheek and she turns to look at me, compassion and guilt vying for prominence. 'You killed my baby,' I say.

Her face crumples. 'I know. And if I could go back in time, take the beating myself, I would do it in a heartbeat. But I can't. All I can do is promise that I'll make it up to you, any way I can.'

I wonder what she could possibly do to make up for the loss of my child.

Except she has already done the only thing that comes close. 'Is he dead?'

Mary looks towards the door, then back at me. The instinct for self-preservation in all of us. 'Yes.'

'Did you call the cops?'

She's quiet for a moment. 'No.'

'Tell the doctors?'

'They asked, I said you'd slipped in the snow, fallen, and collided with a tree.'

I nod, surprised, and a little impressed by Mary's deception. But perhaps I shouldn't be. This woman who is capable of killing her own brother. 'Where is he?'

'Where I left him. You were bleeding so much, getting you to a hospital was my priority. They operated on you straightaway, and I haven't left your side since you came out of recovery around midnight.' Mary looks at her watch. 'It's just past eleven now.'

Hours lost. A life lost. I wonder what else has gone forever. 'Which hospital are we in?'

'Washakie Medical Center,' she says, shifting her gaze. 'I didn't want to go east, back to Buffalo.'

I nod slowly, realization creeping in. We have too many secrets now to go home, to risk seeing people we grew up around. I think about my family. Will I ever see them again? Lying here, such a thought feels like an unfathomable loss, but the truth is, they made their choice long before now. Losing this baby is their fault too. And I won't forgive them for it.

And now I've lost Jonah, except that's a good thing. As long as it doesn't cost me my next chance at life.

'You should go back to the homestead now,' I say. 'Hide his body.'

'I wonder if I should tell someone, now that I know you're okay.'

I shake my head. But I'm calm. Composed. I wonder if this is part of the new me too. Blessed with a ruthless clarity.

'You cannot risk being charged with murder, Mary.'

'But I killed him,' she whispers. 'In God's eyes, I should be punished.'

'In God's eyes, you delivered justice. He killed my baby with his boot, remember. It's only fair that he pays with his life.'

'But how will I live with myself . . .'

'You said you'd make it up to me, didn't you? In any way you can?'

'Yes, and I meant it.'

'Well, that starts now. I gave up my entire family for your brother, and now he's ripped my baby away too. I've only got you. I can't let you go to prison.'

'But he's lying in the middle of your living room,' Mary pleads, her voice trembling. 'There's blood everywhere. What do I even do with his body?'

'You're the most diligent person I've ever met. And no one comes out to the homestead – we've cut ties with everyone, so no one will miss him. You'll have all the time you need to clean the place. There's woodland behind, only a few hundred yards away. Jonah is always going on about the predators in there. Drag him into the woods and let nature do the rest.'

Mary starts to cry, her shoulders juddering as she tries to contain it, but she nods. 'Okay, I will.'

I touch my belly again, as though it's going to steady me,

which is stupid, because it's just jelly now. 'I'll get through this, won't I?' I ask. 'Can you promise me that?'

'I can, I promise.'

'Because I'm not even nineteen yet. My life is only just beginning. I can still have the dream, can't I?'

'Of course you can. You're special, Brianna.'

'All I want is to get married, live in a nice house, have a family. Please tell me it's all going to be okay.' But Mary's face folds. My heart thuds at the sight. 'What? What did I say?'

'You need to talk to the doctor,' she whispers.

'No, tell me now.' That new voice again. Caustic.

Mary's face moves from pale to ghostly. 'It wasn't just your baby they couldn't save. There was too much damage.'

I lift my hand, like I'm fending her off. My head is spinning so much, I can hardly remember my own biology. Then it hits me. 'They took my womb?'

'I'm so sorry.'

'I'm damaged goods, a write-off, at eighteen?'

'No, of course you're not.'

'You think?' I hiss. 'What decent man around here would choose a barren bride?'

Chapter 61

Mary

I killed my brother, caused my unborn niece's death, and took away Brianna's chance of ever being a mother.

What kind of a monster am I?

I rest my forehead on the steering wheel and close my eyes.

I had no warning. One minute I was the good sister, a role I've practiced plenty over the last twelve years, since our dad died at work, crushed by a colleague with undiagnosed epilepsy driving a forklift truck. Especially as the tragedy left us motherless in all but name. Our mom never got over the shock of becoming a widow so prematurely.

Then I made one mistake – and set off a chain of horrifying events.

And now I must face up to the consequences. The child I cooked SpaghettiOs for, who I nursed through chicken pox and two bouts of influenza is dead. And I killed him.

Slowly, I lift my head and turn towards the house. It looks lovely from here. The sun is giving the rusty tin roof a warm glow. There's no hint of the bloodshed inside. I wish I could stay outside for longer, but I have chores to do. Clean the house, pack Brianna's things. Drag my brother's dead body through the back door and dump him in the woods for animals to scavenge on. Burn his possessions until I have removed all traces of him from the property.

I push open the car door, vomit on the frozen ground.

But I promised Brianna I would do this, and I owe her.

She lost the child that's been growing inside her for six months. I've never been pregnant, but I can imagine it, how special it must feel when the baby kicks, or hiccups, knowing that he or she is reliant on you for everything. To lose that connection so brutally is beyond my comprehension.

I hold on to the car door and straighten up. If Brianna can go through all that without breaking, I can do this.

Just like when I stepped up after my dad died.

I was only thirteen. Not old enough to become a parent to three grieving boys, but also too young to get away, so I had no choice but to dig in. To do my best. I thought I'd done pretty well too, but now I see how deeply I failed. I think about Jonah, kicking his own child to death. Perhaps my responsibility for this tragedy started a long time ago.

I walk up the steps to the front porch. There are clues now. Spots of blood on the gray wooden boards. I log a mental note that they will need cleaning, then step over them, and push on the door.

The smell hits me straightaway. Like rotting flesh. It's so pungent that it acts like a wall, a barrier. I feel the fight-or-flight hormone swell through my chest. Except I've got no fight left in me, so I eye my car.

I could drive back to Buffalo, pretend that I spent the week cooking and making curtains for my brother's new home and that nothing bad happened. Except I feel like the word 'killer' is now permanently etched into my face. But I've got savings in the bank so I could go elsewhere. Start again some place new.

Maybe somewhere anonymous like New York or Seattle. Yes, I'd be leaving Brianna with no one, but I've only known her for a few days. She's not family. Not my responsibility. And maybe she'd be better off without me.

Then my eyes return to the crimson spot on the deck, and I remember that I'm not the kind of person who runs away from my mistakes. I walk into the house.

My brother is where I left him. He could almost be asleep if it wasn't for the blood pooling around his head. I screw my eyes closed, the image too distressing, then take a long, slow breath and open them again.

I pick up his feet and pull. I don't look at his face at all. Not as he bobs down the back steps, or as his head flops sideways as I hoist him into the wheelbarrow. And again, when I tip him out in the densest part of the woods. The branches are so meshed together here that there's no snow on the ground, and Jonah sinks into the mulch of wet leaves.

But as I look down at his still body in the dirt, the sight is too upsetting, too lacking in respect. I run back to the homestead, looking for something suitable to cover him with. I find the patchwork blanket that Brianna knitted. I remember her showing it to me on the day I arrived, how proud she was of it. I know she'd hate me for using it to give Jonah some comfort, but I find that I want my brother to lie underneath it. A final kindness before he enters hell. And Brianna will never know.

I carry it back into the woods. As I tuck in the sides of the blanket, I mumble the Lord's Prayer, even though I know it won't help him. Then I walk away without looking back.

I still have a list of things to get done, and I need to get back to the hospital before nightfall.

Chapter 62

Madison

A mistake. How can Lori possibly think that her killing Jonah was a mistake? Yes, he was her brother, but he was also an abusive baby killer. He deserved to die.

And that's what she has always believed too. It's true that she has felt guilty since that day, thirteen years ago, when our lives changed forever. But not for taking Jonah's life. It's what she did to me that has hung over Lori, or Mary, as she was then. Letting it slip that I'd asked her to come to the homestead by mentioning that I'd given her directions, sparking Jonah's shame-induced fury.

And then everything that came after. I lost the baby I was carrying, as well as the chance to have any more children. Lori has always accepted that I was the innocent one, and that she needed to repay me for what I lost.

So what has changed?

'Mommy?'

Matilda pulls on my sleeve, and I lift my arm on autopilot, curl it around her shoulders. She quickly snuggles in, and the intimacy feels both comforting and dangerous, like it might peel away another layer of my skin and expose Brianna underneath. As I think back to that awful time, lying in a hospital bed, mourning my first child – my only child, if I'm brutally honest about it – I wonder how life would have turned out if I hadn't lost her. But the truth is, I will never know.

'Mommy!' Matilda repeats.

'Yes?'

'Does Old Yeller die? Because Mason said he does, but I don't want him to. I love dogs.'

I turn to look at the familiar movie playing on the fabric screen in front of us, the projector softly whirring behind, sending light granules through the dark air. We usually have movie night up here in the den on a Saturday, but with Lori not around, and the children feeling her absence, I suggested we have a bonus extra one tonight too, and Michael was all for it.

Except he's not here yet – late back from work, I guess – so adult attendance has dwindled from the normal four to just two. Cally and me.

'Honey, watch the movie, and I promise you'll love it,' I say. 'It was Daddy's favorite when he was a boy.'

'It was?' Matilda's eyes light up, and I wonder if my second-born daughter will break with tradition and follow her brother over to Michael's camp one day.

It would be heartbreaking, but I know I'd survive it, because being let down by family is familiar territory for me. If my parents had supported my decision to run off homesteading with Jonah, would things have worked out differently? Or if my mom had called me back when I first sensed things were going badly wrong? Or if she'd responded after I impulsively

289

scribbled that card and asked the mailman to deliver it to my family home's address? Of course I don't know if the mail ever arrived – it didn't have a stamp on it – but I have always figured it did. That my parents had just lost interest by then.

After that, I promised myself that I'd never think about my family again. But when my Truly Madison profile started getting noticed, I got nervous about being recognized. I knew I looked completely different – it's amazing what money, time, and aspiration can do – but there was always the chance someone from my past might get suspicious. So I created a cover story for Brianna. I wrote to my parents, told them that I'd split up with Jonah and was moving to Hawaii with my new boyfriend who loved to surf. Piling up more reasons for them to disapprove of me. I then set up an Instagram profile for Brianna Nelson and I still share surfing pictures sometimes – although none of my family have ever followed me.

At the same time, I also blocked everyone I was close to in Buffalo from my Truly Madison account to build some distance. There have been times over the years when I've worried that I've become too famous, that someone will recognize me on TV, or in a magazine, and blow my cover. But no one ever has. It could be my blonder hair, my fuller lips, or the expensive make-up I always wear on my posts. Or it might be because no one could ever believe that the dreamy, fresh-faced teenager they once knew could rise to such heights. Or maybe it's even simpler than that. I feel a world away from Brianna Nelson, so it makes sense that no one else sees her in me either.

Matilda stays snuggled against me but returns her attention to the screen. There's a clatter of gun noise, and I wonder for a moment if *Old Yeller* is appropriate for a six-year-old, whether its status as a 1950s classic Western gives it more leeway than it deserves. Then I imagine Michael's reaction if I shared my concern. I smile at the image, a gallows humor kind of smile, and accept that a dead dog in a movie is the least of my problems.

When I lay in that hospital bed, I didn't know how I was going to get my life back on track. My plan, when I first texted Mary those photos, had been to convince her to hand over some of her mom's huge insurance payout from her daddy's death, enough for me to be a single mom without needing to beg, or apologize to anyone. But I never got a chance to ask. Jonah was suddenly dead, at Mary's hand. And I needed a new plan.

But I knew, with a clarity borne from twenty stitches in my belly and a leaflet on still births in my hand, that I would make one. I had to. And Mary needed to play her part.

I never saw the homestead again. When I was discharged from hospital, my refusal to be involved in my baby's funeral still pounding at my temples, we drove away in Mary's car, her trunk full of my stuff, with a promise that all of Jonah's stuff had been burned in his oil drum. We went north, because we didn't want to go east, and then chose west when the road forked. When Mary got tired of driving, and the tank ran empty, we found a cheap motel and parked up. In a place called Big Timber.

It turned out Mary had some savings, and we stayed in that motel for two weeks. Mary went out hiking most days, while I spent my time scrolling through my phone without Jonah scowling his disapproval. I shut down my Tumblr account straightaway – that needy, vulnerable Brianna Nelson didn't exist anymore – but I rekindled my love of Instagram, which was still new and exciting in 2012. Those self-serving women who never responded to my messages – even @bettymaydickson who'd been pregnant at the exact same time as me – had once again become my inspiration. My educators.

The March ranch was well-known around Big Timber, so it didn't take me long to work out who Michael March was, or that he was single – an ex-wife somewhere, but clearly not his proudest moment – and the sole heir to his daddy's fortune. It felt like a reason to stay.

We changed our names to Madison and Lori, and built our backstories. Two single women from East Wyoming, a friendship forged through our shared love of the church. We rented a two-bedroom cottage on the edge of town, Mary got a cheffing job at the steakhouse on Main Street, and I found ways to bump into Michael. Mary gave me money to look my best – new clothes, new hairstyle, regular trips to the beauty salon – and by the end of summer 2012, Michael and I were dating. We married the following March – the month chosen by Michael of course – and finally I had stunning photos of my own to post on my grid.

For a while, things couldn't have gone better. I had picked a man as rich as he was masculine, a husband whose fear of women's biology means he still has no inkling that I'm not genetically linked to our children, and who has been too wrapped up in himself to properly notice my escalating influencer presence.

But then I got older, and my beauty faded. The affairs started. Arguments grew into fights. Admiration became rivalry. And now Lori has shaken the whole foundation of this life I've built. Lori, the woman who killed her own brother to save me, who has dedicated her life to making sure mine is a success, has turned on me. And in response, I've tied her to a chair and locked her in a windowless bunker.

Matilda toots, then giggles. I sniff my disapproval and extract my arm. Molly is curled up in a beanbag a few feet away, intently watching the movie, preparing herself for its

292

tragic ending. Mason is alone on the small sofa, snuggled into one corner, leaving one and a half cushions free, a shrine to his absent father. And Myron is sprawled across Cally's lap, fast asleep.

Our tutor, the traitor. She's staring at the screen too, but I can tell she's not interested in the movie. It will be too old-fashioned for her, too American. But I'm still glad she's in here. I have no idea whether she believed my story about Lori's little luxury pit stop, but I like being able to keep an eye on her. She's probably waiting for Michael to arrive, desperate to have her phone back, and I suppose I can relate to that. Shame she's going to be disappointed.

Although, where is he? It's nearly nine o'clock, Old Yeller is about to meet his maker, and it's been dark for hours.

My mind travels to Lori, the brutal way Michael tied her up.

He wouldn't do anything more to hurt her while I'm otherwise engaged, would he?

Chapter 63

Cally

This is excruciating. Lori is out there, handcuffed and taken away by Michael. Probably in that bunker of his. And I'm his prisoner too, in a different kind of way. No phone, no money, no allies except maybe a couple of the children. I shuffle under Myron's bulk. In other circumstances, I might enjoy him treating me like a mattress, but right now I'm feeling too claustrophobic for it to be fun.

I look at my watch. Michael is usually here for these movie nights, warning Mason not to cry if things get emotional, throwing Matilda in the air and then telling her off for not settling when he decides its time. I know he went to the ranch this morning because Mason got a couple of welts for begging to go with him, but he can't still be there now. What if he has already come home, but instead of joining his family for movie night, has gone straight outside to see Lori? What if he's doing something terrible to her right now? I shuffle again.

I can't just sit here.

I wrap my arms around Myron to keep him attached to my chest, then push up to standing, his legs dangling either side of me. I continue staring at the movie, and not in Madison's direction, following the childish logic that anyone I can't see can't see me either.

'Cally, what's wrong? Where are you going?'

I sigh. Of course Madison is watching me. I give her the most soothing smile I can manage. 'I think I should take Myron to bed,' I mouth. 'He's exhausted, poor thing.'

Madison narrows her eyes. 'Maybe I should take him.'

'Don't worry, honestly. You and Matilda look so cozy there,' I say. 'I'd hate to break that up. It'll only take me a couple of minutes.'

'So you're coming back?'

'Of course,' I lie.

Madison nods, at least I think she does. It's a tiny movement, but I take it as consent and head for the door.

Once I've wrestled Myron into clean pajamas and made sure he's fallen back to sleep in his wagon-shaped bed, I tiptoe downstairs, trying not to think about the consequences if Madison finds me, or even worse, if Michael appears. Too late, I remember that the knife I stole for protection is still under my pillow. I pause for a moment, considering whether I should go back for it, while also wondering what has happened to me in the last six months that has made a knife feel like a necessary accessory. Then I realize I'm being stupid, again. The kitchen is full of knives. I can just get a different one.

My heart booms as I open the kitchen door, but the room's empty, so I go straight to the knife block and pull out the one Lori uses to carve the meat. I grip it like a warrior, up by my ear, then realize how ridiculous I look, and cautiously slide it down the back of my jeans. Would I even be able to use it, if it came to it? Actually make contact with human flesh and keep pushing? The idea seems crazy, nauseating, but if I was left with no other choice, maybe I could.

I go into the mudroom, put on my thick ski coat, and pull a flashlight from the shabby chic chest of drawers in there. I grab some paperclips and a safety pin, hoping that I'll be able to pick the padlock to Michael's bunker – and if that doesn't work, I'll smash it with a rock until it breaks. There are two sets of car keys in the drawer too, so I shove those in my pocket, just in case we need a getaway car. I still don't know how I am going to face Murphy if I leave here without my fifty grand, but there must be another way to get the money. There are loan sharks who don't care about your credit rating, as long as you pay their crazy interest rates. I could raise the money that way, work three jobs to pay it off. Prove to everyone what I'm capable of, myself included. With an unfamiliar sense of determination, I head outside.

There's full cloud cover tonight, the very definition of pitch black. It's not late – barely half past nine – but I'm still petrified. I don't want Madison to notice the beam of the flashlight through any upstairs windows, so I rely on the weak glow coming from the house to guide me at first. I lost sight of Michael and Lori quite quickly last night, so theoretically he could have put her in one of the barns, but in my gut, I know she's in the bunker.

When I reach Clarabelle's meadow, I turn on the flashlight. It's a relief, something to light up my route, but everywhere beyond its beam descends into total darkness. If someone came up behind me, I would have no warning until they grabbed me.

I twist around on instinct. No one. But Michael is out there somewhere. I can sense it.

I carry on walking. Past the gym. I poke the flashlight into the stables, just in case, but there are just six sleepy horses inside who don't even whinny. But when I walk past the next barn, Clarabelle's winter home, I hear something. And freeze.

296

I can't make out any words, but it's a man's voice, no question.

I switch off the flashlight and crouch down. My heart beats so loud in my ears that I feel like I'm wearing my mom's stethoscope. I only hesitate for a moment before pulling the knife out of my jeans. My arms are shaking, but I grip the handle with both hands. I will do it, I realize with a lurch of shock. If I am attacked, I will fight back.

I just hope with every cell in my body that it doesn't come to that.

Chapter 64

Madison

@mamasanchez88 I've seen the video, and this ain't about the baby
#cheater #scumbag #solidarity #tradwifeMIA

Matilda is sobbing. Mason is pummeling Molly because she accused him of crying. And despite her assurances, Cally hasn't returned from putting Myron to bed.

But the thing that's bothering me the most is that Michael still hasn't shown up. While I'm sure it has more to do with his hunger than hurrying back to see his family, Michael is rarely late back from work. And if he is, he warns me – again, mostly to make sure someone is around to cook a meal. But it's nearly ten o'clock and there's no sign of him.

I run my fingertips over the smooth glass of my phone screen, but as much for comfort as for any intention to use it. I have messaged Michael twice now and a third time would not be appreciated, however upbeat my tone. There are tracking apps of course, but Michael wouldn't just confiscate my phone if he found one of those linked to him, he'd smash the holy hell out of it.

I frown. I'm a smart woman, but I feel adrift right now. It's funny, when I have staff around me – Erica, Noah, Lori, Cally – being the boss comes naturally. But now they're not here, waiting on my instructions, I'm suddenly at a loss.

I do know one thing though. I'm too distracted to put these children to bed.

'Who wants popcorn and another movie?' I learned to make popcorn a couple of years ago, although luckily it's not hard – just kernels, oil and salt. It was soon after we introduced movie night, and I had the brain wave about my reel. Molly designed individual popcorn bags for us all, and Mason – back when he was as cute as Myron – gasped with every pop. My followers loved it. Nowadays it's hard to believe that kind of traditional family life was once clickbait enough.

Mason looks up, his fingers splayed in the air. 'Me!'

'Okay, stop hitting your sister. And you,' I add, looking at Matilda. 'Dry those tears. Is that a deal?'

'It's a deal, Mommy,' Matilda says, stifling a hiccup.

'Molly, you're in charge of choosing the movie from the shelf. And Mason? Keep your hands off Daddy's special shelf. I'll be back soon.'

I give them the best mommy smile I can manage, and head downstairs.

I don't know why I notice the knife missing from the block. It's not like I have an intimate knowledge of my kitchen, but with everything that's going on at the moment, its absence feels unsettling. I check the dishwasher, but that's empty. I inspect the utensil drawer. I even look in the cupboards. But it's nowhere to be seen.

I hear a noise outside. A howl. It sounds terrifying, but animals make sounds like that. When they're fighting, or mating, or in the case of coyotes, all the damn time. But too much has happened for me to brush it off so easily. A man has tried to break in twice. Rose sent me the note that Lori burned. Lori left me. And now Michael is missing, the knife has gone, and Cally is nowhere to be seen.

Do I go outside? Check on Lori? I wonder for a moment if the noise is her in labor. But the bunker is soundproofed, so if it is, that means she's escaped somehow. Or Michael has let her out. Or Cally has found her. Or Rose.

I take a deep breath and walk into the mudroom. I pull on my snow boots, reject my Woolrich trench coat in favor of an older jacket – tonight feels like it could get dirty – and open the drawer to fetch a flashlight.

That's weird. There are normally two flashlights in here – Michael's Surefire Turbo that no one but him is allowed to touch, and the Maglite that everyone else uses. But neither one of them is in here. And I feel that there are other things missing too, but I can't work out what. Is that because Lori has been away from the homestead for two days and she's the only one who puts things back where they belong? Or are both flashlights in use? Are there two people out there, roaming around in the dark?

The feeling makes my stomach flip. But this is my home. I shouldn't feel scared. I check my phone battery – a healthy seventy-one percent – and switch on its flashlight function. Then I push open the back door and step outside.

Chapter 65

Cally

I stumble away, listen to the horses rustling, stomping in their stalls, sensing distress. The flashlight creates crazy patterns in the snow as I try to calm my shaking limbs, to build some distance from the barn.

I'm sure Lori is in the bunker, so I just need to get there and get her out. I'm sure we'll be able to match one of the sets of car keys to a vehicle in the garage. Then we can go to the police, explain everything.

Except what if I can't break the padlock? I should have brought a screwdriver, or pliers, or one of those heavy tools that the cops use to break down doors. Not a few paperclips and a safety pin. Why was I so stupid? I pat myself down. Even the knife has gone.

I pause when I get around the back of Clarabelle's barn. There's a river of footprints in the snow and the sight spurs me on. I start sprinting – maybe adrenalin has been the missing element in past fitness regimes all along – until I hard stop by the cement wall and stare at the bulky padlock clipped over the sliding bolt.

I pummel the door. 'Lori!' I shout. 'It's me, Cally!' I push my ear against the solid metal panel but all I can hear is the whoosh of blood being flushed through my brain. There's no way she can hear me. I quickly realize that the padlock needs a code not a key, so my little metal tools are pointless. I dip the flashlight and move it along the ground until I see a hand-sized rock, then pick it up. But however hard I bash it against the metal shackle, the lock holds.

I throw the rock down and yank the padlock in annoyance. It's a six-digit lock, which means one million possible combinations – and I don't have a clue where to start.

I screw my eyes in concentration. What number sequence might Michael choose?

I try Mason's date of birth first, then Myron's – I know how Michael ranks his kids – followed by Molly's and Matilda's. But none of them work. I know Michael and Madison got married in March 2012, so I try all the different dates in that month, but the shackle still doesn't budge.

I turn, lean against the door, will my brain to come up with something amazing.

As I stare at the black sky, I think back to my first conversation with Michael, when – much to my shame – I was drawn to his love for his home. Five generations had lived here, he told me. The March Homestead. The home he won't leave even when the world turns to shit. When did he say it was built? Could that be the code? I screw my eyes closed. Concentrate. Eighteen something. After the Homestead Act. I open them again. 1870? Yes, that's it.

I twist back, spin each of the wheels on the padlock to 0-3-1-8-7-0, and . . . click. The lock releases. I stare at the swaying curve of metal. I have never been so impressed with myself in my whole life.

I shake out of my reverie, slide open the bolt, and pull open the door. It's pitch black, so I shine the flashlight inside. Lori is tied to a chair. Her face flinches at the bright light, so I quickly tilt the beam downwards.

'Lori!' I cry, surging forward.

'Cally?' she whispers, her voice hoarse and tired. 'Cally, is that you?'

'Yes, it's me. Oh, my God, what have they done to you?'

'My hands, can you untie my hands?'

I skirt around the back of the chair and rip apart the knots with surprising ease. The rope falls to the floor and Lori sighs with relief. I watch her stroke her belly, then slowly push to standing. She drinks from a water bottle beside her.

'I need to pee.'

'Of course, yes. But then we need to get going,' I call after her as she staggers into one of the rooms. 'Is your car here?' I holler. 'It doesn't matter if it isn't. I got some car keys from the drawer; we can take whatever car they unlock.'

Lori reappears, moving with a lot more grace than I would if I had an almost full-sized baby in my belly and I'd been tied to a chair for twenty hours. 'Slow down, give me a second.'

'Sorry. It's just . . . this place. It's like something from *The Walking Dead*.'

Lori reaches for my hand, squeezes it. The woman who has been imprisoned all day is comforting *me*.

'I can't go, Cally, I'm afraid. Not yet. I can't leave my children here by themselves. It's my job to protect them and I know – I mean really know – that I'd never forgive myself if I didn't manage it.'

'But you have to!' Then I soften my voice – the last thing I want is to upset this angel in maternity wear. 'I mean, didn't you leave them once already?'

'You're right, I did. But I only ran away because I thought

that was the way to save them, and Madison. And I always planned to come back, one day, when I felt able.' She looks down at her hands. 'But it's too late for that now.'

'I don't understand.'

'No, you wouldn't,' she says sadly. 'Because your crime was smashing up metal panels welded together to impress men with big egos.' She looks into my eyes. 'I did something much worse, a long time ago, and I have been paying off the debt ever since. I finally had a chance to settle the score for good, but Michael found me before I could do it. So now there's no option but to deal with the fallout, just like before, and only hope that I can do better this time around. But that doesn't mean you should stay. In fact, I think it would be safer if you went.'

I think about the car keys I stole. Could I run away and leave Lori to face the dangers of the March Homestead alone?

But before I get to decide anything, I hear a crash. I turn to the doorway and gasp.

Chapter 66

Madison

@jemimapuddlef_ck97 If my husband fooled around, I would chop his mf dick off.
#cheater #scumbag #revenge #tradwifeMIA

This is not fun. Why does darkness make everything worse? Even the horses sound jittery. And the sky is so goddamn black.

I pull my jacket a bit tighter and walk behind the gym, the most direct route to the bunker. But it's even more terrifying here – further away from the house – and I feel my knees weaken. Except, is this really about the darkness? Or is this my sixth sense screaming that I'm in danger? The same danger I sensed when I watched Lori and Jonah through the kitchen window of my first homestead, just before he killed Brianna. Because the girl I once was, she died that night, no question.

Tears swell in my eyes. I try to blink them away – I'm Madison March now, strong, ruthless, clever enough to reinvent myself completely – but when I look down at my legs, they're still refusing to move.

Actually, I'm going to call Michael. He should be here, helping me deal with this mess. If he has gone to the bar with his ranch hands, missed movie night without letting me know, I might even explode. I take three long breaths – it's important I don't explode prematurely – and press on his number. I listen to it ring, and ring, getting more annoyed with each droning vibration. But then I realize there's something weird about it. Like my phone has suddenly developed surround sound.

Slowly, with a growing sense of unease, I slide the phone away from my ear.

But I can still hear the ringing.

'Michael?' I call out, my fear spiraling. 'Are you out there?' I scan the black void with my phone flashlight, while wondering why Michael's Surefire isn't blasting light every which way. But there's nothing. The ringing has stopped – the call gone to voicemail – so I call again and start walking towards where the sound came from. The closer I get, the more certain I am that Michael isn't with his phone. Which doesn't make sense. Michael doesn't care about his phone like I do, but he has deep pockets, and he doesn't check it every five seconds either.

Suddenly my foot catches on something. I lose my balance and career forward, my phone flying out of my hand. I hit the ground face first. But I barely register the snow burn on my cheeks because I'm too disgusted by what I fell on. Something warm and slimy. I scuttle away from it, grab my phone, and shine it at whatever horrific creature I've just encountered.

And scream.

And scream some more.

Michael. Covered in blood. Pools and smudges. Like Jonah all those years ago, but worse, because Jonah's body was intact – just his head smashed – while Michael has stab wounds in his chest, his shoulder, and his belly.

I need to check if he's breathing. But I can't do it. I can't get that close to him; it's all too horrific. And there's so much blood, too much for him to still be alive, surely. I know he's dead. Just like Jonah was. Except when he died, I was distracted by my own pain. Now I'm fully alert and the sight of Michael's ravaged body is so raw and vivid and gross that it's going to be etched into my eyeballs forever.

Oh, God, why is this happening to me again?

An image flashes up: the missing carving knife in the block. I knew its absence meant something bad. But who delivered the blows?

Cally? No, I can't believe that girl is capable of something as primeval as this. She's vegetarian, for Chrissakes.

What about Rose? She's crazy enough to do it, and she hates Michael. The back door wasn't locked when I went out, so that means she could have got inside the house to steal the knife. The security lights in this place are ancient, so maybe she knows the system from when she lived here, and how to avoid setting anything off.

But of course there is someone else who could have done it. The woman who pulled a gun on Michael yesterday, who has killed before.

Did I not secure the padlock properly when I left earlier? Did Lori find a way to free her hands from those knots I tied after her bathroom visit? It probably wasn't that hard; I only went to Girl Scouts for one term before a place on the cheerleading squad came up.

But even if Lori killed Michael, I still need to find her, and even more desperately now. Because she's the only one who can get me through this trauma. I watched Lori kill Jonah thirteen years ago, and that made me more certain that I wanted her by my side, not less.

I pause. Did Lori do this for me? Again, like she did with Jonah? She knew Michael was threatening to end our marriage, that he'd demanded I stop doing the one thing I love. And she knows what Truly Madison means to me.

Has Lori been on my side all along?

Did she run away because she knew Michael would follow her?

We won't be able to hide Michael's body like we did Jonah's – I'm too famous for that now – but there are always ways to spin the narrative if you live in a remote place like we do and have money to spare. For years, I've been sharing my life with millions of followers, but I only ever show them what I want them to see. And I can control this story too. We can't leave any loose ends, which means killing Cally. It's a shame – she doesn't deserve it as much as Jonah or Michael – but she's far from special. Just another young woman who believes she was born with rights, who isn't willing to earn them. And there are so many like her in Boston, she'll barely be missed.

I need to find Lori. Talk to her. And the first place to look is the bunker. I pick up Michael's Surefire, wipe the blood on my skirt – this dress is past salvaging – and direct the beam at the mound in the distance.

Chapter 67

Cally

A figure stands in the doorway. Just a silhouette in the shadows, but instinctively I know I'm in danger. I drop the flashlight, stumble backwards, and almost lose my footing, but Lori reaches for me just in time. We stand pushed up against each other, like sandbags before a storm, and stare as a man emerges with a foot-long hunting knife in his grip.

'Jonah,' Lori says, lifting her hands. 'I can explain.'

Jonah? Who's Jonah? And how does Lori know him? The man is wearing a bulky hat, low down on his forehead, and in the semi-darkness, it's hard to make out his features. But his blue eyes are bright enough to stand out.

'We had a deal,' he growls, his eyes flitting between us then settling on Lori.

'I know, and I was waiting for you up at Harry Fisher's farm like we agreed. But Brianna's husband found me before we were due to meet and brought me back here.'

And who is Brianna? Wait, Brianna's husband? Michael? Has he been married before? Or is he a bigamist? Is that kind of thing legal in Montana? I feel my brain short-circuiting.

'Well, you'll be glad to know that he won't be troubling

us anymore,' Jonah says, walking further into the room. 'That asshole thinks he can point a gun in my face, call me a pussy, without payback. All I had to do to lure him over was to throw a few stones at his precious truck. He ran after me, cursing, thinking he was in charge. Goes to show how stupid he was.' Jonah is holding the knife out in front of him and it's not shining like it should be. It's dull and grimy. Like it's just been used.

Lori and I move as one unit away from him.

'I'll come now,' Lori says. 'No one else has to get hurt.'

'What?' I say. 'You can't go anywhere with him!'

'It's fine, Cally.' Lori swallows, but her voice still breaks. 'Jonah is my brother.'

My eyes widen. I look from one to the other. 'Your brother? So why is he pointing a knife at you?'

Suddenly Jonah swivels and lunges, sticks the tip of the knife at my throat. 'Because she murdered me.' I nod, as though his nonsensical claim stacks up perfectly, because this man is clearly crazy. It must appease him a little, because he retracts the knife, but only by a few inches. 'Who are you?' he demands.

I wonder for a moment whether telling him would breach the NDA, then decide staying alive trumps the threat of bankruptcy. 'Cally,' I whisper. 'The kids' tutor.'

'You like your boss?'

I look at the knife. Wonder what the best response is.

'Well?'

'Um, she's okay,' I mumble, then have a brain wave, safer territory. 'And the kids are great.'

But his expression morphs from hostile to furious. 'Oh, yeah, Madison's cute fucking family. While my baby died!'

'What?' Lori calls out, incredulous. 'How can you say that when you're the one who killed her!'

310

'You mean like you killed me, or as good as? Knocking me unconscious, leaving me for dead. When you came back the next morning, I thought that you'd found a conscience, that you were going to help me. But no, you dragged me down to the woods when I couldn't speak or move and left me to the animals like I was nothing more than trash.'

'I thought you were dead!' Lori wails. 'Your head was covered in blood; you weren't moving!'

'And you think that makes things better?' Jonah hisses. 'I would have died if Jackson hadn't found me when he was out hunting. I'll tell you something, that man is a hero. He didn't assume I was dead. He checked on me, found a pulse, and then got me back to his cabin. He'd been fending for himself for three decades by then, God rest his soul, and he fixed me up better than any doctor could. I was a stranger to him, but he still spent more than a month getting me back on my feet, and didn't ask for anything in return. While my own sister . . .'

'And now you want your revenge,' Lori interrupts, closing her eyes.

I don't want to believe this man with a knife, but Lori's not denying it, and I guess it fits with what she just told me, that she did something terrible. But attempted murder? Leaving her own brother to die in the woods? I used to think she was amazing, a superhero, but I suppose it wouldn't be the first time my instincts were off.

'I spent six weeks in Jackson's cabin,' Jonah goes on. 'I went back to the homestead when I was able, but all my stuff had gone. Burned, I guessed, in my oil drum. I suppose that was you too? Leaving me destitute as well as dead? No job, no money. My face disfigured. The only thing you didn't find was this knife. I guess it's no wonder I ended up in the slammer.'

'Listen, I can get the money,' Lori says. 'Just let me go now and I'll come meet you tomorrow.'

'No, Mary,' Jonah says, shaking his head. 'You had your chance to save Brianna. And you blew it.'

Chapter 68

Lori

New Year's Eve

I check my mirrors again. But of course Madison isn't following me tonight, not like she did four days ago. She doesn't even know I left the homestead, and she has her hands full with her New Year's Eve dinner party. Nathan's wife Nancy doesn't know about our surrogacy arrangement – even Nathan agrees that she loves gossip too much to be trusted with something like this – so I was told to stay out of the way.

Which suited me fine. With the booze guaranteed to be flowing, I knew it would be my best opportunity to meet up with Jonah without anyone realizing, so once I was certain the kids were fast asleep, I snuck out.

Because after reading the card Jonah sent to Madison, I needed to see him.

I park a block away from the bar and walk up. It's half past ten, and the place is busy, which is both unnerving and a relief. I'm not used to crowds, especially so many drunk men altogether, but at least no one will notice a fat woman with graying hair. I walk up to the bar and order a single shot of Jack

Daniels on ice. I'm not going to drink it but it's the best way to fit in here tonight. My bump is hidden behind Michael's old parka again – although this isn't about protecting Madison's secret anymore. I don't want Jonah to know my vulnerability.

On Christmas Eve, after the security lights were set off, I only followed Michael towards the perimeter fence to make sure he didn't do anything stupid – or at least anything that might create a backlash for Madison on her social channels. But when we found the intruder, his face was lit up in the bright light like a fallen angel, and I recognized him instantly.

Jonah.

Even though I had been certain my brother was dead, and his face was half covered by a trapper's hat, I knew it was him. And he recognized me too. Maybe he already knew that I lived with Brianna, or rather Madison, but I don't think so – he looked too shocked. And his hesitation proved to be his undoing too, because Michael managed to lock and raise his rifle before Jonah even looked at him.

I was reeling when I got back to the house, but I hoped that would be it. That for once, Michael had done something genuinely helpful for Madison and me, even if he didn't know it.

But my optimism wilted the next morning when Noah gave me a card addressed to Madison. He'd found it in the mailbox on his way in and had asked me to pass it on. But the roughly scrawled half-address was too much of a coincidence, the handwriting too familiar. Jonah must have been delivering the note when the security lights went off.

I went to my room and opened it.

Madison March. Quite the reinvention, Bri.
Even got your own armed cowboy to run me out of town.

I bet you thought it had worked, didn't you? That I wouldn't be back.

You blocked Brianna Wyoming on Instagram and thought all your problems would go away.

But what about my problems?

Headaches. Nightmares. Depression.

Ten years in federal prison for freakin standing up for myself. That's what being left for dead does to a man.

You OWE me, Bri. And it's Christmas so I figured it was time for a gift.

I want half a million dollars. Spare change to you and that husband of yours, right?

Unblock me on IG and wait for my message. If you don't, I'm telling him who you really are.

I hid the letter under my pillow, then threw it on the fire as soon as I got the chance. For a fleeting minute, I thought about telling Madison, ask her if she could get the money. But I knew it would be impossible, so what was the point? Madison might earn a fortune, but she has no access to her money. It all goes to Michael – a small price to pay for the lavish lifestyle he provides, according to Madison – and how could she possibly explain needing half a million dollars to pay off an ex-lover, who she thought had been killed by their housekeeper?

But it's more than that. Jonah died thirteen years ago – I killed him to save Brianna, and that gave her a chance to become Madison March. Except he didn't die. And that means I failed. And that this is my job to fix.

However, I needed to find him first. The only lead I had was when Madison questioned Bill after the intruder was first found on the homestead. Before I knew it was Jonah. Bill told us that Jonah had been seen with Rose a couple of times in the bar. So I made up an excuse to visit town as soon as I could get away after Christmas – my fake tooth infection – and went looking for her.

I was nervous, knowing Rose's reputation, but it turned out she wasn't as scary, or crazy, as people say. She was fidgety, yes, and mistrustful. But she seemed more vulnerable than dangerous. She didn't know where Jonah was living, or maybe she wouldn't tell me, but when I asked her if she could make sure Jonah was in the bar on New Year's Eve, she said she would – if I put a fifty on her bar tab.

Except he's not here. And Rose is surrounded by a group of men too intimidating to interrupt. I take a tiny sip of my drink and wait.

Midnight comes and goes, and I'm about to give up waiting, when I see him. He looks towards Rose, then skulks over to one of the booths and slouches into a seat. A moment later, Rose drops a bottle of beer on his table, then walks away without speaking. He clearly wants to keep a low profile. I watch him take a large gulp, then he turns to stare at me across the room. An alarm screams inside my head. Run! But I ignore it and walk over. I don't sit at the table – that's a step too far – but I force myself to look into his eyes.

'Hello, Jonah,' I whisper.

'Mary,' he says. He sounds calm but his neck muscles quiver with tension. 'When Rose told me a woman was looking for me, I hoped it was Brianna, but I'd have put money on it being you. Come here to save that lazy bitch's ass again, have you?'

'I don't want any trouble.'

'Smashing my head in and leaving me for dead is trouble enough, is it?'

'I thought you were going to kill her,' I say. 'She needed protecting.'

316

Jonah laughs, shakes his head. 'I barely touched her. Was just teaching her a lesson about lying.'

'Really? So how come she lost the baby? And the doctors had to remove her womb?'

'Don't bullshit me,' he growls. 'She's got loads of kids. I've seen them on Instagram. So cute, it makes me want to wring their little necks.'

They're only words but they fill me with a primal fear. My children being threatened by the man I played a part in bringing up. How could he have turned into this repulsive human being? And how could I have so badly failed to raise a decent man? Perhaps he was rotten from the start. A bad apple, decaying from the inside out. 'They're not . . .' I run my hand down my front. 'They're Michael's, but they're not hers.'

'I don't believe you.'

'It's true.'

'Says a cold-blooded killer.'

My breath judders out, a mix of fear and frustration. If I hadn't covered him in that blanket, would he have died of exposure? Were those few degrees of warmth the difference between life and death?

But I've learned a lot about resilience since that night. This time I need to get it right. I pause, breathe. 'I can get you the money.'

'Half a million?'

'Like you said.'

'When?'

I don't want Madison, and definitely not the children, to know about this, so I need some time to plan. To say goodbye, just in case I can't go back home. But I know I can't hold him off for long either. 'Madison will need a week to get it together,' I choose.

Jonah leans across the table. 'You see that drunk guy over there?' He nods into a dense crowd of people. I follow his gaze, then suck in a gasp. It's Michael, one arm draped around some girl, the other holding a beer bottle. Why is he here?

'I'm guessing that means you didn't know he was coming,' Jonah says, with a smile that reminds me of a crocodile. 'Well, that bastard made me feel like I was in jail again, flaunting his big gun, treating me like some pathetic stalker. So funnily enough, I'm not big on patience right now.'

I need to get out of here, make sure Michael doesn't see me, or Jonah doesn't announce my presence. But I also need to walk out knowing I have made a deal. 'It's your birthday on January 6th,' I say. 'And wouldn't half a million dollars be the best birthday present? Tell me where to meet, and I promise I'll be there.'

'That date isn't just my birthday,' Jonah points out, running his palm across the front of his hat. 'And I guess there's something poetic about it.' He grabs my hand, pulls it down onto the booth's seating. I feel cold metal, his hunting knife, and wish Michael had taken it when he had the chance. Then Jonah grabs a pen out of his jacket pocket, scrawls some words on my arm, an address. 'Meet me at this farm on January 6th, there are some outbuildings two miles west of the main house. I'll be there, mid-afternoon. Three o'clock. And if you don't show, with all the money, I'll be coming for Madison March and her whole damn perfect family.'

I walk out of the bar without saying a word, but thinking about my children, and what I'll need to do to protect them. I only hope God will forgive me. Again.

Chapter 69

Cally

Jonah lunges for Lori. Suddenly I'm lunging for him in response, leading with my shoulder. If I can barge him hard enough, he might drop the knife. He's not a mountain of a man like Michael, but he's tall, and I'm a size-four woman who never goes to the gym.

My shoulder connects with his. Pain travels up my neck. He tips slightly, takes one step away from me, then steadies himself, the knife still rooted in his grip. I stand stock still. I'm already out of ideas, and all I've done is make myself more of a target, and slow him down by about three seconds max. Great job, Cally.

Except Lori uses those three seconds to knee him hard in the groin. He doesn't relinquish the knife, but he doubles over, lets out a cry of pain. I look around for a weapon. Jesus fuck, there's a whole wall of them. A crossbow, so many guns. But even Michael can't be reckless enough to display them loaded. Well, maybe is, but I still have no idea how to shoot. I spot a glass bottle on the shelf – the kind you use for water at dinner parties – which is way more my level. I grab it, smash it down on the back of Jonah's head while he's still bent over.

The glass doesn't break, but there's a solid thud. His hat slips off; there's a messy square of red knitting sewn to its lining. He howls, straightens up. Rage sparks in those haunting blue eyes. But they're not the standout feature anymore. His head is mangled, out of shape, with a mesh of livid scars across his forehead. I stare at it, in shock. Did Lori do that? He lifts the knife.

I realize just in time that I'm about to die, and surge forward, barrel into him. My shoulder connects with his chest, and he stumbles backwards, winded this time. He reaches out to steady himself, grabs onto a tripod – wow, Madison puts them everywhere – then realizes it's not sturdy enough to help him and flings it at me instead. I lift my hands to protect my face, feel the cool glass of the attached phone as it slams into me. I fumble with it, then push the tripod back to standing, out of my way, but my advantage has gone. Jonah has found the much sturdier table to support himself.

I sense his muscles tighten; his body win the battle against gravity. I try to scuttle backwards, but my feet won't play ball, and I slip. I windmill my arms to stay upright, but it doesn't work, and I tumble backwards. Completely vulnerable.

I'm going to die. Today, at twenty-four years old. Before I've had the chance to achieve anything. Whoever writes my eulogy will have to pretend that my tiny part in the school musical meant something. Murphy won't get his money. And Luke. What will happen to him?

I hear the whoosh of liquid being thrown. Spray lands on my arm, and I feel it start to burn my skin. Then Jonah screams and finally, finally, drops the knife. He lifts his hands to his face, the horrendous noise still spewing out of his mouth.

'Come on,' Lori says. 'We need to go.'

'What was that?' I ask, my eyes wide.

'Bleach. I found some in the box marked "cleaning products", and figured it's my kind of weapon.' She gives me a wink – to the background noise of Jonah's ongoing cries – and grabs my hand. My God, I take everything negative back, this woman is officially awesome. 'But I think this baby might be on the way,' she adds. 'So we should probably get back to the house.'

My head spins. A killer back from the dead, now writhing around in agony. A baby that's not due for five weeks suddenly on its way. Can this night get any more terrifying? 'And what about him?'

'Lock him in here for now. We can figure out the rest when I'm not having contractions every five minutes.'

It seems like a good suggestion.

I slam the door behind us, reattach the padlock, spin the wheels, and guide Lori back to the house as fast as her crushing pain allows.

Chapter 70

Madison

I shine Michael's flashlight at the padlock to the bunker and see that it's locked. I work through what that means. Lori is still inside. Lori didn't kill Michael.

I wonder how I feel about that.

I had convinced myself that it was her, and that she'd done it for me. I'd thought about how we would navigate through the fallout together, spin this into a story that kept Lori out of jail and made my brand even more relevant. But if Lori is still locked up in the bunker, then someone else attacked Michael. And that means I'm in danger.

I spin around, push my back against the safety of the solid bunker door, swing the flashlight wildly at the black night. I have always hated this bunker, but right now I want to be inside it, with Lori and supplies, and a wall full of guns.

I slide the flashlight into my armpit and reach up for the

padlock with both hands. I spin the six wheels to the correct numbers until the lock clicks. With shaking fingers, I flick up the metal shackle, slide the bolt across, and pull open the door.

A tortured scream rushes out. Like a wild animal in pain.

My adrenalin surges again. I take a few steps backwards, my heart racing, then I realize. The baby! Lori must be in labor. Will I need to deliver it? Would Michael have thought to stock latex gloves? Thank God I didn't wear my new Dôen dress today.

I take a breath to steady myself and walk inside.

Except it's not Lori crumpled on the floor, writhing around in pain. It's a man. My heart almost stops with the shock.

I shine the flashlight at him. His eyes are screwed up tight. His face is puffy and raw, the skin bright red and blotchy.

But it looks like . . . No, it can't be. He's dead. Lori killed him thirteen years ago.

Except.

I think about the messages from Brianna Wyoming. If I'm honest with myself, did I always know there was something off about them? Jonah was dead, and no one else knew what Lori did, so it was easy to push those fears away. But if this isn't my mind playing tricks, Jonah is still alive. And pretending to be Brianna would be the perfect way for him to mess with my head. He hated me scrolling on my phone – maybe because he could tell I grew to love it more than him. So seeing me living the life we dreamed of, and with ten million followers adoring me for it, must have felt like torture.

And then it hits me. It was Jonah who came to the homestead, who Bill scared off that first time, and then Michael on Christmas Eve. Was the note from Jonah too?

I stare closer. Jonah opens his eyes.

Whatever Lori did to her brother all those years ago, she didn't kill him. Because he's here. Lying on Michael's bunker floor. Next to the hunting knife I still see in my dreams sometimes. Blisters all over his face.

'Bri,' he whispers, his voice strangled with pain. 'My face. Get water.'

I look at the five-gallon container pushed against the wall in the kitchen area. It reminds me of when I would lug water from the well to the house in Wyoming. Jonah telling me he always did it, when he had no idea how many times it needed filling when he wasn't around. The way he dismissed everything I did, how he constantly accused me of being lazy, no matter how hard I worked. And how quickly he'd disappear if the chance presented itself. He promised me so much. And then he raised his fists when he realized how little he had to offer.

'Does it hurt? Your face?' I ask, hoping he says yes. I don't know what's gone on here, but I can make a wild guess. Lori has always sworn by bleach for getting rid of stubborn stains.

Hardworking, dependable Lori. Always willing to get her hands dirty.

Have I underestimated her again?

And then I made another one.

When Lori told me she'd made another mistake, I thought she meant that she regretted killing Jonah. But it wasn't that. The card she burned on the fire, the secret trip to the bar, running away. She must have found out Jonah was alive. Did he come here for revenge? Did she leave the homestead to protect me? Was she on my side all along?

'It kills, man,' he rasps. 'And it's getting worse. I need water.'

I remember how shocked I was when Jonah punched me. Innocent, trusting eighteen-year-old me. And how quickly that shock turned to fear. Justified fear, as it turned out, his boot killing my chance of ever being a mother in the true sense. Causing me indescribable pain.

I pull a pistol off Michael's display. Jonah slithers on the floor, trying to get away.

He killed my husband. It will be easy to convince people this was self-defense. The police, yes, but more importantly my followers.

And this is about more than revenge. It could do so much for my brand. I'll be a hero. The real American woman who defended her home, her children, and fought off a violent intruder.

A broad smile spreads across my face as I point the pistol at Jonah and pull the trigger.

Five shots. Five bullets. And maybe even five million new followers for @_TrulyMadison_.

Chapter 71

Madison's Followers

Jenna drops onto the sofa, pulls the blanket over her legs, and bites into the gooey chocolate chip cookie. So good. Christmas was excruciating. New Year was disappointing. But this – being back in her apartment, with no one to notice her bra on the carpet, or question her late-night snack choices – is exquisite.

Jenna opens Instagram, swipes through her stories. Swipes faster. Too many annoying friends with exciting lives that almost certainly aren't exciting but still no one needs to see it. Wait. Jenna drops the half-eaten cookie onto the cushion, sits up straighter. @_TrulyMadison_ is doing an Instagram Live. That never happens!

Lisa knows she should put her phone on sleep mode and turn out her bedside lamp. Like she knows that going to bed early because she feels a migraine coming on does not mean scrolling through Instagram for hours, or that having it muted means it's better for her. But this is too addictive.

@_TrulyMadison_ has gone Live, but nothing has happened. At least, not since Lisa started watching. But the backdrop is so different from her usual aesthetic. Gone are the Montana sunsets and cute kids making cookies. It's dark, and grungy, like a basement in a dystopian thriller. Lisa half expects a handmaid to appear or a zombie to climb out of one of those labeled boxes on the side. Hang on, does that say 'ammunition'?

Taylor pulls out her phone. Could this date be going any worse? A big part of her wants to escape now, while he's in the restroom – for the third time; she swears the guy's doing lines of coke in there – but she can't quite do it. She blames her parents, and her church, for making her too much of a flipping good girl.

She taps into Instagram. Scrolls through a few posts. God, why does she follow so many celebrities? How is that supposed to make her feel better about approaching thirty with a job she hates, clothes that keep shrinking, and no significant other? She tries stories instead. But it's more of the same. Until.

Oooh @_TrulyMadison_ is doing an Instagram Live. That will shut those #tradwifeMIA trolls up.

But wow, she looks rough. And skinny. Isn't she supposed to be pregnant? Did she have her baby over Christmas? And who is she talking to?

A shadow passes above Taylor. He's back. Dammit. She puts down her phone, curses Sunday school again, and smiles as he lowers into the seat opposite, his nose twitching.

Alice DeMille desperately wants to scratch her face. This new face peel is beyond itchy. Not that she'll mention that in her reel, of course, not with the twenty grand her agent managed to negotiate for her to say only good things about it. Especially now, after that bitch Madison March made it so hard for her to make any money from this tradwife gig.

Alice scrolls through Instagram. Well, look at that. Madison

March is doing a Live. That's brave of her, or stupid, hopefully the latter. Worth a look either way.

Holy mother of God. Alice blinks – it being the only facial movement the rock-solid peel will allow. Did Madison just shoot a man lying on the ground? It can't be real. Is this a weird brand partnership? An ad for some movie? How much is she getting paid for this?

And isn't she supposed to be eight months pregnant?

Alice listens to the gunfire. Five shots. Screaming after the first two and then nothing following the final three. It's actually pretty gruesome. She knew Madison was a bitch, but she didn't realize how low she'd stoop for a paycheck. Maybe doing the KULR-TV segment with her next week isn't such a good idea after all.

Detective Scarlett Finn of the Sweet Grass County Sheriff's Office came off duty half an hour ago, but she hasn't made it out of the station yet. What's the hurry when there's no one to go home to anymore? Both kids at college now, William taking his leave a decade before. The night, dark and cold. Snow threatening.

She leans back in her chair and picks up her personal phone. She loves her job, but sometimes she worries that it's all she has. No, more than that. That it's all she is. She wonders whether William might not have screwed around if she'd been a stay-at-home mom. Baked cookies and worn sexy lingerie instead of working all hours in an unflattering brown pantsuit.

Like Madison March. That beautiful woman whose values couldn't be further from Scarlett's own, but who she can't bring herself to stop following. Ah, speak of the devil. The queen of the tradwives is going Live.

328

Scarlett leans forward. She can't believe what she's seeing. But she *knows* what she's seeing sure enough; she's been a detective for eighteen years, so she can recognize a murder when it's taking place square in front of her. She drops her phone, sets her jaw, and picks up her police radio.

Chapter 72

Cally

We reach the back door. Lori is pushing out heavy exhales, and the light from the mudroom shows that she's deathly pale. Surviving Jonah's attack gave me such an endorphin rush that I felt invincible as we ran back to the house. But now we're here, reality has kicked in. Lori is about to have a baby five weeks premature, and I'm going to have to break the news to Madison that her husband is dead and his killer is locked in Michael's bunker.

'How do you want to do this?' I ask. 'When I left the house, Madison was watching a movie upstairs with the older three kids. But that was . . .' I look at my watch. Have I only been gone for fifty minutes? It feels like at least a lifetime. 'Not that long ago actually.'

'I can't see Madison, not yet. Not now,' Lori says, shaking her head. Then her face crumples in pain and she curls over her bump, gripping onto her belly as though she might drop the baby right there on the doorstep.

I hold her up, try to hide the panic ripping through my chest. 'Lori, we need to call 911. Get an ambulance.'

'You can't . . .'

'I know it's not ideal, with everything that's happened tonight, but we can't do this by ourselves. What if there are complications? The baby could die. Jesus, you could die. You need to put yourself first for once, Lori!'

'No, I mean you can't because neither of us have a phone.'

Shit. She's right. How can I live in the house of one of the world's biggest social media influencers and not have access to a phone?

'I'm going to have to tell Madison, get her to call them.'

Lori looks scared, but she doesn't challenge me. 'Okay, but be quick,' she says, heading towards the living room. 'Because this baby is not hanging around.'

I take the stairs two at a time. A cold sweat leeches out across my forehead. I race to the door of the den, then force myself to pause, just for a second, to compose myself. I can't have the children freaking out.

I fix on a smile and push open the door.

'Hey, Miss Cally,' Molly says. 'Did you bring the popcorn?'

'Popcorn?' I repeat, momentarily floored by the calmness of the room. Matilda is fast asleep on one sofa, Molly is lounging on a beanbag, and Mason is sitting, regimental straight, on the other sofa. Lassie is running with purpose on the fabric screen.

'Mommy said she was going to bring some up but that was ages ago.'

'Why do you have blood on your sweater?' Mason asks.

I look down. He's right, there's a smear of blood across my white Boston Red Sox hoodie. It must have come from Jonah. Christ, it could be their father's blood.

'Lori's having the baby,' I blurt out. Shit. What do I expect an eight- and ten-year-old to do about that?

'Lori's back?' Molly says, her eyes widening and a smile growing on her face.

'Does Daddy know?' Mason asks. 'Because normally Miss Kate comes when Lori has Mommy's babies. But I haven't seen her.'

'No, the baby is a little early,' I say. 'But I'm going to get an ambulance so there's nothing to worry about. I just need to find your mommy so I can use her phone.'

But Mason isn't listening. He whips past me, and clatters down the stairs. Oh, God, what have I started? I chase after him with Molly a few steps behind.

Luckily Mason heads in the opposite direction from the living room, towards the kitchen. I ask Molly to check on him, to keep them both away from Lori, then race back to her, hoping that popcorn or leftover cherry pie will be enough to distract the children. I'm no closer to finding a phone, but Lori told me not to leave her for long, so I need to check on her.

I hear the wails before I reach the door, and seeing Lori confirms it. This baby is not waiting for an ambulance.

'Miss Cally.'

I turn around. Mason is holding out a pile of fresh towels. Molly has a bowl of warm water. 'This is what Miss Kate always gets,' he explains. 'And now I'll go call 911 from one of Mommy's phones that she keeps in her bedroom drawer.'

'Really?' I say, taking the towels and bowl. 'That's amazing. But won't her phones be locked?'

'Emergency calls cut through locked phones. Didn't you know that?'

Shit. Of course they do. Why is everyone so much smarter in a crisis than me?

'Cally,' Lori shouts from inside the room. 'I need you!'

Oh, God. 'Thank you, Mason,' I say. 'Lori's going to love you forever.'

He beams, then runs, and I turn, pulling off my dirty sweater as I go.

Chapter 73

Madison

@jenna.cookiequeen WTAF did I just watch???

I switch on the overhead bulb and pull the door towards me, not so it's closed, I don't want to be shut in here. But to give me some privacy while I work out what to do. How to set the scene perfectly for my self-defense narrative.

I look at Jonah's corpse in the dim glow. On reflection, maybe I shouldn't have shot him five times. Will people think that was overkill, literally? Maybe it will help if I move his body into a more threatening position. And put the knife in his hand. Yes, that's what I should do.

He's bleeding a lot though, so I need to be careful. It's fine to have Michael's blood all over my dress, the distraught wife kneeling by her one true love's side, almost essential even. But not Jonah's. Him being my one true love is a secret that will go to the grave with me, I swear.

Reluctantly – because being in my underwear makes me feel vulnerable in here – I pull off my coat and dress and fold them onto the shelf furthest away from the crime scene. Then I step over Jonah's body and start rummaging through the box of cleaning products. Ah, there are latex gloves here after all. I pull them on and turn back towards the body.

Except something catches my eye.

The phone that Michael clipped onto the tripod is facing away from me, but in this weak light, I can just make out a glow around its edges, as though the screen is lit up on the other side. Why would that be? I feel a shiver run down my near-naked torso. When I came in here with Michael in November, I remember talking to him about the phone. Feeling a mix of gratitude that he'd thought of my needs, and discomfort that he'd railroaded my privacy by loading up my Instagram account without me knowing.

I remember tapping into the app, seeing all my notifications there, no password required. When I came to see Lori earlier today, I don't recall noticing the phone or the tripod, but I did have other things on my mind.

Wait. Where *is* Lori?

I've been so distracted by Jonah's reappearance, that I hadn't thought about Lori not being here. But the last time I saw her, she was tied to a chair. So where has she gone? I eye the phone on the tripod again.

The sense of foreboding is so intense that I can barely lift my arm. But I manage it. The phone is firmly attached to the tripod, so I twist the whole thing around. Then I take in each fact in turn. The camera is on. There are symbols on the right-hand side of the screen. There is some text overlaying the image.

Madison's First Live!! Aurora borealis in Montana!

Holy mother of God.

My clever idea.

To be filmed when Michael was snuggled up with the kids on bonus movie night.

I start hyperventilating. I can't line up my finger with the button. I'm shaking too much. I swipe, miss, swipe again. Oh, thank the Lord. The live recording stops.

Do you want to save your video?

No, no, no, no, no. I hit discard.

But what have I done? And when did it start recording? I try to remember what time I set it for – my first ever Instagram Live – but my mind is blank.

Please, God, don't let it be before I shot Jonah. Him in pain and defenseless, me looming over him, all five of my shots at close range.

When Bill started talking about the aurora borealis on New Year's Eve, and how it was predicted to be visible over Montana on the night of January 7th, I knew that it would be an amazing opportunity for content. But not in the same way everyone else would do it. Mystical greens and pinks on their story. Boring. Reels set to the *Star Wars* soundtrack, or *Stranger Things*, eurgh, so unimaginative. But if I could bring the dramatic night sky to my followers in real time, so that they felt like they were there with me, all of us gorgeously wrapped up in off-white Montana woolens, it would be the perfect way to make my Instagram Live debut.

But with Lori running away, and Michael going missing, and the weather being so overcast that no one was going to see any kind of light, I forgot all about it. Does the feature turn on by itself? And why did it start on this camera?

I pull my own phone out of my pocket. The notification is there, prompting me to start my scheduled session. Which means it would only take one tap to launch the live feed. Did Lori see the opportunity and take it, her loyalty finally frayed to the point of breaking after hours locked up in here? Or was it an accident in her tussle with Jonah that led to him getting bleach thrown in his face?

335

Is there a chance this could be Cally's work? Someone must have helped Lori escape. Is she a more competent adversary than she seems?

There's another notification on my phone. *Your Instagram Live was successful. Check your activity.* Sweat beads on my forehead. My breath judders out of me in short gasps. Slowly, with a sense of doom throbbing at my temples, I open the page. 1.4 million followers watched my Instagram Live.

1.4 million witnesses to me shooting Jonah.

For a fleeting, crazy, moment, I feel a jolt of excitement at the number. Then my vision blurs. Tears swim, then drop in fat dollops onto my screen.

I hear the sirens in the distance. Getting louder.

Then I rummage in the box marked 'Madison'. If I'm going to be arrested for murder, then at least I'm going to do it in a clean dress.

Chapter 74

Lori

Eighteen months later

'She's here!' Mason shouts, running into the kitchen from the mudroom.

I smile. 'Well, what are you waiting for? Go say hi. And get the others!' I add as he runs into the hallway, half tripping over one of Matilda's crocs on his way through. I'm not as tidy as I used to be, well I'm a single mother of five kids now, so where's the time, but no one around here cares much anymore. I always thought I enjoyed helping people, even when they didn't deserve it, but I've realized lately that I was just keeping the guilt at bay. Now that I've spent some time figuring out what I really want, it turns out I'm more of a cowboy than a cleaner.

As the other three children clatter down the stairs, I lean over the playpen and reach for my daughter. Even now, the feel of her makes my heart skip. The first child I could claim from day one. Michelle. The name was Molly's suggestion, and Mason approved. It was only afterwards, at the hospital, that Cally mentioned who might have inspired Molly's choice, an actual First Lady, and I still don't know whether Mason was aware of it or not. But I hope so.

I walk into the hallway and smile at our guest.

'Wow, I'd almost forgotten that the weather can actually be warm here,' Cally says, dropping her bag with a thud and wiping a sheen of sweat from her forehead. 'But I guess that's why people choose to get married in July.'

I pull her in for a hug. 'Yeah, and not March. I'm so glad you could come.'

Cally grins, steps back, and takes Michelle's pudgy hand. 'I wouldn't miss it for the world. And this one has grown a bit since I last saw her.'

'Of course she has, silly Miss Cally!' Matilda squeals. 'It's been ages. Michelle can walk now. Show her, Mommy!'

'Mommy?' Cally murmurs, as I lower Michelle onto the wooden floor. 'I bet that sounds good.'

I don't comment – just in case tears spill – but I do beam with pride when Michelle takes a few drunken steps towards her sisters. Molly watches carefully, hands outstretched, ready to catch her little sister if she falls, then sweeps her up.

I turn back to Cally. 'So we've got the rehearsal dinner tonight, but is there anything particular you'd like to do before then?'

'No. I'm all yours.'

'Great, a horse ride then.'

'Oh, God.'

The children burst into laughter, then grab Cally's hand, and drag her through the house. Five minutes later, we've got riding gear on and we're heading to the stables, none of us mentioning the bunker half in view beyond it. Other than painting the door a soothing off white, I haven't been back there since the sheriff's office finished their investigations. There's no need. The apocalypse has been and gone, and we survived it.

'Can I take Michelle on with me?' Mason asks.

As I turn to answer him, I catch Cally's raised eyebrows, and I feel a squirm of pride in my belly. Scrubbing Mason clean of his father's influence is an ongoing project – especially with the stakes so high – but I'm making good progress. And I figure I've got another eleven years before it really counts. 'Yes, fine. Her baby saddle can attach to yours. Be gentle with her though.'

He tuts. 'Of course.'

Molly chooses kind-natured Apricot for Cally to ride – after vetoing Mason's sniggering suggestion of our new colt Pedro, proof that he's still my work-in-progress – and the rest of us mount our own horses. We walk them past Clarabelle's meadow, then the children speed up to a canter, leaving Cally and me alone at the back.

'You know, I still can't believe Bill's getting married,' Cally starts. 'I mean, if anyone deserves a happy ending, it's him, but I had him down as the eternal bachelor.'

'I think Bill might have had a thing for Rose for a while actually, but he couldn't act on it when he worked for Michael.'

'Someone else winning at life without that man around,' Cally murmurs.

I smile. 'Rose too. It turns out the final straw in her marriage to Michael was when he struck her, the same night that his daddy had his first heart attack. She didn't leave him though. He blamed her for goading him into it, and then kicked her out. He'd taken away her self-belief by then too, so she didn't go far. Her drinking was a way of coping, and she figured that would be her life forever. But when Michael died, things changed. The closing of a book, she called it. Anyway, once she'd been sober for a few weeks, I gave her a job on the ranch, and she's taken to it like a duck to water.'

'Wow, if I wasn't already happy that Michael's gone, I am now,' Cally mutters. We ride in silence for a while, until Cally picks up again. 'But I'm glad you're running the ranch. Being the cowboy you always wanted to be.'

'And I have Michael's sister Madeline to thank for that, guiding me through all the paperwork. She's a good woman, that one. I don't understand how she's related to the rest of them, but I'm glad she is.'

Cally smiles. 'Well, you totally deserve it.'

'You know, it wasn't a surprise that Michael left everything to Mason. But when I read the will in black and white, and with Nathan appointed as trustee . . .' My voice trails off.

'Yeah, it was kinda handy that he didn't make it to the will reading, wasn't it?'

To my shame, a small giggle escapes. 'I think Michael's murder and Madison's conviction was a bit much for him. That and years of eating bacon for breakfast and steak for dinner most days. I'm surprised he didn't have a stroke sooner.'

'I'm just relieved the court made you the trustee and Mason's guardian rather than Michael's brother. Although I hope being king of the ranch hasn't gone to Mason's head.'

'I haven't told him yet,' I admit. 'That was my first decision as his guardian. And I'm hoping that by the time he turns twenty-one, he'll want to share his inheritance with his siblings.'

'And was your second decision to honor my end of year bonus?' Cally asks, a touch shyly. 'Thank you for that by the way.'

'I'm only sorry I couldn't get it to you sooner. But it sounds like you managed to get that man Murphy off your back?'

'Well, Madeline helped me a little bit too. When she told me that the NDA I signed had more holes in it than Madison's sourdough, I did those magazine interviews. It's amazing how much they were willing to pay for the inside scoop on Madison

March. Thank you for giving me your blessing on that too. You're still sure you don't want to tell your side of the story?'

'Me? Very sure. I think it's good for people to see the chaos behind the camera, but from now on, this family will be staying firmly offline. So how are you spending the money I sent you?'

Cally looks sheepish. 'Actually, I've booked a trip to Asia – Thailand, Vietnam, India. I'm going to ride elephants – they're slower than horses, right? – and eat street food and surf with dolphins. And when I get back, I'll get a proper job. Absolutely, one hundred percent. But life is short, right?'

I laugh, loudly, and I like how it bounces off the mountains. 'It can be, yes. Depends on the context, I guess. It can also be long.'

Cally goes quiet for a moment, and I expect she's thinking about the same thing as me. Madison's arrest for second-degree murder was splashed over every type of media for months. Her pleading guilty saved us all – but mainly her – from a trial and the awkward questions that would go with it. And her ten-year sentence, the lowest a judge is allowed to pass in Montana, shows that Madison hasn't lost her touch. 'Have you heard from Madison at all?' Cally finally asks.

'Not yet.'

'So you expect to, then?'

I look at the children in the distance. Molly out front, leading the pack. Matilda dipped down, hugging her horse. Myron only five and already a natural. And Mason, one hand on the reins while the other protects his baby sister. For years they thought life was about cameras, and aesthetics; about girl versus boy, and corporal punishment. And they've already forgotten those dark days. People are good at rising from the ashes.

'Oh, you know Madison March,' I finally say. 'The queen of the tradwives won't stay quiet forever.'

Epilogue

Madison

I slide the nail file out from under my pillow. I'm not expecting to get out quite yet – that's what my new pro-bono lawyer Hannah Smith is for, organizing my appeal, that and keeping me relevant in the free world. But being in Montana Women's Prison shouldn't mean lowering my standards.

As I move onto my left index finger, there's a meek knock on my cell door. I look up, already annoyed. Our doors are kept wide open when they're not locked shut, so knocking is a pointless exercise. But this is what I've been waiting for, so I summon up a smile.

'Yes?' I say, playing it cool. Prison is different from Instagram when it comes to influencing people. Less is more in here. And you also can't rely on filters.

'I've got it,' the woman says quietly. Lara. Eighteen months for shoplifting diapers and nipple cream. She reminds me of Brianna in some ways – less beautiful but similarly desperate – and I sometimes wonder how my life might have gone if I'd been arrested for stealing Twinkies all those years ago. Except I suppose the point is that I wasn't caught. I have always been smarter than everyone around me. I even brought about my own downfall in a twisted kind of way.

'Come in then.'

Lara checks the corridor one more time, then walks into my cell, half closing the door with her foot. Can she make this any more suspicious?

'Quick,' I say, beckoning her forward.

She slips her hand down her pants – thank goodness I got Hannah to bring me some antiseptic wipes on her last visit – and holds out my prize. Suddenly, all thoughts of germs and errant pubic hairs vanish. It's a phone. A smartphone. My lifeline.

'There's data on the SIM,' Lara says. 'But not much. My sister said social media will eat it up real fast. Sorry.'

'Don't apologize, Lara, you did good.'

Lara shrugs. 'I used to watch you on Instagram and TikTok all the time. Can't believe that Erica woman just shut all those down like you're dead or something.'

'Well, between us, those channels are dead to me. I just need the phone so I can call people.'

'Phone calls?' Lara looks disappointed. She was probably hoping to appear in my new posts – #tradstrife maybe.

'Can you keep a secret, Lara?' I ask.

Her eyes widen and I give her a conspiratorial smile.

'Building my brand on Instagram and TikTok was fun while it lasted, but I need to look forward now. Pastures new.'

'Oh?'

'Netflix,' I say, with a wink. 'I mean, why would I bother making my own content when some big-shot movie producer has offered a million dollars to do it for me?'

Acknowledgements

I was a little late getting to the #tradwife phenomenon but once I arrived, I was all in. So my first thank you is to those traditional wives who have entertained me for hours, primarily on Instagram. If your food tastes as good as it looks, my diary is always free.

The tradwife lifestyle has created debate in the US and beyond. In writing *The Tradwife's Secret*, I didn't want to judge people's choices, only to explore the themes associated with the movement – and of course, write a story that is twisty and gripping enough to entertain my readers. I hope I achieved that.

This book is all about content on the internet, so perhaps it's not surprising that I did most of my research online. I want to thank the dozens of vloggers and bloggers who shared their lifestyles and vacations in Montana and Wyoming on YouTube and various blogging sites. The vivid pictures you created gave me the extra detail I needed to bring both the setting and the characters to life.

The Tradwife's Secret covers some sensitive topics, and I hope I have written them with the respect – and the horror –

they deserve. Domestic violence and violence against women and girls remain a reality for far too much of the world's population. There are many organizations advocating on this issue, but the challenge is huge, and progress is inconsistent. I hope that together we can educate our children, our men, our communities, and our legislators that violence is never acceptable, and that women are due agency, just like men.

Thank you to everyone at HQ who has supported this book with such enthusiasm. Thank you Francesca von Krauland for your fresh perspective on the manuscript, and my incredible editor Cicely Aspinall. Working on this book with you has been a complete delight – even with those deadlines! – and I really appreciate your input at every stage of the process.

I couldn't do this job without support from my fellow authors, so thank you all for being at the other end of a WhatsApp message, or plea to meet for coffee. And thank you to my wider network of friends and family who have given me the time and space to write this book. A special thanks to my mum for listening to my deadline angst, my dad, always my first reader, and to Hannah for being my loudest cheerleader.

And finally, my family. Chris, Scarlett and Finn. You put everything in perspective.